DEMONS DANCING

P.A. PRIDDEY

Contents

Also by P.A. Priddey

The Vesta Mansion trilogy
Book 1 – The Power Inside
Book 2 – Other Worlds
Book 3 – The final Destiny

An Experiment in Emotions: A Short story collection

CHAPTER ONE

Cicero's Dagger

London 1945

Frank Wright sat in his cell waiting for death to come for him. His neck itched in anticipation of the rope. At thirty years old he served with the British army throughout the war and returned for this. Frank felt numb, not because he was about to be executed, but for the fact he was innocent. Found guilty of murder while the real murderer roamed free.

That's when he's not at my home, he thought, in bed with my wife. The woman I love . . . loved.

Frank could only feel hate as he remembered her standing in the dock describing how he beat a man to death. The day he returned from the war they took a walk where they came across the body of a man. It did not faze him as he had seen a lot of death. Laura, his wife, screamed. People came running, she pointed at him and said, *He did it, smashed his head in with a brick.* It broke his heart, and his love turned to hate when she testified in court.

Frank stared at the wall opposite and the small window which he couldn't open nor see through. He heard keys rattle in the door and wanted to shout "I'm innocent", but knew it was pointless. Frank didn't know much about the law, but it surprised him it had only been a week since they found the body. The door opened, and a man in a suit strolled inside. Frank raised both eyebrows as he expected a priest. The cell became cramped as Warden Croft stepped inside.

'This man is from the Ministry of Defence,' said Croft. 'He's here to offer you a deal.'

Frank's heart beat fast . . . there was a chance of freedom. He did not fear death, but wanted revenge. 'What kind of deal?'

Croft shrugged. 'Does it matter? Accept it or you'll be dead in an hour.'

'Call me Jeremy,' said the man from the Ministry, with the air of authority. He had a thin face and pointed nose. 'I need you to go on a mission.'

Frank rubbed his neck as he felt hot. 'I've not long finished my service.'

'This is different . . . I need certain kinds of men.'

'You mean the odds of surviving are very low, so you want men with nothing to lose or no one to care if they die.'

Jeremy nodded. 'If you want to put it like that . . . then yes.'

'What happens if I survive this mission?'

Jeremy opened a case and pulled out some papers. 'You will be pardoned.'

Frank stood. 'I thought the war was over.'

'It is, but parts of Europe are in turmoil which is where you come in. We will send you and another five to Germany near the Polish border. The Germans stole certain religious artefacts. We know the location, but the Americans and Russians are also after them.'

'I thought the Russians occupy that part of the country.'

'They do, and this is why the mission is dangerous. I have papers for you, but if you're caught we'll deny any knowledge of your existence.'

'Won't they have found it by the time we get over there?'

Jeremy shook his head. 'No, we're the only ones who know where it is, the others only know what region.'

'How sure are you it's there?'

'We caught one of the German soldiers who stole it. We made him talk, and he told us his commander had taken a certain artefact, along with other items from a church in France. The commander was a butcher by all accounts, but after touching the artefact he became a religious fanatic. They deserted before the end of the war and hid in a mansion.'

Frank shuddered as he wondered how they made the soldier talk. 'Hiding in Germany, novel if nothing else.'

'We must hurry, are you in?'

Frank stood. 'Yeah, it beats hanging around here.'

Twenty minutes later Frank was driven away from the prison in a blacked out van. He had not seen another prisoner during his stay, nor had he saw the building from the outside. Another two hours had passed when the van stopped. The doors opened, and he climbed out with a hand over his eyes shading them from the sun. He saw a small airfield, and five men wearing black clothes.

'Put these on,' said one, and passed him a bundle of similar clothes.

Frank changed where he stood as Jeremy showed him a picture of a dagger.

'This is what you are to retrieve. The others going with you are Richard, David, Colin, Bert, and Mathew. You are to only use those names, and they already know who you are.'

Frank glanced around at them. He took an instant dislike to Richard and David. The first had narrow eyes. The second looked like a henchman, big with broad shoulders. Colin was an average looking guy, where Bert, grey-haired, appeared too old for any mission. Mathew, small and slim, was the youngest. 'This is a strange group for a dangerous mission.'

Jeremy put the picture away. 'Bert and Mathew have their tasks, you other four will be their guards. Richard will be in charge as he knows more than the rest of you.'

Frank sat with his back to the side of the cargo plane as they flew towards France. There were no seats and sat in threes on the floor opposite each other.

'Are we going there in the daylight?' said Mathew.

'Don't be stupid,' said Richard, 'we'd be seen for miles. It'll be dark when we parachute down, and you better hope it's not a clear night or you might get shot.'

Mathew raised both eyebrows. 'So are you all murderers?'

'I'm not,' said Colin, 'I was set up.'

'Same here,' said Bert, 'but they were going to hang me anyway.'

Frank realised he wasn't the only one who had been set up. 'Are none of us guilty?'

'They were going to shoot me,' said Mathew, 'for deserting. They lined me up against a wall when Jeremy appeared. I got lucky there.'

Frank scowled. 'Many died in the war . . . you're nothing but a coward.'

'Steady on, lad,' said Bert, 'we all have our reasons.'

Mathew shook his head. 'I'm no coward . . . I'm a man of god and will not kill anyone.'

'Enough,' said Richard, 'we need silence on this mission, so you best start now.'

Frank disliked the man and had enough of orders. 'I lost many friends during the war.' He sat there thinking of his wife and her lover. He had only been home once during the war and when he returned all she wanted was for him to be gone. Laura had never told him as much, but it was her idea to go for a walk.

The plane descended before landing in France to refuel. Richard and David climbed off to supervise.

Mathew watched them leave. 'What do you think they did?'

Colin shrugged. 'I've no idea, and you might want to stop asking so many questions.'

'What's that supposed to mean?'

'He means you might not like the answers,' said Bert. 'I have no interest in what they did.'

'Why not?'

'Because I don't want it to happen to me.'

Frank sat listening, but as he felt angry with the younger man he had no intention of talking to him. Richard and David returned before the plane flew off once more.

Richard stared out of a small window into the darkness. 'It is time. Remember when your feet touch the ground, throw yourself to the side and roll over. Do not make a sound however much it hurts.'

Frank fitted his parachute and glanced at Bert holding a tool bag. 'Give it to me.'

Bert pulled it to his chest. 'No, I'm going to need it.'

Frank held out his hand. 'I know that, but if you've never parachuted before you'll find it a little difficult with a heavy bag. I've done it many times so let me carry your burden.'

Bert handed over the bag. 'Sorry, I did worry about that.'

Richard gave Frank a pistol and a rifle. 'David will go first, so when you land wait for him before carrying on, and remember, don't make a sound when you hit the ground.'

Frank put the rifle between the handles of the bag and the pistol in the waistband of his trousers. He stepped over and grabbed the side of the doorway with his free hand before jumping out. He felt the cool air on his face and realised he would have dropped in a different way if he hadn't accepted the mission. Frank saw lights in the distance, but nothing close as he pulled the rip cord. Now he knew Bert and Colin were also innocent it put a different light on the mission. It was no coincidence they were set up, but Laura confused him. Mathew admitted he was guilty of deserting, but would he have been executed now the war was over?

Frank dropped the bag and rifle as he landed and rolled on the ground. He untangled himself from the parachute as David ran over to him. He picked up both items he dropped and carried on forward in the darkness when he heard a loud, painful, scream. They ran and saw Mathew folding up his parachute.

David glared at him. 'Did you scream?'

Mathew glanced up at them. 'No, it came from further ahead.'

'Well leave the parachute . . . it's no good now.'

Frank watched Mathew drop it to the ground and chased after David. They soon came across another parachute and Colin lying unconscious on the ground. His leg twisted out of shape. 'Oh crap, he's broken it.'

'Is he still alive?' said Mathew.

Frank knelt and checked the man's pulse. 'Yeah, he's unconscious.'

'He's of no use to us,' said David, 'we'll have to carry on without him.'

Mathew shook his head. 'We can't leave him here like this.'

'We have no choice,' said David. 'The mission is too important . . . we'll come back for him after.'

'We will,' said Frank, 'let's just hope he doesn't wake until we get back.'

Five minutes later they came across Bert sitting on a rock with Richard further ahead. The older man took his bag back as Frank put the rifle over his shoulder and removed the pistol from his trousers.

Richard stood staring at them. 'You're one short.'

David walked over to him. 'Colin broke his leg, you probably heard him do it.'

'We'll have to make do. Follow me and watch your footing.'

The group moved off at a brisk pace. Frank noticed Mathew had taken the tool bag from Bert who was finding the terrain difficult to navigate in the dark. Frank glanced back as he felt like they were being followed, but saw nothing. Thirty minutes later they approached a lake with a boat moored to a post. On the other side of the lake he saw a large house with dimly lit windows.

Richard stepped onto the boat. 'Get on, David and I will row.'

Frank helped Bert climb on and sat down as the boat traversed the lake. David stopped rowing as they reached the other side and stepped off. The others followed him to a wooded area at the front of the mansion.

Richard turned to them. 'You three are to go inside and retrieve the dagger while David and I keep watch.'

Frank didn't trust him. 'You're not going in with us?'

'No, we have to keep watch in case the Americans or Russians show up.'

'How are we going to find it? We can't go searching if it's full of German soldiers.'

'You won't need to as the room is on the ground floor on the far right.'

'How do you know so much?'

Richard rubbed the side of his head with a pistol. 'Did Jeremy tell you of the German soldier they caught?'

Frank nodded. 'Yes, and he's probably dead now.'

'No, I was the prisoner until we came to an agreement. For my information and help, I'm now a British citizen. Go to the trees on the right of the mansion, and Mathew will get you inside.'

They hurried over trying to keep out of sight. Frank walked ahead while keeping the trees between him and the large house.

'Wait here,' said Mathew, when they were opposite the room on the right. He ran into the darkness and disappeared from view.

'You shouldn't be angry with him,' said Bert, 'he's a good lad.'

Frank shrugged. 'He's hardly that . . . he's a coward.'

'No, he's a man of god and shouldn't have been forced to join the army.'

'You insult me, old man, I wasn't forced. I joined to save my country.'

'I do no such thing . . . I fought in the Great War, but fighting is not for the likes of Mathew.'

'Have you met others like him?'

'Yes, and they're not cowards, but killing is not in their nature.'

Frank stared at the mansion as the window opened and Mathew stood inside. 'Come on, it's time to go.'

They ran furtively over to the window. Bert passed the bag up to Mathew, and Frank helped the older man climb inside.

Frank pulled himself through the window into what looked like a study. He saw Bert make his way over to a safe. 'I wondered why you were here, you're a safe cracker.'

Bert opened his bag and pulled out two thin bars. He took out a metal box and placed it on the floor. 'No, I was a locksmith. I only ever opened a safe when people couldn't do it themselves or lost the keys.'

'What's in the metal box?'

'Nothing, Jeremy gave it me to put the dagger inside.'

'That's a little odd isn't it?'

'Not really, it's old and valuable.'

'No, I don't think it has anything to do with value.' Frank turned to Mathew. 'Did you see anyone else?'

Mathew shook his head. 'No, it's quiet . . . I think they're all in bed.'

'I can't believe that, so where did you learn to break into buildings?'

'On the streets of London when I was fourteen.'

Bert turned from the safe. 'One night you broke into the wrong house.'

Mathew nodded. 'Yes, I was about to climb back out when I heard a voice.'

Frank scowled. 'You call yourself a man of god . . . you're nothing but a common thief.'

'I was fifteen at the time and only took food. The man who spoke was an elderly priest, and he said "take it with my blessing". I was shocked as I did not see him when I entered. I put the food down and begged for his forgiveness. The priest would have none of it and made me take the food. I returned the following day, but I knocked the door. He became the father I never had and taught me to read. A few years later I was forced to join the army, even after I said I would not kill anyone. One day I had news the priest lay on his deathbed and by the time I was given leave to see him, he had died. During my grief after the funeral, military police arrested me for desertion.'

Frank felt his anger grow, not against Mathew but for the injustice he suffered. 'Didn't the one who gave you leave speak up for you?'

Mathew shook his head. 'No, he wasn't there. I had never seen any of them at my short trial, and many of those there hissed at me.'

'Another strange tale, not too dissimilar to mine. Something is unnatural with this mission.'

Bert twisted the bars and the safe clicked open. 'What are you getting at?'

'This isn't natural . . . some devilry is going on here.'

Bert pulled the safe door open and found the dagger. 'You'd get locked up back home for saying such things.'

'I'm telling you this is all wrong. I mean just listen, if soldiers were here they wouldn't all be asleep.'

'I'll take a look,' said Mathew, as he left the room.

Bert held the dagger up and shuddered. 'This makes me feel all funny.'

Frank raised an eyebrow. 'In what way?'

'I don't know, but I feel calm . . . almost at ease with life.'

Frank held his hand out. 'Pass it over.' Soon as he touched the dagger, the anger inside him vanished. All he could feel was sadness. He put the dagger in a jacket pocket.

'What are you doing?' said Bert. 'It has to go in the metal box.'

Frank shook his head. 'That wouldn't be a good idea.'

'Not the supernatural again?'

'Maybe, and even Jeremy said the dagger affected the German commander,' said Frank, as Mathew returned. 'Did you see any soldiers?'

The young man looked shaken, and nodded. 'Yes, they were all dead, it looks like a slaughter.'

'That settles it . . . we cannot let them take the dagger.'

'Why not?' said Mathew.

'Because they'll kill us soon as we do.'

Mathew rubbed his eyes. 'Why would they when we retrieved it for them?'

'Because we won't be needed anymore. What do you know of the dagger?'

'I've been thinking about it,' said Mathew. 'If it's the same one I've read about, it belonged to a Roman guard called Cicero who under orders killed a holy man. He roamed the land for many years suffering from shame and guilt. One day the spirit of the holy man appeared and forgave him. The guard gave the dagger to a priest and told him his story. He thought the dagger would be going to Rome, but the priest took it to France.'

Frank turned to Bert. 'What's the box made of?'

The older man picked it up. 'Lead, I reckon.'

Frank nodded. 'I thought as much. We've been set up, and there's something unnatural about the others.'

'I agree we were set up,' said Bert, 'but you won't have me believing they're demons.'

'I never said they were demons, but why not?'

'Because there's no such thing . . . what you say is madness.'

Frank glanced into the safe at the other items. 'Think about it. We're all innocent of the crimes we were found guilty of. I don't believe you murdered anyone as neither did I. Mathew is no traitor, something he could've told us earlier.'

'Why?' said the younger man. 'No one would've believed me, like those at the trial.'

'You heard what was said on the plane.'

'Yes, but how was I to know if you were telling the truth?'

'Do you think we're guilty?'

'No, I don't believe you're murderers.'

Frank rubbed his chin. 'Who else apart from the priest knew you broke into houses?'

'No one,' said Mathew, 'I was never caught.'

'Damn,' said Bert, 'how did they know?'

Frank glanced out of the window before turning back to them. 'I bet the authorities back home know nothing of the crimes we were found guilty of. Did Jeremy tell any of you how we're meant to escape from here?'

'No,' said Bert, 'and it never occurred to me to ask.'

'We were not expected to leave here but to die. They want the dagger but cannot retrieve it themselves. Both you and I felt something when we touched it, but we're good men. It's those which are evil who are afraid to touch it.'

'The lead box,' said Bert, 'I see that now, but surely they could've got someone from over here to get it for them. Why go through all this?'

'That's what I don't understand,' said Frank. 'I doubt Richard and David are alone out there as I felt like we were being followed.'

Bert took the other stolen artefacts out of the safe. 'I felt that too.'

'A dangerous mission,' said Frank, 'yet the only danger was the parachute drop. Richard said he had been a German soldier, but there was no hint of an accent in his voice. We need to get away from here quickly.'

'I took a look out the back,' said Mathew, 'the lake continues out there, and I saw another boat.'

Frank nodded. 'We'll have to get back to Colin and see if he's still alive. Bert, do you need those tools?'

Bert shook his head. 'No, I'm leaving them here.'

'Empty the bag and put the contents of the safe inside.'

'What? You said you're a good man, and you want to rob the place?'

'No, of course not. I've no idea how we're going to get to France, but I'd like to return the stuff to the church.'

'Is that a crucifix?' said Mathew.

Bert picked up a cross. 'Aye, and covered in jewels by the looks of it.'

'May I hold it as it has been a week since I saw one?'

Bert handed it over and glanced at the window. 'We're too late.'

Frank turned and saw Richard standing outside. 'I thought you were keeping watch.'

Richard scowled. 'Are you thinking of betraying us?'

'Us? I knew you were part of it.'

'Indeed, he is,' said Jeremy as he approached. 'Are you enjoying our little game?'

Frank gripped his pistol. 'I wondered when you would show up, but why go to all this trouble?'

Jeremy grinned. 'It's been no trouble, in fact it's been a lot of fun. I'm sure you would like to know what's going on, so I will tell you. The dagger is powerful, and the only way we can use it is to sacrifice four men. When the last one dies, the power of the dagger will be mine.'

'How do you work that out?'

'You wouldn't understand.'

'Why not get four people from around here to retrieve the dagger?'

'It doesn't work like that,' said Jeremy. 'We need four certain men, the pious man, the hollow man, the broken man, and the angry man.'

'Ah,' said Frank, 'I'm the angry man.'

Jeremy leant on the window frame. 'Yes, and it worked out well. The others are here including the judge and Warden Croft. Shame Laura couldn't make it, but she has a new friend now, in fact she has lots of male friends.'

Frank shrugged, it saddened him, but he wouldn't show it.

'Does it make you angry?'

'Hardly, and I don't think I could get angry at the moment . . . not after touching the dagger.'

'What?' Jeremy snapped. 'Bert was told to put it straight into the metal box.'

'Too late I'm afraid, and you're one man short.'

'Colin's here, he's resting near the cross we're going to crucify him on. Do not worry as we have one for each of you.'

Frank glanced past him and saw hooded figures in the distance carrying large wooden crosses. 'We won't be playing your games.'

'You have no choice, now put the dagger in the box and pass it over.'

Frank grabbed the box and threw it out the window. Jeremy and Richard jumped back as it landed open on the ground.

'We will come in,' Jeremy hissed.

'If that was true you would be in here now.'

'You cannot escape us . . . we will burn you out if we have to.'

'I was thinking of setting the place on fire as it happens,' said Frank, 'I bet it would have the Russian soldiers curious.'

'You have five minutes before we come in and drag you out.'

Frank watched them walk away. 'What do we do now?'

'We can go out the back,' said Mathew, 'and get in the boat.'

Frank shook his head. 'They'll be out there too.'

'Yes, but we have the dagger.'

'And they have many guns . . . We have two.'

'They wouldn't have to kill us,' said Bert, 'just shoot us in the legs.'

Frank took the rifle off his shoulder. 'I'm going to kill anyone who try coming through the window, but I'd like the door barricaded.' He held out the pistol to Mathew.

'Please no,' said the younger man, 'I couldn't kill them whatever they are.'

Frank nodded. 'It's OK . . . you can hold the dagger and keep it safe.' He passed it over and gave Bert the pistol as the older man walked over to a large bookcase.

Mathew took the dagger and held it between his two hands.

'I could do with some help here,' said Bert, with his shoulder pressed up the side of the bookcase.'

Frank glanced at Mathew who appeared to be in a trance. He grabbed the other side of the bookcase and pulled it in front of the door. 'So which one are you?'

Bert stepped over to a table and pushed it in front of the bookcase. 'What are you talking about?'

'I'm the angry man, Mathew is the pious man, are you the broken or hollow one?'

'The hollow one I guess, Colin is the broken man.'

'Why are you hollow?' said Mathew, in a soft voice.

'I lost all my family to a bomb, my wife, children, grandchildren, and my sister.'

'But that was not your fault.'

'What difference does that make? They're dead, killed when I had to go out on a job. I'm hollow because I feel empty inside.' Bert glanced out the window. 'We got incoming.'

Frank turned to the window and saw four men running towards the mansion. He pointed the rifle and fired four times. The men fell backwards.

'Nice shooting,' said Bert.

'Easy targets,' said Frank, 'too easy.'

'Yeah well, more are coming.'

Frank fired once more and another fell. 'I can see that.' He fired three more times. 'What the hell's going on?'

'Getting you to use up your ammunition I guess,' said Bert. 'They would know how many bullets you have.'

'Yeah, and I should've looked for more. I can't believe they're wasting men like this. I'm making sure I have a bullet left for myself.'

'No,' said Mathew, 'it's a sin.'

'Would it be a sin if I was doing it to stop them? I've spent the last five years trying to protect my country, and if I have to . . . I will do it once more tonight.'

'Aye,' said Bert, 'and so will I . . . they're not going to crucify me.'

'There's something evil here, and he wastes men like they're rats.'

Bert shook his head. 'They're not men, they're getting back up.'

Frank saw those he shot climb to their feet, and all had red eyes glowing in the dark. They walked towards the mansion where he fired again, but none fell. The nearest started to climb through the window. He could hear gunfire and shouting outside but could not see as those in the window blocked his view.

'No, demon,' said Mathew, holding the dagger up, 'you will not enter.' A thin mist emanated from it and passed through the window. The demons Frank shot fell to the ground, and after a few moments they crumpled to dust.

Frank saw an army fighting the remaining demons and many soldiers on the ground. The mist spread across the land to the lake and many of the demons fell. The army continued forward, as jeeps drove away from it towards the mansion. They pulled up and soldiers jumped out, shouting in Russian.

'English,' said Frank.

One approached the window. 'Throw down your weapons and get out here.'

Frank took the pistol off Bert and threw it along with the rifle outside. He helped the older man climb out the window and followed with Mathew.

'I am Captain Volkov of the Russian army, now would you like to tell me why you are here and what's going on?'

Frank thought he spoke English as if it was his native tongue. 'We were escorting a holy man to France when those things waylaid us,' he lied. 'We fled here, but what we didn't know is others were waiting for us.'

Volkov glanced at all three of them. 'I see no holy man, and you all look like thieves.'

'It is I,' said Mathew, 'they thought it best if I dress like them. One of our friends is out there with a broken leg.'

'I saw a man lying by a large wooden cross. There are four of them.'

'They were going to crucify us in some twisted ceremony.'

Volkov rubbed his eyes and removed his hat. 'That's disgusting, what kind of men are they?'

'Demons,' said Frank, 'and I don't suppose they have the same morals as us.'

'Demons? Would you care to elaborate?'

Frank pointed at the clothes on the ground. 'They turned to dust when the mist touched them.'

Volkov spoke in Russian and one of the soldiers picked up a robe. Dust fell to the floor, and he made the sign of a cross on his chest.

'I shot him,' said Frank, 'but he got back up and came at us again, until the mist touched him.'

'Yes, we had the same problem.' Volkov turned to Mathew, 'Did you create the mist?'

'No,' said Mathew, 'I'm an instrument for the lord. There are more of them out there, and they will keep coming after us until we get to the church in France.'

Frank listened to him, and he sounded nothing like the Mathew he had known for just a few hours. He sounded older, calmer, more assured, and people would believe what he said.

'So the mist killed them,' said Volkov.

'No,' said Mathew, 'it made them vulnerable to weapons. They are not dead, but sent back to hell.'

Volkov glanced around at his army who had defeated the demons. 'We cannot take you to France, but we can get you to a part of Germany occupied by the British army.'

'Thank you, that is kind.'

'If it hadn't been for the mist, I would've lost a lot more men.'

'There are dead German soldiers inside, who were slaughtered.'

Volkov nodded. 'Wait here while I check on my men.'

Frank watched him walk away. 'This has been one strange night.'

Bert smiled. 'And then some, but I think we got lucky in the end.'

Soldiers walked up to the mansion with all the demons clothes. Frank inspected them but couldn't find Jeremy's and only saw one set of clothes similar to his. He believed they had belonged to David.

Thirty minutes later Frank sat on the back of an army truck with a canvas cover. Bert sat next to him while Mathew was sitting opposite, next to Colin who lay on a stretcher. Frank stared at the mansion as flames tore through the building.

Volkov climbed onto the truck. 'It saddens me to burn such a place down.'

'You did the right thing,' said Mathew, 'evil deeds have been happening there for a long time.'

Frank closed his eyes through tiredness and with his mind at peace for the first time in a week he fell asleep. He woke a few hours later and saw Volkov still sitting there. He rubbed his eyes stretched, and could hear Bert snoring next to him.

Volkov smiled. 'How can you sleep the way this thing rattles?'

'It was the first time I managed any in a while.'

'Father Mathew said they led you on a merry dance.'

'You could say that, but it's not over yet. I didn't see Jeremy's or I believe Richard's clothes.'

'Do not worry about them,' said Mathew, 'even if they escaped they would've been touched by the mist. They should be aware now any weapon could send them back.'

Frank nodded and turned to Volkov. 'Your English is very good.'

'I am also fluent in French and German,' said the captain, 'but I think you mean something else.'

'I sense no Russian accent . . . you could easily pass as British.'

'That's kind of you to say, and it did take a lot of practice. In my previous career I needed to pass as different people.'

The truck stopped near a border crossing as the sky brightened. Volkov climbed off and spoke to a British officer who nodded. Mathew joined them for a moment before they walked back.

'They have a truck to take us to France,' said Mathew.

Volkov returned the pistol to Frank. 'I don't know what happened to your rifle, and you should stop mentioning demons from now on. I believe you as I saw them for myself.'

Frank and Bert carried the stretcher to the other truck while Mathew carried the bag. They climbed on and lay the stretcher down.

Bert sat with his back to the side. 'Is Colin going to be OK? He's been asleep a long time.'

'He will be,' said Mathew, 'I am keeping him asleep. It's not only his body which suffers, but his mind too.'

Frank raised an eyebrow. 'Is that why he's the broken man?'

Mathew rubbed his chin. 'For the last year of the war he was a prisoner. They tortured him until it almost sent him mad. He was rescued and taken home, only to be arrested not long after for murder. His punishment was not death, but torture.'

'Oh crap,' said Frank, not understanding how Mathew knew so much. 'Those creeps know how to screw with your mind.'

'Yes, and then he finds out he has to go to Germany on a dangerous mission.'

'It makes you think,' said Bert, 'did he break his leg in an accident or was he trying to end it all?'

Twenty-four hours after parachuting into Germany they arrived at a monastery in the south of France.

Frank climbed off. 'I thought you said it was a church.'

'It's a place of worship and for Colin to recuperate.'

Frank and Bert carried the stretcher as Mathew led the way and opened the door. They stepped inside and monks stopped what they were doing and stared at them. One approached and spoke in French.

'English,' said Mathew, and the monk walked away.

'That went well,' said Bert.

Frank nodded. 'Let's hope he's gone to get someone who can speak English.'

An elder monk appeared and hurried over to them. 'I am Abbot Stephan, can we help you?'

'Yes,' said Mathew, 'I would like rooms for the night for my friends and more permanent ones for our injured friend and myself. I would also like food for them.'

'You have come to the wrong place. There's a hospital not too far.'

Mathew clasped his hands together. 'No, this is the perfect place for him to recuperate.'

The abbot rubbed his neck. 'This is a monastery, not a hotel.'

'I am aware of that,' said Mathew, 'but this man helped us retrieve certain artefacts stolen from here. Would you reward him by refusing him help? It's not just his leg which needs healing, but his mind too.'

Stephan put a hand to his mouth. 'What artefacts?'

'This is one of them,' said Mathew, and held out the jewel encrusted crucifix.

The abbot's eyes grew large as he accepted it. 'Yes, it is one of ours, and you said there were more.'

Mathew held the bag up. 'We have a few.'

The abbot turned to the other monks and spoke in French. Two of them hurried over, took the stretcher and carried it to another room.

'They will make him comfortable, 'said Stephan. 'If you follow me to the dining area, I will arrange refreshments for you.'

He led them to the rear of the monastery to a small canteen. Frank and Bert sat at a table as a monk poured them glasses of wine.

Mathew placed the bag on another table. 'I believe all the contents of this bag belong here.'

'There is one,' said Stephan, 'which we cherish more than any other. It may have been overlooked.'

'Cicero's Dagger,' said Mathew, 'we have brought it too.'

'You know of it, are you a priest at such a young age?'

Mathew shook his head. 'It is my calling . . . I was in training when the call for me to join the army came.'

'Then you were correct, this is the perfect place for you and your injured friend. We cannot thank you enough or pay for such a deed.'

'The items belong here, so there's no need.'

Frank smiled at the monk who placed bowls of stew and a plate of bread on the table.

Bert grabbed a spoon and tasted it. 'I could stay here for the food.'

'They'd probably let you,' said Frank, 'as it looks like Mathew and Colin are.'

Bert glanced around at the monks. 'No, I wouldn't be able to understand most of them, and it would send me crazy. What are you going to do?'

Frank swallowed some stew. 'Go home, get my belongings, and find somewhere to stay. I can't say I'm looking forward to it.'

Bert broke up a piece of bread. 'Is there no chance you and your wife could work things out?'

Frank thought about Laura. 'After what she's done, I don't think so.'

'You mean what the demons said she did.'

'Maybe, but she was the one who accused me, and testified in court, albeit a fake one.'

'Fair enough, and if you need somewhere to stay I can put you up. I'm living at my sister's house as she was at mine when the bomb hit.'

Frank watched the monks empty the bag with joy on their faces. 'Thanks, I might just take you up on that.'

Mathew joined them. 'How's the food?'

'Very nice,' said Bert, 'but then I haven't eaten since yesterday morning.'

Frank studied the young man. 'Is there anything of Mathew left in you?'

Mathew smiled. 'Of course, I am still him. I am more at peace at the moment and more aware.'

'I see you're going to stay here for a while.'

'Yes, the world needs healing and I'm going to start with Colin.'

Two days later Frank said goodbye to Bert as they walked through London. He carried on after Bert had showed him where he lived. The streets were busy as he stepped down an alley and passed piles of rubble. Frank hoped Laura was out as he did not want to confront her. The house was near, but as he turned right out of the alley he saw her. Laura was not alone as Jeremy stood next to her with Richard who held a knife to her throat.

'We've been waiting for you,' said Jeremy, 'as you ruined our plans.'

Frank felt angry once more, but this time for how they treated his wife. 'No, you ruined them yourselves with your stupid games.'

Jeremy shrugged. 'Richard wanted to kill you at the docks, but I thought it would be no fun. It would be much better if you watched us kill your wife first. Poor innocent Laura never did any of the things we told you about.'

Richard grinned. 'Do you have anything to say to her before she dies?'

Frank pulled out the pistol. 'Only that you'll be sent back straight after.'

'Your weapons cannot hurt us,' said Jeremy, 'you should know that, and you don't have the dagger with you.'

Frank watched as Richard slid the dagger down Laura's arm. It gave him the chance he wanted and pointed the gun. He fired hitting Richard in the forehead and pointed the pistol at Jeremy. 'I don't need the dagger as the mist already touched you.'

Jeremy stepped back as Richard turned to dust. 'No, this can't be.'

Frank shot him. 'Go to hell.'

Laura put both hands to her face. 'They told me you were dead. I'm so sorry for what I did but I had no choice.'

Frank approached her. 'It's OK . . . I know they would've killed you if you didn't follow their instructions.'

Laura shook her head. 'No, I would've died for you.'

Frank rubbed his eyes. 'I don't understand.'

'Quickly,' she said, 'follow me.' She ran down the road, and he followed her to their home. Frank walked inside as she picked a baby up out of a cot. 'Meet your daughter.'

Frank froze. 'How? When?'

'How do you think? The only time you came home during the war. The demons never threatened to kill me . . . they were going to kill her.'

Frank took his daughter and cradled her in his arms. 'What did you name her?'

'Francis, after her father. She hasn't been christened yet, and we don't have any godparents.'

Frank smiled. 'She has one, she has an Uncle Bert.'

CHAPTER TWO

Summoned

Present Day

Detective Inspector Devon Fields stared at the headless corpse. It sat propped up against a small wall in Clifton Country Park. 'Have I become such a cold hard bitch that I'm undisturbed by this?'

Sergeant Chris Doyle shrugged. 'Maybe, but it's more to do with the fact there's no head.'

'What's that got to do with anything?' Devon glanced around park as police officers searched through bushes and among the trees. Behind her was the visitor centre and café.

'When you see a dead body, you look into their eyes and imagine what their life was like. You can't do that here as we only have the body.'

Devon nodded as she studied the body dressed in designer jeans and sweatshirt. She had become hardened to scenes like this after life's trials. Forty-two years old and divorced. When her husband walked out she cropped her hair and started to wear trouser suits. 'True, so where's the bloody head?'

'I've no idea, but he wasn't murdered here, there's not enough blood. It's as if the body's been put on show for us.'

'Not for us,' said Devon, 'someone else.'

Chris rubbed his shaven chin. 'Once we get a name for this one we might know who, which might give us a lead to the killer.'

'Get on to missing persons, and tell them the victim was late teens to early twenties.'

'How can you be so sure?'

'His hands, he didn't do much work if any. Going by his clothes he may have been from a rich family.'

'He could've been a drug dealer,' said Chris, 'selling on the wrong patch, or a gang dispute.'

'I didn't know we had gangs around here. Look at his clothes and hands . . . it doesn't look like there was a struggle.'

'No, this was an execution. So where do we go now?'

'Back to the station and wait. We can't do anything until we know who he was, and I want to see an autopsy report. I doubt very much we'll get a finger print match.'

'The killer must've been some cool monster to do this. He beheads someone, brings the body here, and puts it on display.'

'Or she,' said Devon.

Chris scratched his head. 'I doubt it, look at the size of this guy, I wouldn't try carrying him.'

'There are such things as wheelchairs. I don't believe it to be a gangland killing as this would be the wrong place to put him on display.' Devon turned towards the visitor centre. 'Who found the body?'

'The cook from the café, she stepped outside and saw him. We won't get much from her for a while.'

'She wouldn't know anything. The body was placed here in the last few hours, and the murder occurred a few hours before. Don't bother checking for missing persons too far away, this is local.'

Chris scribbled into his notepad. 'You can travel a good distance in a few hours.'

'Yes, but why put it on display here if it's a statement?'

Devon glanced around the office as she leant back in her chair. No one matching the dead man's description had been reported missing. 'It's probably too soon.'

 Chris put the phone receiver down. 'What's too soon?'

'No one's missing him yet. Who was on the phone?'

'Geoff, he's done an autopsy and agrees with you about the time of death. He also believes the head was removed with one cut.'

'Does he know what with?'

'Probably an axe . . . and it would've been some blow to do it with one cut. When they used to execute people like that, it would normally take a few swings to remove the head. France had a better system with the guillotine.'

Devon shook her head. 'I wouldn't call beheading someone a good system in any sense.'

The door opened and a man's head appeared. 'You had any luck finding out who the body belonged to?'

Devon glanced up at the young detective. 'No, Vine, we're waiting for fingerprint and DNA results to see if they tell us anything.'

'Have you tried dental records?'

Devon threw her pad, but the head withdrew quickly. 'Moron.'

'Taverner put him up to that,' said Chris. 'How the hell did he make inspector?'

'Contacts probably.' Devon stood. 'I'm going home . . . I've had enough for one day.'

'What if something comes up?'

'You know where to reach me. I hate cases like this where there's nothing to go on, but I can tell you now it will have us up all hours trying to solve it.'

Devon stepped through her front door and saw an envelope with her name handwritten on the front. She picked it up, opened it and pulled out a one-page letter.

If you value your life you will drop this case, as death waits with the evil you face.

Pray to your god if you believe, for creatures are here who will deceive.

Heed my words and this warning, for tomorrow will be a bloody morning.

Devon rubbed her eyes. 'What the hell's this about?' She sat on the sofa and fell asleep.

Devon woke hours later when her phone rang. She sat up and picked it up off the table. Chris flashed on the screen. 'Tell me you've got some news.'

'Yes,' said Chris, 'but not what you want to hear. We've got another.'

Devon sighed. 'Is it the same?'

'Not quite, you better come and take a look yourself.'

Forty minutes later Devon steered her car to the right down Meadow Lane where police had blocked it to the public. On the right were expensive looking houses, and to the left she saw trees. Devon pulled up outside the last house where a constable leant over a bush being sick. She climbed out and walked up to the front door.

A constable opened it for her. 'It's not pretty in there, Inspector.'

Devon turned to the officer still retching. 'No, I imagine not.'

Chris stood watching forensics taking photographs. 'You might not want to go in this room.'

Devon walked down the long hall. 'Could it be any worse than this morning?'

Chris nodded. 'Oh yes.'

Devon glanced into the room and took a deep breath at the sight which greeted her. She looked around the room, scarce of furniture, and saw blood splattered over the walls. Body parts lay strewn across the floor. 'You're not wrong there. How could anyone manage to do this?'

Chris shrugged. 'Dunno, maybe they used a chainsaw or an axe.'

'How many victims?'

'Just the one going by the hands and feet we found.'

Devon studied the mess. 'This isn't the same killer.'

'Hard to say, different methods but each murdered by a psychopath.'

'Who discovered this blood bath?'

'We don't know, someone called it in earlier but left no name.'

'Strange,' said Devon, and pulled the letter out of her pocket. 'Read this.'

Chris opened the folded page and read it to himself. 'This is weird, where did you get it?'

'Someone put it through my letter box earlier today.'

Chris handed the letter back. 'Shit, this means the killer knows where you live.'

Devon shook her head. 'No, it means whoever posted the letter knows who the killer of the first victim is.'

'This was the first victim, sometime yesterday.'

'So we've got two killers on our hands, or some messed up psycho. A frenzied maniac who can switch to a calm calculated murderer.'

Chris frowned. 'I don't like either option.'

Devon nodded. 'Neither do I, so what do we know of the victim?'

Chris opened his notepad. 'Gerald Brand, a recluse and wealthy. No family we know of and spent a lot of time abroad.'

Geoff the pathologist pulled rubber gloves off his hands as he stepped into the hall. 'It might be a good idea to find out what his interests were.'

Chris closed his pad. 'Why's that?'

'The only piece of furniture in there is an altar.'

Devon heard someone cough. She glanced down the hall and saw a constable with an open book. 'Shouldn't you be doing something else?'

The constable held the book up. 'I'm trying to find out what his interests were, and his books looked a good place to start.'

Chris laughed. 'Good thinking.'

'Indeed,' said Devon, 'and what's the book you're holding?'

'The Gates of Hell,' said the constable, 'it's about devil worshipping and summoning demons as are many of the books.'

'Write down all the titles.'

'Nice,' said Chris, 'I wonder if the victim is the one who owns the house or a sacrifice gone wrong.'

Geoff shook his head. 'They use chickens for that, and I saw two dead ones in there.'

Devon raised both eyebrows. 'You're not suggesting he summoned a demon up and it did this?'

'No, of course not,' said Geoff, 'but I do believe he tried to. I'd be surprised if he did it alone.'

'You mean he failed and the other person did this to him?'

Geoff rubbed his chin. 'Maybe.'

'Could one man do all that damage?'

'You'd be surprised at what someone gone berserk could do.'

'I guess,' said Chris, 'but could he have calmed down enough to commit the other murder?'

Geoff shrugged. 'As in the way he murdered and left the body on display. It's highly unlikely but not impossible. What we have here is a murder more vicious than any I have ever seen in my years on the force. This one is of brute strength, and from what I can tell he pulled the victim apart.'

Chris shuddered. 'Is that even possible?'

'Yes, and like I said it took brute strength.'

'If one man committed the other murder, he had to be strong,' said Devon. 'I don't want to sound obvious, but this is bad and only going to get worse.'

Chris stared into the room. 'We have to stop him and soon. The only clue we have is a big guy with an axe.'

'I'd like all cameras checked since yesterday,' said Devon, 'and I don't think officers should patrol on their own. It might be a good idea to search the house and see if he kept any animals here.'

'Like a gorilla?'

Devon tried to imagine a large ape causing the devastation and decided against it. 'I don't know, but find out everything you can about this Brand and any known associates.'

Devon searched through the papers on her desk. She saw information on the murders, but none of it of any use. They still didn't have the identity of the headless man so couldn't connect it with the other victim. She pulled the letter out of her pocket and read it again.

'Who are you?' she said. 'What do you know?'

The door opened and Chris entered. 'The chief's not happy . . . he thinks we should be out there searching.'

Devon leant back in her chair. 'Really? Does Mr Jameson know where we should be searching?'

Chris dropped his notepad on the desk. 'No, he wants to show the press we're doing something and not just twiddling our thumbs.'

'He has others for that, we're detectives . . . we solve clues when we get any.'

'He knows and agrees they should only go out in pairs.'

'Are they searching for anything in particular?'

'For anything out of the ordinary . . . and to keep a look out for any big guys.'

Devon sighed. 'God we're desperate, we have nothing.'

'Something will come up, it always does.'

'Yeah, but not until we find another dead body.' Devon stood and put on her jacket. 'Come on, let's go.'

'Go where?'

'We follow Jameson's orders, find a large man and ask him if he has a big chopper.'

Devon yawned as she drove to work. Her night had been restless due to the case. It wasn't natural, and she knew something darker, more sinister, was occurring. Her phone rang and she pulled over.

'Hello, Chris, I'm on my way in.'

'You'll need to make a detour as I'm staring at another dead body. The country park again, only this time in the woods.'

'OK, will see you soon.'

Devon drove off and turned left. She soon passed the sealed off Meadow Lane and drove down a lane opposite. She saw the country park, which was also sealed off, and pulled up. Devon made her way to the wooded area and walked down a path to an open space. Chris stood staring at a dead body, the head wedged onto a tree trunk with the body hanging limp.

'Watch your step,' said Chris, 'the ground's covered in blood.'

Devon glanced down and saw a patch about eight feet in diameter of earth soaked in blood. She turned back to the body and the blood down the trunk. 'This isn't his blood.'

Chris nodded. 'That's what I thought, there has to be another body.'

'Inspector, Sergeant,' said a constable kneeling by undergrowth near a tree, 'you might want to see this.'

'What is it?' said Chris.

The constable stood. 'A dog.'

Devon made her way over while dodging the blood soaked ground. She saw the black and white collie whimpering in pain. 'Hello, little fella.' She noticed it wore a collar with the lead still attached.

'It looks badly hurt,' said the constable.

Devon nodded. 'It looks like it was thrown at the tree. Find a board or a stretcher, so we can get him to a vet.'

'This creep gets worse,' said Chris, 'why take it out on a dog?'

Devon studied the body of the man in the tree and shook her head. She stepped back past the patch of blood and thought of how it happened. 'He had no intention of hurting the dog, but why wasn't this place sealed off already?'

'The chief thought it safe as the other man wasn't killed here.'

'This is different to the others. A couple died last night, a man and his wife.'

'His partner could've been a man.'

'No, his wife. You should pay more attention to hands. He's wearing a wedding ring which he hasn't been able to take off in years.'

Chris knelt by the victim. 'OK, I'm with you on that, but does it give us a reason?'

'Yes, bad luck. They were walking the dog through here with the man holding the lead. The killer came up behind them, slammed the man into the tree which sent the dog flying into the tree over there. The killer turned his attention on the wife and slaughtered her.'

Chris glanced up with a hand above his eyes. 'There's something up in the tree, it looks like a jacket.'

Devon looked up and saw it. 'I want this whole area searched for any more clothing. I have a real, bad feeling about this.'

Chris raised an eyebrow. 'I've had a bad feeling since day one.'

'I mean it's much worse than we thought. Tell me something, where's the other body?'

Chris shrugged. 'Probably dumped in a ditch.'

Devon stared at the patch of blood. 'No, we will never find it.'

'What makes you believe that?'

Devon glanced around to see who was in earshot and said in a quieter voice. 'Whoever did this has eaten her.'

Chris coughed. 'What? That's insane. I reckon the killer went berserk like he did at Brand's house, where he didn't eat the victim.'

'I'll wait for Geoff to get back to us on that. An innocent couple were murdered for what?'

'He's a maniac, does there have to be a reason?'

'Yes, if this maniac was on a killing spree, he wouldn't stop here.'

Chris rubbed his chin. 'If the reason's what you believe then the maniac is an it, not a he. I wouldn't go telling Jameson just yet.'

'Why are you so against the idea? There have been many cannibal killers in the past.'

'Yeah, but they never ate a whole person in one sitting.'

Geoff strolled over to them. 'Are we having a lovers tiff?'

Chris frowned. 'Not a term my wife would like . . . and you're late.'

Geoff shook his head. 'No, I get here when I can, unless you would like to perform the autopsy.'

'I'll give it a miss,' said Chris, 'and besides the inspector here has already solved it.'

'Oh good, maybe she can solve the little conundrum back at the lab.'

Devon clasped her hands together. 'What conundrum?'

Geoff scratched his head. 'We took the body parts back and placed them on the table, and I blame this on the blood.'

Devon studied the pathologist's expression, one of uncertainty. 'Go on.'

'We put the arms either side of the torso and the legs below.'

'Nice,' said Chris.

'Anyway,' said Geoff, 'they looked odd. We have a body, a head, two legs and two arms. The problem is one of the legs is shorter than the other. We cleaned them off and found the shorter one to be shaved where the other is hairy.'

'Two people murdered,' said Chris, 'and we found women's clothing in a bedroom.'

Geoff nodded. 'So what happened to the rest of them?'

Devon turned to Chris. 'You can tell him.'

Devon lay in the bath contemplating about the grizzly events of the past two days. They had returned to the station as Superintendent Jameson called them in for a briefing. After they told him most of what they knew, he came to the conclusion a wild animal was on the loose.

She heard the letter box shut, and she jumped out of the bath. Devon grabbed a robe and ran to her bedroom window. A hooded figure stared up at her before walking off into the darkness. Devon dried herself before going downstairs and as she expected an envelope lay on the floor. She picked it up and pulled out the letter.

Did you not heed or understand? The beast is free and roams the land.

It matters not if night or day, as humankind is its prey.

Listen good and listen well, before your world becomes your hell.

Thousands of years it has waited, for its thirst to be sated.

Weapons to kill it will not be found, unless you lure it to hallowed ground.

Devon drove towards the station but stopped off at the nearest church. She climbed out the car and walked up the dark path. Trees stood either side, with a garden area for wedding photos, but no cemetery. Devon sensed she wasn't alone and three hooded figures stepped through the trees. She could take two she thought, although unsure how good they were.

One stepped forward. 'Wrong church.'

'What do you know about the murders?'

'You read the letter,' said the figure, as they shuffled back through the trees.

Devon walked into the station after nine. She stepped into her office where Chris sat with his feet on a desk. 'Comfortable?'

'Not really, but then I didn't get to go home like some.'

'I needed a bath . . . it helps me think.'

'Good, so you solved it then.'

Devon shook her head. 'Not quite.'

Chris opened his notepad. 'We may have a name for our headless body.'

'Finally, who is he?'

'Mike Hughes, son of business man Alan Hughes.'

Devon walked over to the window and stared out into the darkness. 'The father sounds familiar.'

'He's known to us, a small-time crook until he got a lucky break and became the owner of a business.'

Devon nodded. 'Didn't it have to do with some dodgy deal, but it couldn't be proved?'

'Yeah, a business for sale, and he paid less than what others offered.'

Devon sat on the edge of her desk. 'What do we know of the son?'

'Twenty-one, at university until his death.'

'The father's the reason the son's dead, but why?'

Chris shrugged. 'Dunno, but I do remember Hughes being mentioned in a murder case years ago.'

'He's not the one who murdered the others, and that's what we need to concentrate on.'

'The chief agrees . . . he sent Taverner and Vine to interview Hughes.'

Devon rubbed her eyes. 'I'm sure there are more tactful officers than those two.' She pulled the second letter out of a pocket and handed it over.

'Another one,' said Chris, and read it. 'He's no poet laureate . . . did you see him?'

'From the upstairs window, but he wore a hooded top.' Devon stood and walked around the office. 'I stopped off at a church on the way here, where I saw three of them.'

Chris leant back in his chair and watched her. 'Are you mad? It could've been a trap.'

'No, the letters are more than that, I wasn't in any danger.'

'He's trying to tell us the killer's a monster, and if we don't stop it soon we never will.'

'Something like that, the end of days as we know it.'

'Are you going to show this to Jameson?'

'Not yet, he might have my house watched.'

'Would that be a bad thing?'

'Yes, I might not get any more messages.'

'From what I've read they're not much help.' Chris glanced at his pad. 'Some of Brand's neighbours said he had a maid, but they believed she may have been more than that.'

Devon rubbed her chin. 'Get the area map up on your computer . . . there's gotta be a pattern to this.'

Chris turned to his computer screen and clicked the mouse. 'There are only two crime scenes, well three but two were in the park.'

'I know, but forget about Mike Hughes for now, let's concentrate on the others.'

'You don't think his murder is part of it.'

Devon stood behind him and stared at the map on the screen. 'I do, but for different reasons. See Brand's house is the last on the edge of town, and if we go north we find the country park.'

Chris rubbed his eyes. 'Shit, this thing's moving north, and we've got men out there.'

'Zoom out . . . I want to see where it might be heading.'

Chris did and a larger map appeared. 'There's not a lot out there apart from Lockwood House.'

'I've heard that name before.'

'It used to be a big thing before you moved up here, but since Lord Lockwood was murdered you hear nothing of the place anymore.'

'Yes, I remember reading about it.'

'They never caught the killer, and the place would've been left to his daughter, but she vanished the same night and hasn't been seen since.'

Devon smiled. 'It's all falling together, and starting to make sense,' she said, as the door opened.

A grey-haired, uniformed, officer stepped into the room. 'That's what I like to hear. Do we have a suspect?'

Devon shook her head. 'Not yet, but we were talking about Lockwood House.'

'The chief's the man to ask,' said Chris, 'he knows all about what happened there.'

'I will tell you all about the mystery there another time,' said Jameson, 'but we have a more pressing case at the moment.'

'It's part of what's happening now,' said Devon, 'I just need some information.'

'Are you serious?'

Devon looked out of the window again. 'I'm joining up the dots. I have all the dots but I need to connect them.'

Jameson turned to Chris. 'Do you know anything about this?'

Chris held his hands out. 'No, but I can't wait to hear it.'

Jameson sat in Devon's chair. 'OK, what do you want to know?'

'The history and what happened the night of the murder.'

Jameson put his hands together and interlocked his fingers. 'The mansion has belonged to the Lockwoods for hundreds of years. Frederick Lockwood made his money trading overseas although many thought him a pirate. He returned here a rich man and bought the mansion. He had no other family and hoped to make a large one, but it never worked out that way. Frederick married the daughter of a lord and eventually became one himself. They had two children, a boy and girl. The boy inherited the mansion, and he only had one child. The family was never blessed with many children even up to Edward, the last Lord Lockwood. His only child, eighteen year old Vanessa, vanished the night of his murder. I was part of the search for her, and I can tell you she was not at the mansion dead or alive.'

Devon nodded. 'Could she have killed her father?'

Jameson shook his head. 'No, she was too fragile for that. Her father was brutally beaten before the killer stabbed him.'

Devon knew Vanessa didn't die that night. 'She may have fallen in love and got her lover to do it.'

'There was no lover, and she adored her father. He was a friend of mine and a good man. What does this have to do with the case you're on now?'

'I'm getting there . . . I wanted to make sure she was innocent all those years ago.'

'What difference does it make? We believe she died that night.'

Devon imagined the incident over in her mind. 'No, not that night. Who inherited the mansion?'

Jameson scratched his chin. 'Raymond Barlow, a distant cousin, who also inherited the businesses belonging to Lockwood. He had no interest in those and sold them off.'

Devon smiled. 'Was he ever a suspect?'

'No, he was living overseas at the time.'

'He could've paid someone else to do it, giving him an alibi.'

'We looked into it, but found nothing as we didn't know who the murderer was.'

'Do you know who bought the businesses?'

'No, he didn't sell them for months after the murder and I took no interest. He has become a recluse and the only people anyone sees from the mansion are the servants.'

Devon passed the letter to the superintendent. 'Before I go on, read this. It was posted through my door earlier.'

Jameson read the letter before putting it on the desk. 'Please tell me you don't believe this nonsense.'

'Something inhuman is killing people. You yourself believe it to be a wild animal.' Devon chose her words carefully, although part of it she didn't believe. 'A wild animal would've been seen by now, so what if it was a trained one.'

'Maybe, but why did it kill the couple?'

'They were unlucky as it looks like those from the mansion have lost control of it.'

Jameson folded his arms. 'You ought to be careful with your accusations, Barlow is a rich man. I also told you he has become a recluse.'

'You can't know that for certain, and we have no idea what he gets up to at the mansion. Why do you think they sent me the letter?'

'To throw you off the scent.'

Devon shook her head. 'If it was a monster, what could I do about it? They know we have armed police who will stop an animal.'

'I agree with that, but why?'

'Look at the map, it's going back. They're either afraid or want to distance themselves from it.'

'Don't you mean him as in Barlow?'

'Yes, but I don't believe he's working alone. Now we've solved the case . . . we need to stop the thing.'

Chris coughed. 'When did we solve anything? All we know is the identity of the headless body.'

'Indeed,' said Jameson, 'do enlighten us.'

Devon sat on the edge of the desk again. 'You said the Lockwood murder happened twenty years ago.'

Jameson rubbed his chin. 'Longer, Vanessa would've been forty this year.'

Devon considered it. 'That night a petty crook was offered a deal he couldn't refuse. He failed in part but got lucky. The crook was Alan Hughes, and if he killed Lord Lockwood and his daughter he would be a rich man, the owner of one of the businesses.'

'The dodgy deal,' said Chris.

Devon nodded. 'Yes, but he didn't kill Vanessa. She must've seen what was happening and ran. She found a safe haven and stayed hidden until a few days ago.'

'It can't be,' said Jameson. 'Where could she have gone?'

'Look at the map,' said Devon. 'Vanessa ran towards town and knocked on the first door she saw.'

Chris stared at the computer. 'Brand's house.'

'Yes, she found a place to hide, and Brand found the perfect helper. If she had knocked any other door, she would've been safe in the hands of the police.'

'I can't believe it,' said Jameson, 'all these years and she was alive.'

'I'm sorry, Chief, but those from the mansion must've found out and had her killed along with Brand. The same night they got their revenge on Hughes.'

'How the hell will we pin it on him?' said Chris.

'We find the animal killing people and those at the mansion might blame him. Hughes may also confess to get his own back on them.' Devon stood. 'Is there a church between the park and Lockwood House?'

Jameson looked weary. 'Yes, an old one, and it has a cemetery.'

'We best go and check it out.'

'No, it's too dangerous . . . I will have armed officers go.'

'We'll be fine,' said Devon. 'We're just going to check it out, and I'm sure the car will be faster than any animal.'

Chris started up the engine. 'What the hell was that all about?'

Devon turned to him. 'Excuse me?'

'Yeah, you solved the case and made it sound easy, but there's no way you think it's an animal.'

'No, but I couldn't tell Jameson that. This might be the only chance we have of stopping the creature if we believe the letter.'

Chris drove off down the street. 'How can you believe the letter when he makes it rhyme?'

'Maybe he thinks himself as a poet.'

'He should study more, and I'd feel a lot better with armed officers.'

'If they show up first the creature might not.'

'Do you think Brand managed to summon this thing up?'

Devon nodded. 'It goes against everything I believe, but I can't help thinking it's a demon.'

Fifteen minutes later Chris drove down a country lane with the park now behind them. Devon glanced out the window as fields passed by when Chris slammed on the brakes.

She lurched forward. 'What the hell?'

Chris reversed the car. 'I just saw a caravan on its side.'

Devon stared through the driver's side window as Chris pulled up and saw the caravan. She grabbed a torch and climbed out the car. They made their way forward with the torches pointed across the field and climbed over a wooden fence.

'It looks like the door's been ripped off.'

'More like half the side.' Devon shone her touch inside and saw blood everywhere.

Chris turned away. 'Shit, we better get back and call it in.'

'You've got a phone.'

Chris took his mobile out an inside pocket and hurried back to the car while making a phone call.

Devon followed at a slower pace and climbed into the car. A few seconds later Chris put the phone away and drove off at speed.

'Slow down,' she said, 'what's got into you?'

'What do you think? It didn't use a can opener . . . it tore the door off. I want to put some distance between us.'

'I know, but I would like to get to the cemetery alive. Anyway, we're most likely heading towards it.'

Chris slowed the car down. 'Great . . . that makes me feel much better.'

'Don't worry . . . we'll be at the church soon.'

'How come it took so long to get here?'

'It probably doesn't want to be seen and still needs food. Remember what the letter said about it being sated? So maybe the more it eats the stronger it gets.'

'That's comforting, after seeing that guy stuck to the tree I wouldn't have thought it needed to get any stronger.'

'Yes, and that's why it need stopping now. If it feeds any more, there will be no chance of stopping it.'

Chris pulled over. 'We're here now.'

Devon climbed out and stepped over a small wall. She glanced around at the church and gravestones. 'It's not very big.'

'No one has been buried here for over fifty years.'

'Let's just hope it's hallowed ground.'

Chris rubbed his head with the torch. 'We might have a problem.'

'Like what?'

'The letter said weapons wouldn't hurt it unless on hallowed ground.'

'Yes, I know.'

'We have no weapons, and I don't think I'd be able to punch it to death.'

Devon stared at the church. 'Let's have a look around, and we might find something.'

Chris shone his torch on the ground. 'You want to fight a demon with a stick?'

'Maybe the poet left us something.'

'Or he could be hiding with the others you saw, this could be a trap.'

'We could go back if you want.'

Chris glanced over at the car, his eyes growing large. 'I don't think that option is open to us anymore.'

Devon turned and saw the beast. She could also see through parts of it. The demon looked like a hyena, with arms and legs, and twice the size of the car. 'We're still in time.'

'I can see that, but we have nothing to kill it with.'

'It's staying the other side of the wall . . . I think the demon's too afraid to enter.'

'Not afraid,' said another voice, 'just wary.'

Devon turned and saw eight hooded figures outside the cemetery. 'So the riddles were just a trick to get us here?'

'Yes and no. I didn't write the message this one next to me did.' He pulled back his hood to reveal red eyes and sharp-pointed teeth.

Chris sighed. 'More demons?'

Devon nodded. 'It would appear so.' She glanced towards the other demon which hadn't moved, and turned back to the others. 'Why choose me?'

'What the letter said was true,' said the red-eyed demon. 'The Devourer needs to be stopped, and it can only be done on hallowed ground. It's a dumb creature but would never enter where you are unless for a special meal.'

'What's that supposed to mean?'

'The Devourer knows what you are, the daughter of a demon hunter.'

Devon shook her head. 'You're mistaken, my father was a detective.'

'Yes, and he also hunted demons. We hid your scent for the most part, but the beast knew you had been to the park.'

Devon remembered her father had been stabbed to death when she was a child, and the murderer was never caught. Her uncle had brought her up as her mother died a few years before. 'The Devourer didn't stop at the park though, as it was coming after you at the mansion.'

The demon hissed. 'How do you know where we're from?'

'It wasn't difficult. So you're here to kill it once it enters the cemetery?'

'Yes, after it has eaten you. It will be fun to watch, but that is not the reason why. The Devourer will go into stasis for a few hours which will make it easier for us.'

'I don't get it,' said Chris, 'you're all demons.'

'Yes, human, but we are not all the same. The Devourer is a mindless killer and will never stop, which wouldn't be good for our plans.'

'The days of man will soon be the past,' said the hooded demon next to him, 'for demon kind are coming fast.'

'There's your poet,' said Chris, as the Devourer appeared restless.

'It senses hallowed ground,' said the first demon, 'but doesn't understand what it is. I think it has waited long enough.'

Devon heard sirens. 'Armed police are on the way.'

'They're going to the caravan, not here.'

Devon shook her head. 'You're wrong . . . they're coming here on their way to the mansion. Our superintendent wants a word with Raymond Barlow.'

The demon's eyes grew bigger. 'What does he know of him?'

'Everything, as I know what happened.'

The demon laughed. 'Not such a great detective then as Barlow is dead. He never made it here, he died before Lockwood did.'

Devon shrugged. 'Just replace Barlow with demon and it's the same result. Not so good for you as they will search every inch of the mansion and its land looking for him.'

'You will pay for that.'

'Isn't being eaten by that thing enough?' said Chris, 'I think we should try to get inside the church now.'

'No, you will not,' said the demon, as it pulled out a dagger. 'Try and you will be dead before you reach the door.'

Devon watched as most of the other demons pulled out daggers. 'What I don't understand is why you killed Hughes's son out of revenge and not Hughes himself. I would never have linked Lockwood to the case if not for his murder.'

'It was not revenge as we knew Hughes never killed Vanessa. The sacrifice of his unborn son was always part of the deal. We gave him time as it would not happen until his twenty-first birthday. He was happy with the deal at the time, but as the day grew closer he tried to get out of it.'

'You refused, so he turned to Gerald Brand who summoned up the Devourer.'

'Almost correct, he tried summoning another demon, but we made sure it went wrong.'

Devon rubbed her eyes. 'I think it went wrong for you, as my colleagues will get here before you destroy it.'

'It's coming,' said Chris, and they stepped back towards the church.

'Stop,' said the demon, waving the dagger, 'we do not miss.'

'I'd rather take the knife,' said Chris, as the Devourer approached.

The church door burst open and a grey-haired man ran out. 'No, demon, you will not harm them.' He held up a shard of glass and beams of light shot out hitting all but one of the demons and the Devourer. The hooded demons ran, and the Devourer chased after them.

Devon watched as they vanished into the darkness and turned to the man. 'Uncle Benjamin, what the hell are you doing here?'

Benjamin smiled. 'Hello, my dear, Robert called when he thought you had a demon problem.'

'Robert?'

'Your chief, Robert Jameson.'

'Are you saying he knew they existed all along?'

'Of course, your father and I were his friends a long time ago.'

Devon saw blue flashing lights drawing near. 'Was my father a demon hunter?'

Benjamin shook his head. 'No, not really. He hunted some men who killed a young family. It upset him as the daughter was like you back then, and he wanted to capture them. He didn't know they were demons until he met another man who gave him this piece of glass. He sent me a message saying he knew where they were, but I got the message too late, and he went alone.'

Devon rubbed her eyes. 'My father was killed by demons?'

'Yes, when I got to him, he was lying on the floor with a dagger in his chest. He told me he sent four back before one got him.'

'How do you mean he sent them back?'

'You cannot kill demons, as far as we know, you send them back to where they came from. Most weapons will not harm them as the bodies they use are not like ours and the wounds will heal quickly. Certain objects like this glass changes things, and they will turn to dust when they receive a fatal blow.'

'What is it?'

Benjamin handed over the glass. 'I've no idea, but it's yours now. Your father asked me to give it to you when you were old enough.'

Devon accepted the glass and raised an eyebrow. 'I've been old enough for a long time.'

'I know, but you weren't ready. If I had told you all those years ago you would've gone after them.'

'No, I would've thought you mad.' She saw police cars arrive, and they made their way over to the road.

Superintendent Jameson opened a window. 'Are you OK?'

Devon put the glass in a pocket. 'The thing was here and it looks like it chased the others to the mansion. You won't find Raymond Barlow there as they killed him years ago, but it gives us a reason to search the place.'

'Good, let's go and put an end to this.'

Chris drove towards the mansion where they saw flames light up the darkness. Police officers forced the gates open as they all drove through. They parked up at a safe distance and climbed out.

Devon stared at the burning building. 'Let's hope they were all inside.'

Benjamin nodded. 'If they are, those touched by the light at the church will be sent back.'

'What about the poet?' said Chris. 'I wonder if he was in there.'

Devon shrugged. 'Who cares? He's a demon who set us up.'

'Maybe, or maybe not. For all we know he knew your uncle was in the church.'

'I doubt it,' said Benjamin, 'demons cannot see inside a church unless they enter.'

Chris scratched his head. 'Neither can I.'

'You can see through windows.'

Chris shook his head. 'Not church windows, anyway about the poet. He may have set us up, but what would've happened if we didn't come here tonight?'

Devon considered it. 'The Devourer would've fed and become whole.'

'Yes, and it would be unstoppable. The information he gave was the only chance of doing so, and I hope the white light worked on it. Remember his last rhyme about the last days of men . . . I think that was a warning.'

'I know, but what does that have to do with anything?'

'Why bother telling us if he thought we were about to die? He knew we were safe.'

'True, and I'm sure the light didn't touch him.'

Devon woke to the smell of breakfast. She smiled as it brought back memories of her uncle Benjamin cooking for her. She climbed out of bed and wrapped a dressing gown around her before going downstairs.

'Morning,' said Benjamin, as he placed a fried breakfast on the table.

Devon leant on the frame of the door. 'Should I be upset with you for not telling me about demons sooner?'

Benjamin placed another breakfast on the table. 'You could if you wanted, but would it do you any good?'

'I guess not, and besides I haven't tasted your cooking in a long time.'

Benjamin picked up a pot of tea. 'I haven't cooked for anyone else since Melanie died.'

'Have you been coping OK?'

'Yes, been keeping busy. There's a letter for you in the living room, I thought your postman was early until I noticed it had no stamp.'

Devon turned and saw it on the coffee table. She picked it up, returned to the kitchen, and sat at the table.

'Anything important?' said Benjamin.

'It's from the poet.' Devon opened the letter and read it out.

'You survived the night and live today, for the beast has gone away.

The Lockwood mystery has now ended, but the human race is undefended.

Will you now choose your fate? For destiny will not wait.

Earth will be covered by demon hoards, if you fail to stop the demon lords.

You must protect and help the weak, while retrieving the items you must seek.

Others will help who are true, so let me help you with this clue.

Spells woven spells cast, blood soaked earth from battles past.

Tree of death, sword of life, a broken window and a sacred knife.

Demon lords which number three, on this we all agree.

A dark witch and a humped back man . . . are all part of their evil plan.'

Devon put the letter on the table. 'I will need to ask Jameson for some leave.'

Benjamin sat down. 'You're going through with it then?'

'I have to . . . you can't leave me a puzzle like this and expect me to ignore it.'

Benjamin smiled. 'I know a few people you should meet.

CHAPTER THREE

Entrapped

Do not ignore this letter. Fail to comply with the instructions, and your wife will receive certain photographs of the night you spent at the Raven Inn.

Dan Miller smiled as he remembered the night and continued reading.

You are to log onto your computer and transfer one hundred thousand pounds to another bank account. Details are given at the end of this letter and must be completed by midnight. Enclosed is a photograph of you and the woman you slept with.

Dan removed the picture and saw Kelly, the woman he met at the pub. It had not long been refurbished when he decided to see what it was like. It turned out to be date night, and the inn had rooms available. They took one but neither stayed the night as they had to be up early for work. His only regret was not getting her phone number. He screwed up the letter and threw it in the bin.

Judy Miller stepped into the room. 'Nothing important I see.'

Dan shook his head. 'No, just some scammers. There wasn't a stamp, so they're probably just trying their luck.'

~ ~ ~ ~

Stuart Jones stared at the photograph, his hands shaking. 'Shit, if Victoria sees this picture she'll divorce me. I've done it too many times before and have run out of chances. Her father would sack me on the spot. A hundred grand, yeah I've got it, but only just.'

Stuart read the letter again and switched on his computer.

~ ~ ~ ~

Alison Townsend rubbed her eyes as she read the letter. Due to whom your husband is, we will send a copy of the pictures to the press when we send him his.

This will destroy me, she thought, because of one moment of madness. The handsome charmer made me feel young again. I can see the headlines now, Counsellor Townsend's wife in bed with another man.

Since turning fifty, Alison felt old. Years ago she always tried to get her picture in the papers, now she hated seeing herself.

She sighed and opened up her laptop.

~ ~ ~ ~

Dan Miller stared up at the extension he had built. A shaven headed man carrying a bag stepped out. 'Are you off now?'

John put the bag over his shoulder. 'Yes, boss, I'm off out tonight.'

'OK, and be careful as I need you in early tomorrow.'

John scratched his head. 'You're joking right? It's Saturday tomorrow.'

Dan yawned. 'Is it really? I seem to be losing track of time.'

'What do you expect with all the hours you put in? That wife of yours will end up killing you?'

Dan shook his head. 'No, it's not her, and I have a deadline to meet. I'm also trying to raise enough money for Ben's operation in America.'

'I thought you had enough now.'

'I do, but he won't be going alone so flights and accommodation will cost.' Dan picked up a tape measure. 'I received a letter from someone trying to scam me the other day. They wanted a hundred grand.'

John whistled. 'That's a lot of money, did they leave contact details?'

Dan shrugged. 'Dunno, I only read a few lines and threw it in the bin. It makes you wonder where they thought I could get my hands on such an amount in a short time.'

'You own a building business and have good contracts.'

'True, so where you off to tonight?'

'The Raven Inn, it's date night so Tim says. He went there last week and said it's been done out.'

Dan thought about the pub. 'Yeah, I went in the first night it reopened.' He remembered Kelly and wanted to join them, but work came first. He also knew the picture was taken from there. 'As I said be careful, you get the feeling you're being watched.'

Dan walked into the house on Sunday afternoon and could smell a roast dinner being cooked. 'Something smells good, what we having?'

'Beef,' Judy shouted from the kitchen, 'and there's another of those letters on the sideboard.'

Dan put his bag down and picked up the letter. He opened the envelope and pulled out a piece of paper before reading. For failing to complete the first task in time, you have a further one. Dan screwed up the letter and threw it in the bin.

'Another scammer?' said Judy.

Dan nodded. 'Same people, I'm going to take a shower before dinner.'

Dan glanced up from his dinner. 'Anything exciting happened around here lately?'

Judy sliced a roast potato in half. 'Have you been away somewhere and I didn't know?'

'No, I've been too busy to watch the news.'

'A man from a few streets away was murdered yesterday . . . he had his throat slit open. He was married too, with three children.'

'How horrible, did they get whoever did it?'

Judy shook her head. 'No, and a homeless man died in a fire in a shop on the high street the other day. The police say he sneaked in for the night, but did not start the fire.'

'Anywhere near our shop?'

'It happened at the other end of the high street. Helen, from church, told me it happened down south. Her sister lives there and says a string of murders and fires took place a couple of months ago.'

'I hardly think it's the same person.'

'So you say, but for all we know there could be a serial killer around here.'

'I'm sure the police will know who has moved up here from there.'

Judy pushed her empty plate away. 'Reverend Simon says we should be extra vigilant.'

Dan laughed. 'I did wonder what you lot get up to at church, or is it a detective agency?'

'We're just concerned, and Simon said it would be nice to see you there one Sunday.'

'You know I'm not one for church, and besides when do I ever get a Sunday off?'

~ ~ ~ ~

Alison Townsend watched her husband leave for work on Monday morning before taking the envelope out of her pocket. It arrived earlier that morning. She breathed deep, opened it, and pulled out the letter. Alison unfolded it and started to read.

Due to unforeseen circumstances you have a new task. Because of this, your money has been returned. For your new task you must seduce a young man called Tim at the Raven Inn. His picture is enclosed, and the task will be over when he has fallen in love with you. A room will be reserved.

Alison rubbed her eyes. 'What the hell? I'm being blackmailed for being unfaithful, and now I'm being blackmailed to do it again.'

She took the photo out the envelope and saw the picture of a skinny young man about twenty years old. 'I'm fifty, how am I supposed to do that?' Alison sighed. 'I don't know what I've gotten into, but see you soon, Tim.'

~ ~ ~ ~

Stuart Jones's hands shook as he opened the envelope. He found it on the door mat an hour earlier, but needed two vodkas before he could read it. He sat in the bathroom with sweat dripping down his face.

Due to unforeseen circumstances you have a new task. Because of this, your money has been returned. For your new task you are to go to the high street tonight and set fire to a shop. At the rear you will find a can of petrol and the door unlocked.

He sighed in relief. 'I can do that, and would gladly do it for a hundred thousand.' He continued reading.

~ ~ ~ ~

Dan placed a tool bag in the back of his van. He saw John change his boots for trainers while Tim stood waiting. 'Good work today, lads, and as we got the job finished early you can have tomorrow off.'

'Thanks,' said John, 'but what about wages?'

'You'll be paid, just think of it as a bonus. I'm going to the manor to talk about the annex we'll be starting on Wednesday.'

'Nice one,' said Tim, 'It looks like I'm going to the Raven tonight.'

John patted him on the shoulder. 'You might as well move in there.'

Tim raised both eyebrows. 'You can talk . . . you've already spent the night there.'

'True, but don't worry I'm sure your time will come soon.' John put the boots in his car. 'I might even come with you tonight.'

'How about you, boss?' said Tim, 'fancy joining us?'

Dan decided not to tell them the scam letters came from the Raven as neither would care if someone took photos of them. 'It would have to be early as I'm taking Ben to the cinema.'

Dan climbed down the stairs as the front door opened. Judy entered, pushing a wheel chair in front of her.

A boy of five looked up from the chair. 'Daddy,' he shouted.

41

Dan knelt in front of him. 'Hey, mate, are you OK?'

'Yeah, and I got lots to tell you.'

'Good, you can tell me all about it when I get back.'

Ben frowned. 'I thought we were going to the pictures.'

Dan ruffled his hair. 'Of course we are . . . I just have to pop out for an hour first.'

Judy removed her coat. 'Where are you going?'

'The pub, but don't worry I'm only going for one as the lads want to celebrate getting the job finished.'

'I'll drive to the cinema and pick you up on the way at seven.'

Dan decided against a jacket and picked up his phone. 'Good idea, I'll get a taxi.'

Dan stepped through the doors of the Raven Inn and saw five people inside. Two of them were John and Tim. He often smiled when he saw them working together. John was a big lad in his mid-twenties and Tim, a skinny lad at nineteen. He walked over to the bar and bought three pints of lager before joining them.

'Cheers, boss,' said Tim, 'you sure you don't want to stay longer?'

Dan sat down. 'No, Judy's picking me up at seven, and besides I would only cramp your style.'

John laughed. 'You can't cramp Tim's style . . . he doesn't have any.'

Dan glanced at the door when it opened wondering if Kelly would show up. He hoped she wouldn't as it may be awkward as he had to leave soon. He saw Tim start on his fresh pint. 'You might want to take it easy, it's still early.'

'You're only young once,' said Tim, 'and besides I won't be stopping all night.'

Dan hoped it was true. He paid Tim well and didn't want him spending all his money on beer. He thought of the night he met Kelly and where they sat in the photograph. Dan wondered where the photographer sat. It would've been from the table next to theirs, but it was empty.

'There's one for you, Tim,' said John.

Dan looked up and saw a middle-aged woman stroll over to the bar. She was attractive and had a certain grace. 'A little too old, don't you think?'

'Na,' said John, 'not for our Tim, he likes the more mature type.'

Tim grinned. 'She's nice.'

Dan stood and shook his head. 'I best be off as Judy will be waiting.' He finished off his pint and stepped outside. He saw Judy parked up and climbed into the car.

Judy drove off. 'When did that place reopen?'

'A few weeks ago, and it must've cost a few bob.' Dan turned to Ben in the back seat. 'Did you choose a film?'

Ben beamed at him. 'Yeah, and it's got monsters in.'

~ ~ ~ ~

As Alison strolled over to the bar in the Raven Inn she saw him. The young man she was meant to seduce sat with two older men. She paid for a white wine and turned to find another table. Alison sat down and sighed in relief as the oldest of the three men walked out. She glanced around the lounge at the stylish décor. The tables were in front of cushioned benches around the wall. Alison noticed a red-haired woman buy a drink and approach her table.

'Are you Alison?' she said quietly.

'I am . . . who wants to know?'

'I was told to find you as I'm part of it.'

Alison frowned. 'You're one of the blackmailers?'

The woman shook her head and sat down. 'No, I received a letter too. I'm Kelly and have to help in your task.'

'I don't understand . . . how can you help me?'

'I have to entertain the other one, and I have to say I got the better deal.'

Alison felt relieved she wasn't alone. 'You could say that, so what do we do?'

Kelly took a sip from her glass. 'We drink and wait for the beer to give them courage to chat us up.'

'You make it sound so simple.'

'I believe my task will be, but I don't envy yours.'

'I can't say I do, but I was relieved to get my money back.'

'Yeah, same here,' said Kelly, as she smiled. 'Did you know we already have rooms booked for the night?'

'So the letter said, but I haven't checked.'

'I did, and the keys are behind the bar.'

They sat chatting for the next couple of hours when the biggest of the lads turned to them.

'Will you ladies be OK getting home?' he asked.

'We're not going home,' said Kelly, 'we got rooms booked for the night. Why don't you bring your drinks over here?'

As the next hour dragged on Alison watched Kelly all over John, while Tim chatted in her ear. Kelly winked at her as she dragged John off to a room. Alison turned to Tim who had his hand on her leg. She moved it under her skirt.

'Would you like to see my room?' she said.

Tim's eyes grew big. 'Oh yes.'

~ ~ ~ ~

Dan woke at three in the morning to the sound of someone banging on the front door. He hurried downstairs and opened it to find a police man standing there.

'Are you Dan Miller of Miller construction?' said the constable.

Dan yawned as Judy approached while pulling her dressing gown together. 'Yeah, that's me.'

'I have to inform you there's been a fire at your premises on the high street.'

'Oh crap, how did that happen?'

'I'll take over here,' said an officer in a suit, who looked like he had not long woken up. He studied Dan. 'I'm Inspector Collins . . . can you tell me where you were around midnight?'

'In bed,' said Dan, 'fast asleep.'

'Don't even go there,' said Judy.

Collins raised an eyebrow. 'I'm sorry, but go where?'

'You know what I mean. If you think this is an insurance job, you better ask the landlord. The shop is rented to advertise the business and used as an office. All we owned in there was an old computer, a phone, a radio, and a coffee maker. It wouldn't be worth claiming for any of it.'

Collins rubbed his eyes. 'Fair enough but I do have to ask these questions. Do you know of anyone with a grudge against you?'

'I can't think of anyone,' said Dan, 'but I'm sure this is related to the other fire on the high street.'

'If it is, it's not the same person who set fire to the other shop. I know that for a fact.'

'What fact is that?'

'I'm not at liberty to say at the moment, but we will be releasing a statement in the morning.' Collins pulled a card from an inside pocket. 'I've disturbed you long enough, but if you remember anything give me a call.'

Dan took the card and watched the inspector leave. 'Could be worse I suppose, what files have we lost?'

'None,' said Judy, 'I back everything up on an external hard drive and bring it home.'

'Good thinking, so we didn't lose anything really.'

'Only my coffee maker and radio.' Judy stared at him. 'Why didn't you mention the letters?'

Dan shrugged. 'I doubt scammers had anything to do with it. They only had to go inside and work out for themselves it wasn't worth the effort.'

Judy climbed the stairs. 'Maybe, but it wouldn't hurt you to tell the inspector.'

'OK, I'll think about it.'

~ ~ ~ ~

Alison woke the following morning and realised where she was, and who lay next to her. The night was a disaster. Tim may have been drunk, but only lasted seconds before falling asleep. The lack of sex didn't bother her as she really wasn't interested in him. The thought of sex with anyone had left a bad taste in her mouth. What bothered her was the young man had not fallen in love with her yet. She slid her hand down his waist and his eyes opened.

'Morning,' she said.

~ ~ ~ ~

Dan stared at Ilkstone Manor, a large Gothic style building. His attention was the boarded up windows at the back. An annex destroyed by fire over ten years ago. Next to him stood two older men. 'I can't see there being a problem getting it done in time.'

'I told you,' said Councillor Townsend, the taller of the two men and stouter, 'Dan's your man. He finished the work at the cricket club in time.'

Dan smiled. 'You're too kind.'

'No, you did a great job, and Mr Grimshaw has given us permission to use the grounds for our fete when the work is finished.'

'Please call me Albert,' said Mr Grimshaw, 'and how could I refuse when you helped me get the property?'

Dan turned to him. 'Did you have trouble buying it?'

'Yes, a little. I had already agreed a price with the owner, but he decided to sell it to someone else for more money.'

'I found out,' said Councillor Townsend, 'and did a little digging. The other buyer is a property developer. I sent him a letter saying the manor is a listed building and no planning permission would be given to build on the land. He pulled out of the deal.'

'The owner came back to me,' said Albert, now smiling, 'and I bought it for less than we originally agreed on.'

Dan glanced back at the old building. 'Surely any property developer would know he wouldn't get permission.'

Councillor Townsend nodded. 'He was a shady character from what I read about him. As you may have noticed you cannot see the land from the road, and we were worried he might start without getting permission.'

'Clever,' said Dan, 'once you sent the letter he knew you'd be watching.'

'Yes, and we have drones.'

'We'll be here in the morning, as I want the foundation down for the new annex.'

The following morning Dan drove to the manor and stopped to pick Tim up on the way. The young man climbed in bleary-eyed and slumped in the passenger seat.

Dan drove off. 'You had a day off and should be looking fresh . . . did you go out again?'

Tim yawned. 'No, but because I stayed in bed until late I struggled to sleep last night.'

'You had a good night in the Raven on Monday then.'

'It was alright, I just drank too much. You were right about that woman, she was way too old.'

'Of course she was, and as I said there's no rush, the right woman will come along for you.'

'John got lucky again, he pulled a red-head called Kelly, and they soon buggered off to a room.'

Dan felt his stomach turn. 'Really, and he left you alone in there?'

'I've been in there on my own before, but I was waiting for a taxi anyway.'

Dan turned right to a set of gates which were open and drove up the long drive.

'Wow,' said Tim, 'this looks posh. Does it belong to a lord?'

Dan pulled over near John who stood talking to an older man. 'No, well not yet anyway. He owns a chain of supermarkets.' He climbed out of the van and greeted the older man with a handshake. 'Glad to have you with us, Pat.'

The older man smiled. 'It'll be nice to be doing something. I thought you would've had one of your other brickies working on it as I've not done it for a while.'

'They're on other jobs, and I'm sure you still have it. My father used to say you were the best in the business.'

'He was a good man, and I'm pleased he left you the business, but I can't see me laying any bricks today.'

'No, I've got a digger coming so John and Tim can do the foundation. You and I are going to decide on how to blend the new building to the old one.'

~ ~ ~ ~

Stuart Jones sat staring at the television. He rubbed his face before squeezing his hands together.

'Police have confirmed,' said the reporter, 'that Nigel Willis who was murdered last week, was also the man who set fire to the shop on the high street where a homeless man died.'

'Shit, did you hear that?'

'What part,' said Victoria, playing with her phone, 'the murder or the fire? They both happened last week?'

'I know, but the victim is the arsonist.'

'Yes, he had his throat cut open, probably revenge for the fire and killing the homeless man inside. Are you going to work today?'

Stuart decided it would be safer to stay in. 'Not yet, I've got things to do.'

Victoria stood. 'Well I'm going out for a while.'

Stuart trembled as she left and glanced back at the television. Is that my fate? He thought. Burn down a shop and get my throat cut.

~ ~ ~ ~

Alison Townsend glanced out of a bedroom window in the Raven Inn, and saw Tim dawdle away. She had spent every afternoon, after he finished work, since Monday with him. She believed her task was over as the young man appeared smitten with her. She left the inn through the back and walked over to her car where she saw an envelope on the seat.

How, it's locked? Alison thought and opened the door. She picked the letter up before climbing inside. Alison opened the letter and shivered.

'Now your task is over you have one more to complete. Tomorrow on Friday night you will take Tim to the old church near Ilkstone Manor with the promise of sex. Do this late in the evening and once you're inside you are to kill him. The method is your choice, and you will find the instruments beneath your seat. One is a knife, and the other is a bottle of laced with poison. Failure to comply and your husband will receive the photos while you're entertaining.'

Alison dropped the letter and put her face in both hands.

~ ~ ~ ~

Stuart Jones saw the envelope in the letter box on Friday morning. He grabbed it before Victoria came down, stairs and took it into the kitchen. He hadn't left the house since he saw the news and knew he had another task. Stuart opened the letter, his hands shaking as he did so.

47

Your final task will be tonight. Go to Ilkstone Manor and make your way to where the new building will be. Wear gloves and take the builder's hammer before making your way to the old church on the edge of the grounds. Inside you will find Albert Grimshaw looking for his daughter. Kill him with the hammer and your wife will inherit everything. Fail to do so and your wife will receive the photos.

Stuart stuffed the letter into a trouser pocket. Shit, I've been too frightened to go out for the fear of being murdered, he thought, and now I have to go out and kill my father-in-law.

~ ~ ~ ~

Dan sat on the back of the van as he removed his boots. He glanced at John. 'You off to the Raven tonight?'

John opened the boot of his car. 'Na, I might go up town instead.'

'I thought you liked the place.'

'No, not really.' John threw his bag into his car. 'To be honest the place gives me the creeps. The woman I met on Monday night was all over me and no one there batted an eyelid.'

Dan put on his shoes and tied up the laces. 'I didn't think that would bother you.'

'It didn't on Monday night, and she was hot. The thing is she was so easy, almost as if it was her job to seduce people. She and the other woman had rooms already booked.'

'The other woman?'

'The older one Tim liked.'

Dan raised an eyebrow. 'It's a good job he took a taxi home.'

'Did he tell you that? He lied as he spent the night with her.' John stretched his arms. 'I don't like to tell on him, but I'm just surprised he didn't say so.'

'Probably just embarrassed.'

Dan stepped through the front door just after seven and climbed the stairs for a shower. Thirty minutes later he walked back down in clean clothes. On the table he saw a letter with his name handwritten on the front. He picked it up and unfolded it.

Dan, I've been trying to ring you because I saw something important on the news. It said the man who was murdered also had one of those blackmail letters on him. Call the police and tell them of yours. Another of those envelopes arrived with my name on the front. It's also on the table with pictures of you and a woman inside. You will need to get this sorted.

Dan checked his phone and saw it had gone off. He put it on charge and took out the card Collins gave him. He waited a few minutes and called the number off it.

'Inspector Collins here.'

'Hi, it's Dan Miller, I've got some information for you. I also received some of those blackmail letters.'

'OK, Mr Miller, I will get to you as soon as I can. I would prefer it if you remained indoors as your life may be in danger.'

'Don't worry about me, I can handle myself.' Dan picked up the envelope addressed to Judy and took out the pictures.

$$\sim \sim \sim \sim$$

Alison Townsend pulled up outside the church and wiped her eyes. She climbed out and saw lights on inside. Nervously she edged up to the door and opened it. Inside six people stopped what they were doing and stared at her.

A priest hurried over. 'My dear, what is troubling you?'

'I've come to give confession.'

He passed her a tissue. 'You're at the wrong church, I'm Reverend Simon.'

Alison wiped her eyes with the tissue. 'Oh, I didn't know that.'

Simon led her over to a pew where she sat down. 'I will listen to what ails you.'

'I'm Alison and have got myself into a right mess. I've betrayed my husband and now I'm being blackmailed because of it.'

Judy Miller stepped over to them. 'Aren't you Councillor Townsend's wife?'

Alison nodded. 'Yes I am.'

'You should go to the police.'

'I know, and I don't care what happens to me, but it might destroy my husband. What I've done is nothing to what the blackmailers want me to do next. I had to seduce a young man about the same age as my own son who's at university.'

Another woman stepped over. 'What's this young man's name?'

Alison wiped her eyes again. 'Tim.'

'I knew it,' said the woman, 'you harlot, that's my boy.'

'Now, now, Helen,' said Simon, 'this is a place of god.

'You heard what she did to my boy . . . I thought he'd been acting strange lately.'

Judy took her arm. 'Tim will be fine, he's a growing lad.'

Helen pulled her arm away. 'Your Dan has to take some of the blame in this.'

'Don't you dare blame him . . . he gave your son a job when no one else would. He has got his freedom and it'll do him good in the future.'

'Ladies,' said Simon, 'there's something sinister here. You should be worried why someone would blackmail this lady to do such a thing. If we listen, Alison might tell us.'

Alison shook her head. 'I can't tell you why only what's happened. It started last week after my bad decision. I received a letter where they demanded one hundred thousand pounds, which I paid. A day or so later I received another letter with another demand, but they also gave me the money back. You already know of their second demand, but it's the final one which has brought me here. You see there's no way I could ever go through with it.'

Helen folded her arms. 'It sounds like you're making excuses for what you've done.'

'No, I make no excuse. My final task, as they call it, is to lure your son to the old church near Ilkstone Manor and kill him.'

Helen put a hand to her mouth. 'You're going to kill my boy?'

'No, of course not, it's why I'm here.'

'Calm down,' said Simon, 'Alison wouldn't have come here if she was going to do such a thing. Tim has only gained life experiences through this.'

Alison raised an eyebrow. 'You're not what I expected.'

'I like to think of myself as modern.'

'This is worse than you think,' said Judy, 'the man who was murdered last week also had one of those letters. Dan received two, but he tossed them in the bin. One came for me with pictures of Dan and a woman in bed.'

'Oh no,' said Helen, 'that must've been horrible for you.'

'I never looked too close, but they had a duvet over them.'

'There's something else,' said Alison. 'I found the letter for the final task in my locked car.'

'But why my Tim?' said Helen. 'He's never hurt anyone. We should call the police.'

'No,' said Simon, 'they won't be able to stop them. I knew it would happen again and it looks like they're back.'

Judy scratched her head. 'Who are back? What's happened before? I've never heard of anything like this happening.'

Reverend Simon clasped his hands together. 'It would've been different back then, as they weren't sending letters. Over two hundred years ago St Stephen's church was not the one you are standing in now, but the old building on the land of Ilkstone Manor. People believe they just built this one because it's closer to town, but the real reason is a lot darker. Back then a young boy ran to the village screaming "demons killed my father". The villagers marched to the church and found not only the boy's father had been murdered, but also the priest and many others. They had been sacrificed by creatures with red eyes and sharp teeth.'

'Good lord,' said Helen, 'you don't believe such tales?'

'Of course, as it has happened a few times since, and always at the church. I have no doubt if Alison had followed their orders they would've killed her next. I have to go now so please see that Alison gets home OK.'

Judy stood in front of him. 'And just where are you going?'

'To the old church, of course, I have to send the creatures back. My grandfather did before and now it's up to me.'

A grey haired man walked over to them. 'You won't be going alone, as I'm coming.'

'Yes, Henry, I am too,' said Judy, 'I just wish Dan was here.'

'Are you not worried about his safety?' said Alison, 'You said he received the letters.'

'I wasn't until I found out it was demons.'

~ ~ ~ ~

Dan waited for two hours but the police still hadn't arrived. He stared out the window when his phone rang. He saw a name flashing on the front, and he answered it. 'Hello, John, what's up?'

'It's Tim, he said he had a phone call off the woman he slept with and now he's panicking. She told him someone was about to kill her, and he's gone on a rescue mission. I'm going to try to rescue him.'

'Something sounds wrong there, did you phone the police?'

'Yeah, but the woman who answered didn't believe me and ended the call.'

'That doesn't sound right either.' Dan glanced out the window and saw a car pull up. 'I've been waiting for the police and it looks like they've arrived. Where's Tim going?'

'Back to the manor, do you know the old church?'

'Yeah, I'll meet you there.' Dan stepped outside as Inspector Collins opened his door. 'I wouldn't bother, it's happening at the old church and I'm going there now.'

'You better get in,' said Collins, and closed the door.

Dan climbed in and put on the seat belt. 'Some weird shit's happening tonight.'

'Tell me about it, so what's happening at the church?'

'Friends of mine have gone to save a woman from being murdered there.'

'Oh no, why didn't they call us?'

'John did, but the woman who answered didn't believe him.'

'I'll check it out when I get back. They've had a few crank calls over the past week from people claiming to have done this or that. I would've gotten to you earlier but have been on a manhunt. Some guy beat his wife almost senseless because he found one of those letters.'

Dan wished he had kept the letters. 'Who the hell are these people?'

'I thought you might know as you received one of those letters.'

'I've no idea, and they sent me two. I only read a few lines before throwing them into the bin.'

'Even now you know they wanted you dead, you still can't think of anything?'

Dan raised an eyebrow. 'They never mentioned that in the parts I read.'

'No,' said Collins, as he drove at speed, 'didn't the constable I sent to your house earlier tell you about it?'

'He didn't show up and I stood waiting for any news.'

'It was a she.'

'Maybe the same one who answered the phone.'

'I'm going to have a word when I get back. The letter we found on the murdered man said his task was to kill you.'

'Nice, when was he meant to do it?'

'It wasn't dated, but we believe it was Friday night.'

'I received the first letter on Wednesday, which I ignored, so they decided to have me killed. The man refused to do it, so they killed him instead. It looks like they changed their mind about me as I received the other letter on Sunday. I ignored that one too and Judy had pictures sent to her.'

'That must've been nice for her,' said Collins, 'and now we might be getting somewhere.'

Dan thought about the pictures. 'They were taken at the Raven Inn, and I'm guessing the others spent the night there.'

'I wouldn't know,' said Collins, 'the only other two we know of being blackmailed are either dead or in a coma. Soon as we sort out what's happening at the church I'm having the place raided.'

'My friends, John and Tim, both spent the night there and are on their way to the church.'

'There it is,' said Collins, 'and someone's outside.'

Dan stared ahead. 'It's John, but I can't see Tim.' The car stopped and he jumped out. 'Have you seen him?'

John shook his head. 'No, and he's not answering his phone.'

Collins opened one of the church doors, and they saw it was dimly lit by candles. Tim stood a few feet away scratching his head. Dan noticed Albert Grimshaw near the front where another man approached from behind with a hammer.

'Albert, look out,' he shouted, and ran forward. He dived at the other man, and they crashed to the floor. The man dropped the hammer and curled up like a baby.

Albert put both hands to his face. 'What's going on?'

Dan picked up the hammer and dragged the man to his feet. 'He was going to kill you with my hammer.'

'Stuart, you coward, you're fired.'

Stuart squirmed under the tight grip of Dan's hand. 'They made me do it, I had no choice.'

Dan slung him to the floor. 'You always have a choice, I did.'

Albert frowned as he clasped his hands together. 'He's my son-in-law, is my daughter in on it too? She called me earlier to say she was stuck in here.'

'No,' said Dan, 'this is something else. Why did you come alone?'

'There was no one else, the few staff I have are out for the night.'

'She's not here,' said Tim, 'I don't get it.'

'You don't need to worry about that,' said a voice near the altar, 'as you're going to die soon.'

Dan turned and saw seven hooded figures. 'Who are you?'

'Who do you think?' said the one in the middle. 'You failed to fulfil any of your tasks and for that you die tonight.'

'I don't think so,' said Collins, 'you're under arrest.'

The hooded figure laughed as they all pulled back their hoods to reveal red eyes and sharp teeth. 'You have no power over us and you will be sacrificed. So which one of you wants to be the first?'

'Are you insane?' said Collins, and turned to Dan. 'What the hell are they?'

'I don't know, but I don't think they're human,' said Dan, as Stuart Jones ran for the door, only for it to slam shut on him, and he fell backwards.

'You will come forward,' said the hooded creature, 'or we will drag you over here.'

Dan saw a metal spike on the floor and picked it up. He stood in front of Albert Grimshaw and turned to the creature. 'I'd like to see you try.'

Six of the creatures ran forward, and Dan swung the hammer. He smashed one across the head, and as he turned he drove the spike into another's chest. Both fell to the floor. He glanced across and saw two of them trying to drag Collins down and the other two grappling with John and Tim. He hit one of those fighting Collins across the back of its head, and threw the spike at one grappling with Tim. It hit the creature in the neck and it dropped. John lifted the other and slammed its head into a wall. Dan grabbed the one off Collins and threw it towards the altar.

'Nice shot, boss,' said Tim, as the creatures scrambled to their feet and ran back.

John stared at the creature who spoke. 'Is that all you've got?'

Dan sighed. 'I wish you hadn't said that.'

'Why, we just beat them?'

Dan shook his head. 'Really? They shouldn't have been able to get back up.'

'We were just testing you,' said the creature, as seven more appeared from the shadows. They pulled back their hoods and Dan saw a red-eyed Kelly.

'Oh shit,' said John, 'she's one of them.'

'It would appear so,' said Dan.

John's eyes grew big. 'Boss, you didn't?'

'If it makes you feel any better,' said Collins, 'one of them is the constable I sent to your house.'

'Enough,' said the first creature, 'you will be sacrificed.'

Stuart Jones climbed to his feet as the door burst open, and he was sent crashing to the floor again.

'No, demon,' said Simon, as he stormed into the church, 'you will not sacrifice anyone.'

Dan raised both eyebrows as he saw five others follow him into the church, and turned back to those at the front.

The demon snarled. 'What are you going to do, priest, kneel and pray? I, however, thank you for bringing us more sacrifices.'

'Oh look,' said the Kelly demon, as she stared at Dan. 'It's your wife Judy, did she like the pictures?'

Dan laughed as he realised they sent the pictures to the wrong person. 'She's my sister, you idiot, my wife divorced me and took the house.'

Judy shook her head. 'A demon, really?'

'Time to die,' said the main demon, as the others pulled out curved daggers.

Reverend Simon stepped forward and pulled out a shard of glass. It glowed and white lights shot out hitting the demons. 'I will not kneel here or before you.'

'A nice light display,' said the demon, 'but it can't hurt us.' Four of the demons vanished, their clothes dropping to the floor. The demon hissed. 'A mistake we won't make again, you have no real weapons to finish us.'

'I do,' said Henry, the grey haired man from the church pulled out two guns. He fired with great accuracy and the demons turned to dust.

Reverend Simon stared at him. 'Where did you get those from?'

'The car,' said Henry, 'I like to keep them handy. The last priest never got to face any demons, but he told me all about them. We spent many hours discussing what we would do if they returned. I've waited a long time to do that.'

'You might want to put them back in the car,' said Collins. 'I won't be reporting it . . . in fact I can't report any of this. I can't take a bag of dust to the station and say it's over.'

'It's not over,' said Dan. 'Remember the Raven Inn? I bet you'll find all the blackmail photos and other stuff there.'

Collins smiled. 'Of course, there may even be some of them left there. Do you need a lift back?'

Dan shook his head. 'No, I want to get Albert back safely first, but you might want to get his son-in-law away from here.'

Collins glanced over at Stuart rubbing his head. 'I will, I'm not sure if I can arrest him though, this would look weird in court.'

'Just get him away from me,' said Albert, and smiled at Dan. 'It's kind of you to get me back safely.'

'I can't let anything happen to you now can I?'

Albert winked. 'A man after my own heart, you know my daughter will be single soon.'

Dan thought about his ex-wife and the demon Kelly. 'I'm giving up on relationships for the foreseeable future.'

Alison approached Tim. 'I'm sorry for what I did and making you fall for me.'

Tim scratched his head. 'You didn't, yeah I had fun but that's all it was. I started to feel guilty as I thought you might be married.'

Alison smiled and walked out the church.

Helen grabbed Tim's ear. 'I brought you up better than this.'

Tim pulled away. 'If we all listened to our mothers we'd still be in the stone age. We would never have put a man on the moon or found the North Pole.'

'No, we don't stop you doing those things. What we do is teach you not to be twats.'

Dan choked back a cough. 'I'll keep an eye on him.'

Helen sighed and walked away. 'I give up.'

'What's that supposed to mean?'

'Well,' said John, 'at least Alison was human.'

Dan scratched his head. 'Good point.'

'Just think of it as a life experience,' said Simon, 'Tim will be better for it.'

'Dan too,' said John, 'and you never said anything.'

'What, and compare notes?'

Albert glanced around. 'Why does this place still stand?'

'The previous owners of the manor,' said Simon, 'all thought it bad luck to knock down a church.'

Albert turned to Dan. 'When you get five minutes.'

Dan thought of driving the digger at the building. 'Sure, but I'm going to church on Sunday as I need cleansing.'

'Yeah, and me,' said John.

Simon smiled. 'Good, as I'd like a chat, and there are some people I would like you to meet.'

CHAPTER FOUR

The Familiar

Jack Flint stared into the burning embers of the small campfire. He sat in deep thought after being woken by another vivid dream. The campsite, next to a forest, was situated in the Lake District. A piercing scream shook him from his thoughts, and he leapt to his feet. Jack looked around to see where it came from when he heard another, it came from the forest. He picked up a torch near his tent and ran.

Jack pushed branches away and saw lights ahead. As he neared, he noticed they were solar lamps scattered around a small campsite. The tents lay flattened and belongings slung everywhere. He saw blood splattered all around but no body. Bushes surrounded the site with a path on the other side. He made his way over being careful not to touch anything. Jack stood listening for any sounds when he heard footsteps behind.

'What the hell happened here?'

Jack turned and saw his younger brother Jamie. 'Dunno, but don't touch anything there's blood everywhere.'

'Where are the campers?'

'Can't be far, I was here within seconds.' Jack shone his torch down the path but saw no blood.

'Where are you going?' said a woman.

Jack glanced back and saw Elisabeth, his oldest friend. 'To see if I can find them.'

'Are you mad?' said Gary, Elisabeth's husband. 'We need to leave this place untouched and wait for the police.'

'Yeah we should,' said Jack, 'but it'll be too late for them by then.'

'By the looks of all this blood I'd say it already is.'

'He's right,' said Elisabeth, 'and you don't know who did this nor where they went.'

'There's only two ways they could've gone, and I'm sure I would've seen someone being dragged off from that side.'

'Leave it until the police get here, or you could end up anywhere in the dark.'

Jack knew she spoke the truth. 'I know, or I would've already gone.'

Elisabeth walked over to him. 'You were first here, was you awake again?'

'Yeah, I had another dream.'

'What was it about?'

'Same thing, I was a soldier who failed.'

'Does it have anything to do with when you were in the army?'

Jack thought about his dream and the armour he wore. 'No, I never had a gun, as I was fighting with a sword. In the dream I'm protecting a priest who gets killed. I always wake up with a deep feeling of sadness and guilt for failing. There's something else in the dream but I can't see what it is.'

'You were using a sword?'

'Yeah, and I was good with it. My enemies fell before me.'

'Let's hope you weren't sleepwalking.'

Jack smiled. 'Don't worry . . . I was sat in front of the fire when I heard the screams.'

'Have you ever used a sword before?'

'No, but I'm good with a knife.'

'Who do you think they were?' said Jamie. 'I wanted to check their belongings, but Gary told me not to touch anything until the police get here. He's gone to get a signal to call them.'

Jack nodded. 'At least he got that right, but I've no idea who camped here.'

'Why don't you give Gary a break?' said Elisabeth. 'He does try you know.'

'I know, but sometimes his way of doing everything right can get tiresome.'

'It's his way, and he wanted to be more like you. He tried joining the army but his health put a stop to that. You were good friends once.'

'And his best man,' said Jamie, 'I remember that.'

Jack glanced at his excitable younger brother. Eighteen years old and brought up by Elisabeth and Gary. Jamie was only eight when their parents died while Jack was in the army. 'Things change.'

'What things?' said Elisabeth. 'I've never known you to have bad words with each other.'

'He nearly got you killed because he couldn't keep things to himself.'

Jamie raised an eyebrow. 'When was that?'

'Years ago when they lived in the Bronx.'

'The Bronx?'

'A council estate,' said Elisabeth. 'We had a flat there not long before we started looking after you.'

'A flat which had a petrol-bomb put through the letter box,' said Jack, 'all because someone had to tell the police about everything he saw.'

'He's anti-drugs, just like you are. The kids on the estate were buying them.'

'I know, but he should've put your safety first. Everyone knew it was him telling the police.'

Elisabeth smiled. 'Yeah, but we got a house because of it.'

Jack frowned and shook his head at her. 'That's because I gave you my house.'

'The police are on their way,' Gary shouted, 'but might be a while.'

Jack shone his torch around the edge of the campsite and into the bushes. 'I just don't get it.'

Jamie pointed his own torch. 'What are we looking for?'

'They must've left other tracks with all the blood here.'

'Maybe they didn't spill any more. So what do you think happened?'

Jack stared at the carnage. 'Dunno, but there were at least three campers here, so where are the bodies?'

'There could've been an argument,' said Gary, from the other side of the small camp, 'and two of the campers killed the third.'

'I thought of that, but why leave their stuff behind?'

'The screams, they must've known someone would come running.'

'Maybe, but I've carried a body before and it's not easy to do in the dark.'

'We'll see better in daylight,' said Gary, 'and how sure are you the screams came from here?'

Jack raised an eyebrow. 'I think the blood is a big giveaway. There's something else, the two screams I heard came from different people.'

'Are you coming back over here?' said Gary. 'The police will be here soon.'

Jack sat on the ground with his back resting up a tree. 'No, if I do that they won't let me through this way.'

The police arrived as morning light broke through the trees, and Jack stared down the dirt path looking for any clues.

'I need you to move away from the site,' said an officer, 'but don't go far as we will want to speak to all of you. Does anyone know who were camping here?'

Jack sighed, stood, and stretched. He glanced back at the camp and saw the blood on the low hanging branches. His eyes searched through the trees and saw a body hanging over a large branch. 'I've found one.'

The officer followed his gaze and frowned. 'I need you all to return to your camps, this is now a murder scene.'

Jack walked down the path and turned right to follow the direction of the body. He wanted to go and search for the other campers.

'Jack,' said Jamie, as he ran to catch him, 'we're meant to go back to camp.'

'I know, and to do that I have to find another way, so I don't walk through the murder scene.'

'You're kidding right?'

'Yes, but it gives me an excuse to find any others.' Jack patted his brother on the shoulder. 'Keep your eyes peeled.'

'How can anyone put a person up a tree like that?'

'I don't know . . . the question is why would they want to?'

They walked on for another five minutes when they came across an open area.

'Another,' said Jamie, and pointed a hand to the left, 'in the tree over there.'

Jack turned and saw a half-naked body bent over a branch. 'What the hell's going on?'

Jamie took out his phone. 'You want me to call the others?'

Jack marked the path. 'Yeah, I'm not going back yet.'

Jamie stared at his phone. 'No signal, I'll go back and tell them.'

'OK, but stick to the path. Whoever did this, has gone in the other direction.'

Jack watched him walk away as he tried to work out a direct line between the bodies. He walked through the clearing to the right of the body. The trees were spread far enough apart to let plenty of light through. After five minutes he saw a group of hikers all staring up, and he knew what they were looking at. A third body hung over a branch.

A woman wearing a cap approached him. 'Do you have a phone as we need to call the police?'

Jack shook his head. 'No, doesn't one of you?'

'We don't allow them on our hiking trips. Have you seen anything like this before?'

'Yeah, it's the third one this morning.'

'What? Oh crap, there's a maniac on the loose. Do the police know?'

'They arrived when we saw the first body. This place will be crawling with them soon.'

'I'm Chloe,' she said, and removed her cap to show shoulder-length blond hair. 'Were you looking for more?'

'I found their camp a few hours ago when I heard screams. It was covered in blood and I knew there would be other bodies.'

'This trip gets weirder,' said another hiker, 'first the tree and now this.'

Jack felt the urge to see it. 'What tree?'

'One we saw yesterday, a horrible looking thing which I've never seen before.'

'It's true,' said Chloe, 'our hiking group has been here many times, but none of us have ever seen it on previous visits.'

Jack raised an eyebrow. 'I've been here a few times and don't recognise any trees.'

'You'd remember this one. Branches sticking out like arms with a skirt of lower branches as if it's concealing something. I love trees, but I never went close enough to see what was behind them.'

'Sounds interesting,' said Jack, 'where is it?'

'Straight ahead for about a mile, you can't miss it,' said Chloe as she stared up at the body. 'You said their camp was covered in blood, so it looks like we were lucky the killer didn't attack us.'

Jack glanced around the group. 'Not really, there were only three tents and there must be at least twenty people in your group. Anyway, I best go and look at this tree.'

'You're going alone?'

'Yeah, I doubt the killer hung around.'

Jack walked on not believing his last statement. Something was eluding him, but he couldn't work it out. He blamed it on the lack of sleep and the dreams. The tree came into view. It stood out from the other trees almost as if they didn't want to be near it. Like Chloe said many of the upper branches looked like arms, and had a skirt of smaller branches around the middle pointing to the ground.

Jack noticed a large black bird sitting near the top. 'Hello, Mr Raven, what secrets do you know?'

'The tree is ancient, as old as the forest,' said a voice.

Jack almost jumped. He turned and saw a woman in old-fashioned black clothes and using a branch for a walking stick.

'It has always been here, but not everyone sees it.'

'How do you know, old crone?' said Jack, and nearly choked on the words. 'Sorry . . . I've never said that to anyone before.'

'You have, Sir Jack, have you forgotten calling it me all those years ago?'

Jack rubbed his eyes. The woman being here made no sense. 'You have me mistaken for someone else . . . I've never seen you before.'

'Haven't you, Sir Jack? You know the tree, you and I go way back.'

'I've no idea what you're talking about.'

'Jack,' Elisabeth shouted, 'what the hell are you doing coming here on your own?'

'Remember, Sir Jack,' said the old woman, 'not everything is as it appears.'

Jack shook his head and turned to his friends, which included his brother Jamie, Gary, and Chloe who had brought them here. 'I'm just taking a look at this tree.'

'Are you mad?' said Elisabeth, 'There's a monster on the loose. Who were you talking to?'

'This woman,' he said, and glanced around to see she had gone. 'Well there was a woman here, an old one with a walking stick.'

'You must be seeing things,' said Gary, 'we saw no one.'

Jack shrugged. 'Not everything is as it appears.'

Jamie stared at the tree. 'What's that supposed to mean?'

'I've just realised the woman and the tree were in my dreams.'

'What dreams?' said Chloe. 'Have you been having nightmares?'

Jack considered it. 'Not nightmares, but they were quite vivid. I thought it was the despair which kept waking me up, but it was the shadow.'

'What kind of shadow?'

'I don't know, but it fell all around me.'

'We better go,' said Elisabeth, 'there are police everywhere, and an inspector wants a word with you.'

'What for?'

'Probably to ask you the same questions he asked us.'

Jack walked back with them. 'I don't suppose they know the cause of death yet.'

'Hardly,' said Gary, 'the bodies are still in the trees while they wait for forensics to get here. The first looks like he had his back broken.'

'That's what I thought, and I didn't see much blood on any of them.'

'What's that got to do with anything?' said Elisabeth, as police came into view.

'The blood at the camp, of course, we're missing another body.'

'True, but you might not want to say anything to the police.'

Jamie grinned. 'I wouldn't mention the old woman you saw either or they might lock you up.'

Jack put an arm around his brother's neck. 'You could be right as she called me Sir Jack.'

'You must've been daydreaming,' said Gary, 'how could she know your name?'

Jack released his brother as the police let them through. 'I don't know, but it's who I am in the dream.'

'Inspector Richards,' said Elizabeth, as a balding man in a suit approached.

'Are you Jack Flint?' he asked.

Jack stopped in front of the inspector. 'That's me.'

'I hear you were first on the scene.'

'Yeah, I got there in less than a minute'

The inspector rubbed his chin as police taped off the area. 'So soon, weren't you asleep?'

'No, I'd been awake about an hour when I heard the screams.'

'What did you see when you got there.'

Jack thought back to the early hours. 'The same as the others, but it's what I couldn't see which confused me'

'How do you mean?'

'You know how quickly I got there, yet I saw no one or any tracks leading from the camp. The trees and bushes are dense in that part but I heard nothing moving through them.'

Richards looked Jack up and down as if working him out. 'Is that why you wandered off?'

'I wanted to see if I could find them, but I guess I was always too late.'

Richards glanced at his notepad. 'Did you see any sign of a fourth body?'

Jack knew the other would never be found. 'No, just the three.'

'How do you know there were four?' said Elisabeth.

'The park ranger told us he saw them earlier in the day,' said Richards.

'Couldn't the fourth person be the killer?'

'Not unless they did it after losing so much blood.'

'And super human strength,' said Gary.

'Just like Jack,' said Jamie, 'he's strong.'

Jack stared at his younger brother. 'Thanks for that.'

Richards smiled. 'I really don't think he's in the habit of leaping into trees with a body over his shoulder.'

'Only it was four bodies,' said Jack, 'so was there more than one killer? I only heard two screams, yet the state of the camp meant there was a struggle. I just don't understand how they got away so fast.'

'Could be many reasons how,' said Richards. 'We don't know if all the campers were attacked in the camp, or if the first was taken while the others slept. I think you should go back to your camp now and stay there until we decide what happens with the place.'

Jack woke in his tent hours later. They returned earlier to find others had moved onto the site, and police everywhere.

'You're awake then,' said Jamie.

Jack sat up and rubbed his eyes. 'It would appear so.'

'Did you dream again?'

'No, not that I remember. Have I missed anything?'

'I'm famous, I've been talking to reporters, and been on camera.' Jamie grinned. 'Your dinners waiting for you, Elisabeth cooked it.'

Jack sighed. 'What was Gary thinking?'

'He's busy talking to the press, and everyone else to be honest.'

'Have none gone home yet?'

Jamie glanced out of the tent. 'I don't think so, and the police don't want anyone moving on until they know which way the killer went. Only the hikers are upset by it as the others are happy to be in such a big group.'

'I can understand that, so what's for dinner?'

'Instant mash and tomato soup.'

'Lovely.' Jack stood and stretched. 'I hope there's some beer left.'

'We could do with a proper campfire,' said Jamie, 'so we could sit around it and tell stories.'

'We're not allowed them,' said Elisabeth, 'only these small ones.'

Jacked sipped from a bottle of lager. 'Get everyone to put their solar lights in a pile.'

'Great idea,' said Jamie, and walked off.

'I was joking,' said Jack, 'and we don't have any stories.'

Chloe approached. 'We get one every night we camp.'

Jack smiled at her. 'Are they any good?'

'I like to think so. Arthur knows a lot of legends from around the UK, and tells them well. We're camping here tonight so you might get to hear one.'

Jack glanced over at Jamie collecting solar lights with others. 'I know someone who would like to hear a good story.'

'The police will let us carry on tomorrow, as they reckon the killer has gone in the other direction to where we're going.'

Jack opened another bottle of beer and passed it over to Chloe who accepted. 'I don't think it's going anywhere.'

Elisabeth stared at him. 'What do you mean, it?'

'You called it a monster earlier.'

Elisabeth raised an eyebrow. 'I meant a human monster, and what makes you think he's still here?'

'No human could put the bodies up the trees like that.' Jack rubbed his chin. 'Imagine if the beast came from its lair last night and killed those people. It leaves three in the trees for another night and takes the other back.'

'That's disgusting,' said Elisabeth.

'And a little far-fetched,' said Gary. 'If something like that lived here we would've heard about it before now.'

Jack knew it sounded ridiculous but no human could have done it. 'How do you know that for a fact? You all saw the tree earlier, yet none of us have seen it before.'

'It's true,' said Chloe, 'a tree like that would be in the brochure and quite famous.'

Elisabeth stood. 'How much of what you say is because of your dream?'

'The woman and tree were in my dream. You may have not seen the woman but you did see the tree. You know from the bodies we found something unnatural is happening here.'

'Are you lot ready?' said Jamie. 'There's an old guy who's gonna tell us a few stories he knows.'

'His name is Arthur,' said Jack, as he glanced over at the admirable makeshift campfire. They made their way over and sat within hearing distance.

Arthur, a grey haired man sat waiting for everyone else to find somewhere to sit. Police officers moved closer, so they could hear the story.

'How strange,' said Elisabeth, 'I didn't think so many people would be interested in a campfire story nowadays.'

'Lack of Wi-Fi,' said Jack, 'and some might want to listen to take their minds off what happened last night.'

'Good evening, I am Arthur Pendrift and have spent many years travelling these parts. During this time I have learned many stories and myths from the area. Tonight I have a couple for you, but the first I have never told before. I will do so now because of last night's events. The story is of Black Mary who once roamed these forests and many believe she still does. She was so named because of the black clothes she always wore.'

Jack nudged Elisabeth on the arm, and she shook her head at him.

'A long time ago,' Arthur continued, 'a village was situated around here. No one is sure where, as there were more trees back then. The village sat on the edge of the forest with many having homes inside. It was a time of chivalry and men fought with swords. They were happy living here until people started vanishing. Those living in the forest ran out screaming "Witch, Monster", and the village elder sent for help.

Father Godfrey from the abbey, which no longer exists, received the messenger. He learned of the monster, and the witch the villagers had named Black Mary. Godfrey was sceptical when it came to witches, and of the innocent women who were killed for it. Missing people, men, women and children, were a different matter. The monster, a dark shadow from above, chilled his blood. He believed the villagers were in mortal danger, but the creatures were beyond him, so he turned to the lords of the land for help.

He travelled with a monk to find those who would come to their aid, but none did. The lords refused as none had any men spare to help them, they were away at war. With a feeling of dread, but a stout heart he travelled back to the village to face the evil. He had faith in God and was a good man. As they rode back on a cart, he saw a boy lying on the side of the road. The monk pulled the reigns and stopped the cart. Godfrey climbed off and saw the boy had been stabbed in the chest. He was barely alive and the priest bandaged him the best he could. They took the boy to the abbey to be cared for before going onto the village.

Most of the villagers waited outside the forest too frightened to enter on their own. Godfrey told them he was their only help and six of the men followed him. The priest entered the forest armed with only his faith. To his horror he saw bodies hanging over branches, and a tree which looked like it came from hell. Branches, gnarled and twisted, stuck out like arms. Smaller branches covered in dark leaves skirted around the bottom of the tree hiding the main trunk. An old woman, back bent and wearing black clothes, stepped through the branches.

She gave him a sickly grin. *Do not worry about those, as my pet will take care of them.*

Godfrey held out his crucifix. *You will pay for what you have done . . . your evil deeds will not go unpunished.*

The witch laughed. *Not by you, priest, you have no power*, she said as a dozen armed men stepped up behind her. *I warned the villagers to stay out of my forest, or they will all die.*

Godfrey glanced at the men, scruffy looking mercenaries. *The forest does not belong to you. They enter because of their faith, something you will never break.*

I care nothing for such things, said Mary, *where has your faith got you?* She turned to the mercenaries. *Kill them but leave the priest for my pet . . . it has never eaten a holy man.*

Godfrey held firm as a dark shadow fell around him and the armed men stepped forward brandishing swords. The thunder of horses sounded behind the priest and three mercenaries fell as arrows pierced their chests. The others ran as mounted soldiers rode up and soon chased them down.

Godfrey clasped his hands together. *Sir Edmund, how is it you are here? I was told you were away at war.*

The knight dismounted, followed by his men. *The war is over.*

How did you know to come here?

We are here because of your kindness. Sir Edmund stared at the tree. *What happened to the witch?*

A soldier moved one of the low hanging branches with his sword. *She ran in here.*

Do not enter, said Godfrey, *the tree is ungodly.*

Burn it down, said Edmund.

The soldiers placed dry branches and straw around the tree and set them alight. The tree soon caught fire and after a few minutes they heard a shrieking scream.

Thank you, said Godfrey, *but what kindness do you speak of?*

Edmund patted the priest on the shoulder with a large gauntleted hand. *Before I returned home, I learned my son had been taken. We rode after those who were responsible and caught one. He told us they took him for ransom but their leader changed his mind and stabbed the boy. We went in search of the body, but he had gone, so we followed the tracks of a cart to the abbey. I learned you saved his life and of your call for help. I will forever be in your debt.*

Over the next twenty years the villagers lived in peace. Sir Edmund's son, Jack, would visit Godfrey often. The visits became less frequent as Jack matured, fell in love, and married. He had two children when war came again. Jack, now Sir Jack, rode to battle. It was during this war when people of the village started to vanish once more. Godfrey, now in his sixties, was too old to travel far, so he sent others for help. When no help came, he travelled to the village with a younger priest.

They entered the forest with a few of the villagers and to the priest's horror, the tree had returned. Black Mary soon appeared from beneath the branches along with the mercenaries. Godfrey swore they were the same ones from twenty years previous, only this time they had red eyes. Like the time twenty years before the priest heard horses charging into the forest. Only this time the mercenaries did not fall to the arrows nor did they run. The soldiers attacked with sword and many fell to the unholy men as their weapons had no effect. Sir Jack leapt off his horse and fell the demons with his sword, the only weapon which hurt them. He slew them all, but not before one released an arrow which hit Godfrey in the chest.

You will pay for this, Sir Jack, said Mary, *I will return and end your line.*

Jack swung his sword and beheaded the witch. A dark shadow fell around the knight and before he could react a large winged creature bore him away. The villagers carried Godfrey out of the forest, and Sir Jack was never seen again. The duke sent in an army and once again the tree was burnt to ashes. They dug up whatever roots remained and burnt them too. Father Godfrey died days later from the wound to his chest, but not before he warned Jack's wife of what Mary threatened. She moved south, and many believe overseas. Wherever they went, you will find no trace of them today. Many say Mary still roams the forest, and pray a black shadow never falls around you.'

Most of those listening gave Arthur a round of applause. Jack shuddered as he had dreamt most of the story.

'How creepy was that?' said Jamie. 'It had people hanging from trees and you saw Black Mary.'

Jack nodded, as Arthur told another story. 'So it would appear.'

'He should've saved that one for another time,' said Elisabeth, 'I doubt many here will be put at ease by it.'

'No,' said Gary, 'and I don't think the police will appreciate it.'

'Oh I don't know,' said Jack, 'it might keep people out of the forest. I know I wouldn't want to go back in there.'

'Good point, and she called him Sir Jack, isn't that what she called you?'

'Yeah, but I'm the only one who saw her.' Jack sat listening to the other story without paying much attention. When Arthur finished Jack walked back over to his tent and opened another beer.

Chloe approached with Arthur not far behind. 'I hope you don't mind, but I told Arthur about your dream.'

Jack wondered if he was going mad. 'Does he think I need locking up?'

Chloe smiled. 'No, but he was interested in who you spoke to earlier.'

Arthur held out his hand. 'You must be Jack.'

Jack shook the hand. 'You heard about my dream.'

Arthur nodded. 'Yes, but I wouldn't worry too much as it could be a natural occurrence.'

Jack raised an eyebrow. 'None of this feels natural to me.'

'No, I do not believe it would. Certain events leave a residue where people with a talent can pick up on them. That is only a theory, of course.'

'Would that include me talking to the witch when I'm awake?'

'No, and that is why I needed to talk to you. What did she say?'

'She called me Sir Jack and I called her old crone, something I've never said before. She also said not everything is what it appears.'

'So she is back, and believes you're a descendant of Sir Jack,' said Arthur, as he rubbed his chin. 'I do not understand the last part.'

'Maybe it's because she or the tree shouldn't be here.'

'No, it is something else. Is that all she said?'

'Pretty much, I did see a large raven on the tree.'

'Yes,' said Arthur, 'it would be a bird.'

Jack took a drink from the bottle. 'What would be a bird?'

'Her familiar, what she called her pet.'

'I thought they were cats.'

Arthur shook his head. 'A familiar is a demon a witch summons up. They will look like a small animal but will be a lot worse. You must understand you are in great danger being here.'

'I don't see how as I'm not in the forest. I also walked through it alone today.'

'Yes, but they play games. It would be no fun to kill you without you knowing why.'

'That would make my brother a descendant too.' Jack glanced over at Jamie. 'How can they be here if they were destroyed?'

'She is not here, only her spirit. It has something to do with the familiar and until it is sent back she will keep returning.'

'Give me a gun,' said Jack, 'and I'll get rid of it.'

'Guns will do you no good, only certain weapons can send them back.'

'What about Sir Jack's sword,' said Chloe, 'would that work?'

Arthur clasped his hands together. 'Yes, if wielded by one of his descendants. The problem is we have no idea where the sword is.'

'It's gotta be here somewhere,' said Chloe, 'if there's any truth to your story. The creature flew off with Sir Jack but I doubt they left the forest.'

'Yes, but the forest was a lot bigger back then.'

'What difference would it make?' said Jack. 'The sword's long gone now, probably picked up by someone else.'

Chloe stared at the forest. 'If that's the case we might as well leave this place and forget it happened.'

Jack couldn't make her out. 'What else can we do? We have no idea where the sword is and the police won't let us go back in there.'

'If we could go back, I know of some caves where the sword could be hidden.'

Jack drank the remainder of the beer from the bottle. 'If I were suspicious, I'd be wondering why a stranger was so eager to get me back in there.'

Chloe frowned and nodded. 'I see your point, but I know you'd regret not going.'

'I've had the dreams, so they must mean something.'

'I know some in the police force,' said Arthur, 'I believe they will let us in.'

Jamie walked over. 'The others are not as good at telling stories, so what's happening?'

'I'm going to bed,' said Jack, 'and in the morning I'm going to check out some caves.'

Jamie grinned. 'Cool, it'll beat hanging around here.'

Jack wanted to argue, but he couldn't protect his brother if he wasn't with him.

Jack swung his sword and the mercenaries fell. His soldiers lay on the ground as their weapons had no effect on the red-eyed demons. Jack's sword broke those of the demons and turned the creatures to dust before him. One released an arrow which flew past him, and he saw the priest drop to his knees. Jack destroyed the demon and turned to the witch. *You will pay for this she shouted . . . I will end your line.* Jack cut off her head when a dark shadow fell around him. He felt sharp claws dig into his shoulders.

Jack woke with a start, sat up and rubbed his shoulders.

Jamie stared at him with both eyes large. 'Bro, that's one freaky way to wake up.'

Jack stretched and stood up. 'I had another dream, and you're up early.'

'No, you're late . . . the others are waiting for you.'

'Have I missed anything?'

'Armed police are here, and someone said they heard shooting in the night but I never heard anything. You got bacon and eggs for breakfast.'

Jack finished off a mug of coffee and glanced around the camp. Most of the hikers were ready to leave. Chloe and Arthur walked over.

'The police are allowing them to go,' she said, 'but only if it's in a different direction.'

Jack put the mug down. 'You're going to be insistent on searching through those caves?'

Chloe nodded. 'Of course, I've a good feeling about today. The sword's here, I just know it.'

'I agree,' said Arthur, 'do your dreams tell you anything?'

Jack rubbed his shoulders again. 'No, the furthest I've got is when the beast from above grabs me.'

Gary smiled. 'A treasure hunt it is then.'

'It's no treasure hunt,' said Jack, 'and only a small group is going.'

'Isn't it?' said Elisabeth. 'Searching for an old sword sounds like a treasure hunt to me. It'll be just the six of us and two others. Gary's sorted it all out.'

Jack raised an eyebrow. 'Who are the others?'

'Police officers,' said Gary, 'they won't let us go without them.'

Jack patted him on the shoulder. 'Good work, how did you get them to agree to it?'

Gary shrugged. 'Bugger all really, I think they already knew and offered to help.'

'Odd,' said Jack, 'do they know something we don't?'

'Yes,' said Chloe, 'they know we're not going anywhere near the bodies. We go south along the forest before going inside.'

'They want us gone,' said Gary, 'and if we're far from the murder scenes all the better.'

'I can see that,' said Jack, 'but we'll still be in the forest.'

'Yes, as will others. It appears the forest is too big to cordon off. Not all the police are happy about it.'

'Here they are,' said Chloe, as a man and woman in potholing gear approached. 'Constables Gavin and Holly will be going with us.'

Jack rubbed his eyes. 'I hope we won't need to use that stuff.'

'It never hurts to be prepared,' said Gavin.

'It looks like you already were . . . how did you get it so soon?'

'We're on holiday,' said Holly, 'or was. We were about to go exploring elsewhere when the inspector asked us to accompany you. We jump at any chance to explore caves we've never been to.'

'I'm confused,' said Jamie, 'why would you need that stuff to explore caves?'

'Because of what you seek,' said Gavin. 'The inspector believes if we find the right cave whatever you're searching for will not be on show. We may have to go down some small holes to find it.'

'It won't be that small if Jack's gotta go down it.'

Jack smiled. 'Don't worry, they don't have enough equipment.'

'Hold on,' said Jamie, and grabbed his backpack.

'What you got that for?'

'It's got lunch inside.'

They walked south along the forest leaving the campsite behind. It wasn't long before Chloe turned right and entered the forest along a path. Jack followed, unsure of what to expect and curious to how much Chloe knew. He said nothing. It bothered him how a police inspector allowed two constables to go searching for an ancient sword. Did the inspector know something he didn't? They soon approached a sign pointing to caves, and Chloe walked past.

'What's wrong with those caves?' said Jack.

'It's not in any of those, too many people having been in them,' said Chloe as she walked off the path towards a small hill just over head height.

Jack tried to work her out. She was attractive, but also hiding something. 'Are none of you worried about being here?'

'No,' said Jamie, 'it's daylight, the place is full of police and many have guns.'

Chloe stopped in front of the hill surrounded by bushes. 'This is the one we need.'

Jack glanced around. 'Where, I can't see anything?'

Chloe grabbed part of a bush and pulled it back to show the opening of the cave. 'Right here.'

'Amazing,' said Gavin, 'I never knew that was here.'

Jack switched on a torch. 'Good, let's hope not many others did either.'

They all stepped inside shining their torches. The cave was about fifteen feet in diameter.

'This would make a great place to stop,' said Gavin, 'and perfect in bad weather.'

Arthur nodded. 'I have no doubt it has been shelter to many over the years.'

'We'll come back when it rains,' said Jack, 'but I don't think what we seek is in here.'

'Over here,' said Chloe, standing by a large rock.

Jack hurried over and saw an opening hidden behind the rock. It was too small for any of them to get through, so he placed his back to it. He turned his body to get some purchase on the wall and pushed. The rock moved slightly, and he pushed again. The rock moved further away giving them room to pass through.

'Thank you, kind sir,' said Chloe, as she walked through the opening.

Elisabeth smiled as she followed. 'Sir Jack.'

Jamie grinned. 'Bro.'

Gary stepped through followed by Arthur, Holly, as Jack and Gavin took the rear. They walked down a tunnel until they came to an open area with two passages leading off.

Jack stood in front of them. 'Which one?'

Chloe stepped over to the one on the right and moved down it. 'This one, it's in here.'

Jack caught up with her. 'Have you been here before?'

'Sort of.'

Jack threw his arms up. 'What's that supposed to mean?'

'Look,' she said, 'it's getting lighter.' Chloe ran on.

Jack could see without the torch and switched it off. 'Wait, you don't know what's there. It can't be daylight as we've been going downwards.'

He realised she most likely did know and gave chase. He found her in another room with a pool of water. The pool stood two feet off the ground as the rock formed a wall keeping the water inside.

'Wow,' said Jamie, 'where's the light coming from?'

'Phosphorous in the walls I'd guess,' said Gavin, 'but I've never seen anything like it before.'

'It's nice,' said Jack, 'but it's empty.'

'It's not here,' said Gary, 'we best check the other tunnel.'

'No,' said Chloe, staring into the pool, 'this is the right place.'

Jack walked over to her. 'I can't see anything, and the water's clear enough.'

'Look at the back of the pool, there's a tunnel.'

Jack sighed and removed his top. 'There's no point in everyone going.' He emptied his pockets into Jamie's backpack before stepping into the pool. He expected it to be cool as he lowered himself down, but found it pleasant and relaxing. After a few seconds, he saw the others staring at him.

Elisabeth shook her head. 'I thought you were going through the tunnel.'

'I know, but this feels lovely.'

'You might want to see if the sword's here first.'

Jack ducked under the water and swam through the tunnel. His head surfaced a few seconds later and his feet touched the ground. He stood and walked up a ramp out of the water. The room he stepped into was lit up like the last one and only a little smaller. He glanced to the right and saw it. An armoured skeleton sat on the floor with a sheathed sword leaning up the wall. The armour on the shoulders was bent out of shape.

'Sir Jack, we finally meet.'

The skeleton did not reply.

'I need to borrow your sword to avenge you and destroy the creature.'

The skeleton still didn't reply.

Jack picked up the sword. 'Rest in peace.'

The skeleton crumpled to the floor and the lights dimmed. Jack hurried down the ramp and dipped below the water. He swam through the tunnel to the pool where he had to dodge many feet. He stood and saw the others relaxing in the pool.

Chloe smiled up at him. 'You found it then.'

Elisabeth frowned. 'You were way too quick.'

Jack climbed out and put his t-shirt on. 'You might want to hurry up . . . it's going to be dark in here soon.'

Jamie stood. 'The water's gone cold, what did you do?'

'I took the sword, and I think the pool was the last shield protecting it.'

'Yes,' said Arthur, rubbing his arms, 'I felt so calm I didn't want to go anywhere.'

They all climbed out and grabbed their clothes, as Jack switched on his torch and walked back up the passage. By the time he reached the opening the others had caught up with him.

Jack walked towards the path, but he felt uneasy. 'Something's wrong, it looks different.'

'There are more trees,' said Chloe, 'and the undergrowth's a lot thicker. How can that be?'

'That's neat,' said Jamie, 'but at least my brother can cut us a way through with his sword.'

Jack shook his head. 'No, mate, this is a lot more serious than that.'

'Indeed it is,' said Arthur. 'I believe the forest is how it was back in Sir Jack's time.'

Jack walked on searching for the path. 'Are you saying we've gone back in time?'

Arthur stood with hand on chin. 'I do not believe so, but neither are we in our own time at the moment. Something happened when you took the sword, but I do not know if it is the power of the weapon or of the witch. We must tread carefully as you are Sir Jack, and we are your soldiers as it was back then.'

'That's a charming thought,' said Gary, 'none of them survived.'

Jack pushed a branch to the side. 'The path's here, let's find an open space.'

They walked on in silence listening out for any noise or for the sign of police. Branches hung over the path as daylight only just managed to break through the top of the trees. Jack slowed as he saw the tree, with its gnarled and twisted branches, ahead. It stood alone in an open space.

'Strange,' said Chloe, 'how did we get here?'

'Not everything is as it appears,' said Jack. 'It's the same tree, but this isn't where we saw it before.'

'I believe this is where the tree originally stood,' said Arthur, 'before they burnt it down and dug up the roots.'

'Indeed it is,' said a woman. The low hanging branches of the tree parted as Black Mary stepped through. Twelve men, wearing tatty clothes, all armed with swords, followed her. One of the men held a bow.

Jack stood in front of his friends with sword over his shoulder. 'Hello, old crone.'

The witch cackled. 'Is that you, Sir Jack? Have you taken over his body? It would be so much sweeter for my pet if you have.'

Jack gripped the sword handle. 'What are you talking about? I came here for a holiday. Sir Jack has gone . . . he died a long time ago.'

'No, he's here or you would never have found the sword.'

Jack noticed Gavin pull out a gun. 'Go for the archer first.' He gave Mary a hard stare. 'I see your men do not have the red eyes like they did when Sir Jack defeated them.'

'No, because these are the men his father defeated.' Mary grinned. 'You do not have knights with you and your friends will die slowly. Do not worry as it will be over soon for them, but not for you.'

Jack checked his watch, and pulled the sword from its scabbard. 'I think not, we may only have one sword, but we are more advanced than you.'

'It will not aid you today.' Mary glanced at the men. 'Kill them, but leave Sir Jack for my pet.'

The archer strung an arrow to his bow as the men moved forward. He fell to the ground as Gavin fired his gun. Another of the soldiers fell when Holly fired hers, and the remaining men backed away.

'Impossible,' said Mary, 'you cannot have those here.'

'If you say so,' said Jack, 'yet, they are here and can kill your men.'

'You cannot kill what you cannot see,' Mary screamed, and a mist formed around her and the men.

Jack found himself running into the mist, as bullets shot past either side of him. He swung the sword killing any mercenaries he saw as others fell to bullets. The mist thinned out with all the mercenaries dead and Mary badly injured on the ground.

'You will suffer,' said the witch, 'my pet will make sure of that.'

Jack saw the shadow fall around him and turned quickly. Large talons slashed down at him, and he dived out the way. The sword fell from his hand as he rolled over to see a huge bird like creature land. It had the body of a giant raven, but the head had jaws with razor-sharp teeth. The beast turned to him as Gavin and Holly fired their guns, but they had no effect.

Chloe ran over to the large sword and picked it up with ease.

'It's of no use to you,' Mary laughed, 'only a descendant of Sir Jack can wield its power. You cannot stop my pet and while it lives so do I.'

Chloe ignored her and swung the sword down at the familiar's neck as it attacked Jack. The blade bit through the feathers and into what looked like flesh. The demon reared up in pain as she hacked it again and it fell.

'No,' Mary screamed, as the familiar turned to dust.

'I also had the dream,' said Chloe, 'I saw what happened to Sir Jack when the creature took him off. He managed to wound it and fell to the ground. Sir Jack dragged himself away and found the cave where he died.'

The witch along with the mercenaries vanished as did their clothing, and the air around them changed. It grew brighter as Jack noticed the forest thin out.

'That was amazing,' said Jamie, 'but what happened to their bodies?'

Jack climbed to his feet and dusted himself off. 'I've no idea.'

'The familiar was a demon,' said Arthur, 'Chloe sent it back. The witch and the mercenaries were not in this time as you can see we have returned to the present.'

'What about all this dust?' said Elisabeth. 'What do we do with it?'

'Nothing,' said Arthur, 'it is just dust.'

Jack turned to Chloe who passed him the sword back. 'Is it mine or yours?'

'Yours,' said Chloe, 'I'm not lumping it around.'

Jack picked up the scabbard and sheathed the sword. 'You have some explaining to do.'

Chloe nodded. 'I wanted to tell you, but something kept stopping me.'

'It worked out well,' said Arthur, 'as the witch wasn't expecting it either.'

'This should be fun to write up,' said Holly, as a woman in a suit approached.

'You will not need to report this,' she said.

Holly smiled. 'As you wish, Inspector, I hate making reports.'

'A cover up,' said Jack, 'you can't brush away the murder of four people.'

The inspector shrugged. 'You are free to tell the world what happened here, I'm sure the papers would love the story. They might want proof, of course, you do have some?'

'Jack will not be talking to the press,' said Arthur, 'we're going to have a long chat.'

Jack frowned at him. 'I don't think a conversation will cover up what has happened here.'

Arthur bent over and scooped up a handful of dust. He let it fall through his fingers before he tipped his hand over. 'That was just one of them, but there are many more. You have a weapon only you and Chloe can use.' Arthur smiled at him. 'It is in your hands to send many more of these things back.'

'Do it, Bro,' said Jamie, 'it's what you are.'

Jack glanced at his brother who could've easily been one of those he saw dead in the trees. 'What do I have to do?'

'Come with me,' said Arthur, 'there are some people I'd like you to meet.'

CHAPTER FIVE

Demons Three

'Ten dead, many injured,' said the reporter, 'as train derails before entering Stockton Station.'

Rachel Cooper put a hand to her mouth as she stared at the television. Shit, she thought, Sean was on that train.

She grabbed her keys, ran out the house and jumped into her car. Rachel drove off at speed just missing a car at the end of the road. Twenty minutes later she arrived at the station but had to park down a side street because of all the emergency vehicles. Paramedics treated people outside as she made her way to the entrance. Rachel squeezed through into the packed station with her eyes darting left and right searching through the crowd. Most of those there sat dazed while the more seriously injured had already been taken to hospital.

'Miss,' said a man, 'if you're here to catch a train I suggest you go home. There'll be no more running from here today.'

Rachel turned and saw a police officer. 'I'm trying to find my fiancé, he was on the train.'

The constable reached for his radio. 'What's his name?'

'Sean Evans, he was on his way back from a meeting.' Rachel stood on tiptoes trying to get a better view while the constable called in.

'Sean Evans,' she heard him say, but too anxious to listen. Rachel had been with Sean for three years and was due to marry him in a month.

'Miss,' said the constable, 'Miss.'

Rachel rubbed her eyes. 'Sorry.'

'We don't have his name down for any of those seen yet, so he must be here somewhere if he was on the train.'

Rachel sighed. 'Thank god.' She put a hand to her mouth. 'That must've sounded horrible after what's happened to some of the other passengers.'

The constable shrugged. 'Relief has that effect on people, and we all have our own way of coping. Could you give me a description of your fiancé?'

'He's six-five, broad, with short brown hair. He's wearing a black suit . . .' Rachel saw him through the crowd, sitting on a bench. 'It's OK, I've found him.' She pushed her way through to him. 'Sean, are you OK?'

He glanced up at her and rubbed his eyes.

'Sean, it's me Rachel.'

He blinked.

'You remember me, I'm your fiancée.'

'I know that, give me a minute I'm all fuzzy.'

Rachel saw blood on his head. 'You've taken a knock, you need it seen to.'

Sean stood and towered over her. 'I've been checked over and told I'll be fine.'

Rachel embraced him. 'Come on, let's get you home.'

'You brought the car?'

'Yeah, it's around the corner.' Rachel took his arm. 'What happened?'

Sean shrugged. 'I don't know, one minute I was reading a paper, the next I was lying on the ground with the train all twisted. You're gonna have to bear with me for a bit.'

Thirty minutes later Rachel kissed his cheek as he lay in bed. 'I gotta go to work, but ring me if you feel any worse.'

Sean nodded and closed his eyes. 'I'll be fine, I just need some sleep.'

Rachel left the house and climbed in the car, she worried about Sean and his bang to the head. She would've stayed, but being a nurse she knew they expected her in early and was already late for her shift.

Rachel stepped through the doors of ST Mary's hospital and saw Doctor Tim Bennett staring at a clipboard.

He glanced at her. 'Good of you to join us, you do know what's happened?'

Rachel walked over to him. 'Of course, Sean was on the train.'

'My god, is he OK?'

'Yeah, he took a bang to the head, but whoever checked him over said he'll be fine. I took a look myself, and he had a small cut. He was a little groggy though.'

Tim lowered the clipboard. 'I've seen a lot of that today, mostly through shock.'

~ ~ ~ ~

Erin Brown danced down the road with the street lamps lighting the way. 'Come on, Kay, we're gonna miss the party and all the fun.'

'I'm sure it'll still be on.'

'Yeah, well I need a drink.'

'You've had enough already.'

Erin glanced over the wall to the railway line as she danced along. 'Don't be a bore . . . Keith will be there.'

'Like I care . . . and I don't know why you do, he's never shown any interest.'

Erin threw her hands in the air. 'God you know how to bring someone down, I don't know why you bother coming out.'

Erin walked on without reply. 'Are you sulking?'

Still no reply, so Erin stopped and turned around. Kay was nowhere in sight. 'Oh come on, you know I didn't mean it.'

She glanced down the road and realised Kay should still be in sight as there were no side roads. On the other side of the road was Stockton Park, with an eight-foot steel fence all around. The gates were open, but she knew Kay wouldn't go through such a place at night. Erin didn't know which way to go, look for Kay or head to the party. She saw a man at the end of the road which led to the party. A tall skinny figure and Erin turned to go back when a large stocky man appeared at the other end of the road.

Erin ran across the road to the park and open gates, she carried on towards the play area where she saw someone sitting on a swing. As she approached Erin saw it was Kay, slumped on the seat, and heard a noise behind. The tall skinny man stood by the wall on the other side of the fence.

Erin glanced around not sure where to run, she had sobered up quickly and knew the man couldn't have put Kay on the seat and be where he was. The skinny figure walked towards the fence and leapt it with ease. She saw him more clearly now, legs unnaturally long as were his arms. He didn't have hands but long claws. He stared at her with red eyes, cackled a laugh, and her blood ran cold. She saw movement to her right as the big man in a hat walked into the park.

'Can I have this one?' said the skinny man.

'No,' said the one in the hat, 'she's food for the maggot.'

'You shouldn't call it that.'

Erin couldn't think straight, and was too frightened to run. She saw something slither along the ground, and she stepped back. It looked about six-foot long, like a fat caterpillar. The face was a large round mouth full of needle sharp teeth.

The skinny man leapt over and knocked her to the ground. He put a foot on her chest, and she couldn't move. 'You should feel privileged, not everyone gets a chance like this.'

Erin felt tears fall down the side of her face and wanted to scream. The creature shuffled over to her, its body stretching then shrinking as it moved. It sank its teeth into her arm, and she did scream before everything turned black.

<p style="text-align:center">~~~~</p>

Kevin Roberts glanced up at the wall clock. Two minutes to go, he thought, and my shift will be over. Being stuck at work until midnight on a Friday sucks.

He grabbed his bag and waited to clock out. The last bus would come at five past, and he would have to hurry. The clock changed to twelve, and he put his card in the machine before returning it to the holder on the wall. He walked out of the factory and ran down the road. It took him three minutes to reach the stop but the bus was already leaving.

'Wait,' Kevin shouted, 'you're early.' He bent over to catch his breath as the bus carried on. 'Thanks a lot . . . it's an hour's walk from here.'

Damn, this is all I need, he thought. Kevin had no money for a taxi and couldn't call his wife to pick him up. Friday was her night out and there were rumours she was seeing someone else. Ten minutes later he saw a field which would cut the time getting home down by half. It would also be tricky as it was dark and a large field with many obstacles.

Fifteen minutes later after using his phone as a torch he approached a set of garages on the edge of Frimley housing estate. He put the phone away and walked along the tarmac between the garages.

'What do we have here?' said a voice from above.

Kevin glanced up and saw a man sitting on top of a garage. He decided to carry on without answering, but the man jumped down in front of him.

'Where are you going, Kevin?' said the tall skinny man. 'Your wife's car is parked outside that house again, are you going there to kill them?'

Kevin stopped, nervous at the sight of the man. 'What? Who are you?'

'Spring-heeled, they call me, would you like a knife to kill them?'

Kevin shook his head. 'I'm not going to kill anyone.' He noticed the man didn't have hands but claws, and he backed away.

A big man in a hat approached. 'Then you're just food to us.'

Spring-heeled grinned, his eyes turning red. 'I want you to meet our friend.'

Kevin looked for an escape, but he doubted he could outrun the strange man or whatever he was. He heard clicking noises behind and turned to see a creature so unnatural it didn't look possible.

Click, click, the beast approached. It stood three feet high and walked on four limbs. Its body was almost flat it looked like a table with the head of a bald rat. It opened its jaws to show two long fangs pointing down.

Kevin turned to run but Spring-heeled knocked him to the ground and ripped open the clothes on his back. The creature hurried over and sank the fangs into his shoulder. He saw Spring-heeled jumping around before he passed out.

~ ~ ~ ~

'Watch out,' Kerry Jenson shouted.

Her husband, Dean, slammed on the brakes and turned the steering wheel to avoid the dog. The car veered off the road and into a ditch. 'Shit, did you have to scream down my ear? I could see it for myself.'

Kerry undid her seat belt. 'I couldn't help it . . . the thing came out of nowhere. And don't shout at me, it was your idea to travel at this time of the morning to beat the traffic.'

Dean put the car in reverse but it wouldn't move. He opened the glove box, took out a torch, and opened the door to get out. 'There's a good chance we won't be going anywhere now.'

'Where are you going?'

'To see what bloody damage the car has taken.' He climbed out and shone the torch at the front wheels to see the driver's side was off the ground. 'You better call for help.'

'Dean,' said Kerry, as she stared through the windscreen, 'get back in the car.'

'Why? What's up?'

'There's something out there.'

Dean glanced up and saw two red dots. He shone the torch and saw a man hanging upside down from a branch. His eyes were red and his hands looked like claws. He dropped out of the tree and landed on his feet. Dean stepped back to the car when he heard the sound of breaking glass and Kerry scream. He turned to see a large man drag his wife through the passenger window. He threw the torch at the man and ran to her, but the skinny one jumped on his back. Dean fell on his face and was dragged around to the other side of the car. He was put in a seated position next to Kerry who was unconscious.

'You bastards,' he shouted.

'Tut, tut,' said the skinny man, 'such language. We have a friend who wants to meet you.'

Dean felt something drip onto his head. He glanced up and saw a dog like creature hanging from a branch with its jaws wide open. More saliva dripped down on him. He felt hands grab his ankles and was pulled away from the car. Dean fell onto his back and the creature flew down at him. Its jaws latched onto his mouth, and he felt his life ebb away as darkness took him.

~ ~ ~ ~

Rachel Cooper grabbed her jacket from the locker as the door opened. Sharon Keane entered and put her bag down.

'You're late . . . I hope Doctor Bennett didn't see you.'

Sharon removed her own jacket. 'I've seen him, but I wasn't late. An ambulance arrived when I did with two young women inside. One had a bad knock to the head and the other had a nasty looking bite mark on her arm.'

'What do you mean nasty looking?'

'There's a lot of puncture marks, too many for a normal bite.'

'Don't sound like a bite,' said Rachel, 'what do the police, or to be precise your fella say?'

'Rob reckons they got drunk and fell asleep in the park. They weren't sexually assaulted and their clothes untouched.'

Rachel tried imagining it. 'So one fell and banged her head, and the other was bitten by some animal.'

'Something like that, but apart from the puncture wounds there are no tearing wounds like an animal would make.'

Rachel smiled. 'Since when did you become an expert?'

'I've seen dog bites, and this wasn't one of those.'

'Give me a call later if you find out as I've got to go and check on Sean.'

Sharon pulled her hair back and put a band around it. 'Is he ill?'

'No, but he was on the train which crashed and took a bang to the head.'

Rachel hurried home to check on Sean only to find a note on the table. 'Hi, honey, I woke up feeling fine, so I've gone to work, love Sean.' Rachel sighed. 'I can't even get to nurse him better.' She took a shower and went to bed.

Rachel stared at her phone in the late afternoon as she hadn't heard from Sean since she read the letter. The phone rang with the name Sharon flashing on it.

'Hi, Shaz, not too busy over there is it?'

'It's quietened down a little,' said Sharon, 'how's Sean?'

'OK, I think, he'd gone to work when I got home.'

'What? They got a cheek asking him to go in when it was their train which crashed.'

'Yeah, but that's Sean for you, he's a workaholic. I guess they're going to be busy trying to sort out what's happened.' Rachel glanced out of the window. 'So what about the girls, did you find out what happened?'

'That's why I called you . . . some weird crap must've gone down last night.'

'How do you mean?'

'Are you working tonight?'

'No, I'm off until Monday.'

'Same here, come to the pub tonight, and I will tell you what's been happening. Bring Sean as Rob will be there.'

'I'll have to let you know when he ever gets back.'

'Is everything OK between you two?'

'Yeah, it's great,' said Rachel, 'I just wish he'd let me nurse him now and then. I've never known him to be ill since I met him.'

Sharon giggled. 'Come out tonight, and you'll be glad you've got such a big fella.'

Rachel stepped inside the Swan public house just after eight in the evening. She saw Sharon, and her husband Detective Rob Keane, sitting at a table. Sharon waved and pointed at the table to show they had already got the drinks in. Rachel removed her jacket and sat down.

'No Sean?' said Rob.

'He'll be here soon, but can only stay for one.'

Rob sipped on his beer. 'I bet it's hectic over there with the crash. I haven't had a chance to go there since it happened because of last night.'

'Here he is,' said Sharon, pointing at the door.

Rachel turned and saw the hulking figure of Sean approach. She smiled as he leant over and kissed her cheek.

'Grab a seat,' said Rob, 'I got you a lager.'

Sean sat next to Rachel. 'Cheers, I need it, shame it's only the one.'

'You got to go back?'

'Yeah, it's been a nightmare.' Sean picked up his pint and took a swig. 'I hear strange things are afoot.'

'You're not wrong there.' Rob leant forward on the table. 'Of course, I'm not supposed to tell anyone but Sharon and Rachel work at the hospital. Sharon knows as much as I do, and Rachel will soon anyway.' Rob glanced around the bar. 'If one person had told me what happened I wouldn't have believed them and put it down to drink or drugs. Since around nine o'clock last night, five people were attacked.'

Rachel rubbed her chin. 'Like the two girls who were brought in this morning?'

Rob put his glass down. 'Yes, but also different. Four gave short accounts of what happened, the other only remembers being hit on the back of the head. The attacks happened in three different parts of town. The four witnesses gave similar descriptions of two of the attackers. One's a big man in a hat, and the other is skinny with long arms. Three of the witnesses said he had claws instead of hands, and red eyes.'

'Could be costumes,' said Sean, 'a pair of creeps going around terrifying people.'

'It's possible,' said Rob, 'but these were vicious attacks and the victims are lucky to be alive.'

'You said two of the attackers,' said Rachel, 'were there more?'

'That's where it gets weirder,' said Sharon, 'along with the injuries they caused.'

Rob nodded. 'Three of them gave different descriptions of the third attacker. The first, a young woman, said it was a giant maggot which bit her arm. The wound has many puncture holes and her arm has turned purple. The second said the attacker had limbs either side of its flat body. It bit into his shoulder which has also turned a funny colour. Both of them lost a lot of blood. The third couldn't describe the attacker too well as he was the weakest we spoke to. He also looked the worst, with his grey looking skin. He said it flew out of a tree at him and sucked his breath away. His mouth is swollen and blotchy. We're waiting to see if they can tell us more as all three are unconscious again.'

'I take it you've ruled out drugs,' said Sean.

'They all said they never touched them. One had not long finished work and two were going on holiday. It was five in the morning when their car veered into a ditch because of something they saw in the road. The wife who was dragged through a window said she saw an animal. The guy who had been to work until midnight said the skinny man called himself Spring-heeled.'

Sean took another swig from his drink. 'Spring-heeled Jack, I've read about him.'

Rob raised an eyebrow. 'I can't say I have.'

'A myth from around the country in Victorian times. He could leap great heights too.'

'One of the victims said he leapt over the fence at Stockton Park.'

'That must be eight feet high.'

'So the men are real,' said Rachel, 'but the others sound ridiculous. Could they have built some models to look like monsters? Whatever they used could have infected the victims.'

'We're not ruling anything out at the moment,' said Rob. 'Doctor Bennett, thought it possible, but he also believes there were traces of saliva. We'll no more when he gets the test results.'

Sean drank the remaining lager from his glass. 'It appears they're dressing up as myths from the past.'

'You could be right,' said Rob, 'but who could the big guy in the hat be?'

Sean kissed Rachel on the cheek and stood. 'I've no idea, but I gotta go back to work now. Will you make sure my fiancée gets home safely?'

Rob smiled. 'Of course, we'll get a taxi together.'

Rachel watched him leave. 'He's got loads of books at home on mythology . . . we should go and take a look through them.'

Rob glanced at his empty glass. 'That sounds like work to me.'

'True, but we have plenty to drink.'

'A free bar, my favourite kind of work.'

Rachel flicked through the pages of a book. 'Nothing in here.'

'Same here,' said Sharon, 'try the internet.'

'Good idea.' Rachel put the book down and opened her laptop. She powered it up and waited. The internet browser came up. 'What should I type in?'

'Spring-heeled Jack,' said Rob, 'let's see what he looks like.'

Rachel typed it in and the page changed. She clicked on images and a new page loaded.

'That's one creepy looking dude,' said Sharon, 'and something like him is running around town attacking people?'

'It would appear so,' said Rob. 'He's quite famous, and I'd never heard of him until Sean mentioned it. He could be right about it being a copycat.'

Rachel nodded. 'I see that, but why?'

Rob shrugged. 'Who knows, maybe they get a kick out of terrorizing people.'

'So we know who he is,' said Sharon, 'but who's the other meant to be?'

Rachel rubbed her chin and typed "Mr Hyde" into the search bar. The page changed and pictures of a large man in a hat appeared.

'Clever,' said Sharon, 'what made you think of him?'

'Apart from Dracula, he's the only other one I could think of.'

'A strange looking pair,' said Sharon, 'you'd have thought others would've seen them.'

'There will be a lot more officers patrolling tonight,' said Rob, 'So if they're out again they'll be seen.'

Rachel woke the following morning and turned to see Sean fast asleep. She thought about waking him up but decided to have a shower. Afterwards she went downstairs to make breakfast. Rachel poured boiling water from the kettle into two cups when she felt hands go round her waist.

Sean kissed her neck. 'Something smells nice.'

Rachel smiled. 'It's called coffee.'

'I wasn't talking about that.'

She turned to him. 'Have I finally got you to myself?'

'For a while, I've got to go in later.'

Rachel sighed. 'You never work on a Sunday.'

Sean stepped to the side and leant back on a cupboard. 'I know, but there's never been a crash since I've worked there. It'll all die down soon.'

Rachel turned back and stirred the two cups of coffee. 'I guess so.'

'How did your night go? Did you solve the case?'

'No, we come back here to look through your books on myths, but couldn't find the right ones.'

Sean picked up a cup of coffee. 'You should've tried the spare room . . . they're in a box as the bookshelf fell down.'

'Yeah, I remember. We looked on the internet instead, but didn't find much, just who the big guy might be masquerading as.'

Sean took a drink of the coffee and put the cup down. 'I'm going for a shower . . . I'll be back down in a bit.'

Rachel watched him climb the stairs when her phone rang. She jumped and knocked her coffee over. She answered the phone to Sharon, and soaked the coffee up with a tea towel. 'Hi, Shaz.'

'Have you been watching the news?'

'No, not switched the telly on yet, what's happened now?'

'Three more attacks,' said Sharon, 'only this time the victims died.'

Rachel put a hand to her mouth. 'Oh shit, do you know how they died?'

'Not yet, but Rob's gone into work.'

'Does that mean you're stuck home alone all day?'

'Not sure, Rob said he'd be back soon but that means nothing when he's on a case.'

'Sean's going to work later, so we should meet up.'

'Yeah OK, I'll give you a call when I find out what's happening.'

Rachel opened the washing machine to put the wet tea towel inside and saw a pair of trousers covered in mud. She placed the towel inside, and made another coffee.

She saw Sean enter the kitchen not long after. 'What happened to you last night?'

Sean sat at the table. 'How do you mean?'

'The state of your trousers in the washing machine.'

'Oh that, I fell over a gravestone.'

Rachel shook her head at him. 'What on earth were you doing in a cemetery?'

Sean rubbed his damp hair. 'The car broke down, so I took a shortcut.'

'I don't think that was a good idea when the police are looking for a big guy.'

'It's OK, I don't wear a hat, and you're my only skinny friend.'

'I'm hardly skinny, and you might want to know there were three more attacks last night, three people were murdered.'

Sean raised an eyebrow. 'Do we know who?'

'No, Sharon's trying to find out.'

Sean stood. 'You don't think I had anything to do with it?'

Rachel shook her head and embraced him. 'Of course not, you're my big teddy bear.'

Sean smiled. 'Why don't we invite the others over for Sunday dinner?'

Rachel released him. 'What others?'

'Rob, Sharon, Tim, and Wendy.'

'I can ask, but the men might be a little busy. I'm gonna need to go shopping now to have any chance of getting a roast cooked.'

Sean stared out of the window. 'No, that's too much hassle. Ask them if they can get away for an hour for a barbecue.'

'I prefer that idea, and everyone needs a lunch break.' Rachel arched an eyebrow. 'Are you being sociable, or is this about something else?'

'Both, as they know more of what's happening than we do.'

'True, but we still need to go shopping.'

'Not yet, I think we should go back to bed first.'

'You haven't had breakfast.'

Sean glanced at the empty table. 'We must be having cereal, it can wait.'

Doctor Tim Bennett stood outside the back. 'This is pleasant, and your garden is so much bigger than ours.'

Rachel glanced down the garden, and the neatly trimmed lawn. The smell from the barbecue drifted around. 'Yes, because you bought one of those new town houses.'

'That's how they build them now. You've had this place a while.'

'Yeah, ever since my parents gave it to me, as it had too many bad memories for them.'

'Don't you have those memories too?'

'Yes, but it's the good memories I try to remember. They always wanted to leave after what happened, but couldn't sell the house. Once I was old enough to live on my own they gave it to me and moved to the coast.'

'You're life savers,' said Rob, 'I'm gonna be stuck at work for the rest of the day and night.'

'Tell me about it,' said Sean, 'I've got to go in soon.'

Rachel turned around where Rob, Sharon, and Wendy Bennett sat at a table drinking juice. 'That's nice, we've got maniacs on the loose, and they're leaving us home alone.'

'You'll be fine,' said Sean, as he tended to the barbecue. 'You can have a girls night in.'

'I have to be out there,' said Rob, 'we need to stop these creeps.'

'Tim's working,' said Wendy, 'so I'm off to my sister's for a few days.'

The doctor sat down. 'I don't have much choice in the matter.'

'I thought they were dead,' said Rachel, 'I mean the three from last night.'

'They are, but it's the three from the night before. None of them have regained conscious since yesterday morning and the infections are a lot worse.'

Sean turned burgers over on the barbecue. 'I don't want to sound obvious, but how certain are you the murders are connected?'

'No witnesses have come forward for the attacks last night, said Rob, 'but the wounds the victims suffered are pretty much the same.'

Tim nodded. 'A man with puncture marks on his arm similar to those of the young woman on the first night. A second with a bite mark on his shoulder, which also matched one of those from the first night. We believe the assailants took blood, but last night they took too much.'

'Took blood,' said Rachel, 'you don't mean like a vampire?'

'We have no idea how they took it,' said Rob, 'as for the third, it's as if he was drained of all his energy. I knew the young man, Calvin Johnson, who liked to jog at night because he didn't like going out in the day. He was nineteen, but if he hadn't got ID I would never have recognised him. His skin was all wrinkled, and he looked about seventy.'

Rachel shuddered. 'What the hell could cause that?'

Rob leant forward on the table and clasped his hands together. 'The witnesses were adamant the creatures were real. We've had sketch artists trying to draw them but the pictures look ridiculous.'

'They could be deformed animals,' said Wendy, 'there must be some that drink blood.'

Tim shook his head. 'They would be too small, and I wouldn't want to come across a six-foot-long leech. The thought of it is pretty terrifying. There were bigger animals, but they're extinct now.'

'We can have a look on the net after we've eaten,' said Rachel, and turned to Sharon. 'Are you staying here?'

'Yeah, if it's OK, I don't fancy sitting in the house on my own.'

Rachel sipped on coffee as she sat in her living room with Sharon. 'I wonder if there will be any more attacks tonight.'

'I hope not,' said Sharon, 'but after what's happened it's possible. Let's hope people use common sense and stay in.'

'Yeah, but it's not that simple. Pubs are open, even some shops, and what about people who need to get to the hospital for whatever reason?'

'True I guess.' Sharon picked up some pictures from the table they had printed off. 'What do you think . . . giant insect or a prehistoric monster?'

Rachel leant back on the sofa. 'I hope it's neither.'

'I know, did you see the hagfish, if it's a big one of those I'm off to Wendy's sister's house too.'

'Are you stopping the night?'

Sharon smiled. 'If that's OK, as Rob won't be home until the morning.'

'Of course it's OK.' Rachel sat forward. 'Listen to us all scared of what's going on while our men are out. We're not doing much for women's lib.'

Sharon raised an eyebrow. 'You're not suggesting we go and search for this freak show?'

Rachel climbed off the sofa to look out of the window into the darkness. 'No, but we could go to the hospital and see what's happening.'

'Sounds good to me, and we could show the witnesses these pictures.'

Ten minutes later they were driving down a country lane when the lights from a parked car lit up in the night.

Rachel slowed the car. 'That's Pete's recovery truck, he brought Sean's car home earlier.'

Sharon stared out of the passenger window. 'It looks like he hit a tree.'

Rachel stopped the car to see what happened to him.

The back door opened and a grey haired man scrambled inside and shut the door. 'Drive,' he shouted, 'get away from here.'

Rachel put her foot down without looking.

'Watch out,' Sharon screamed.

Rachel turned to the road and saw a tall skinny man just as she hit him.

'Don't stop,' said Pete, 'whatever you do, don't stop.'

Rachel drove on and glanced in the mirror. She saw the tall skinny man climb to his feet, and was soon joined by a larger man. She noticed Pete touching a cut on his head.

'What just happened?' said Sharon.

'The weirdest thing,' said Pete, 'I've never crashed a car until tonight.'

Sharon reached over with some tissues. 'Press these over your cut . . . we're taking you to the hospital.' Sharon took out her phone. 'I'll call Rob.'

Rachel glanced in the mirror at Pete holding the tissues to his head. 'Are you OK?'

'I think so, but it shook me something funny.'

Rachel waited for Sharon to finish her call. It only took a minute.

Sharon put her phone away. 'For some reason he wasn't happy about us being out. He's got some officers going to check out the crash and will meet us at the hospital.'

Rachel nodded and glanced in the mirror. 'What happened, Pete, did they make you crash your truck?'

'I don't know what it was, but I saw it flying just ahead of me. It looked like a dog with wings. I turned sharply and hit a tree. I was trying to get my bearings when the passenger window exploded inwards and a big man lunged in. I managed to get out when you drove up. I'm not one for being frightened easy but the guy coming through the window scared me. He must've been as big as your Sean.'

'Did you see his face?'

'No, he wore a wide-brimmed hat. He would've got me if the window wasn't too small for him.'

Rachel saw blue flashing lights heading towards them which soon passed by. Ten minutes later they arrived at St Mary's hospital where they helped Pete into the accident and emergency department. They walked past people waiting to be seen and approached the counter.

'Hi, Carol,' said Sharon, 'we've brought you a patient.'

The nurse raised her glasses. 'Are you going out finding them now, only we're a little busy?'

'Yeah, I can see that, and it's why we're here. Can we take him through as the police will be here soon to talk to him?'

'He doesn't look like a vicious criminal.'

'No, that's because he's a victim.'

The nurse looked him up and down. 'OK, take him through.'

They took him to a cubicle where Rachel removed the tissues to show a lump and a one-inch cut. She picked up a surgical wipe to clean the wound.

'This might hurt a little.'

Pete shrugged. 'It already does.'

Rachel cleaned off the blood. 'I don't think it's life-threatening.'

'This is some girls night in,' said Rob, as he marched towards them with Sergeant Carling.

'Hello, dear,' said Sharon, 'nice to see you're concerned for us. Don't you think we're much safer here?'

'How? No one's been attacked in their home.'

'Not yet, but when they can't find anyone on the streets it'll change.'

'I don't like to interrupt,' said Pete, 'but if these ladies hadn't come along when they did, I'd be dead now.'

Carling rubbed his unshaven chin. 'You can't be sure of that.'

'I beg to differ, as you weren't there or saw that thing.'

'What thing?'

'A flying dog,' said Sharon.

'I never said that,' said Pete, shaking his head as Rachel tried putting butterfly stitches on the cut. 'They'll put me in a straitjacket. I said it looked like a dog with wings.'

'Same thing,' said Carling. 'Could it have been a bat?'

'I suppose, if a bat had four legs and was the size of a German Shepherd.'

'Pete,' said Rachel, 'can you keep still for a moment?'

'Sorry, my dear.'

Rachel put the last stitch on. 'There, finished.'

Rob watched her. 'What does Sean think of you being here?'

'He doesn't know,' said Rachel, 'as he's still at work. What does it have to do with anything? I'm a grown woman and can go out when I like.'

'The inspector didn't mean it like that,' said Carling, 'we have warned everyone not to go out tonight.'

'That worked, did you see the waiting room. Besides, the attack on Pete happened five minutes from my home, and that's too close.'

'Yes, I agree,' said Carling, 'but it's not the reason you're here, you're more interested in what's going on.'

Rachel shrugged. 'Yeah, I won't deny I want to know more.'

'We want to know more,' said Sharon. 'I brought some pictures to see if the witnesses recognise any.'

Rob sighed. 'What pictures?'

'The ones we printed off the net.'

'The creatures the witnesses said attacked them were not real.'

'On the contrary,' said Doctor Tim, as he approached. 'Whatever animal caused those injuries, are real. Sadly none of them will be looking at any pictures for a while. The three are still unconscious due to the infections. The other two suffered no infection just received bad knocks to their heads, and they've gone home.'

'We know that,' said Rob, 'but what makes you believe they were real?'

'Saliva, as I said before, but we have no idea what it's from.'

'Like a Komodo dragon,' said Pete, 'it bites its prey and waits for them to die.'

Tim nodded. 'Something like that.'

'Well what I saw was real, even if it did look weird.'

Carling turned to Sharon. 'May I have a look at the pictures?'

'Sure,' said Sharon, and took them out of her bag before passing them to him.

Carling glanced at the pictures. 'Some of these are hideous, and I'm sure this is a fish.'

'It is,' said Rachel, 'but it's the closest we found with lots of teeth.'

'I can't see anything here which looks like the one with limbs either side of its body.'

'We couldn't find any creature like that, all I can imagine is a table with a head.'

Carling laughed. 'It's all we could come up with.'

'I'm getting more officers here,' said Rob, 'I want those already hurt protected in case the freaks come back for them.'

Tim rubbed his chin. 'What makes you think they would?'

'What Pete said about the dragon. Maybe the infections were no accident, but a chemical to do something to them.'

Tim raised an eyebrow. 'An interesting thought, I will do more checks and keep an eye on them.'

'You might want to check for parasites while you're at it, maybe it laid eggs.'

'Nice,' said Rachel, 'people being used as incubators.'

'It could well be,' said Tim, 'have you two come in to work?'

'Yes,' said Sharon, 'but we forgot our uniforms.'

'Grab a couple of white coats from my office, they will suffice for tonight.'

'It makes me feel happier,' said Rob, 'it means we won't have to keep an eye on them.'

Sharon shook her head. 'I'm quite sure you said they might come here for the others.'

'Yes, dear, but there will be police here too.'

Rachel walked down the corridor while fastening the buttons on the white coat. 'Is your husband always so arrogant?'

'No,' said Sharon, 'you know Rob, but this shit has shaken him. It's never bothered him if I go out or even where I am because he trusts me. He wants to protect me, but he can't be here to do it himself.'

'I guess, but I hate being treated like a child.' Rachel stopped. 'I'm sorry, but it would've been nice if Sean showed as much concern.'

'He thinks you're at home.'

'True, so where do we go first?'

'The mortuary, I wanna see the bodies.'

Rachel shook her head. 'You get more gruesome every day.'

'No, I want to know if there's been any change in them or deterioration.'

'They're dead, and besides you never saw them when they were brought in.'

Sharon put her hair in a band. 'Rob mentioned the survivors might have parasites, if so the dead might have them too.'

They made their way to the mortuary at the rear of the hospital. This side was new and only had one floor.

Rachel noticed the door to the mortuary was slightly open and the room in darkness. 'Something's wrong, the lights are off.'

'Not really, someone may have just turned them off.'

'Have you ever known them to be off in there? I know I haven't.' Rachel opened the door and the light from the corridor shone into the room. There was a metallic sound of something crashing to the floor. She looked over at one of the dead bodies where a strange-looking creature leant over it. It turned to her with its large rat like head and snarled. Its body was almost flat with limbs sticking out each side. It stood with its legs bent out sideways, and arms bent at the elbows.

'What the hell?' said Sharon.

Rachel froze as the creature stared at her with black eyes. It dropped to all fours and scampered out a door at the back.

Sharon pulled Rachel out of the room and closed the door. 'I hope Rob's still here.' She took out her phone and called him.

Rachel rubbed her eyes. 'That was the table monster.'

Sharon nodded while holding the phone to her ear. 'Rob, you still here? ... We just saw one of the creatures in the mortuary ... No, it's gone now ... OK, just hurry up.' She ended the call and put the phone in a pocket. 'They're coming.'

A few moments later they heard footsteps running down the corridor, as Rob and Carling came into view with uniformed officers.

'Where is it?' said Rob.

Rachel pointed at the door. 'It ran out the back if you can call it running.'

Rob opened the door and stepped inside. He flicked the light switch, but they didn't turn on. He switched on a torch and shone it around the room. The lights hung down, smashed. Carling hurried past him to a woman, in a white coat, lying on the floor.

'Doctor Medway,' said Rachel, as she ran over and knelt by the woman.

'You should've waited in the hall,' said Carling.

'I'm a nurse and have to see if she's OK.' Rachel put a finger on the doctor's neck and felt a pulse. 'She's alive . . . we better get her out of here.'

Sharon pushed a trolley over to them and two constables lifted the unconscious doctor on to it.

Rob turned to the officers. 'Escort them to wherever they need to go and join us outside.'

Rachel sat in the canteen drinking a strong coffee when the two detectives walked in.

Rob shook his head. 'We searched everywhere, but found no sign of the creature.'

Sharon squeezed her hands together. 'If you had seen it you would know.'

Carling sat down. 'What did it look like?'

'Exactly how the witness described it,' said Rachel. 'It stood on two legs, but I don't know how as it seems impossible.'

'How do you mean?'

Rachel held her arms out sideways and let them drop at the elbows.

Carling scratched his chin. 'You appear to have mastered it.'

'Yeah, now try doing it with your legs.'

'Its face was horrible,' said Sharon, 'it had black eyes with an odd shape mouth.'

'They were more like jaws,' said Rachel, 'like a large bald rat.'

'How's the doctor?' said Rob.

'She should be OK,' said Rachel, 'she wasn't bitten, just took a knock to the head. It looks like she was in the way.'

'We have police guarding the doors to the mortuary and where our three living victims are. We best get back out there, but it might be more productive if we stuck close to you two.'

Sharon shrugged. 'Are you worried we might solve the case for you?'

'No, but you're like magnets to these things tonight. Please don't go anywhere alone.'

'That would be hard,' said Rachel, 'the place is full of police.'

Rachel glanced at her phone as she walked down the corridor. It was almost ten o'clock, and Sean still hadn't called.'

'He's probably still at work,' said Sharon.

Rachel put the phone in a pocket. 'Are you psychic now?'

'Just a guess,' said Sharon, as they entered a room where Doctor Medway sat in a chair.

Rachel smiled. 'How are you feeling?'

The doctor rubbed the side of her head. 'Terrible, my head throbs and I've no idea if what hit me was real or from a dream.'

'Real, for definite, we saw it too but it ran off.'

'So I owe you my life.'

Rachel considered it. 'I don't believe so . . . it was more interested in one of the dead bodies.'

Medway rubbed her eyes. 'What on earth is going on?'

'We don't know, but would you say the bodies are infected with anything?'

'Yes, I was going to perform an autopsy, but decided to have them quarantined first.'

Rachel put a hand to her mouth. 'Is it contagious?'

'I'm not sure, but it's possible. They were murdered last night but boils appeared on their faces not long ago. I don't want anyone going in there until we know it's safe to do so.'

'It's a bit late for that,' said Sharon, 'the police are already there.'

Medway stood. 'We best get back there and make sure the room's clear.'

They hurried to the back of the hospital where they saw two officers standing outside the mortuary.

'I'm sorry, Doctor Medway,' said a constable, 'we have orders not to allow anyone in.'

Medway stood in front of him. 'That's fine, Terry, as I have no intention of going in there at the moment. What I do want is for you to open the door and make sure only the dead bodies are inside.'

'They are, and we have two officers outside guarding the exterior door.'

'Good,' said Medway, with her arms folded, 'now be a dear and check for me.'

Terry switched on his torch and opened the door. He stepped inside and shone the torch around. 'Oh crap, the bodies have gone.'

Rachel followed the other constable inside with Sharon and Doctor Medway. Terry ran over to the other door and opened it.

Rachel saw two officers on the ground and hurried over to the nearest. She checked his pulse. 'He's alive.'

Sharon knelt by the other and put her fingers on his neck. She looked up and shook her head.

'No,' said Terry, 'you have to try something.'

'There's nothing we can do, he's been dead too long.'

'Officer down,' the other constable shouted into his radio, 'outside the back of the mortuary.'

'We need to get this one inside,' said Rachel, 'and get him treated.' She glanced around in the dark. The lawned area outside went fifty feet to the back fence. It continued around the sides of the hospital as a place for patients to walk. She saw lights approach from the right side as officers hurried towards them.

Rob reached them first. 'What the hell happened?'

'I don't know,' said Terry, 'whoever did this made no sound.'

Rachel watched as other officers put the unconscious constable on a trolley.

'And the other,' said Rob, 'I don't want him left out here.'

'Sir,' said a constable with a radio next to his ear, 'they've been spotted.'

'Where?' said Carling.

'Heading towards Stockton Station.'

Carling nodded. 'Let's get the creeps.'

'Wait,' said Rob, 'how were they travelling?'

'Does it matter?' said Carling.

'Yes, Sergeant, they've got three bodies with them.'

The constable shook his head. 'Whoever called in never said.'

'I don't like it,' said Rob, 'I want half the officers to remain here.'

'Rob,' said Rachel, 'Sean's still at work.'

Rachel stood outside the front of the hospital with phone in hand. She had tried to call Sean and tell him of what she knew, but he never answered. Sirens sounded in the distance as a paramedic approached.

'Are you Miss Cooper?' he asked.

'Yes, Steve, how long have you known me?'

'Two years I guess, but I didn't know your surname.'

Rachel laughed. 'I never considered that, and I don't know yours either.'

'It's Olsen, and some guy gave me this letter for you.' He handed over an envelope.

Rachel took the letter. 'Thank you, did you recognise him?'

Steve shook his head. 'I've never seen him before.'

Rachel stepped inside and walked to the canteen, so she could read the letter.

'What you got there?' said Sharon, as she sipped on a coffee.

Rachel sat at a table. 'Steve the paramedic gave it me . . . some guy gave it to him.'

'I'd say it was strange, but I don't think that applies anymore.'

Rachel opened the letter and read it.

The demons three it is said, like to feast upon the dead.

Three victims each they must take, for the demon lords to wake.

Return they will for the three who live, for a plague the world they give.

You are marked for the last, because of your family's past.

You must hurry and leave this place, or disease and death you will face.

If all else fails trust no other, but to the love of your brother.

Tears fell down her face, and she wiped them away.

Sharon put her cup down and reached over the table. 'What's wrong?'

Rachel pushed the letter over. 'Read it.'

Sharon picked it up and did so. 'Shit, this is weird, and it says you're one of their next victims.'

Rachel shrugged. 'I know.'

Sharon scratched her head. 'It's not that part which bothers you is it?'

Rachel shook her head. 'Read the last part.'

Sharon glanced at the letter again. 'The part about your brother, I never knew you had one.'

'Not many do, he died when I was ten. Whoever wrote this letter knew of him, and Sean's the only one I told.'

Sharon arched her eyebrow. 'You don't think he wrote it?'

Rachel thought about Sean. 'It's not his writing. I'm just being silly as the letter threw me.'

'What happened to your brother?'

'I don't speak of him often as it always saddens me. Justin was my big brother who died when I was ten. He could always make me laugh but that changed when he turned sixteen. The laughter stopped, and I often heard him crying at night. One day he gave me this.' Rachel pulled out a necklace which had a small bottle, no bigger than a thimble, attached to it. 'He told me it contained his last tears as he would never cry again. I thought he meant the laughter would return, but he was found hanging from a tree that night. They said it was suicide but I never believed it. He told me demons were trying to make him do horrible things, but he refused.'

'That's horrible,' said Sharon, 'and it looks like he was telling the truth and the demons have come back for you.'

'I can't believe that,' said Rachel, 'not when so many others have already been attacked.'

'The letter said you're to be the last.'

'Where's Sean?' Carling demanded, as he approached their table.

Rachel raised an eyebrow. 'At work as far as I know.'

'He's not,' said Rob, 'we went to the station to see if he was OK, but they told us he hasn't been in since before the crash.'

Rachel felt her stomach flip. Sean had never lied to her before, or so she thought. 'Then I've no idea.'

'Don't try blaming this on Sean,' said Sharon, 'I've known him a few years and you couldn't meet a nicer guy.'

Carling rubbed his chin. 'I would've thought the fiancé would be the one to defend him.'

'Sharon's trying to protect me,' said Rachel. 'I love Sean with all I have. He's never lied to me until now and I feel betrayed. None of it means I am without hope. Sean might be a big guy, but he's also gentle.'

Carling shrugged. 'Many psychos act in the same way.'

'Enough,' said Rob, 'he's a friend of mine and I'm sure Sean will have a good explanation. He hasn't lied to the police, apart from me but I wasn't on duty.'

'He also had a bang to the head,' said Sharon, 'and that can make people act funny.' She turned to Rachel. 'Show them the letter.'

Rachel pushed it over. 'I was given this not long ago.'

Rob picked it up and read it before passing it to Carling. 'That settles it. We believe the sighting of these, whatever they are, was just to get us away from here.'

'Do you know why this hospital is called St Mary's?' said a voice.

Rachel turned to see a grey haired man sitting at the next table. She had no idea anyone else was in there.

'Excuse me?' said Carling.

'I said do you know why this place is called St Mary's?'

'A question for another time,' said Rob, 'only we're a little busy at the moment.'

Rachel looked at the man who wore a dark grey suit. He had a distinct air about him. 'Why is it called St Mary's?'

The Man clasped his hands together. 'It was the name of the church which once stood here.'

'What?' said Carling. 'There's never been a church here.'

'I have to agree,' said Rob, 'I'm a bit of a historian when it comes to Stanton and I've never read anything about one being here.'

'You never will either, as the church burned down long before anyone here was born.'

'Sounds fascinating,' said Rob, 'and I'd love to hear more, but we have to get the ladies away from here.'

'Rob's right,' said Sharon, 'from what the letter says we need to get you far from here.'

Rachel stood. 'I know, but I also want some answers.' She passed the letter over to the man. 'Who are you?'

'I am Charles Edwards,' he said, and put on a pair of glasses before reading the letter. He put it down and removed his glasses. 'You have to do as they ask and get away from here now.'

'I will, but why was the church burned down?'

'Because of what happened. Nothing has ever been written about it, just the story passed down over the years. Over three hundred years ago Stanton Village, as it was called then was a much smaller place. Three people were attacked and the following day three more was murdered. The people back then were superstitious, and thought it the work of a witch or even demons. They buried the dead the same day, but on the third day someone had dug them back up.'

'Similar to what's happening now,' said Carling, 'something the public doesn't know about, yet you do. I'd like to know how, and how much you do know.'

'Pretty much everything,' said Charles, 'but that's not important right now. You need to worry about getting these ladies away from here. What is also important, are the three live victims. When the villagers learned about the unholy grave robbing, they marched to the church.'

Carling rubbed his eyes. 'Like a mob with flaming torches?'

Charles nodded. 'In a sense, as it was night. They were marching to it as the first three victims were being taken care of there. When they arrived, they saw strange creatures outside with nine victims. The three dead were emaciated shells, and the three injured were covered in boils. The final three were knelt with hooded figures holding knives to their throats.'

Rob raised an eyebrow. 'They were being sacrificed.'

'Yes, but the villagers were not alone as the local squire had gone for aid and soldiers arrived. The hooded figures were killed by arrows, and the other creatures were not strong enough to fight.

They grabbed the three victims covered in boils and dragged them into the church. The priest ordered it burnt down as it was no longer a house of God.'

Rachel shivered. 'They burned it while the three lived?'

Charles clasped his hands together. 'Yes, once the boils appeared, there was no hope for them. Boils meant only one thing back then.'

'The plague,' said Rob, 'Like it says in the letter.'

'Luckily no one else was infected.'

Carling sat on the edge of a table. 'Why were the creatures not strong enough?'

'They were not whole, like the ones now. They are demon lords, and the two doing all the work are guardians who protect them and find the food.'

Sharon coughed. 'Food? You mean the victims?'

'Yes,' said Charles, 'as horrible as it sounds. Of course, we're not completely sure, but we do surmise. Once they have their final victims nothing will stop them and pestilence will cover the land.'

Carling shook his head. 'Are you saying demons are going around killing people?'

'Yes, and like I say you have to ensure the other three are protected.'

'They're safe,' said Rob, 'we have them guarded.'

'I doubt the guards will be close enough when the boils appear. You do need to get the ladies away as I believe they want to perform the sacrifices where the old church stood.'

'I don't know who you are, old man,' said Carling, 'but I don't believe any of it.'

'Does it matter?' said Rob. 'Whatever they are we have to get these two far away.'

The lights flickered and Charles glanced up. 'It may be too late . . . they are trying to cut the power.'

Rachel and Sharon followed Rob out of the canteen with Carling behind them. Tim approached with four officers.

'They've gone,' said the doctor.

Rob rubbed his eyes. 'Who have gone?'

'The first victims, I had to quarantine them the best I could as boils appeared on their necks and under the arms. The hall outside the room was guarded as was the outside of the window, yet no one saw anything.'

'Damn,' said Carling, 'why was no one inside with them?'

'Because we don't have the proper facilities to quarantine anyone here.'

Rob turned to the officers. 'Sergeant Harris, I want the whole place searched, they're still here. Search in fours and find out where the power box is.'

The lights flickered and went out. The emergency power came on and dim lights lit up.

'Too late,' said Carling.

'The light here won't get any better with the emergency,' said Tim, 'as we need the power for more vital equipment. I will show the officers to the power room.'

Rob carried on forward with the others which now included two constables.

Rachel looked back. 'Where's Charles?'

'I don't know,' said Carling, 'and we're not going back for him. He's got something to do with this, I'm sure of it.'

They carried on when there was an explosion ahead. Rob ran through a pair of doors into another hall. Rachel followed and saw half a wall and ceiling had collapsed.'

'It's blocked,' said Rob, 'we have to go another way.'

Carling turned to Rachel. 'You work here.'

'It's not hard, just find the next turning going left or right and follow it until you reach a corridor which leads to the front. You should worry about what's happened, and if those on the other side are OK.'

A constable spoke into his radio but got no response.

'Let's go,' said Rob, 'we best hurry.'

Carling led the way and walked right at the first turning. They soon turned down another corridor only to find it was also blocked.

'I don't like this,' said Sharon, 'it must've been a bomb.'

Rob rubbed his eyes. 'Maybe, we better go back.'

Rachel shook her head. 'No, we try one of these rooms.'

'How will that help?' said Carling.

'These are offices on the far right of the hospital. Inside them you'll find windows which open to the outside world.'

Carling grinned. 'Good thinking.' He grabbed a door handle and rammed the door with his shoulder. The door did not give. He tried again with the same result.

'This way,' said Sharon, holding another door open, and they followed her inside.

Rob walked over to the window and opened it. 'There's no one out here.'

'Where the hell are they?' said Carling.

'I've no idea, but it's too quiet.' Rob glanced back. 'I don't know what's happening, but you might want to lose those white coats.'

Rachel removed hers before climbing out of the window. She felt cool air on her face as she tried looking around in the dark. 'This is wrong, the hospital looks fine.' She checked her phone for a signal.

'No good,' said Sharon, 'I've got no bars.'

Rob switched on his torch. 'We best get down there and see what's happening.'

'Wait,' said Carling, shining his torch, 'something just moved.'

Rob shone his torch around. 'Where are the officers patrolling?'

'Inside, I guess,' said Carling, 'searching and trying to get through the blocked corridors.'

Rob shook his head. 'No, it's something else, have you heard any sirens?'

'There,' said Sharon, pointing to the left.

Four torches shone in the direction to show what looked like a large dog, the size of a horse.'

'No way,' said Carling, 'it can't be real.'

Sharon grabbed Rachel's arm. 'That's one big dog.'

'There's another,' said a constable, 'and it's got red eyes.'

'We better get back inside,' said Rob, 'if we have to fight I'd rather do it in there.'

Rachel glanced at the window they climbed out, and saw a figure inside closing it. 'We're too late, unless you're going to break it.'

'No,' said Rob, 'I doubt we would all get inside before they reach us. We have to go round the back and hope there's a way in.'

'I reckon I could take one,' said Carling.

'Don't be crazy, look at the size of them . . . they'd snap you in half.'

The group ran down the side of the hospital and turned left when they reached the end. Further ahead they saw a hooded figure holding a flaming torch with what looked like bodies on the floor.

'I think we found our victims,' said Carling.

Rob glanced around. 'Yeah, but we can't do anything about it now. Get ready to run as I'm going to charge into those doors.'

'You can't,' said Sharon, 'they're made of glass.'

Rachel looked over at the doors when she saw a man inside. He opened a door and looked out.

'You might want to hurry,' said Charles.

They all ran, not caring what was inside. Carling took the rear and slammed the door shut once they were all in. Rachel stared through the glass as the dog-like creatures trotted past.

Charles sighed. 'Well this is not going to plan.'

Carling scowled. 'What are you playing at?'

'I'm not playing at anything, this is very serious.'

'I can see that. You vanish without saying anything, and now you're here just as we go past.'

Charles shook his head. 'I did not vanish as I was still in the canteen when you left. The reason I am here is to find where the church stood.'

Carling rubbed his chin. 'You said it was here.'

Charles sighed again. 'Yes, my boy, but it was only a small church compared to the size of the hospital.'

'So where was it?'

'At a guess, I would say it is where they are now.'

Carling leant back on the wall. 'Great, just where we don't want to be.'

'Tell me,' said Rob, 'Why are you still here? I thought once we got the women away, it would be over.'

'Oh come now, Detective, did you honestly believe that. I did hope you would get the young ladies away from here, but it would be far from over. The demons didn't go through all this just to give up when they didn't get the right people to sacrifice.'

'I don't get it,' said Rachel, 'why did we need to leave if they're still going to do it?'

'They will try to complete the ritual,' said Charles, 'and we may thwart them with some luck.'

Rob stared through the door. 'How will we do that?'

'We get away for a start,' said Charles, as he walked down the corridor.

Rob hurried after him. 'You said they'll just choose three others.'

'Yes, but have you seen anyone else on this side of the barriers?' Charles pushed open a door to the next corridor as they all followed him. 'They will have to take three of your group or drop the barriers.'

'You mean where the walls collapsed?' said Sharon, 'How did they manage to do that?'

'Magic, at a guess. It means they have a more powerful demon with them. Of course, most of what you've seen will have been illusions.'

'Were those dog things illusions?'

'I do not know . . . the problem is you would need to touch one to find out.'

Rob approached one of the barriers which looked like a collapsed wall. 'If they're using people for food why don't they go on a killing spree?'

Charles stared ahead. 'It doesn't work like that. These creatures are summoned over as mindless shells waiting for their hosts. They are also weak and only take a little from the first victims, and as you know a lot more from the second victims. The final three will be at the ritual where all of them will be drained of everything. The ones helping them are different as they are lesser demons.'

'Lovely,' said Sharon, 'and I thought they wanted me for my purity.'

'I'm hardly pure,' said Rachel, 'I've been living in sin with Sean for a few years.'

'The sacrifice of the virgins,' said Charles, and shook his head. 'It makes no difference, but pure of heart is another thing.'

Carling put his hand on the rubble. 'It feels real, but I can't hear anything from the other side.' He took a bar off the floor. 'We best try and break through.'

Rob grabbed another bar and turned to the constables. 'Phil, you go and keep watch, and Colin, keep in sight of us and him. I don't want those things sneaking up on us.'

The constables walked off only to return a minute later.

'We've got a problem,' said Phil.

Carling sighed. 'What problem?'

'We got smoke heading this way . . . it looks like the place is on fire.'

Rob slammed the bar into the floor. 'This is ridiculous . . . the rubble shouldn't be holding us back.'

'Demon magic,' said Charles, '

'I can see the smoke,' said Carling, 'they're herding us.'

Rob nodded. 'I know, but we have no choice.'

'No,' said Sharon, 'we can't let them do this to us.'

Rob took her arm. 'If we stay here the smoke will kill us. Out there we still have a chance to fight.'

They all ran and Rachel felt her stomach turn again at the thought of Sean being out there. She saw the doors Charles had opened for them, and they stopped.

Carling sniffed the air. 'It doesn't smell like a fire.'

'No,' said Charles, 'another illusion.'

'Then we stay here,' said Rob, 'an illusion won't kill us.'

The smoke grew closer and a dagger flew out of it. Phil, the constable, crumpled to the floor with the dagger stuck in his chest.

Carling ran over to him. 'Phil,' he shouted. 'We have to get him outside.'

Colin helped him carry the constable out where Sharon checked on him.

'How is he?' said Rob.

'Alive, but only just. He needs proper treatment.'

Rachel stared over at the creatures but the hooded figure had gone. Bodies lay on the ground, but she couldn't see how many.

'I am sorry, my dear,' said Charles, 'I should have been more open with you earlier.'

Rachel gasped. 'I don't understand, are you saying you knew they were after me?'

'We had an idea as the priest I told you about was an ancestor of yours.'

Rob pointed the bar at him. 'You knew and never told us?'

Charles nodded. 'Yes, I only told you so much as some of you disbelieved what I had already said. You may have dragged me off if I told you more. I knew Rachel had been chosen, but I also believed you would get the ladies away.'

Rachel rubbed her eyes. 'Do you know who sent me the letter, and how they know so much about me?'

'We know about him,' said Charles, 'but not who he is. He has helped us in the past.'

'You keep saying we,' said Rob, 'who else is involved?'

'Just a few friends who have certain knowledge of these things.'

'Yet, you're here alone, what would you have done if we had got away?'

Charles glanced around. 'I was hoping help would come. I also left the weapons you and Sergeant Carling are carrying in case the help didn't arrive. I never knew they would put barriers up and hoped the other police here would use them if my other help never came.'

Carling walked over to them with his bar. 'Are you trying to tell us you left these?'

'He did,' said Rob, 'these bars don't belong in a building like this. I have to say they're not much of a weapon though.'

'They are made of iron,' said Charles, 'and will send demons back, but not the more powerful ones.'

'What about those things which have been feeding,' said Rachel, 'will they get rid of them?'

Charles nodded. 'Yes, but not once the final sacrifice has been made.'

'Interesting,' said a voice. 'I will enjoy dealing with you after the final two sacrifices have been made.'

'Show yourself,' Carling shouted, and the hooded figure stepped forward.

Charles put a hand to his face. 'What do you mean the final two sacrifices?'

The demon pulled his hood back to show it had red eyes. 'I have already performed the first, and will do the last two shortly.'

Rob stood in front of the women and pointed the bar at the demon. 'You won't touch them.'

The demon glared at him. 'The only reason you live is so the lords can feed upon you. There is nothing you can do to stop us, just ask the old man.'

'It is true,' said Charles, 'if the creature is not sent back before it rises as a demon Lord we won't be able to stop it.'

'Nice try,' said the demon, 'but you won't have the chance. Take them now.'

Rachel turned quickly, and saw the constable knocked to the ground as Spring-heeled leapt out of the darkness. Rob and Carling ran over when a hulking figure barged into them.

Sharon screamed as Spring-heeled kicked Rob when he tried to get up. The demon leapt at her and Rachel grabbed the iron bar Rob had dropped. Carling scrambled to his feet and ran at the skinny demon as the big one loomed forward at Rachel. She swung the bar at the hulking beast, which just knocked it out of her hand.

Rachel fell backwards as he loomed over her. The demon was sent crashing to the ground as a large man smashed into it. Sean pinned the demon down with one hand, and plunged the bar into its chest with his other. The demon turned to dust as Spring-heeled tried to fight off Carling. Rob picked up the other bar and pushed it into the demons back. Its clothes fell to the floor.

'It won't do you any good,' said the third demon, as it strode forward, 'those bars cannot hurt me.'

Sean grabbed it by the throat and pulled an arrow from the inside of his jacket. The demon screamed as Sean rammed the weapon into its chest. He let go as the robes fell to the ground.

Rachel saw movement to the left and watched as the table monster change shape. It grew as the body filled out. Its arms and legs stretched and moved into a normal looking position. The demon roared, and stood twelve feet high.

'A demon lord,' said Charles, as the demon marched towards them. 'Run, there's nothing you can do.'

'What about the arrow?' said Carling.

'It might work, but you would not be able to get close enough to use it.'

'We've got to try or God knows how many it'll kill.' Carling picked up the arrow from the robes and ran at the demon. The huge beast swung out an arm and the sergeant flew across the ground as he dropped the arrow.

'Carling,' Rob shouted, as a ghost like figure of a boy appeared.

'Justin,' said Rachel, as the apparition floated in front of her.

Throw the bottle at it, he whispered.

Rachel grabbed the bottle, pulled hard, and the chain snapped. She threw it at the demon and it smashed open on its hard leathery chest. It screamed as a mist covered it, and the beast started to shrink until it was no more.

'Quickly,' said Charles, 'You must send the other two back.'

Rachel wiped her eyes as she watched Sean and Rob run over to the other demons. They put up little fight as they were sent back. The lights in the hospital turned on as police came running outside.

Sharon put an arm around Rachel. 'Are you OK?'

Rachel wiped her eyes again. 'I can't believe my brother was here.'

'It's over, and he saved us. He can rest in peace now.'

Rachel nodded and turned to Charles. 'Is it over?'

'The battle here is over,' said Charles, 'but not the war. The fight against the demons and the oncoming darkness still goes on. Tonight we were lucky.'

'You mean there are more of these things.'

Charles glanced out into the darkness. 'Oh yes, many more.'

Sean and Rob carried Carling over and passed him to medical staff.

Rachel watched as they took him in the hospital. 'Is he going to be OK?'

'I hope so,' said Rob, 'he took one heck of a hit.'

Rachel turned to Sean. 'You have some explaining to do, as you haven't been to work.'

Sean scratched his chin. 'No, I haven't, because someone had me searching for something.'

'Ah, yes,' said Charles, as he retrieved the arrow, 'that was my fault.'

'That's evidence,' said Rob.

Charles winked. 'I'd love to see the report where you explain all this.'

Rob shook his head. 'On second thoughts, you keep it.'

Charles put the arrow inside his jacket. 'I met young Sean after the train crash, which was caused by the demons. I saw him all dazed with blood coming from a cut on his head. On the ground his wallet lay open showing a photograph of Rachel. I tended to his wound while asking him a few questions.'

'A few,' said Sean, 'you never stopped. Then he tells me if I don't find an arrow by midnight on Sunday, Rachel would die.'

Charles smiled. 'At least you believed me.'

Sean rubbed the bump on his head. 'I'm not sure what I believed as I was dazed.' He turned to the others. 'I searched all the places Charles thought it might be but I had no luck.'

'What's so special about the arrow?' said Rob.

'It was one of those which sent the demons back before,' said Charles. 'There are others, but we believe the archer retrieved those. One of those chosen for sacrifice had grabbed the other for protection.'

Rob stared at the older man. 'For a story only passed on by word of mouth, that's pretty descriptive.'

'Yes, but it's an important part of the story as many have searched for it over the years.'

'And you believed Sean would find it in a few days?'

'I hoped he would, as the one who sent Rachel the letter also sent me one. I am intrigued to know where he found it.'

Sean gave Rachel a weak smile. 'I'm sorry I lied to you, but I couldn't tell you the truth. Telling the woman you love she's going to be murdered in a ritual just didn't seem right. I had almost given up tonight and was going to drive you far away.'

Rachel smiled at him. 'But you didn't give up.'

'No, I ended up in St Bartholomew's cemetery. I think I worried a few people until Father Nick came to me. He had guessed I was looking for something, probably someone's grave. We talked about what's been happening and I told him Rachel was a descendant of the priest from the old church.'

'Was that wise?' said Rob.

Sean shrugged. 'From what Charles told me they already knew of Rachel and the only person I was putting in danger was myself. I told him and his eyes lit up. He said, "Do you think the demons are back?".'

Rob raised an eyebrow. 'That should've been your cue to get out of there . . . he's only been here two years.'

'I know, but I also needed to find the arrow. He knew of the old church burning down, but not why. I told him all I knew, and he took me to a room at the back of the church full of old books. He picked one up, an old diary of sorts, and read from it.'

Rachel felt a shiver, she was happy with Sean but also confused about her ancestor. 'What did he say?'

'I can't remember,' said Sean, and smiled. 'Father Nick might tell you, he's here with the book but the police won't let him through.'

'It's too dark out here to read a book,' said Rob, 'let's go inside.'

Charles was introduced to the priest, as they made their way to the canteen and took seats at a table.

Nick, a young priest, placed the book down and opened it. 'I found this not long after I took over at St Bartholomew's. It took me a while to work out what it read.'

'Is it foreign?' said Sharon.

'No, just old writing.' Nick put a finger on the first line. 'I write this in haste as my time on earth is nearly over. The snow falls outside and I feel the cold creeping into my bones. It was different twenty years ago when I stood outside St Mary's church watching it burn down. I received a visitor today, an old friend. He told me the demons will return one day, only stronger and wiser. They will be invulnerable to most weapons, but none which has sent them back before.

The arrow must be hidden until the day the demons return. I have hidden it, but I cannot write the location down. So if you are of pure heart and seek the arrow, you will find it in plain sight.' Nick closed the book and looked up.

'Of course,' said Charles, 'the priest was the one who took it. I never considered the arrow would have been taken to the church on the other side of town. Was there any more clues?'

Nick shook his head. 'No, and I searched everywhere to no avail. The Lord must've been smiling down at me a couple of weeks ago. We had a storm with strong winds and I heard something crashing down outside. I went out to investigate to find the weather vane had fallen, and then I saw it.'

'Clever,' said Charles, 'on view for all those years and no one saw it for what it was.'

Rob sighed. 'I can't put any of this into a report.'

Charles smiled. 'Do not worry, my boy, I can help you there. We have contacts in the police who will do it for you. As you all know of what we face, I would like you to meet some friends.'

CHAPTER SIX

Trail of Lost Souls

The constable opened his notepad. 'Do you know if she was on any medication or took recreational drugs?'

Tarin Barkley stared at the lifeless body of her friend Gina. Thirty six years of age, but she looked old and grey. 'No she never touched either. If she ever felt ill Gina would take herbal remedies.'

'When did you last see her?'

'Last Saturday, but we spoke over the phone yesterday.'

'What was her state of mind like?'

Tarin rubbed her eyes. 'Cheerful as always. She even had a date last night but I doubt she made it.'

The constable scribbled into his pad. 'Who did she have a date with?'

'Gina never said, but it was someone she met on an internet dating site.'

'What time did you talk to her?'

'Lunchtime,' said Tarin, 'she was on her break.'

A man wearing a suit stepped into the room and stared at the body. 'Hello, Jenkins, have forensics been?'

'No, Sir,' said the constable.

'It looks like she's been dead a while.'

'Miss Barkley here said she spoke to her yesterday.'

The detective turned to Tarin. 'Are you sure?'

Tarin hated the way they spoke about Gina. 'I'm quite sure. She worked at Fletchers on the high street . . . they will tell you what time she finished.'

'What was her name?'

'Gina Donaldson.'

'How long have you known Mrs Donaldson?'

'Miss, Gina was single. Over twenty years, we've been best friends since school.'

'Was she ill at all?'

Tarin shook her head. 'No, Gina jogged most mornings before work.'

A woman in a white coat entered the room. 'Could you have the conversation somewhere else?'

The detective nodded. 'Sure, Kim, and before you ask we know she was alive yesterday.' He turned to Tarin. 'I'm Detective Inspector Jim Murray . . . could you show me to the kitchen?'

Tarin walked out the room and led the way to the kitchen where she sat at the table.

Jim stood opposite. 'Can I get you a glass of water?'

Tarin shook her head. 'No thank you.'

The detective sat down. 'You were the one who found Miss Donaldson?'

Tarin wiped her eyes with a tissue. 'Yes, I got here around ten and found the front door open. I thought it unusual and called out her name. When she didn't answer I took a look around and found her.'

Jim glanced at his notepad. 'You didn't call us straight away.'

'No, I screamed and cried a lot first.'

Jim nodded. 'Did you have plans?'

'Shopping and lunch, where Gina was going to tell me all about her date.'

'Do you know who with?'

'Some guy off a dating site I guess, she joined one a few weeks ago. You should find any messages she shared as there's a little book with all her passwords on the computer desk.'

Jim placed his notepad on the table. 'I'll get someone to take a look, but you do realise there may be some sensitive material on the computer.'

'I don't think Gina will mind.' Tarin sighed. 'I need to get my head around this . . . I mean could someone actually do that to a person?'

'I've never seen anything like it before, but we will find out.'

The pathologist stepped into the kitchen. 'Are you sure she was alive yesterday?'

Tarin nodded. 'Yes, we chatted on the phone for over forty minutes.'

'Has she ever done —?'

'No,' Tarin interrupted, 'Gina never touched drugs and drunk about three glasses of wine a week.'

'Has she been abroad recently?'

'We went to Italy three months ago, we are . . . I mean, were more interested in sightseeing.'

Kim rubbed her chin. 'Was it you who opened the window?'

'No, it was already open.'

'Are you sure?'

'Yes, I thought it might've been gas until I saw the window.'

Kim leant back on a cupboard. 'I'm having the body taken back, I'm not happy with it.'

Tarin snorted. 'I don't think Gina's over the moon about it.'

Kim grimaced. 'Sorry, I didn't mean to put it like that. I have to find the cause of death and make sure it's not contagious.'

'Could a disease have done it so fast?'

'Not that I've ever seen. I will need to do a toxicology test. Your friend may not have taken drugs, but it doesn't mean someone else didn't give them to her.'

Constable Jenkins walked into the room. 'I've just spoken to Fletchers, and they told me Miss Donaldson left at five pm, and in high spirits.'

Jim nodded. 'Thank you, Jenkins, it narrows the time down.' He glanced over at Tarin. 'I will need your name, address, and phone number. I would also prefer it if you didn't speak to the press for the moment.'

Tarin laughed. 'That might be a little difficult as I'm a reporter for the Standard.'

Tarin drove home after she stopped off to buy two bottles of wine. She lay on the sofa feeling numb for the loss of her friend. If it had been anyone else but Gina lying in the bed she would've been more interested in the story.

She dozed while trying to piece it together and woke with no answer. Tarin climbed off the sofa and switched on the computer. She ignored the wine as an investigative reporter investigates. She typed strange deaths into the search engine, and clicked images to see if any were similar to Gina's. After a few minutes of scrolling down she clicked back to see if any sites reported them, and found plenty.

Bodies found in trees, was a witch to blame?

Spring-heeled Jack and the diseased bodies.

The case of the headless corpse and the body wedged into a tree.

Tarin clicked on the first site and what surprised her were the dates, all recent and in the UK. Tarin read everything on there while taking notes. She tried other sites and one claimed demons were to blame for the murders. Tarin came to the conclusion there was a maniac on the loose. The site stated the culprits had been stopped, but the police refused to divulge any information on them. The murders stopped in an area after a while which made her feel it was the same killer.

As he come here? Tarin thought. She studied the map on the site, but found no pattern. Sitting back in the chair she tried to remember the dating site Gina had joined and typed "Treasured Love" into the search bar. She glanced at the results. A site for like-minded people who love historical buildings. Tarin signed up, put a few details in and switched off the computer.

She looked out of the window into the night sky before returning to the sofa. Tarin opened a bottle of wine. 'This one's for you, Gina.'

Tarin woke the following morning with a headache and a dry throat. She had drunk a bottle of wine and a glass from the other without having anything to eat. She lumbered to the kitchen and drank a glass of water before going for a shower. Forty minutes later she drove to work. As a reporter, Sunday was just another day. Tarin had no intention of working, but finding out any information on the strange murders. She walked through the building straight to the editor's office.

Leaning on the frame of the door she saw the balding man sitting at his desk. 'Hi, Norm, can I have a word?'

He glanced up at her. 'Hi, I wasn't expecting to see you today.'

'I know, but shit happened yesterday and I need to piece it together.'

Norman removed his glasses. 'What happened?'

'I found Gina dead in her flat.'

Norman stood, and stepped over to her. 'Good grief, how did it happen?'

'I don't know . . . the police took her body away but haven't said anything yet. They also told me not to talk to the press.'

'Don't worry . . . as much as I like a good story I've no appetite to put pictures of Gina on the front page. I can't believe she's gone, Gina always looked so healthy.'

'She didn't yesterday, she looked old and grey.'

'I don't know what you can do until you know the cause of death.'

Tarin nodded. 'I know, but I'm not sure if the police will tell me what they find after the autopsy.'

Norman rubbed the bridge of his nose. 'Why wouldn't they?'

Tarin took her notepad from a pocket and opened it. 'Do you still have friends in Stanton and Clifton?'

'Yes, but friends might be pushing it, more like associates.'

'Have they mentioned any strange deaths in those areas?'

'Cyril at the Stanton Gazette mentioned a few but the murderers are dead.'

'Yes,' said Tarin, 'but the police gave few details and I found out more on the net than would've been reported in the paper.'

'Of course, you'll find more on any internet site as they won't care if it's true or not. You have to remember you'll find conspiracy theories on everything on the internet.'

'I know, but there's also a lot of truth in this, other sites corroborated the stories. In Clifton, they found a headless corpse, a man wedged into a tree, and still have missing victims.'

Norman shook his head. 'You're trying to find something which doesn't exist. You want to justify Gina's death. The murders you've been looking into have nothing in common.'

'They're all unusual, and two of the survivors were quarantined but the disease they had disappeared.'

Norman smiled. 'You're missing the point where the culprits are now dead.'

'Or it was covered up. The names given for the murderers are of people with no personal records. You know I'm not one for flights of fancy, but something strange is happening.'

Norman leant on his desk. 'Do you want to go there for a story?'

Tarin shook her head. 'No, it's over in those places. I believe it has started here now and I want to know if there are any more strange deaths.'

'If I hear of any I'll let you know.'

Tarin logged onto the dating site and regretted joining up. She had twenty-two unread messages, and hadn't uploaded a picture. She ignored them and clicked on forums when her phone rang.

She answered it. 'Hello.'

'Miss Barkley, Inspector Jim Murray here. I just wanted to let you know we have ruled out the man Gina was meant to go on a date with.'

'Should you be doing that so soon?'

'We have spoken to him, and he told us she stood him up. He had sent her messages but received no reply. He spent the night in the pub with many witnesses.'

Tarin sat back in the chair. 'Thank you for telling me, but is it because Gina was my friend or the fact I'm a reporter?'

There was a pause before Jim spoke again. 'Both, as I'm sure you have joined the dating site by now.'

Tarin put a hand to her mouth to stifle a cough. 'I thought it might be worth having a look. Inspector, are you aware of the strange deaths around the country?'

'Yes, but nothing like your friend's, and I do believe the other cases are now closed. I would have to warn you to stay away from those.'

'You can't warn a reporter to stay away it makes them want to investigate further. Anyway I'm looking for new ones.'

'If there are any more, and I would warn you about how dangerous they are.'

Tarin scrolled down on the dating site and deleted her account. 'You have to admit we have our own.'

'An unusual death yes, but we do not know if it's murder yet. Gina may have died from an illness. Kim has not yet found the cause of death, but there are no bruises or injuries.'

'I'm sorry I was out of sorts yesterday or I would have asked more questions.'

'I have a feeling you will make up for it.'

Tarin smiled. 'Do you believe Gina left her flat after she returned home from work?'

'No, it appears she was in the middle of getting changed when she decided to have a lie down.'

'Don't you think that strange with the front door still open? Gina was highly security conscious . . . you must've seen all the locks.'

'Yes, but she may have just forgot, and there was no sign of any struggle.'

'So if anyone else was involved, Gina must've known them?'

'If someone else was involved. We're waiting on tests to tell us anything, or if Gina's behaviour may have been erratic.'

Tarin switched off the computer. 'Are you saying, from the time Gina left work and until she reached home a toxin got into her body? I don't see how that would happen. I believe this is something else.'

'If it is a toxin. It could've happened before that, and she didn't know. Miss Barkley, I have read some of your articles and you appear to be a shrewd woman. I believe you are letting your emotions control your thought process.'

'Here we go, do you say that to all the women?'

'No, of course not. I'm not ruling anything out at the moment including someone knocking on her door.'

'Gina would've only opened the door to someone she knew.'

'Yes, I believe that, and it's why you are our number one suspect.'

Tarin nodded. 'At least I know you're doing your job.'

'I've got to go,' said Jim, 'something else has come up. Nothing related to the other case.'

'OK, Inspector, and thank you for letting me know.'

Tarin sat pondering over what happened and the inspector was right. She had dived in head first to save Gina who was already dead. She was trying to ease her own conscious when she failed to save Gina while she lived. Tarin knew monsters didn't exist, but she wanted the other stories to be true to explain her friend's death.

Her mobile phone rang and she answered it. 'Hi, Norm, have you got something for me?'

'Yes, but nothing about earlier. We have a breaking story and I want you on it.'

'What's it about?'

'A five-year-old girl went missing lunchtime yesterday.'

'Oh no,' Tarin sighed, 'that's over twenty-four hours, and you know what that means.'

'Yes, normally, but this is different. I want you to take this as you're the best man for the job. The child was playing outside in the back garden one moment and gone the next. The thing is she was in view of her father in the living room for all but two minutes.'

It piqued Tarin's interest, something didn't sit right. 'Are you sure about the time?'

'No, but I only know what I've been told. The parents are a mess with many fingers pointed at them.'

'What's the address?'

'Forty-three Moorpark Lane.'

Tarin grabbed her car keys. 'OK, I'll go and take a look.'

She drove to Moorpark Lane only to find it blocked off. Television cameras and reporters filled the street along with the police. Tarin parked up in the next road and walked to Moorpark Lane. She saw an alley leading to the back and made her way down it. At the end of the alley she saw garages to the left, and to the right a fenced off path behind the houses. The wire fence stood eight feet with trees and bushes blocking any view of what lay beyond it.

Tarin turned left down the drive with the garages opposite the back gardens. She walked along the small path with many broken slabs. At the end she saw a police car blocking the only entrance by road. Many of the gardens had high fences which she could not see over. One with a small fence had police inside. Walking up to the gate Tarin studied a patch of mud where a slab should have been.

'Sorry, Miss,' said a voice, 'you cannot enter here.'

Tarin glanced and saw Constable Jenkins. 'I have no intention of doing so.'

'Miss Barkley, I forgot you're a reporter. The other press are out the front waiting for a police statement.'

Tarin raised an eyebrow. 'Have there been any developments?'

Jenkins shook his head. 'No, it will be more of an appeal to the public.'

'It won't be of any use as all the clues are out here.'

Jenkins nodded. 'It's where the child was playing and it's why I'm out here.'

'Good, can you tell me when it last rained?'

'Yesterday morning, I think.'

Tarin rubbed her chin. 'Do you know if the child ever played out here?'

Jenkins leant on the gate. 'She wasn't allowed, and had to stay in view of the window.'

Tarin glanced at the window but couldn't see anyone inside. 'That only works if someone is watching. If either of the parents were, they would've seen their daughter walk out of the gate.'

'You believe she did?'

Tarin pointed to a small footprint in the mud just past the gate. 'That was made while the ground was still wet.' She walked on in the direction of the footprint to where the police car was parked, and the constable followed. Beyond the car was a main road and to the right a petrol station. 'I take it you have checked their CCTV cameras.'

'Yes, but no one was seen leaving or entering at the time.'

Tarin pursed her lips. The camera from the station could only see the entrance where they stood. She turned back, garages to her left and houses on the right. 'Have you searched all the houses?'

'Yes and the garages.' Jenkins rubbed his nose. 'The father said he only left the room for two minutes.'

'I take it he needed the toilet?'

'No, someone knocked the door. He answered it as the mother was in the kitchen preparing lunch.'

'Really?' said Tarin, with some interest. 'Who was at the door?'

'Just some canvasser,' said Jenkins, as two men in suits approached, one Tarin recognised.

'Constable Jenkins,' said the other, 'are you in the habit of giving information to the press?'

'No, Inspector, this is Miss Barkley.'

'I know as Inspector Murray told me.' He stared at Tarin. 'Are you here for another story?'

Tarin frowned. 'No, I'm here to find a missing child.'

'That is kind of you, but the job's already taken.'

'Yet, over twenty-four hours later you're still here.'

'Miss Barkley found a footprint,' said Jenkins.

The inspector folded his arms. 'So did Inspector Murray.'

Jim smiled. 'This is Inspector Logan who asked me to help in the search.'

'Don't worry, Jim,' said Logan, 'I believe Miss Barkley has solved it for us.'

Tarin shrugged. 'Not quite, but I'm getting there.'

Jim shook his head. 'Are you serious?'

'You saw the footprint, what did you make of it?'

'Small, made by a child, but there are many children around here.'

Tarin smiled as she stepped past them. 'This is no opportunist child abduction . . . they waited for their moment and took it.'

'What do you mean "they"?' said Logan. 'Child abductors work alone. What you're suggesting is kidnapping and that usually requires a ransom. You only have to take a look around here to know there won't be one.'

Tarin stared at the footprint once more. 'I'm sure abduction is the same as kidnapping, but I know what you're getting at. This has nothing to do with money. There were at least two people involved, and they knew about the station's CCTV camera.' Tarin turned to Jenkins. 'How long was the father away for?'

The constable rubbed his chin. 'Two minutes, or so he says.'

'Let's call it three.' Tarin glanced at the fence by the passage along the back of the houses to the right of the alley. 'What's on the other side?'

'A road,' said the constable, 'and a field.'

Tarin walked on and grabbed at the fence which didn't give.

Jim followed. 'What are you doing?'

'This was planned, and the abductors had only a small window of time to get away.' She moved along pulling at the fence when part of it came away.

Jim grabbed the fence and held it open. 'How could you know?'

'They never left by car from here, so they had to make their own exit from the scene.' Tarin stepped through the gap in the fence. They had already cut their way through here before they took the child.'

'I'm sorry,' said Logan, 'but it's all a little far-fetched. What you say makes sense, but what's so special about this girl?'

Tarin walked on through the trees where she came to a road. Opposite was a field and to the left country lanes. 'I can't give you an answer to that only to how they took her. When we find the abductors you can ask them yourself.'

'We will do,' said Jim, 'but how did you know they came this way?'

Tarin glanced at him. 'I thought you were a detective. The chances of someone taking the child in the three minutes without knowing where the father was are too implausible. Whoever did this knew exactly where he was. The footprint was a ruse to fool you, but it didn't work because no one saw it until today. The child's foot was pressed into the mud to make you think she went that way.'

'I considered it,' said Jim, 'but the chances of someone else stepping on it ruined the idea.'

Tarin shook her head. 'It was placed where no one would, or would most likely step over it. The print is right next to the fence where someone coming out the garden would miss it and below a slab where most would step over it. They just wanted you searching in a different direction.'

'OK,' said Jim, 'and that's why you knew there would be an escape through the fence.'

'No, it was the three minutes which made me believe there had to be an exit close by. When the father returned he would've noticed his daughter gone and ran straight out to find she was nowhere to be seen.'

'It didn't take us that long to get here,' said Logan.

'No, but they had to make sure the father had left the room, and put the fence back in place.'

'Agreed, but that doesn't mean it took two people.'

'Look around,' said Tarin, 'where would they go from here? Leaving a car parked would be too big a risk.' She turned to the detectives. 'The one abductor waited here until the other picked them up. It wouldn't take them long to get here after speaking to the girl's father.'

Jim sighed. 'The canvasser was part of it.'

Tarin nodded. 'Yes, and soon as the father shut the door the canvasser jumped in the car and drove here.'

Jim stared down the road. 'They'll be long gone by now.'

'Maybe,' said Tarin, 'or maybe not. This was planned, and they might've been waiting days or weeks for their chance. It would mean they had to be staying nearby. What's down this road?'

'Not a lot,' said Jenkins, who rubbed his eyes, 'apart from the old factory, of course. It's been empty for years.'

Tarin remembered going to the factory after it closed down. 'I know the one.'

'Call it in,' said Logan, 'we'll search it from top to bottom.'

'No,' said Tarin, 'if they are there, you'll be putting the child in danger.'

'The odds are we're already too late.'

'I refuse to believe that. They wouldn't go through all this trouble just to kill her.'

'It's true,' said Jim, 'we also need to leave without alerting the press.'

'We can take my car,' said Tarin, 'it's parked on York Drive.'

'I will get it,' said Jenkins, 'while you wait here.'

Tarin took the keys from a pocket and passed them to the constable. 'You know what one it is?'

Jenkins smiled. 'The black Nissan and I did want to drive it.'

Jim turned to Tarin. 'I don't suppose you'd like to wait here while we take a look?'

Tarin watched the constable disappear through the trees. 'Not a chance . . . and you wouldn't want to leave a reporter behind.'

'I thought you would say that?'

The Nissan appeared a few minutes later as Jenkins drove it round the corner and pulled over. He climbed out.

'You drive,' said Tarin, as she opened the back door, 'it'll be nice to have a chauffeur.'

They all climbed inside as Jenkins drove off. Tarin stared out the window as the fields disappeared and were replaced by trees.

'We did search out here,' said Jenkins, 'had a helicopter searching too. I think they would've said something if they saw cars parked outside the factory.'

'What's the girl's name?' said Tarin.

'Jemima Lawson,' said Jenkins.

Logan, sitting in the back turned to her. 'You wait until now to ask for her name?'

'I didn't want my emotions getting in the way, just ask your colleague about that.'

'And a name would make that much difference?'

'Yes, it makes it even more personal.'

The factory came into view five minutes later. Tarin had seen the building before. It had two floors, the upper being offices and the lower manufacturing. It was a busy textile factory until the eighties, when the owners moved to a more modern building.

'Drive past,' said Jim, 'let's see if there's another way in.'

Jenkins drove on. 'I know just the place . . . the back entrance has been overgrown for years.'

'People have been here though,' said Logan, 'the front is far from overgrown.'

Jenkins pulled over near a set of wooden gates, three feet high, almost covered in grass and bushes. 'We had to remove travellers from there a few times.'

Tarin climbed out. 'Why, they weren't hurting anyone?'

'It's private land, and the owners wanted them gone.'

Tarin approached the fence with the factory hidden from view by the trees.

Jim walked up to her. 'It might be best if you stayed here.'

Tarin grabbed the top of the fence and climbed over. 'No bloody chance.'

Jim sighed and followed her over the fence. 'At least let me go first.'

Tarin did and Logan joined Murray as they made their way through the thick undergrowth. The rear of the factory came into sight as they stepped over to the edge of the trees. A set of double doors were open with one hanging off its hinges. They led to a corridor with glass windows either side.

Jim leant up a tree as he scanned the factory. 'We need to get over there quickly and quietly.'

They ran forward, covering the distance in seconds, and entered the corridor. Tarin ducked beneath the windows. Part of the ceiling had collapsed as they edged ahead.

'Keep low,' said Jim, 'I just saw something move in one of the offices.'

Tarin scurried on keeping beneath the windows. The light was fading as night was near. They reached the end where a set of swinging doors, with glass windows, barred their way. Jim stood as he looked through a window before he pushed a door open. They all followed as he stepped through to a wide hall and saw a car and van parked inside. To the right were wide stairs leading up to the offices. Jim indicated with his hand for them to stay while he climbed the stairs to another set of doors. He glanced through the window and waved his hand for them to follow.

Tarin hurried up and entered a wide room with doors on the outer walls. She guessed this was the main office, but all the furniture had gone. Jim and Logan walked over to the central doors where they heard voices from the other side. Tarin stepped over to the one on the left of it and heard crying. She noticed a key in the door and turned it. The door opened, and she saw a small child sat on the floor with both arms wrapped around her legs. Tarin put a finger to her lips when she heard a voice behind her.

'What do we have here then?'

Tarin turned and saw a scar faced man with a gun.

'Police,' said Jim, 'and you're under arrest.'

The man waved the gun at them and laughed. He stared at Tarin. 'You get out here.'

Tarin stepped out of the room as the other doors opened. A man and woman walked out and joined the gunman.

'Back up is on the way,' said Jim, 'so I would quit now.'

The gunman sneered at him. 'No, you came here on the off-chance and are all alone.'

'Hardly,' said Logan, 'did you think the footprint would fool us? It was obvious the canvasser was part of it, and it didn't take long to find the gap in the fence. I'm afraid you were too elaborate in your plans for this girl. We knew more than one person was involved.'

'Shit,' said the woman, 'they know.'

'We do,' said Logan, 'but I'm surprised the child is still here.'

'Not for long,' said the gunman. 'When my colleague returns with instructions on where to take the girl, we'll leave. When your colleagues arrive, they'll find your bodies.'

Tarin knew they had to get the gun before his friend returned. 'You won't get far, as the police have the numbers to the vehicles down there.'

'Nice try, but you only saw them for the first time when you got here. You should let the detective do the talking as he knows how these two did it.'

Tarin shrugged and tapped a front pocket of her jacket. 'Yes, and it only takes a few seconds to send a picture. You can take a look for yourself.'

The gunman snarled. 'Give it to me now.'

Tarin took the phone out of her pocket and tossed it over. As the man caught it she swung her leg up and knocked the gun out of his hand. She spun fast and the back of her heel caught him on the chin knocking him over. The other man and woman tried to run but Jenkins and Logan blocked their way and handcuffed them. Tarin checked the gunman who was unconscious.

They heard footsteps on the stairs as Jim grabbed the gun and hid behind the door. It opened as a large man entered. Soon as he saw them he reached inside his jacket.

'Don't even think about it,' said Jim, as he held the gun to the man's head.

The man pulled his hand out and put it in the air with the other. Logan approached and took the man's gun from his jacket.

'Jenkins,' said Jim, 'call it in.'

Tarin stared at the man. 'Where were you taking the girl?'

The man spat on the floor. 'I'm not telling you anything.'

'Inspector Murray,' said Tarin, 'if he refuses to answer in the next few seconds would you be kind enough to shoot him in the head?'

The man laughed. 'Sorry, girly, the police are not allowed to do that. I also have connections and will be free soon.'

'I reckon a shot to the knee first,' said Logan, 'and if he still isn't cooperating, one to the stomach.'

The man stepped back to the door. 'You wouldn't.'

Jim stood in front of him with gun pointed low. 'It would be called self-defence, and it's not my gun. We would be thought of as heroes for killing child abductors. Now talk.'

'I don't know who they are,' said the man, now pale. 'We were just told to take the child to the motorway services where someone else would collect her.'

'Why go to all this just for one little girl?'

The man shrugged. 'I don't know, but they said she was special.'

Tarin walked back to the room where Jemima sat crying. She picked her up. 'Hey, honey, you're safe now.'

'I want my mommy and daddy.'

'I know, and I'm taking you to them now.'

Jemima rubbed her eyes. 'Are they angry with me?'

'Of course not, they're just sad you're not there.'

'She will need to be looked at by a doctor first,' said Logan.

'Send one to the house,' said Tarin, 'this little one has been through enough.'

'If you give me a few minutes,' said Jenkins, 'I'll fetch your car.'

Tarin smiled. 'Thank you.'

Logan turned to Jenkins. 'You go with them, and make sure they get through.'

'You've got a story,' said Jim. 'One you solved . . . thanks for that.'

'I'll write it up,' said Tarin, 'but I won't be taking any credit.'

'Why not?' said Logan. 'If it wasn't for you they would be out of the area and long gone.'

'I'm a reporter, and the public would feel a lot safer if they thought police solved the crimes.'

Tarin stepped outside the front still holding Jemima as Jenkins pulled up. Police cars arrived as she put the girl in the back and climbed in after.

Ten minutes later Tarin carried Jemima down the path of forty-three Moorpark Lane when a door opened. A man stood in shock.

'Daddy,' Jemima shouted, as Tarin passed her over.

Tarin grabbed her keys the following morning when her phone rang, and she answered it. 'Hello.'

'Miss Barkley, it's Jim Murray, I wondered if I could have a word.'

'Sure, I was just off to work.'

'I don't want to talk over the phone, could you meet me at the Full House Café on the high street? I'll buy you a coffee.'

'Give me ten minutes . . . white, no sugar.'

Tarin stepped through the doors of the café and saw Inspector Murray sat at a table with two mugs of coffee. There were only two other customers inside. She made her way over.

Jim stood as she approached. 'Thank you for coming.'

Tarin sat down. 'I'm a reporter who was asked to meet at a café, of course I would come. I also want to know if you found out anything about Gina. So why this place?'

'I come here most mornings for my breakfast.'

Tarin raised an eyebrow. 'That's healthy. So did you find out who they were taking Jemima too?'

Jim shook his head. 'No, Logan and his team waited but no one came. The couple who took her had only ever met the two gunmen, Loughton and Farron. They had only ever spoken over the phone to the ones who ordered the abduction.'

Tarin smiled as she sipped on her coffee. 'You trust me with this information?'

'If not for you we wouldn't have anyone in custody, and the girl long gone. It's not the reason I wanted to see you.' Jim leant on the table. 'I don't want to sound insensitive, but was Gina gay?'

Tarin stared at him. 'No, and you already know she had a date with a man. Would it be a problem if she was?'

Jim leant back. 'No, of course not, but we found another body last night, a man, in the same condition as Gina's.'

Tarin's mind raced back to the strange deaths she found on the internet. 'Another?'

'Yes, and he was also a member of a dating site, it was all on his phone. He was found on the back seat of his car down an alley. His ID said he was twenty-six, but looked about seventy.'

'I don't believe gender has anything to do with it. Was it the same dating site?'

Jim shook his head. 'No, a different one. Of course, we still have no idea how they died.'

'Someone did it to them,' said Tarin, 'I know that much. The dating sites are too much of a link.'

'We are trying to find out if anyone is a member on both sites.'

Tarin watched as a woman with grey hair moved tables and sat at the one next to them. She was smartly dressed in a grey suit.

'You are on the right track,' she said, 'but the child is more important than the killer at the moment.'

Tarin frowned. 'I don't know who you are, but I take offence at you saying the death of my friend isn't important.'

The woman smiled. 'I never said that, and I meant no offence. Your friend has gone, but the girl is here and still in danger.'

'Maybe we should have this chat down at the station,' said Murray. 'You appear to know more than you should.'

'Indeed I do,' said the woman, 'just like I knew you were meeting a reporter here. How I know does not matter, as I said the child needs protecting.'

'Who the hell are you?'

'I am Elouise, and would like to help.'

Jim pushed his empty coffee mug away. 'Thanks for the offer, but we have the culprits locked up.'

'Maybe, but not the ones who paid them to do it . . . and they will be back.'

'What about my friend,' said Tarin, 'do you know who killed her?'

Elouise rubbed her chin. 'I cannot give you a name, but I guess it was a succubus.'

Jim sighed as his phone rang. 'Great, I'll tell the chief we have a monster on the loose.'

'A demon to be precise,' said Elouise.

'What?' said Jim, into his phone. 'How did that happen? OK, I'm on my way.'

Tarin watched him put the phone away. 'What's happened?'

Jim stood. 'Loughton and Farron are dead.'

Tarin considered it. 'How could someone kill them in a police station?'

'They wasn't in the station, someone had released them. They were found in a side street with their throats cut open.' Jim picked up his keys. 'I have to go, will you be OK?'

'I'll be fine, and I haven't finished talking to Elouise.'

Jim turned to the older woman. 'Monsters apart, are the links to our other deaths the dating sites?'

'In a way, but the killer will not be a member. They were both lonely souls which it feeds on.' Elouise rubbed her hands together. 'Remember what I said, Inspector, the child still needs protecting.'

'Even with those two dead?'

'Yes, I have no doubt they were murdered for failing, and also to make you think the girl is safe. Be careful what you divulge, as it may well have been another officer who released the two men.'

'Who the hell are these people?'

'We best call them a devil worshipping sect for now.'

Jim shook his head as he hurried out the café.

Tarin swapped tables and sat opposite the woman. 'Devil worshippers, are you saying they want to sacrifice her?'

'Yes, but only because they like sacrificing people. What do you know of what's been happening lately?'

'Not a lot. I've done a little research of events in other areas like Stanton.'

Elouise smiled. 'A colleague of mine was there. The creatures you read about were real but dealt with. You have your own problem here now.'

Tarin sipped on her coffee. 'You said a succubus killed my friend, I thought they were female who preyed on men.'

'Very good, and an incubus preys on women. What we have here is a demon which appears as the person of your dreams and sucks your life away.'

'That's how Gina looked.' Tarin rubbed her eyes. 'How do we stop this thing?'

'We have the means to send it back, but we have to find it first.'

Tarin sat back. 'I'm single, I could be bait.'

Elouise shook her head. 'Being single is not the same as being lonely.'

'Why, when I live alone?'

'You choose your lifestyle, and I take it you're happy.'

'I was until I lost Gina.' Tarin put the mug on the table. 'How do you know so much about me?'

'I only know a few things, like how you figured out how the little girl was taken.'

'Was it Logan or Jenkins?'

'Constable Jenkins told me earlier.'

Tarin frowned. 'I thought he was one of the good guys.'

'He is, and the good constable wasn't spying on you. He told me you would make a great detective. You have already connected the deaths from other towns to the ones here.'

'The only connection is they're weird.'

'Indeed, and it is the best connection when it comes to demons. Shooting or stabbing someone isn't enough, they like to play games.'

'So you're going to send it back?'

'Hopefully, once you have located it, of course.'

Tarin raised an eyebrow. 'How am I supposed to do that?'

'The same way you found Jemima I guess.'

'The abductors left clues, this creep is leaving nothing. Two deaths in three days, I best find out where the second body was found.'

Elouise passed her a card. 'Here's my number, I already have yours.'

Tarin drove towards the police station through the busy high street. Temporary traffic lights flashed green as she carried on past the road works. Many reporters gathered outside the police station trying to get information on the murdered men. She parked up and climbed out of the car.

Tarin walked over to a fellow reporter from the Standard. 'Hi, Bill.'

'Hey, you're late getting here. I know this is your story as you did the first, but Norm asked me to do it.'

'It's yours . . . I'm too busy at the moment.'

Bill nodded. 'I've got a whiff of another story I'm going to look into later. Three people dead. One found in her home and another in his car near the Dog Inn. The third was found in a hedgerow on Thornton Park. They're all connected from what I hear because of how they look.'

Tarin rubbed her nose trying to hide her surprise at the news of the third body. 'Sorry, Bill, I'm already on that one.'

Bill sighed. 'I should've guessed. When did you find out about it?'

'Saturday morning, as the first was my friend Gina.'

'Oh crap, sorry about that.'

'Don't lose any sleep about the story as Norm won't print much about it.'

Tarin returned to her car and took a map of the town from the glove compartment. She studied it to see where the three bodies were found. Thornton Park was further into town than the other two.

She tapped the map ahead of the park. 'It looks like I'm going out for a drink tonight.'

Tarin sat in the Black Horse Inn, drinking an orange juice. She glanced at her watch and saw it was nine o'clock. She decided to leave and try another pub as there were only three others inside. The next pub was busier but after thirty minutes she gave up.

This is stupid, she thought, I don't even know what I'm looking for. She walked down the high street towards her car which she left parked at the Black Horse. Tarin could see a man and woman arguing ahead as she felt as if someone was following her. She walked past the unhappy couple and stopped outside a Chinese takeaway. Tarin pretended to read the menu in the window, and glanced up the road to see two men hanging back as if they were waiting for someone.

Tarin walked on wondering if they were the ones who killed Loughton and Grimes. She crossed the road in the opposite direction of her car as she tried figuring away to turn the tables on the men. She could get more information by following them. Tarin saw a passage between two shops ahead. Behind the shop facing her was an eight-foot wall with a wooden gate. She slipped down the alley, ran at the wall and leapt up. She scrambled over and waited. A minute later she heard the sound of running feet enter the alley.

'Where the hell did she go?' said one of the men.

The handle of the gate turned but it did not open. 'Not here, it's locked.'

'Come on, she must've ran through.'

Tarin heard the footsteps fade as she climbed the wall. Without a run up it took longer than she expected. Tarin shook her head as she sat on the wall and realised the men were too far to follow.

Tarin made her way back to the car when she heard a noise. She turned and saw two figures in hoods. They stood ten feet apart and held curved daggers.

'Don't you know it's dangerous to be out on your own?' said one.

'Dark things come out at night,' said another.

Tarin tried to work them out as street thugs wouldn't talk like that. They stood far enough apart she had to move her eyes to watch their movements. She shrugged. 'I can handle myself.'

They removed their hoods to reveal red eyes and dark leathery skin.

'We're hungry,' said one, as it licked the end of a dagger.

'We will feast on your flesh,' said the other.

Tarin stepped back not expecting this, demons like Elouise said. She needed to get both in view without having to move her head. 'There's a takeaway on the high street.'

'No,' said one, as they edged forward, 'we want to feast upon your heart.'

Tarin shuddered and realised they were probably faster than anyone she had fought before.

'It has stopped speaking,' said a demon, 'maybe it doesn't want to play anymore.'

'No,' said the other, 'and it hasn't screamed yet.'

Tarin ignored the conversation as she concentrated on their movements. The one on the right ran at her. She waited until the last moment before she spun away and her heel connecting with the back of its head. The demon somersaulted onto its back. The other charged but had to jump over the first only to find Tarin's foot connect with its chin. It fell back as the other started to get back up.

Tarin stepped away knowing she was in trouble . . . she hit the one with all she had.

The demon grinned. 'You're fast, but you cannot hurt us. Your death will be slow and will breathe your last breath when I remove your heart.'

Tarin edged back as the other climbed to its feet, and they approached. She heard the sound of brakes screeching and saw the headlights of a car hurtling towards them. It drove straight into the demons sending them flying across the car park. A man with a sword jumped out and ran to the creatures before plunging the blade into each of their chests.

A woman climbed out of the car. 'You had finished playing with them?'

Tarin scratched her head. 'What the hell just happened?'

'We are here for another reason but saw them. I'm Chloe, and he's Jack.'

'I'm Tarin, just how many of these things are there?'

Chloe shrugged. 'I've no idea, but something is meant to happen soon and more of them are appearing.'

Jack approached. 'Nice moves, but you don't want to fight them without a proper weapon.'

Tarin watched as he put the sword in the car. 'I didn't have much choice as they were waiting for me.'

Jack leant back on the car. 'So you don't know about them?'

'Not those two, I've been searching for a succubus.'

Chloe raised an eyebrow. 'How are you going to manage that?'

'I was using myself as bait. It was here today I'm sure of it.'

'Be grateful you didn't find the thing as it'll be a lot more powerful than those two.'

'I'm only meant to locate it as someone else will get rid of it. What are you going to do about the bodies?'

'Nothing,' said Chloe, 'they're just dust now.'

Tarin stared over at the clothes. 'Are you demon hunters?'

'Sort of, but we've only been doing it a few weeks. What about you?'

'I'm a reporter.'

Jack shook his head. 'So you're just after a story.'

Tarin laughed. 'What paper would print it? The thing killed my friend and I want it stopped.'

Another car drove up, stopped, and Jim climbed out. 'Tarin, what the hell are you playing at?'

Tarin folded her arms as Logan got out the other door. 'Excuse me.'

'I had two men watching you, but you managed to lose them.'

Tarin gasped. 'You had me followed?'

'No, I said watched. You were seen by undercover officers, and I knew what you were up to. They were only watching as I actually thought you might find the killer.'

Tarin watched Logan inspect the clothes on the floor. 'You should've called to say it wasn't a pair of maniacs following me.'

'They were clumsy . . . you were not meant to see them.'

'What happened here?' said Logan, holding up a hooded top as dust fell to the ground.

'Demons,' said Tarin, 'they were wearing them when they attacked me.'

Chloe's eyes grew big. 'You might not want to be so specific.'

Jim sighed. 'You're not still going on about the succubus?'

Tarin folded her arms. 'No, these were different, and I'd be dead now if these two hadn't shown up when they did. I saw the faces on those things and the red eyes. You may have noticed they turn to dust when sent back.'

'Or they were set on fire,' said Logan, 'how do you think it would look in court?'

'Pretty silly,' said Jack. 'How would you explain the undamaged clothes?'

Chloe put a hand on his arm. 'Do you know Inspector Devon Fields?'

Logan whistled. 'That's a blast from the past. Yeah, we know her.'

'Give her a call, she'll explain everything.'

'I'd love to, but I don't have her number.'

Chloe took out her phone and scrolled through the contact list before passing it over. 'Tell the inspector, Chloe and Jack send their best, and she'll tell you what we're up against.'

'Let's say they're demons,' said Jim, 'I would have to stop you searching for them.'

Tarin laughed. 'Are you going to lock me up in the station where prisoners just walk out?'

'This is no joking matter.'

'Don't you think I know that after what happened to Gina?' Tarin watched Logan walk around with the phone next to his ear. 'Whether you like it or not, they're here and need to be stopped.'

'I've seen some of the victims,' said Chloe, 'these things are pure evil and will kill anyone.'

Logan approached and passed the phone back. 'It's true, Devon says we are to believe these and a woman called Elouise.'

Jim nodded and turned to Jack and Chloe. 'Do you have anywhere to stop tonight?'

'Yeah,' said Jack, 'in the car. We're going to watch a house where a little girl is in danger.'

'Jemima,' said Tarin.

'That's the one.'

'You do know she was already abducted, but we got her back?'

'Yeah, it's how we know of her.'

Logan scratched his head. 'We have officers already there.'

'We know,' said Jack, 'but others are worried they could be moved away at any time.'

Jim shook his head. 'That won't happen.'

Jack pointed at the demons clothes. 'The two we just sent back were here for a reason. What would've happened if they had gone on a rampage killing everyone they came across?'

'We'd have the whole force out.'

'You have to remember something,' said Chloe, 'if they get desperate they'll try taking her by force. Your officers are not equipped to fight them. The swords in the car are two of the only few weapons which can stop demons.'

'There's a dagger,' said Jack, 'it has the power to make them invulnerable to all weapons.'

'That could be handy,' said Tarin, 'where is it?'

Jack shrugged. 'We've no idea, as it was stolen from a monastery in France years ago.'

Tarin felt her interest pique. 'Does it have a name?'

'Cicero's Dagger, I think.'

Tarin smiled. 'Thanks for stopping those things . . . I'm off home now as tomorrow might be a long day.'

Tarin parked outside her house and climbed out of the car. She walked up to the path when she sensed someone there. She sighed. 'Here we go again.'

A hooded figure stepped into view. 'Do not be alarmed, as to meet you I am charmed.'

Tarin rubbed her eyes. 'What?'

'Ignore me if you choose, or heed my warning and the clues. When the sun is at its peak, the succubus will be weak. The biggest clue I believe, is what lived but did not breathe. Green in life and brown in death, after the touch of the demon's breath. Seek help to defeat this beast, or on your life it will feast.'

'What's that supposed to mean? And why talk in riddles?'

The hooded figure mumbled something and stepped back into the shadows.

'Wait,' said Tarin, but he had gone. She hurried into the house and grabbed her notepad. Tarin had a good memory and wrote it down before reading it over. She switched on her computer and searched for Cicero's Dagger.

After a few phone calls the following morning, Tarin made her way to the Full House café. She sat at a table and ordered four mugs of coffee. She took out her notepad and waited for the others. Five minutes later Elouise, followed by Constable Jenkins, entered.

'Hello, constable,' said Tarin, 'I wasn't expecting to see you.'

Jenkins smiled. 'I've been asked to escort Miss Elouise around town. It's not a problem is it?'

'No, of course not, but I didn't order enough coffees.'

'That's OK . . . I've had enough for one morning.'

Elouise sat down. 'I take it you have some news, which I never expected so soon.'

Tarin nodded as the two inspectors walked in. 'I went out last night and met two of your friends.'

'Yes, they told me.'

Jim picked up a coffee. 'What's happened since last night?'

Tarin sipped on her drink. 'I had a visitor . . . he was waiting for me outside my house when I got back.'

Jim grimaced. 'He never harmed you?'

Tarin rubbed her nose. 'No, he gave me a message. I wrote it down soon as I got inside.' She opened her notepad and read out the riddle.

Logan gave out a whistle. 'It's all a bit weird.'

Elouise smiled. 'He's back then, I did wonder if he would help us again.'

Tarin put her notepad away. 'You know him?'

'Not quite, but he's helped us out before. We call him the rhyming demon, but I think he would prefer to be called the demon poet.'

'Shit,' said Jim, 'a demon knows where you live.'

Tarin shrugged. 'I know, but what I don't understand is why a demon would help us.'

'If he is,' said Logan, 'it could be a trap.'

'It's no trap,' said Elouise, 'as I said he has helped before. We have no idea what his intentions are.'

'Why would it be a trap?' said Tarin. 'I was alone last night when he appeared. What I want to know is why they're after Jemima.'

'We believe she is linked to the dagger,' said Elouise, 'but are not completely sure.'

Tarin leant on the table. 'You mean Cicero's Dagger?'

'The very same . . . you know of it?'

'Jack mentioned it last night, but what difference would it make if it was linked to the child if it's a weapon?'

'It's more than that, and only certain people can use it. Demons also believe with certain rituals they can use its power.'

Tarin sighed. 'Does that mean they have it?'

Elouise shook her head. 'No, but they are searching. If they do find it, nothing will stop them taking the child.'

'I'll be searching for it after we've sent this thing back.'

'Don't be ridiculous,' said Jim, 'you can't go off just like that.'

Tarin felt anger build up. 'I can do what I like . . . it has nothing to do with anyone.'

'It's madness, I don't like it.'

Tarin stood. 'You don't have to like it, as I doubt very much it'll be in your jurisdiction.' She turned to Elouise. 'I'll phone you when I find the demon.'

'How are you going to do that?' said Logan, 'the clues give us nothing.'

Tarin shook her head. 'They give us plenty. What lived but did not breathe? What's green in life but brown in death? I'm going to search for some dead trees where the demon has been staying.'

Tarin walked out of the café and hurried up to her car. She didn't lose her temper often and Inspector Murray had got close to doing it. At the same time it put her in a bad mood.

Logan hurried over to her. 'Please don't take it to heart what Jim said. He's a good man who cares too much.'

Tarin opened her car door. 'I don't need a babysitter . . . I can look after myself, I've been doing it long enough.'

'I know . . . I've seen you in action.'

'There's one thing I hate, and that's people telling me what I can or can't do.' She climbed into her car and drove off.

Tarin leant on the railing of a metal fence as she glanced across Thornton Park. Although she believed the succubus had moved on she wanted to see evidence of dead leaves as the third body was found here. Something felt wrong, had the demon moved on? She took out her phone and made a call.

'Hello, Tarin,' said Elouise, 'have you found something?'

'Not yet . . . is the constable with you?'

'Yes, I will put you on loudspeaker.'

'Hello,' said Jenkins, 'what can I do to help?'

'Has a fourth victim turned up yet?'

'Not that I know of.'

Tarin rubbed her eyes. 'How sure are you of the order of deaths?'

'I don't understand what you mean.'

'Do we have times of death for them?'

'No, only the order they were found.'

Tarin sighed and made her way back to the car. 'We've got this wrong, the demon isn't moving on but still in the same place.'

'How do you know that when the murders occurred further through town?'

'But they haven't.' Tarin climbed in the car and opened up the map. 'Three murders over three nights, yet you found two of them on the same day. I'm in no doubt one of those victims was murdered the second night but wasn't found until twenty-four hours later.'

'It couldn't be the one found in the back of his car as he would've been seen.'

'No, so he was the third victim, the one in Thornton Park was the second. Where are you?'

'Bluebell lane, Inspectors Murray and Logan are searching the small wooded area down here.'

'You're on the wrong side of town, the succubus is somewhere between where Gina lived and Thornton Park. Looking at the map I'd say it's the field near Hunt End.'

'OK,' said Jenkins, 'I'll tell the inspectors. How far away are you?'

'Ten to fifteen minutes at a guess.'

'You might want to wait as it will take us almost an hour with the roadworks.'

Tarin put the map down. 'You're the police, I'm sure you get through such things quicker than the rest of us.'

'If you locate the demon,' said Elouise, 'please wait as I have someone on the way with a weapon to send it back.'

Tarin drove off with the intention of waiting, but she decided to wait at hunt end. Ten minutes later she drove down an area waiting for development. Old houses were boarded up, as was the pub she parked up in front of. She climbed out and walked around the side where she saw the field. Beyond it was a housing estate, and in the middle a copse of trees. Most of the leaves were brown, and she knew the demon was nearby. After seeing the two demons the night before, Tarin decided to wait in the car.

'You'll find it in the trees,' said a male voice.

Tarin turned back as a young woman appeared from behind the pub.

The woman pointed towards the field. 'You want me to go in there?'

'Yeah, I left you a present, but you have to find it.'

Tarin walked towards her. 'Wait, don't go near those trees.'

'What do we have here then?' said the male voice.

Tarin turned and saw three men in hooded tops. She couldn't tell their age as the hoods were up.

'Are you a cop?' said one in a blue top.

Tarin shook her head. 'No.'

'What you doing here then?'

'None of your business.'

Blue stepped closer. 'You're lying.'

Tarin could smell alcohol and cigarettes on his breath. 'Just go away.'

'I've never had a cop,' said one in a grey top, 'grab her.'

Blue lunged forward, hands reaching for her, but Tarin brought her knee up fast. It connected hard between his legs. He howled in pain and dropped to the ground.

'Bitch,' shouted one in a green top, 'I'm gonna have you.'

Tarin sighed. 'You might want to start running as the police are on their way.'

'Liar,' he said and pulled out a knife, 'I'm gonna cut me some pig flesh.'

'How charming,' said Tarin, as grey moved to her left and picked up a short length of scaffolding pipe.

Green ran forward with knife in hand. Tarin sidestepped him and rammed her elbow into the back of his head. Grey leapt at her, swinging the bar sideways. Tarin ducked beneath it and punched him in the stomach. He bent over as Tarin stood and brought her knee up, smashing into his jaw, and he crumpled to the ground. She stepped back making sure none of them tried a second attack, none did.

The young woman ran back. 'You cow, what have you done?'

Tarin raised an eyebrow as the girl knelt by Green. 'I did warn them. You should go home and keep away from scumbags like these.'

'Glyn's not scum, he's my boyfriend.'

'Really? Didn't you hear what he wanted to do to me? I doubt very much he cared about you as he sold you to buy more beer.'

The woman pushed hair away from her face. 'He would never do that.'

'But he did, why were you going over to those trees?'

'He said there was a present in there for me.'

'Oh yes, and you would've found the present in the form of a man, one much older. You would never have left those trees alive.'

The woman's face turned pale. She stood and kicked her boyfriend. 'You bastard,' she said, and stormed off.

The three men struggled to their feet and hobbled away. Tarin turned towards her car where she saw a man ahead of her, and she froze. He was the blandest looking man she had ever seen. There was nothing attractive or anything to make him look ugly.

'You shouldn't have done that,' he said, 'I was going to have fun with her.'

Tarin frowned. 'You're disgusting . . . she's at least half your age.'

'Age matters nothing to me, life energy is all the same.'

Tarin shuddered, as the boring looking man is the succubus. 'I thought you only wanted lonely souls.'

'It's what I prefer, but I also like to see the fear in their faces.'

'How the hell can you attract anyone?'

'You know too much about me, but I will tell you anyway. I look like this as no one gives me a second glance. I can also appear as the man or woman of someone's dreams. Would you like to see who yours is?'

'That'll be hard as I don't have or want one,' she said, trying to sound cocky, while hoping for the sound of sirens.

'You are wrong there, but as you ruined my fun you will see my real form as I drain your energy.'

The demon started to change in front of her. Its clothes fell away as it grew to ten feet. The skin bubbled as it turned dark and leathery like a lizard. The front jaw stretched forward as the head grew larger. Its hands nearly reached the ground with long clawed fingers.

Tarin glanced around, the creature stood between her and the car. There was no way she would outrun the thing. It charged forward, she dived sideways and rolled on the ground. As she stood Tarin grabbed the scaffolding bar and faced the beast. It lunged at her once more, and again she rolled out of its reach.

Tarin looked for an opening, but its arms were too long. She saw something move on top of the pub. The distraction was all the succubus needed and it was on her. It grabbed Tarin by the shoulders and lifted her off the ground. The demon pulled her closer as its large mouth stretched open. She felt hazy as it breathed in, and she rammed the bar upwards. It entered the demons head below the jaw and it dropped her.

Tarin fell to the ground and scrambled away backwards to the pub. She watched the demon trying to pull the bar out when an arrow dropped in front of her. She glanced up when the scaffolding bar bounced off the wall a few inches away from her head. Tarin grabbed the arrow and leapt to her feet. The demon charged at her once more, and she realised the long sharp claws were no threat as it wanted to drain her energy. Tarin ducked inside its long arms and rammed the arrow into its chest.

The succubus backed away trying to grab at the arrow, before the beast turned to dust. She retrieved the arrow and sat back on the ground with her back to the pub wall. A shadow fell over her.

'I'm sure I said . . . come alone and end up dead.'

Tarin glanced up and saw the hooded demon from the night before. She still couldn't see his face. 'I was waiting for the others when it crept up on me. Do you want the arrow back?'

'No, my dear, keep it for the fight, an arrow is best served when in flight.'

Tarin smiled and studied the arrow. 'Thank you.'

'You will find in your search, the dagger is linked to a church. A fake priest showed his hand, stole the knife and fled the land. Greed for money was his plan, but it spelled the end for this man. Before he died he gave confession, but no dagger was in his possession.'

Tarin concentrated as she tried to memorise the riddle. She waited for more but only found silence and glanced up. The demon poet had gone. She heard noises to the right and saw the three lads walking back with friends. Tarin counted eight and looked over at the scaffolding bar.

No, she thought, I'll get in the car and run them over instead. She was about to stand when she heard police sirens. The lads also heard them and turned back. Cars screeched to a stop as she saw Jim jump out of the first.

He ran over to her. 'Are you OK?'

Tarin nodded. 'Why shouldn't I be?'

'You're sitting on the ground outside a boarded up pub for a start?'

'I know . . . I'm having a rest. After all the fighting, I believe I deserve one.' Tarin saw the others approach, as a man with a bow, and a priest studied the pile of dust.

'How many were there?'

Tarin glanced at the lads running away. 'Three of those for a start, and then the succubus decided to have a go. I was going to wait but stuff happens.'

Elouise smiled at her. 'You sent it back?'

'Yes, our friend came along and gave me this arrow.' Tarin passed it over. 'I believe it would be best if your man with the bow should have this.'

Elouise nodded. 'A special gift he gave you, and I accept gratefully for the cause. Did he say anything else?'

Tarin repeated the riddle and Jim offered his hand. She took it and stood. 'Thank you, kind sir.'

Jim shook his head. 'I never realised you would be so much trouble when I met you.'

Tarin smiled. 'Don't worry . . . I'm off to find the dagger soon.'

'I know, and you won't be going alone, I'm coming with you.'

'It'll be nice to have some company,' said Tarin, and realised she was still holding his hand.

CHAPTER SEVEN
Despair

Sarah Jacobs stared at the walls of her bedroom, something moved, and she stepped back. Not again, she thought, not now.

The wallpaper moved, shapes appeared, hands pushing and stretching the paper. Faces, distorted, protruded as if trying to break through. Sarah screamed and ran out of the room, straight to her fiancé Lee.

He grabbed her arm. 'Sarah,' he snapped, 'what is it?'

Sarah shivered. 'Monsters, they're back.'

Lee shook his head. 'Not this again.' He marched her back to the bedroom. 'Where are they? Show me.'

Sarah looked around the room, but couldn't see them. 'They were here.'

Lee scowled at her. 'We've been through this before, it has to stop now. I can't have my associates thinking you're a lunatic. If I hear any more about monsters, the wedding's off.'

'But . . .'

'No, buts, I got you out of the hospital because you said you were better. Do you want to go back? Is this what it's all about?'

Sarah lowered her head. 'No.'

'Then I'll hear no more about it. I have an important meeting tomorrow and will be away for a few days.' Lee stormed out of the room.

Sarah lay in bed with Lee who snored. She stared at the walls in the darkness, and saw movement. She knew they were there, and wanted to scream but squeezed her eyes shut instead.

Sarah woke in the morning and Lee had gone. She grabbed some clothes and ran into the living room. Noises came from the bedroom as she dressed.

Join us Sarah, said a voice, *be one of us. Let us feast on your soul.*

The voice, Sarah thought, the same voice from before saying the same thing.

The wall shook, the bedroom door swung open and banged. Sarah put her trainers on quickly as the shapes appeared once more, stretching the wallpaper in the living room. She ran out of the flat and down the three flights of stairs as fast as she could.

A cool wind blew in her face as she stepped onto the pavement. She stared up at the front window of the flat and saw the curtains move. She hurried down the road opposite a park when a bird flew down onto a wall. It stared up at her, only it wasn't the head of a bird, but more like that of a small human with dirty long hair.

Join us, Sarah, let us feast on your soul.

She ran as rain fell. She didn't care, just had to get away. Sarah slowed down through exhaustion, with wet hair plastered to her face. Her clothes soaked through, as she forgot to put a coat on. The high street came into view as she bumped into a man but carried on walking. She never reached the high street as a car pulled up and a couple she knew climbed out. Karen and Neil, Lee's friends.

'Sarah,' said Karen, 'I thought it was you. What on earth has happened?'

'Shopping,' said Sarah, 'gotta go shopping.'

'Oh no, you can't go anywhere like that, you'll catch your death. We'll take you home.'

Sarah shook her head. 'Not home, shopping.'

'No, dear, and I bet you don't have any money with you. Lee's at an important meeting today, and he wouldn't be happy if he knew. We'll take you back and get you dry.'

Sarah wanted to run, but knew she would tell Lee. She had no choice but to go back and wait for them to leave before going out again.

'It's for the best,' said Karen, 'we don't want you getting sick again.'

Sarah remembered being ill with a fever, not long after she started seeing the monsters. They took her to a hospital for the mentally ill where she stayed until Lee got her out.

'You wouldn't want us to call Doctor Bilson? Poor Lee would have to rush back from his business trip.'

'No,' said Sarah, as rain dripped down her face, 'I'll be fine . . . I've only been out a few minutes.'

Karen opened the back door of the car. 'That's good then. We'll soon have you home in the warmth.'

Sarah climbed into the car followed by Karen. She wiped her eyes and pulled hair away from her face.

'I know you think you see things at home, but I bet you see them out here too. The flat is much safer than out here with the real monsters.'

Sarah's eyes grew big. 'Monsters?'

'Yes, rapists, murderers, it's not safe out here for a beautiful young woman like you. Did you take your tablet this morning?'

'Yes,' Sarah lied. 'I always take my tablet.'

'Good girl, we'll have you home soon.'

Sarah glanced out the window and saw the car still parked outside. Karen had waited until she dried and changed clothes before leaving. Sarah wanted to leave, to run away but couldn't while they were there. She walked to the kitchen as she thought the monsters wouldn't appear because of all the cupboards.

The noises started again as she sat at the table. Whispering voices taunting her. There was no running this time because of Lee's friends. Sarah did not care about the wedding anymore, but the thought of going back to the hospital and Doctor Bilson terrified her. She put her hands over her ears as she tried blocking out the voices. The cupboard doors swung open and banged shut. Sarah hummed and closed her eyes.

She sat there without moving, not knowing how long. When she did open her eyes, the room was dark. Day had turned to night, and she ran to the front room of the flat to look out of the window. The car was still parked below, and she sagged to the floor. Shapes appeared in the wall once more.

Join us, Sarah, said a voice.

She scrambled across the floor back to the kitchen. Sarah sat at the table once more and fell asleep.

Sarah woke the following morning with her head resting on the table. Soon as she sat up the cupboard doors banged again. 'Leave me alone,' she screamed, and ran into the front room.

Join us, Sarah, *let us feast upon your soul.*

She ran out the door and down the stairs barefoot. Sarah opened the front door of the block and ran down the street not caring who was there. She had only been out a couple of minutes when she heard footsteps as a van pulled up just ahead. Someone grabbed her from behind, and a hood was put over her head as she was thrown into the van. Sarah heard the door shut as the van drove off. A minute later it stopped and the door opened. She was dragged out and carried over someone's shoulder for a couple of minutes before being thrown on the floor. Sarah heard a door slam as she removed the hood. She was back in the flat.

Join us Sarah, let us feast on your soul. Doctor Bilson will be here soon as Lee does not want you anymore.

Sarah sat up, wrapped both arms around her legs, and rocked to and fro.

'Demons dancing in my head . . . will not stop until I'm dead. Demons dancing in my head . . . will not stop until I'm dead.'

~ ~ ~ ~

Are you tired, Joe? Would you like to rest?

Nineteen year old Joe Wright turned on his side as he tried to sleep. His room was on the second floor of the psychiatric hospital. 'Go away.'

You can rest, Joe. You need peace, let us give it to you.

'What do you think I'm trying to do? I haven't slept in days because you won't shut up,'

Shapes appeared on the wall, stretching the wallpaper. *It's the wrong place, Joe, you will just wake up here again.*

Joe turned away from the shapes. 'I said go away.'

It's easy, Joe, just like escaping from here.

'Yeah, that'll be a cinch with windows barred and door locked.'

Kill yourself, Joe, and end the pain. Stop the madness in your mind and you will suffer no more.

Joe shook his head. 'No, it's a sin.'

No, it's not, as you do not believe.

'I never said that, and anyway if you're real so is God.'

We're not real, Joe, it is all in your mind.

'Go away and leave me alone.'

We cannot do that, Joe, you have to end it tonight. What have you got to live for? Sarah won't be coming back and will end it soon. Lee will not marry her and she dies tonight.

Joe sat up, he remembered Sarah as he fell in love with her soon as he saw her beautiful face and sad eyes. 'What happened to her?'

She saw demons again and it sent her mad. Her mind couldn't take any more and will end it soon. There's nothing left for you, Joe, no hope, just despair. You're better off ending it now.

Joe turned to the face stretching the wallpaper. 'How can I do that while I'm locked up in here?'

We can bend the bars on the window so you can climb out.

'You can do that?'

Yes, and you can jump.

'This is the second floor, I'm sure I'll survive.'

You have to climb up the pipe which is covered in vine . . . it will be easy for you.

Joe walked over and opened the window. 'How can you bend the bars?'

Watch, said the voice, and the bars broke away from the top and bent down.

'How did you do that?'

Did we do anything, Joe? It is all in your mind.

Joe reached down and picked up his flat shoes. He put them on while standing.

Why do you need those if you are going to jump?

Joe reached out the window and grabbed hold of the drain pipe. 'I'm not climbing in bare feet.' He managed to manoeuvre out the window and clung onto the pipe with both hands. He glanced around and scurried down the pipe.

Joe, where are you going? You need to climb up.

He ignored the voice and ran into the darkness. A high wall surrounded the hospital and Joe knew the best place to climb over. He had seen the tree from his window and thought many times of climbing over but never had a chance until now. He found it in the dark and reached for the lowest branch where he pulled himself up. He stretched across to the wall and climbed on top.

Come back, Joe.

Joe glanced back at the hospital and saw many lights being switched on. He dropped to the other side and ran out onto a street. Joe looked for the best way to run and hide as being seen in the hospital clothes would not be a good idea. He saw an alley across the road and ran down it. People approached from the other side and Joe climbed over a fence to hide.

Drunken voices approached and Joe grinned. Stupid demons, he thought. I'm the one who was locked up, and they expected me to climb up and jump.

He waited for the voices to pass by and climbed back over the fence. Joe hurried down to the end while trying to figure where he was and the best way to Sarah's home. He knew the address as she sent him a letter once. He blamed Lee for the fact she never sent any more and hated him for it. He should have liked him for getting Sarah away from the hospital, but he never trusted him.

Joe crossed another road and ran to the end where he saw the park. He knew Sarah lived on the other side and made his way across. He also knew Sarah had seen the demons as she told him, but Doctor Bilson said she had been cured. The doctor let Lee take her home as she had no family. Joe saw the buildings ahead and ran to the trees at the edge of the park. A car pulled up and two people climbed out. They walked up to the block in the middle and entered through the open door.

Joe ran over and checked the number before entering. He climbed the stairs to the third floor where he saw an open door. He approached and heard Lee.

'It's over . . . I will not marry you now. Get up and decide your fate.'

Joe crept inside and saw Lee glaring down at Sarah. Another man and woman stood there, and both men were a lot bigger than Joe.

Sarah rocked back and forth. 'Demons dancing in my head . . . will not stop until I'm dead.'

'Hello, Joe,' said Lee, 'I wondered where you had gone. I don't know how you found us, but it will save us time looking for you.'

'Leave Sarah alone,' said Joe, 'she's done nothing wrong.'

'I know,' said Lee, his eyes turning red as did those of the other two. 'We are not here to harm her . . . it will be Sarah's choice.'

'No, you're wrong. Sarah's not well at the moment because of you. When she knows demons are real, she'll be OK.'

'It matters not,' Lee hissed, 'when she jumps out of the window her soul will be mine.'

'No, it'll be murder as she won't know what's happening. Why do you want her soul anyway?'

'We will rule the earth soon and demons have a hierarchy. The more souls I collect the more powerful I will be. I will add yours to Sarah's.'

Joe screwed up his nose. 'You sound like the one at the hospital, and I'm still not going to jump.'

'You will, just to stop the torture.'

'You don't frighten me, and it won't be suicide if I did it to escape.'

The female demon pulled Sarah to her feet.

'You say that,' said Lee, 'but what if it was to save Sarah?'

'You're a demon, and will kill her for fun.'

Lee growled. 'He tires me, take him.'

The other demon stepped forward.

'I don't think so,' said a voice from behind.

An arrow shot past Joe hitting the demon in the chest. The clothes fell to the floor. The female demon released Sarah and ran only to be hit with another arrow. Joe swooped down and grabbed the first arrow and leapt at Lee. He plunged the weapon into its chest and turned the demon to dust.

Joe turned and saw a man with a bow, a priest, and a woman. He stepped over to Sarah. 'It's OK, we all saw the demons, and they can be killed.'

Sarah turned to him with an almost blank expression. 'A lowly demon has a plan, to destroy the world of man. Its power will grow it is said, as it leaves demon lords for dead. A secret known to but a few, will allow all demons to pass through.'

Joe scratched his head. 'I think it might take longer than I thought.'

'No,' said the priest, 'I believe she knows of a prophecy.'

'This is Reverend Simon,' said the woman. 'I am Judy, and the one with the bow is my brother Dan.'

Joe passed Dan the arrow. 'How did you know we were here?'

'We had a tip-off,' said Dan, 'and friends of ours always check up on certain people as some demons like to name themselves after someone famous.'

Joe rubbed his nose. 'I've never heard of a Lee Dickens.'

'The demon called himself Charles, then Charlie and finally Lee.'

Joe raised both eyebrows. 'And they said I was mad. You should go to the hospital as I met John Wayne, Superman, and Jesus.'

Judy took Sarah's arm. 'It's time we got you away from here.'

Joe shook his head. 'You can't take her back to the hospital.'

Judy smiled at him. 'No, my dear, no hospital for either of you, just a safe place without demons.'

CHAPTER EIGHT

Chains

The humpbacked man stood by the wall in the dark alley as four hooded figures spread out in front of him.

One threw a rock, grazing his arm. 'Give us your money.'

The old man put up a hand trying to protect himself. 'I don't have any, someone else already stole it.'

'Too bad,' another hissed, 'then you are of no use to us.'

The man cried as a rock hit him on the head, and he fell back. The four figures stepped forward as an engine roared down the alley. They turned as a motorbike screeched to a stop. A large iron chain flew through the air hitting the closest in the face, and clothes dropped to the ground. The iron links swung through the air again wrapping around the neck of another. The chain went taut and the demon turned to dust, as the other two ran off.

A large biker climbed off the bike and approached. He pulled the links to him before putting them over his shoulders. He looked down at the old man. 'Are you OK?'

The man tried to look up, but his back was too bent. He rubbed his head as blood fell from the cut. 'Yes, thank you, I think they were playing with me.'

The biker removed his helmet and shoulder-length hair fell down. He rubbed his beard. 'I wouldn't call that playing, they wanted you dead.'

'Oh yes, but two were a little reluctant. You know about demons I see.'

'I've had dealings with them before.'

'What's your name?'

'My friends call me Chains, and I've never known demons to be reluctant about killing anyone.'

'I'm Peter, and it was the two men who were hesitant. The demons tried to get them to kill me.'

Chains glanced down the alley. 'I wasn't sure if they were or not as they had their hoods up. Luckily for them they ran. So were the demons after you or the men's souls?'

'Both I guess.'

Chains helped the man over to his bike. 'I better get you away from here, where do you live?'

Peter shook his head. 'I'm not going home, I have somewhere to go and I'm in a hurry.'

Chains scratched his chin as he studied the humpbacked man. 'No offence, but I can't imagine you getting anywhere in a hurry.'

'Thanks, I know that, but I still have to go and retrieve a weapon which kills demons.'

'What on earth possessed you to come down here? You should've got a taxi.'

'I did, and the driver dropped me here after taking my wallet.'

'A reason for me to come back,' said the biker, as he wrapped the link of chains around the back of the seat.

'Lucky for me you came when you did.'

'I saw the taxi pulling away at speed and came to investigate. I hope it won't be too uncomfortable for you to ride on here with me.'

Peter rubbed his head. 'I'll be fine, but it's a big bike and I might need some help to get on.'

Chains picked Peter up like he was a child and sat him on the back of the bike. 'I don't know where you're going, but we need to sort out your cut. We can't do that here as we may have company soon.'

The biker put on his helmet and climbed on the bike. They rode off as hooded figures ran out behind them. Chains rode at speed to the edge of town when he felt Peter's grip on his waist loosen. He pulled over and the old man almost fell off. Chains grabbed him and sat the unconscious man in front before riding away. He travelled down country lanes until he saw lights in a field. Chains rode through an open gate towards a camp site with many bikes parked up. He stopped and climbed off with Peter before walking over to the camp where bikers sat around drinking.

A grey haired man stood in front of a large square tent. 'Who have you got there?'

Chains removed his helmet. 'He needs help, Gyp, he's taken a bad knock to the head.'

A woman stepped out of the tent. 'You should've taken him to a hospital.'

Chains shook his head. 'I couldn't, Jess, the ones who did this would find him there.'

'Bring him inside.'

Chains did and lay Peter on the ground. 'I'm sorry, but I had nowhere else to take him.'

'Never apologise to us, my friend,' said Gyppo, 'we've been through too much together.'

'I know, and it was our old enemy who did this to him.'

Jess soaked a cloth in water. 'Is this a demon wound?'

'No, a man threw a rock at him.'

'A man,' said Gyppo, 'I thought you said demons.'

'There were two which I sent back, the men were scum who would do anything for money, but they ran off.'

Jess wiped Peter's head. 'It doesn't look too deep, but he could do with proper care.'

'The demons wanted him as he was going after something.'

'Something the demons didn't want him to retrieve,' said Gyppo, 'did he say what?'

'A weapon he was in a hurry to find.'

Gyppo scratched his chin. 'What kind of weapon?'

Chains shrugged. 'He said it killed demons, but not what it was. When he wakes, I'll go with him.'

'It won't be tonight,' said Jess, 'you best let him sleep.'

Chains nodded. 'Let's hope they don't know where it is.'

Gyppo patted him on the shoulder. 'We can't do anything at the moment, so come and have a beer.'

They stepped out of the tent where other bikers stood watching. Chains liked most of them from their last meeting, but one he had never met before looked him up and down.

'You shouldn't have brought him here.'

Chains stared down at the biker. 'Really, why's that?'

'No, Dirk,' said Gyppo, 'he did the right thing and is always welcome here.'

Dirk scowled. 'Others will follow.'

Chains folded his arms. 'Who will follow?'

Dirk rubbed his mouth. 'The police, they'll be swarming all over this place.'

Gyppo passed Chains a can of beer. 'Let them, we have nothing to hide here . . . unless you do.'

'No,' said Dirk, and walked away.

The other bikers went back to what they were doing, mostly drinking.

Chains pulled the ring of the can and took a swig. 'He's not been with you long.'

Gyppo shook his head. 'Dirk joined up a month ago when we started out. For the most part he's quiet, but I nearly kicked him out after a week. He tried to get a few of the younger ones to rob an off-licence. I think some of them were up for it until I stepped in. If he tries anything else he's gone. This lot might be bikers, but they're no gang. They're here to ride the roads and camp at night for a few months until it gets cold.'

'Not all of them . . . some have been following you for a few years.'

Gyppo nodded. 'Some good lads and lasses, but it's not like when we rode together. It's all seasonal to them.'

Chains smiled. 'Don't worry, old friend, the peace will soon be over. The two I sent back earlier are only part of it. I have sent many more back over the last few months.'

'Something must be happening soon, and I'll be ready.'

'I know, but you can't leave yet. There's something about Dirk I don't like.'

'Jess said the same thing. He gives her the creeps.' Gyppo took a drink from his can. 'I'll keep an eye on him like I have been doing. We've bought a house too.'

Chains arched an eyebrow. 'What's the point if you're never there? Where is it?'

'Not far from Doc's, I thought it would be nice to live near friends.'

Chains sat watching the embers of the fire. Gyppo lay on the ground beside him as Peter occupied his bed. The other bikers had turned in for the night. Chains heard a noise behind the tents on his right. He stood, stretched his arms, and walked to his bike on the left. He picked up the iron links and made his way behind Gyppo's tent. The big biker crept along to where the noises came from and saw four hooded figures. He knew what they were and swung the chain. It caught the nearest in the face and it dropped to the ground.

The other three spread out and ran at him. He whipped the chains to the side catching one around the neck, and snapped his arm back. The demon flew apart as its clothes drifted to the ground. A dagger flew past straight into the head of the third. The fourth was almost on Chains who grabbed its top and slammed the demon onto the ground. Gyppo leapt over and shoved a dagger into its chest.

'Were you expecting them?' said the grey haired biker.

Chains lifted his hand with the clothes still in his grip as dust fell. 'No, but I had a bad feeling about it. The question is how did they know?'

Gyppo shrugged. 'We best burn these clothes.'

The two bikers collected the four sets of clothes and shoes before returning to the campfire. Stood there were Jess and Dirk.

'See, I told you,' said Dirk, 'they were here because of you.'

Chains was about to say something when he heard the engine of a car. He turned and saw headlights approach at speed. The car stopped and a woman jumped out of the driver's door, and a man climbed out of the passenger side.

The woman pointed a gun at them. 'I'm Detective Inspector Devon Fields,' she said, 'where is he?'

Chains threw the clothes on the fire. 'Where's who?'

'Peter Skelton, I know you brought him here.' Devon stared at the fire. 'What did you just throw on there?'

'Clothes, their previous owners no longer need them.'

Devon glared at him. 'What do you mean by that?'

'Peter's asleep,' said Jess, 'he took a bang to the head, but he'll be fine.'

Gyppo dropped the other clothes and patted Chains on the shoulder. 'You're getting slow.'

The big biker nodded and turned to the inspector. 'How did you know I brought him here?'

She took out a glowing piece of glass from her pocket. 'CCTV cameras showed you leaving town. This camp is known to many, but they didn't know it was a demon camp.'

Gyppo laughed. 'You are so wrong there.'

Chains stared at the glowing shard. 'Not quite, I believe the piece of glass detects them.'

Devon nodded. 'It glows in their presence, and it makes them invulnerable to normal weapons.'

'How does that work?'

Devon held it up and a light shot from it, covering Dirk. His eyes became red as he turned to run. A dagger flew through the air and the demon turned to dust. Jess walked over and retrieved her blade.

'I'm getting old,' said Gyppo, 'I never noticed he was one of them.'

'I have to admit I was unsure,' said Chains, 'I had an idea he was when the others turned up.'

Gyppo nodded. 'Dirk must've called them.'

'You know of them I see,' said Devon, as she put the glass, no longer glowing, away.

'We've had a few run-ins over the years. I'm Chains, this is Gyppo, and the lady with the knife is Jess.'

Devon put the gun away. 'This is Benjamin. Can you tell me why you brought Peter here?'

'It's the safest place for him at the moment. I was not going to risk leaving him in a hospital. Is he a friend of yours?'

Devon shook her head. 'No, he left a message with people we know that it was time for him to retrieve an item. They didn't like him going alone, so they asked us to escort him. He had gone by the time we got there and had no idea of his destination. I had to check the CCTV cameras to see if he passed through the town. I saw him on the back of your bike and you do know it's illegal without a helmet?'

Chains shrugged. 'I'm quite sure I had mine on. I would've let Peter use it, but I thought it might aggravate his cut. May I ask what you know of the demons?'

'Only what I've learnt over the last couple of months, but many more are appearing. My uncle here is somewhat of an expert on them.'

'Something is going to happen,' said Benjamin, 'and it needs to be stopped. We can't do that until we find out what it is.'

'Demons are always up to something,' said Chains. 'I've seen many more recently, and sent them back.'

Devon rubbed her chin. 'It sounds like you've been fighting them for a while.'

'You could say that, but they've been quiet for many years. I'll take Peter to retrieve the weapon he seeks.'

'We will be coming with you,' said Devon, 'it looks like the demons know what he was doing.'

'You best find somewhere to sleep,' said Jess, 'he's not going anywhere tonight.'

'I'll be fine in the car,' said Devon, 'I'm getting used to it.'

Chains woke on the ground near the fire to the sound of voices. He opened his eyes and saw Peter, with a bandage wrapped around his head, chatting away with Benjamin. Chains sat up and rubbed his eyes.

'You're awake,' said Peter.

Chains stretched his arms. 'It would appear so, how's the head?'

'Throbbing, but the lovely lady did a good job and also made me a wonderful breakfast.'

Chains sniffed the air. 'Something smells good.'

'You don't,' said Jess, 'you might want to wash up.'

Chains sniffed his top. 'I smell fine, but if you have somewhere for me to do so, I will.'

'There's a tent behind you with soap and water inside.'

Thirty minutes later Chains stood by his bike. 'Are you sure you want to come with me and not travel in the car?'

Peter put a helmet over his bandaged head and lifted the visor. 'Oh yes, I'm looking forward to it.'

Chains lifted the humpbacked man onto the bike. 'So where are we going?'

'Kingsley, it's hidden at Albrath House.'

Chains held his helmet above his head. 'I've some bad news for you . . . it's been a ruin for a long time.'

Peter nodded. 'I know, as I hid it there.'

'It could've been found by now.'

'No, it's private land and the ruins are protected. You did know Albrath House was a church, and the land is sacred. Demons will not go there.'

Chains rode the bike down country lanes and through a village until he reached a set of gates. He pulled up and helped Peter off the bike before removing his helmet. Chains rubbed his sides as his passenger might not have been big but had a strong grip.

'Are you OK?' he asked.

Peter removed his helmet. 'Yes, that was fun.'

The car pulled up behind where Devon and Benjamin climbed out. 'Were you trying to lose us?' she asked.

'No,' said Chains, 'but I did forget you was following us a few times.'

'This way,' said Peter, and pushed open one of the gates.

Chains followed along with Devon and Benjamin. He stepped through the gates and saw the ruins. The highest part was only three feet with the bricks lying all around. 'This was a big church.'

Peter nodded. 'Albrath House was an abbey.'

'What happened to the place?' said Devon.

'The civil war,' said Peter, 'but neither side admitted to it.'

'Not a recent thing then,' said Devon, 'but why destroy the building and not just come inside with their army?'

'Now that's the question,' said Peter, 'why didn't they? The answer is because they couldn't.'

'If demons did this they must've been after something.'

Chains walked through the ruins stepping over broken parts of the walls. 'It was a holy place . . . maybe they just didn't like it.'

'No one knows,' said Peter, 'nothing was ever written about it, and there were no survivors.'

'None you know of,' said Devon.

'True, but people did come when they saw the flames. They searched but only found dead bodies, and those who destroyed the building had gone.' Peter stopped at the back of the abbey by a pile of bricks. 'Here we are.'

Chains scratched his head. 'Where? It all looks the same to me.'

'Beneath these rocks is a cellar.'

Chains sighed. 'You want me to move them?'

'Yes, please, they will be too heavy for me.'

Chains reached down and picked up a large block before putting it to the side. 'How is it you managed to hide it here in the first place?'

'I was much younger then, and my back was straight.'

Benjamin sat on part of a wall as he watched. 'You weren't born like it then?'

Peter shook his head. 'No, I was thrown against a tree by a demon. They would have killed me if not for Elouise and Charles. They sent the demons back and took me away.'

'I'm no doctor,' said Devon, 'but would such an injury give you a hump like that?'

Chains laughed as he tossed a rock to the side. He turned and saw all three sitting down. 'I'm getting the hump right now.'

Peter smiled at him. 'The injury caused a cyst, and it grew. The doctors could do nothing to stop it.'

Chains pulled another large part of a wall away and saw a wooden trap door. Part of it had rotted away, and he removed the remaining rocks. He grabbed the handle and pulled it open to show concrete steps.

'That was quick,' said Peter.

Chains turned to them. 'Who wants to go first?'

Devon stood and passed him a torch. 'I'm not going to let you do all the work and find the treasure myself. It's only right you should be the one to retrieve it.'

'Thanks,' said Chains, and switched on the torch. He shone it down the steps as he walked down brushing cobwebs aside. Rats ran past his feet when he reached the bottom. The light lit up the walls showing they were made up of large bricks of different sizes. He could see no weapon, just broken barrels and smashed crockery. 'Where is it?' he shouted.

'Right in front of you,' said Peter, 'it's stuck in a barrel.'

Chains glanced around and noticed a stick poking out of a barrel. He pulled it out and saw it was a broken spear. 'Is this it, half a spear?'

'Yes, well done.'

Chains shook his head and climbed the steps. 'It doesn't look much.'

'No,' said Peter, 'but in a warriors hand it will be deadly. It will send many of the demons back as it has before.'

'Why hide it if you were fighting demons?'

'We had the ones we did use, and there weren't so many demons around at the time. They will search for weapons such as that to stop us using them.' Peter stood. 'It may not look like a safe place to hide it, but demons cannot see onto sacred lands.'

Devon pulled out her gun. 'We better get going, and be careful as I saw someone move out there.'

Chains gave Peter the spear who tried to hide it under his coat. 'Where?'

'He ran past the gate towards the field.'

Chains glanced to his left and saw movement behind a hedge twenty feet away. 'There's more than one out there.'

Peter rubbed his bandaged head. 'It doesn't sound good, what are we going to do?'

'They're not demons,' said Devon, holding the shard of glass.

Chains walked on dodging the rubble. 'We carry on, and see what they want. What is that piece of glass?'

Devon put the glass away. 'I don't know . . . none of us do, but it looks like part of a stained-glass window.'

'There are at least four of them,' said Benjamin, 'no, make that six.'

Chains nodded as he saw six men move away from the hedge. 'Not demons, but it appears they don't want us to leave here.'

'That's far enough,' said a short-haired man, 'throw out what you found.'

Chains eyed the six men, who looked like they were in their twenties. 'Why don't you come and take it?'

'We will once we have killed you,' said the one who spoke, and pulled out a gun as did the others. 'If you want to live, throw it out now.'

'Tell me,' said Chains, 'what is it you believe we have found?'

'A weapon, a special one.'

Chains laughed as Peter held up the broken spear. 'You would kill for this?'

'That's not it,' shouted another, 'they wouldn't pay us so much for that.'

'Shut up,' said the first, 'if that's what they want, that's what they get.'

'You know of the curse,' said Chains, 'otherwise you would be in here now.'

'What are you talking about, hippy? Throw it out now, or we'll kill you.'

'If you kill us, and try collecting the spear you'll never leave with it. If you kill any of us, and we throw the spear out it'll turn anyone who touches it to dust.'

The man shook his head and waved the gun. 'That's bullshit.'

'Really? You must've seen us arrive. How long did it take us to find the stick? They paid you a lot of money to wait here instead of retrieving it. They can't do it themselves as they can never enter here.'

The man turned to his friends to consider it, and they appeared to argue.

'What are you talking about?' said Peter, 'I've never heard of such a curse.'

Chains nodded. 'I made it up as I'm playing for time.'

'What good would that do us?' said Devon. 'We're stuck in the middle of nowhere and I'm the only one of us with a gun.'

'Throw the spear out now,' said the gunman, 'we're tired of your lies.'

Chains heard a loud bang and the man screamed. The gun fell to the ground as the man grabbed his arm.

'Drop your guns,' Gyppo shouted, as he and Jess approached with six other bikers, all armed. 'Try anything and you all die, now drop them and go.' The five men still with guns did, and the man with the injured arm chased after them.

Devon turned to the big biker. 'You planned that.'

'No, Gyppo did,' said Chains, as they walked amongst the rubble towards the gate where the bikers joined them. 'I noticed they were following a few miles back.'

'We thought it was time for a change of scenery,' said Gyppo, 'Jess and I are going on to Doc's.'

Chains nodded. 'I'm going with Peter to this safe house. I'd like to know what's happening and these people appear to know a lot more than I do.'

Gyppo clasped his hand. 'Ride safe.'

'You too, my old friend.'

Peter put on the helmet and lifted the visor. 'Wouldn't you like to use the spear?'

'Let someone else use it,' said Chains, 'I have a weapon.'

'True and you are very good with them. They are made of iron, but I sense something else.'

Chains shrugged and lifted the humpbacked man onto the bike. 'Maybe, but I've had them since I was young, and they're part of me now.'

Chains followed Devon for an hour when he rode through a set of gates and up a long drive to a large manor house. Trees surrounded the front of the house from what he could see.

A young man with shoulder-length hair walked over to them. 'Welcome to the house of Charles and other old people.'

'Joe,' said a young woman, 'don't be rude.'

'Sorry, Sarah, I was only welcoming them.'

Chains removed his helmet. 'Thank you for the welcome.'

Joe stared up at him as he climbed off the bike. 'My, you're a big one.'

'I've seen bigger,' said Chains, as he helped Peter off the bike.

Joe's eyes grew large. 'Wow, you're well crooked.'

'No, Joe,' said Sarah, 'that's too much.' She turned to Peter. 'I'm sorry, he's not usually so rude, but sometimes he can't keep things to himself.'

Peter removed his helmet and grinned. He reached up and patted Joe on the shoulder. 'This place has needed someone like you for a long time. I can't wait to hear your story.'

Chains sat at a large wooden table in the meeting hall of the manor house. He sipped on a mug of coffee as he glanced around the room. Also seated, were Devon, Benjamin and others he had been introduced to. The owner Charles, his sister Elouise, Arthur, Jack, Chloe, and Reverend Simon. He listened to recent events involving demons.

Charles turned the spear over in his hand. 'Thank you for saving our friend and retrieving this spear. May I ask what your plans are?'

Chains put the mug on the table. 'I'm going to travel north to see some friends, do you need my aid?'

'Two of our friends, Tarin Barkley and Jim Murray, have gone in search of a special artefact we need for the fight ahead. They are without a weapon to defeat demons and it might be a good idea for them to have this spear.'

'Where are they?'

'We're not sure at the moment. Tarin will call in later, but she believes it to be somewhere near Wales. We will give you a phone, so we can let you know.'

Chains rode up to the Travellers Rest public house at eight in the evening and saw a dozen bikes parked up. He stepped inside where a group of bikers, none he recognised stared at him. He counted twelve, eleven men and one woman. The landlord had his back to him.

'I hope your beer is more tasteful than the décor in here.'

The landlord turned and raised an eyebrow. 'You won't find a better pint for miles.'

Chains nodded. 'I can believe that as I didn't see another pub for miles.'

The landlord poured a pint of lager and placed it on the counter. 'Try that.'

Chains picked up the glass, took a long swig and nodded. 'It's a mighty fine drink, and I could easily stay here all night.'

The landlord smiled. 'It's been a long time, big fella.'

Chains reached over and grasped his hand. 'Too long, Doc, how's it been going?'

'Quiet, but business has been good. Where have you been the last few years?'

'Travelling, searching things out. I've seen Gyppo and Jess a few times, and they've bought a house near here, so he told me.'

'Yes,' said Doc, 'it's a nice place to retire, but I have a feeling that won't be for a while.'

'He's a big one,' said a woman leaning up the bar, 'but will he buy a girl a drink?'

'Behave, Cheryl,' said Doc, 'your fella is over there and I don't want any marital problems in here.'

She shrugged. 'I doubt Jed would care, he hasn't noticed me since those other guys started coming in here.'

Doc poured Cheryl a drink. 'He has become thick with them, but a lot of bikers are like that.'

'Yeah, and most of them have partners. Not this lot, have you ever seen a woman with them? Jed goes out with them after the pub, but I've no idea where.' Cheryl took her drink and joined the others.

Chains sipped on his lager. 'Are they new in town?'

Doc nodded. 'The gang are, been regulars for a month now. I'm not over keen on them, but they're quiet. Jed and Cheryl are, or was, a happily married couple before they came along, and now I want to know what they get up to after closing time.'

Chains glanced back as one of them stepped out of the pub. 'It won't be anything good.'

Another man appeared behind the bar. He stood six feet, slim, and wore a black t-shirt. He reached over the bar and shook Chains' hand. 'It's about time . . . I've been a little bored around here.'

'Don't worry, Blades,' said Chains, 'I've a feeling that's about to change. Where are your weapons?'

'Here,' said Blades, 'under the bar.'

'I think you'll need them,' said Chains, as he turned and leant up the bar.

The biker returned inside and shut the door. He stood there and nodded to the others. The bikers, apart from Cheryl and Jed, stood. Their eyes turned red.

'Damn,' said Doc, 'how did I not notice them? Have I lost my touch?'

'No, old man,' a demon hissed, 'we're stronger. We've been waiting for your friend to arrive, and he has left his weapon outside.'

'I don't need them,' said Chains, 'you're not that much stronger. I sent enough of you back last night to know that much.'

The demon snarled. 'You won't be sending any more back after tonight.'

Cheryl stood. 'What the hell are you?'

'Hold her,' the demon snapped, 'she can die after.'

Jed tried to stand but a demon knocked him down as the other demons pulled out curved daggers. One held Cheryl by the arm.

Chains rubbed his bearded chin. 'Tell me, has someone opened a door to let you all out?'

'Not yet,' said the demon, 'but you should be more worried about being gutted alive. When we do that, the Lord of Chaos will reward us.'

'Reward you how?'

'That you will never know, as you're about to die.'

'I don't think so,' said Doc, and put four knives on the bar.

The demon scowled. 'Throw them on the floor now or watch the happy couple die.'

'I'm quite sure you already said you were going to kill them,' said Chains, 'but that won't happen. You made a mistake in thinking there were only three of us.'

'We know there are more, but only three are here.'

Chains grinned. 'I always know when my friends are nearby.'

The door burst open sending the demon standing there flying across the room. A link of chains shot through catching a demon in the head and it turned to dust.

Gyppo stepped into the bar. 'I've always wanted to use these.'

Blades and Doc climbed over the counter as Jess stepped into the room and threw a knife at the demon holding Cheryl. It turned to dust as four more bikers, three women and a man, ran into the room. They carried blades in each hand and were too fast for the demons. The one woman leapt over a table and caught two of the demons across the throat before she landed. The male biker, with short hair and a pointed beard, slid under the swinging arm of a demon as he plunged his needle-shaped dagger upwards. It entered the demon's head just below the jaw and it turned to dust. The other two women jumped in the middle of the remaining demons and dust flew everywhere.

Blades put the knives back on the bar. 'I forgot how fast they are.'

Chains took a swig from his drink. 'They're a joy to watch.'

The four new bikers stepped away from the dusty clothes. They all wore black leather jackets, as did Gyppo and Jess.

The biker with the pointed beard put his daggers inside his jacket. 'It's been a long time.'

'Too long, Ice, but it's good to see you again.' Chains turned to the three women, Tempest, Raven, and Mistral. 'I have missed you.'

'Yet you never call,' said Tempest, 'and a girl can get in trouble when she's bored.'

'Here you go,' said Doc, holding a leather jacket, 'it's been too long since you wore this.'

Chains removed the one he was wearing and took the other. He looked at the picture on the back, a red moon above a howling wolf.

'OK, big guy,' said Raven, 'where are we going?'

Chains put the jacket on. 'Wales, it's time for The Lords of Night to ride again.'

CHAPTER NINE

Following the Dead

Tarin Barkley glimpsed around the wall of the alley as eight hooded figures walk towards them. 'They're getting closer.'

Inspector Jim Murray looked, shook his head, and laughed. 'You're one intelligent woman, but really?'

Tarin rubbed her nose. 'What do you mean?'

Jim took her arm and walked out of the alley. 'They're monks, there's a monastery here.'

Tarin grinned as they walked past the monks. 'I can't be right all the time.'

'Let's hope you're right about being here. I still think it's a longshot.'

'I know,' said Tarin, as they walked along the picturesque street with old buildings, 'but we know the one who stole the cross came here.'

'How sure are you of that? He could've sold it to someone else who came here.'

Tarin shook her head. 'No, I don't believe that. He sold it to a dealer, and we only know of the one. The dealer said he never knew the man he bought it off, a man who didn't know it's true worth.'

'We'll soon find out,' said Jim, as they crossed the road to the Red Dragon Inn. 'Let's just hope Sergeant Fred Talbot is in here.'

They entered the pub, to the right sat two couples, and in the far left corner sat a grey-haired man nursing a pint.

'That's him,' said Tarin.

Jim nodded as they approached the table. 'Sergeant Fred Talbot?'

'Just Fred now,' said the man, 'I'm retired.'

'Can I get you a drink?'

'I'll have a pint of draught ale, but I can't promise you any answers.'

'Of course not,' said Tarin, as Jim stepped over to the bar, 'but you know more than we do.'

'I don't see how,' said Fred, 'you've read my report.'

Tarin sat down. 'You were here, so that's a start. You were also the one who interviewed Stan Morris before he died.'

'As did the press, but he was not the hero they made him out to be. He wasn't a bad guy either, just the owner of an antique shop.'

Jim placed three drinks on the table and pushed one over to Fred before sitting down. 'I wouldn't call him a hero, but he did the decent thing.'

'Aye,' said Fred, 'he handed the cross into us, but he wasn't happy about it. Morris knew it was stolen when he bought it, although he never admitted it. He had never met the man who sold it to him before and the name he got was made up. When the picture of the cross appeared in the papers, Morris knew he couldn't sell it, so he brought it to us. He got his own picture in the paper and might've done well out of it if he hadn't got himself killed.'

Tarin took a sip from her glass of wine. 'Did he have any enemies?'

Fred shrugged. 'Who knows in that trade, but we never looked for any. Morris died in a fire at his shop and the doors were locked from the inside.'

'It could've been made to look like an accident.'

'I don't know how. The shutters were down on the back door, and keys were in the inside lock on the front door. All the windows were closed.' Fred took a swig of his pint. 'What's this all about? It can't be Morris or the cross.'

Tarin shook her head. 'We're trying to find anything we can about the man who sold it to him.'

'It was over twenty years ago and Morris didn't give a good description of him then. He's most likely dead now, just some petty thief who probably spent the money on drink. I can't see why you're interested in him as the cross is back at the monastery.'

Tarin could sense the retired police officer was hiding something. 'He was more than that . . . a petty thief doesn't go to another country to steal valuable artefacts. We're not after him but something else he stole that day. An ancient dagger and the monastery want it back. It would help if we could trace his steps.'

Fred sipped from his glass. 'Maybe Morris bought it too, and it was destroyed in the fire.'

Tarin considered it. 'No, it would take a lot more than fire to destroy it.'

'Strange the monastery never mentioned a second item being stolen.'

'They didn't want certain individuals knowing about it.'

Fred looked at them both in turn. 'Is that why you believe the fire was no accident?'

Jim nodded. 'Yes, as it happened not long after his picture appeared in the paper. Whoever started the fire, thought Morris knew where the dagger was.'

Fred took a long swig of his ale. 'And you just want to return the dagger?'

'It will be going back to the monastery where it will be kept safe.'

Fred rubbed his chin. 'OK, I've no idea where the dagger is, nor do I want to know.'

'Why's that?'

'I'm not a superstitious man, but after what the thief told me I could never touch it.'

Tarin raised both eyebrows. 'You met him?'

Fred nodded. 'I did, by chance, a year or so later.'

Tarin clasped her hands together. 'Who is he?'

'He was Robert Stokes, dying in hospital. I had gone there for another reason when he saw me in uniform. A nurse came over and asked if I would hear is confession. I thought it strange, but I also thought he wanted to confess to a crime.'

'What was wrong with him?'

Fred picked up his glass. 'Everything by then, but it was this stuff which done for him in the end.'

Jim rubbed his chin. 'You made no report of this?'

'No, and maybe that was wrong of me. What he told me is why I had no interest in finding the dagger, and maybe I didn't want anyone else finding it either. It might sound like nonsense, but judge me after what I tell you.'

Jim nodded. 'Of course.'

Fred took a notepad out of his pocket. 'I followed the nurse to his room where I saw a man lying on the bed with different tubes attached to him. He was conscious, but I knew he wouldn't be for much longer. I sat next to the bed when he spoke.' Fred opened the pad and pushed it across the table. 'Only I have ever read this, but now it's time for someone else to do so.'

Jim picked up the notepad and read it out quietly so only they could hear.

'I am Robert Stokes, forty-two years old, and have a confession I need you to hear before I die. Most of my life I've been a thief and never cared who I stole from. I've never worked a day in my life, I've hurt people, beaten them, and never gave them another thought. You would think of me as scum as I lie here dying, and probably believe I want forgiveness. It's not what I want as my sins came back to haunt me over a year ago, and I will die without forgiveness.

Stokes closed his eyes for a few moments and breathed heavily, until he opened them and carried on speaking.

I will not tell you of all my crimes even though I remember each one like they were yesterday. I want to tell you of a certain crime, a robbery, one which gave me a slow death. Being known to the police as a thief became too risky where I lived, so I decided to travel. I also needed to get away as I owed people money. I decided on France as it's easy to get to. It wasn't as easy as I thought but after a few days of driving around I came across a monastery open to the public. I walked around and saw a stunning jewel encrusted cross and knew I had to take it. I had to wait as it was locked in a glass cabinet and people were walking around.

I found a back door which I unlocked and saw a set of monk's robes or whatever they're called. I put them on and waited for the public to leave. Monks were still inside, of course, but they disappeared to do whatever monks do. I was soon inside on my own with the cross in front of me. The cabinet, I found out, wasn't locked. My instincts screamed at me to get away as it was all too easy. I didn't and put the cross inside my jacket. I noticed an antique looking metal box and decided to take it too. I ran from the place terrified I was being followed, but by the time I got to my car I found I wasn't. I drove back to England without being stopped once.

I decided to sell the cross soon as I could and far from where I lived. I came across Morris Antiques and decided to try my luck in there. The owner of the shop inspected it and I expected him to rip me off. He may well have done, but he offered me more money than I ever had in my life. I took the offer and left him holding the cross as if it was the Holy Grail.

I travelled home to Wales and paid my debt before hiding low for a while. I forgot about the other item I had taken until a week later. I don't know why I forgot, but maybe it was all the drinking I had done since I returned home. One night I noticed it at the side of my bed and picked it up. Inside was an old dagger which looked like nothing of value, but I realised it could link me to the robbery, so I decided to get rid of the thing.

I took the dagger out of the box and my life changed in that instant. Not for the good you understand. A strange feeling came over me, a wave of emotions, but mainly guilt. All the crimes I committed, all the people I had hurt over the years, all came back to me. It tore me in two, burning into my soul. My life became a blur after that as I drank more than ever to block out the guilt. I finally rid myself of the dagger and came back here to see if Morris still had the cross, but I found out he died not long after I sold it to him. That was my fault, so I drank more until I ended up in this bed.'

Jim closed the notepad and passed it back. 'Is that all?'

Fred nodded. 'Yes, I did ask him about the dagger, but he said it was hidden and didn't want anyone else to suffer. Not long after he fell asleep, and never woke up again.'

'You were right . . . I wouldn't have reported it either.'

'I would have if the monastery reported it stolen, but they never did.'

Tarin glanced at her notepad. 'Do you know where in Wales he lived?'

'Somewhere south I think. His sister lives there, or she did back then.'

'Thank you,' said Jim, 'can I get you another drink before we leave?'

Fred smiled. 'A pint of ale, please.'

'You amaze me at times,' said Jim, as they walked back to the car.

Tarin rubbed her nose. 'Thanks, but that was more to do with luck.'

'Maybe, but it was your idea to come here and talk to the ex-sergeant.'

Tarin grabbed his arm. 'I know, but it was our only lead. At least we don't have to visit any antique shops to see if they know anything.'

'So it's Wales in the morning, and I've booked us a couple of rooms in a bed and breakfast for tonight.'

'You're such a gentleman.'

Jim smiled. 'I know, it's hard being me at times.'

'Well there's something you've gotta do before you go to sleep.'

Jim raised an eyebrow. 'What's that?'

'See where Robert Stokes's sister lives.'

Jim drove west towards Wales the following morning. 'Do you believe his sister will know anything?'

Tarin glanced up through the window at the blue sky. 'I doubt she'll know anything about the dagger, but she might know where he hung out getting drunk.'

'His confession mentioned his bed, so he might've been staying at her house.'

It took them an hour to reach Wales and find the village where Stokes's sister still lived. A row of houses gave way to spaced out cottages. They drove slowly past a shop and a pub.

'It's quiet here,' said Jim, 'not the type of place where you did things and others wouldn't know about it.'

Tarin turned to him. 'Maybe we should find the local gossip and buy them a drink.'

'Let's talk to the sister first, if we ever find the house that is.'

'You have to drive through the village, Stokes Cottage is further out.'

Jim drove on, and they soon saw the cottage with the sign above the gate. There was a car parked on the drive, and he pulled up. They climbed out and saw a woman kneeling in the garden with a trowel in her hand.

Tarin approached the gate. 'Mrs Stokes?'

The woman turned her head to them but didn't get up. 'Miss Stokes, I've never been married.'

'Sorry, we are here to ask you a few questions about your brother.'

Miss Stokes frowned. 'I don't have a brother, he lost the right to be called that long before he died.'

'You didn't get along?'

Miss Stokes threw some weeds into a bag. 'He was nothing more than a thieving scumbag. I know I shouldn't speak ill of the dead but it's true all the same.'

Tarin rubbed her chin. 'You still feel like that after all these years?'

'Oh yes, he broke my parents hearts and mine. He wasn't always like that. Robert was my sweet little brother until he met that lot down the road. The Gibson gang they called themselves, thieves and scum I called them. Robert met them when he started senior school, and was soon out stealing with them. He was expelled from school at just fourteen.'

'It must've been hard for you and your parents.'

Miss Stokes removed her gardening gloves and stood. 'It made my mother ill, and she blamed herself for what he did. She died believing it. He didn't care, and when my father lay in bed dying, Robert stole his medals and sold them.'

'Did you call the police?'

Miss Stokes shook her head. 'No, what was the point? What do you want with him after all these years?'

'He came back here not long before he died, and we just want to know where he stayed.'

'It wasn't here I can tell you that.'

'Are the Gibson's still here?'

Mist Stokes nodded. 'Yes, but not the same ones, of course. Most of them grew up and moved away. The eldest took over the house when their parents died. His children and their cousins are the trouble now. I'm sorry if I sound bitter, but all I wanted was my brother to show some remorse for what he had done. I've never even visited his grave.'

Tarin realised the woman wasn't bitter, but heartbroken and stubborn. 'I'm sorry he didn't come to see you before he died, but he did show remorse in the end. He even gave a confession.'

Miss Stokes raised an eyebrow. 'He must've known he was dying to do that, thought it might get him into heaven.'

Tarin shook her head. 'It wasn't a priest he confessed to but a police officer. It was the guilt which killed him, the pain he felt for all those who suffered because of him. You should visit his grave, not for him but for yourself.'

Miss Stokes wiped her eyes. 'Why would I want to do that?'

'To say goodbye, it'll ease the pain you still feel. You're a good woman and shouldn't be suffering after all these years.'

'Who are you people?'

'Police,' said Jim, 'but it's nothing to worry about, just loose ends.'

'There is one place he may have stayed. Just past the Gibson farm, on the other side of the road, are woods. There's an old hut he used to stay in. Continue down the lane and you'll soon find the place.'

Tarin smiled. 'Thank you.'

'Before you go,' said Miss Stokes, 'would you tell me where the cemetery is?'

'I thought you were a reporter,' said Jim, 'not a psychologist.'

Tarin glanced out the car window at the fields. 'I could see she was still hurting, and like her mother she blamed herself. She could never forgive her brother because he never said sorry. It's a five letter word some people hate saying.'

Jim smiled. 'I've said it quite a lot since I met you.'

'Miss Stokes has been a lonely woman for a long time. She never married and I doubt she's the type of person to ever go for flings. It looks like it was only her parents and brother in her life, and they have long gone.' Tarin noticed a field on the right with a farm set back. She saw cars and many motor bikes parked up. 'We've found the Gibson farm.'

'I doubt they do much farming,' said Jim. 'We best give them a miss and find the old hut.'

Jim slowed the car as they approached the wood on the left. He pulled into a lay by and parked up.

Tarin climbed out and removed her jacket as the sun shone down on them and put it in the car. She stepped over to the edge of the trees as the inspector joined her. 'It's a nice day for a walk in the woods.'

Jim pushed a low hanging branch out of his way. 'The last time I walked through any woods, before I met you, we were searching for a missing woman. It wasn't a pleasant day as it rained. Her husband was frantic with worry.'

Tarin turned her head from side to side looking for any sign of the hut. 'Did you find her?'

'Yeah, she was at a hotel, in bed, with another man.'

Tarin watched Jim navigate through the woods for ten minutes. 'Do you know where the hut is?'

'No, I'm following a well walked path. There are even tread marks from a bike.'

Tarin glanced down and saw what the inspector meant. 'We might make a detective out of you yet.'

Jim walked on. 'One can only hope, but I'm surprised you didn't spot it.'

'I'm not one for woods.' Tarin noticed something dark through the trees further ahead on the left. 'That could be it.'

'Maybe, but we have to follow the path as the undergrowth is too thick.'

The path veered left and Tarin saw the wooden building. 'That's a hut?'

Jim walked forward. 'It's a cabin, but not the one Stokes stayed in. This one's too new.'

'True, but there's a good chance it's the same place the other one was.'

'Who would put one here in the first place? This isn't private land and anyone can walk through here.'

'You're trespassing,' said a voice.

Tarin turned to the right and saw a bald man with a snake tattoo on his head.

'I don't think so,' said Jim, 'this land doesn't belong to you.'

'No, but the cabin does.'

'Really, and did you get permission to put one here? If not, it'll be taken down.'

The man frowned. 'Who are you?'

'Detective Inspector Murray, the police,' said Jim, and the man ran away.

Tarin watched him disappear through the trees. 'It makes you wonder what he gets up to here.'

Jim hurried over to the cabin and opened the door. 'You might want to see this.'

Tarin followed and looked through the door. On top of a table she saw large bags of white powder with smaller bags nearby. 'Oh crap, they're drug dealers.'

'It would appear so. I better call it in and get the woods sealed off.'

'That might work out better for us, and we can search in peace.'

Jim reached inside his jacket. 'We could have more pressing problems. I'm guessing Snakehead is part of the Gibson clan, and I saw a lot of bikes parked up at the farm.' He searched another pocket. 'I've left my phone in the car.'

Tarin raised both eyebrows. 'So did I, we better get to the car before he tells the rest of the gang.'

They ran back through the woods for a few minutes when there was a loud bang.

'What the hell was that?' said Tarin.

'Back,' said Jim, as he stopped and pulled out a gun, 'that was my car. Snakehead must've phoned his friends.'

'If they saw the car from the farm they may have already been on their way to keep us away from the cabin. They took a chance blowing up the car when we may have already called for backup.'

'Not if they looked inside first and saw our phones.'

Tarin heard the sound of a motorbike. 'We can take them.'

There was a bang and a bullet flew past them. They ran back and continued past the cabin and could hear noises behind them. Tarin saw a bank, and they ran down to the thick undergrowth at the bottom.

Jim knelt behind a bush and glanced up. 'It might be a good idea to see what we're up against.'

Tarin looked around for an escape route when she heard the bikes getting closer. A man appeared at the top of the bank. Another joined him and they both had guns.

'Come out, come out, wherever you are,' said one.

'I could get both of them,' Jim whispered, 'but where's Snakehead?'

Tarin saw him approach. 'There he is, with three others.'

'Big mistake,' said Snakehead, 'leaving your phones in the car. I have men all around the woods and you won't be leaving.' He pointed his hand in different directions and the others moved away.

'They're going around us,' said Jim, 'we need to move.'

'This way,' she said, and pointed at a gap in the undergrowth.

'Let's hope they don't have enough men to watch the perimeter of the woods, and search inside.'

'I'd like that, but I bet they keep men by the cabin.'

'It's not the same one anyway. Let's move as I need a better view, but be careful not to disturb any branches,' said Jim, as he followed her through the dark shrubbery.

They made their way for a few minutes until the bushes thinned, and they could see ahead. The trees here were further apart.

Tarin managed to stand and glance around. 'We must be near the edge by now . . . the woods can't be that big.'

'It looks big enough to me,' said Jim, as he stood. 'The way was slow and not straight.'

Tarin felt something underfoot. She glanced down and saw a bottle under the grass. 'Look what I've found.'

'Nice,' said Jim, 'maybe you can throw it at them.'

'It's a whiskey bottle and I bet a certain person was here.'

'You could be right, and the space between the trees would support it.'

Tarin rubbed the dirt off her jeans. 'How do you mean?'

'It's overgrown now, but cars used to come through here. We know Stokes drove here.'

Tarin nodded. 'We have to follow it.'

Jim sighed. 'We have to get away from here.'

'I know, but which way? As you said he drove here, so it must lead to a road. The question is left or right?'

Jim scratched his head. 'Good point, I've no idea. I'm sure we passed a side road before we came here, so it could be left. We have no idea what's further ahead, so it could be right.'

Tarin glanced around again to make sure it was clear and walked to the right. 'This way.'

'Oh no, Miss, I see your game.'

Tarin turned and smiled at him. 'Whatever do you mean?'

'Don't smile . . . we're in a bit of a pickle if you haven't noticed. You want us to go right because if Stokes drove in from the left we would find nothing going that way.'

'True, but if he drove in from the right we'd find nothing going that way.'

'We can search after we get out of here and come back with help. Any of them could turn up looking for us. They can even wait us out as they can get food, and we have none.'

Tarin knew he was right. 'OK, you decide.'

Jim looked left, right, and straight ahead. 'We go right.'

'Are you serious after what you just said?'

'It's darker in the other directions. It might not mean much, but it could mean the edge of the woods is closer that way.'

They walked on close to bushes trying to keep out of sight. Tarin searched in every direction for the hut and the gang. They carried on for a few minutes when they saw the old hut, not much smaller than the cabin, behind a tree with low hanging branches. Jim hurried ahead and pulled on the door. He had to force it open as it hung on the top hinge.

'It's clear,' he said, 'if you want to take a look.'

Tarin raised an eyebrow. 'Very MI5, I like it.'

'I'm after a promotion. You take a look and I'll keep watch.'

Tarin stepped inside and could smell damp. She could see a single bed and a table turned upside down. She looked under the bed trying not to touch anything. There was no sign of the dagger, so she lifted the table and saw nothing underneath. She was about to lower it when she saw marks on the top and flipped it over to see a message scratched into the wood.

I write this as I'm leaving here for good. I'm free of the dagger now, but not the guilt. I tried throwing it into the sea, but I couldn't. I hid it in a dark place in the cliff itself as I did not want anyone else to suffer like I did. It is the reason for this message as the only warning I could think of. If you find the dagger, do not touch it, or it will curse you too.

It's a shame you didn't understand what it did to you, Tarin thought, and heard voices outside.

'I'm sure that door wasn't open earlier,' said a man.

'It wasn't,' said another, 'we better check it out.'

Tarin moved behind the door and saw two armed men approach. As they neared the hut, Jim ran out of the bushes and hit one of the men on the back of the head with the butt of his gun. He fell to the ground as Jim pointed the gun at the other man.

'Drop it,' he said.

The man did as Tarin stepped out of the hut. Jim handcuffed the two men together and picked up the guns. Tarin slipped back into the hut and turned the table over before going back outside.

'It's time to go,' she said.

'Maybe I should knock the other one out too,' said Jim, 'soon as we go he'll start yelling.'

'Let him, the others will come running here and not where we're going.'

Jim nodded and passed her a gun. 'True, but it's a shame these don't have phones on them or I could've called it in.'

'It doesn't matter at the moment,' said Tarin, 'we need to leave.'

'What about the dagger?'

'It's not here.'

They ran on while keeping low, and heard the conscious man start yelling. Jim pulled her into the bushes, and seconds later two men ran past. They waited a few moments before running on. Tarin soon saw the edge of the woods and a man standing by an off-road motor bike.

Jim knelt behind a bush. 'That's our way out of here.'

'Yeah, but while he's looking this way there's no chance of jumping him before he starts shooting.'

'I know, so where's the dagger.'

Tarin scanned all around looking for any others from the gang. 'In a cliff, somewhere along the coast.'

'You do know how much coast we have?'

'Yes, but it would be the nearest from here.'

The man by the bike grabbed a walkie-talkie from his pocket and spoke into it. As he did he walked about, and Tarin ran around the bushes while his back was to her.

'They haven't come this way,' he said into the walkie-talkie, and put it back in his pocket. He turned to see Tarin pointing a gun at him and leered at her. 'Why don't you hand it over before you hurt yourself?'

Jim crept up behind and hit him across the back of his head with his gun.

Tarin watched the man crumple to the ground. 'I think you're starting to enjoy doing that.'

Jim climbed on the bike and started it up. 'Come on let's go before he's missed.'

Tarin got on behind him. 'You can ride one of these?'

'Yeah, I've got one at home.' They rode out of the woods into a field.

Tarin held onto Jim with one hand while looking back and saw two other bikes leave the woods. 'We've got company.'

'I thought we might have,' said Jim, 'hold on tight, I'll try to lose them.'

Tarin saw a hedge ahead as Jim rode towards a small hill. She put both hands around him, even though she still held the gun, and the bike flew over the hedge. Tarin turned back and saw the other bikes leap over. The riders both had guns and fired them. The bullets missed as Tarin pointed her gun and fired. She missed and fired again. The nearest biker went down after the fourth shot and the other biker stopped.

'We've lost them for now,' she said.

Jim nodded and rode on for another five minutes before slowing the bike down and stopping.'

Tarin glanced around. 'What's up?'

'Just getting my bearings,' said Jim. 'See the road on the right . . . it's the same one we drove to the woods on.'

'That would mean we're going in the right direction to the coast. It might be quicker if we were on the road.'

'We don't have helmets, and they have cars.'

They rode on for twenty minutes, but had to stop a few times to pass through gates or find gaps in hedges. Jim stopped the bike again.

'What is it now?' said Tarin.

'We have to walk from here, we're out of fuel.'

Tarin sighed and climbed off the bike. 'Oh joy, we're in the middle of nowhere.'

'I know, and we've lost sight of the road.'

Tarin brushed her hair back with her fingers. 'When did that happen?'

Jim pushed the bike into a hedge. 'When we had to go along the river, but we can't be far from it.'

They walked on seeing the odd farm-house and village. It started to turn dark when they saw lights in the distance.

'Civilisation at last,' said Tarin.

Jim nodded. 'I thought we might have to find somewhere to stay in a village. I didn't want to as the Gibson gang might have friends there.'

'You still think they're after us.'

'There was over a million pounds worth of drugs in the cabin, and it would get them locked up for a long time.'

'Yeah, but it won't be there now.'

'It doesn't have to be. We know their secret, and they won't want the authorities knowing anything about it.'

'We can't do much about it at the moment, and I'd rather not have to give statements while we're searching for the dagger.'

'Don't worry,' said Jim, 'I've no intention of doing so, but I don't want those drugs reaching the streets.'

Tarin removed the gun from the back of her jeans. 'You best take this as I can't hide it. I shot four times, and I've no idea if there's any bullets left inside.'

Jim took the gun and put it in a jacket pocket. 'We can't leave it here even if it's empty.'

'Let's hope we're near the coast.'

'We are . . . I can smell the sea air.'

Tarin sniffed. 'I can't smell anything.'

'I was joking,' said Jim, 'but I don't think we're too far. If we are, there'll be many places to eat.'

Tarin approached a wooden fence and saw houses opposite. 'I hope so, I'm starving.'

'I might be able to pick up a cheap phone.'

Tarin climbed over the fence to a street. 'Who you gonna call?'

Jim followed over the fence. 'Charles for one, and let him know where we are. I'd also like to let Logan know about the drugs.'

'You can remember their phone numbers.'

Jim shook his head as they walked down the street. 'No, they're in my . . . oh right, I forgot about that,' he said, as they turned a corner and saw a row of bed and breakfast hotels.

'This is definitely a holiday town,' said Tarin, 'but which one?'

'Glamford,' said Jim, 'the big sign over there says as much.'

'Let's find a shop selling maps, and then we can go for something to eat.'

'I'm sure we'll find somewhere to eat without a map. I don't want to go anywhere which looks posh as I feel grubby after the day we've had.'

'You look fine,' said Tarin, as they walked onto a busy high street. 'My jeans are ripped.'

'I thought it was the fashion, I'm just happy I never left my wallet in the car.'

Tarin nodded. 'Same here.'

Jim raised an eyebrow. 'You have a wallet?'

'Yeah, is there anything wrong with that?'

'No, not really, in fact I think all women should have one. You carry a purse and you're going to end up carrying a load of loose change in it.'

Twenty minutes later they were sat in a pub studying a map as food was placed in front of them.

Tarin glanced up. 'Thank you.' She turned back to the map. 'If we're in Glamford, we're miles away from where we should be.'

Jim picked up a chip from the plate. 'I know.'

Tarin shook her head. 'You knew we were going off course?'

'I had an idea, but we needed to get somewhere we could stay the night. I didn't want to be stuck out there and you haven't got a jacket. It won't make much difference as we can go in the morning by taxi.'

Tarin folded up the map. 'We could go now.'

Jim leant back. 'I don't think my feet could take any more tonight, and we might never find it in the dark.'

The following morning Tarin bought a new pair of jeans, top, and a jacket. She changed clothes in the shop and walked to the door. She stopped as a bald man walked past. Snakehead, she thought, and waited for him to go down the street. She left the shop and crossed the road to a men's store. Jim held up two short-sleeved shirts as she entered, one white, the other light blue.

'Which one?' he asked.

'Neither,' said Tarin, 'you better buy a hoodie.'

Jim glanced out the window. 'It's gonna be too hot for one of those.'

'Not today as I just saw Snakehead.'

Jim put the shirts back and chose a cream hoodie. He put it on the counter next to a pair of jeans. 'They haven't given up then.'

Tarin grabbed a cap and added it to Jim's clothes. 'Did they follow our trail or were they just hoping to find us?'

'I've no idea.'

Jim paid by card and changed in the shop. They walked out into the street and Tarin put the old clothes in a bin. She put on the cap as Jim pulled the hood over his head.

Tarin crossed the road towards a taxi rank. 'The sooner we get away from here the better.'

Jim nodded. 'Let's hope they never saw the message as some of them could be waiting for us.'

'I turned the table back over, anyway we've got guns, and it'll be a public place.'

'That was quick thinking, and there's one number I know off by heart.'

'If it has only three digits forget it, we don't know who to trust at the moment.'

'True,' said Jim, 'I'm surprised we haven't seen any demons yet.'

'We can't be sure of that, but I've been trying to figure how much they know. The demons killed Morris when they found out he bought the cross. Stokes had kept the dagger for a while before he touched it, so they never knew about him.'

'They may have found out since,' said Jim. 'I don't mean from the sergeant, but some other way. From what we know there are more of them appearing so it's a good chance there weren't many of them back then.'

'They may also be able to sense the dagger's power while it's away from the monastery. They must know something as they tried to take Jemima.' Tarin stepped over to a taxi. 'Meridan Beach.'

'Sure thing,' said the middle-aged taxi driver wearing a Hawaiian shirt, 'jump in.'

Tarin climbed in the back as Jim got in the other side. She glanced out the window and saw Snakehead talking to a man on a bike.

'You might want to choose somewhere else,' said the taxi driver, 'Meridan isn't the nicest beach, it's mostly shale.'

'We're not interested in sunbathing,' said Tarin, 'just trekking along them.'

The taxi driver nodded. 'The wife likes hiking across fields and over hills . . . if she did it along a beach I might join her.'

They drove on for thirty minutes when the traffic slowed and the driver stopped the taxi. He leaned out of the window to take a look. 'There's been a crash, and we might be here a while.'

Jim leant forward. 'How far are we from the beach?'

'Not far,' said the driver. 'You can see it from the ridge over there on the left. Are you thinking about going on foot from here?'

'Yeah, we got a thing about walking.' Jim handed him a twenty pound note. 'Keep the change and you should be able to turn around before the traffic builds up behind.'

They climbed out and walked across a grassy area towards the ridge. Tarin glanced over at the crash and saw two badly damaged cars. 'It doesn't look good.'

'No,' said Jim, 'the sports car must've been going too fast.'

'What sports car?'

Jim pointed to the right of two cars. 'Over there.'

Tarin saw the car turned upside down. 'Oh yeah.' She reached the crest of the hill and saw the sea. 'What a gorgeous view.'

Jim nodded. 'I love the ocean, but I'm not keen on the beach down there.'

Tarin saw the shale on the beach, and to the left the view of the ocean was blocked by a hill. 'Yeah, but we don't want a popular spot. The fewer people the better while we search. Would you say the hill to the left of the beach is a cliff?'

'Could be, but you have to remember the message was written by a drunk.'

Tarin walked to the road and saw wooden steps leading down to the beach further up. She made her way towards them.

'Where are you going?' said Jim. 'I thought you wanted the beach.'

'I do, but Stokes came here to throw the dagger into the sea, but something stopped him. His first thought was to get rid of it. I don't think he wanted to run across the beach and throw it into the sea but up here. He could park on the road and walk to the edge of the cliff.' Tarin reached the steps but made her way to the top of the cliff. She glanced down a twenty-foot drop. 'It's not that high here, but the beach isn't very wide. This would be a good place to throw it away.'

Jim stepped over to her. 'Yes, but the message said he didn't throw it.'

'I know as something made him change his mind. I'd guess that would be the dagger, and he decided to hide it instead. If it happened like that, where do you go to hide it?'

'If you're going to hide it in the cliff you would go down the steps. What I want to know is how do you hide something in a cliff?'

Tarin walked down the steps when an eerie feeling came over her. 'The dagger's here.'

Jim followed her down. 'How do you know?'

'I can sense it, I don't know how but I'm sure of it.'

'Look ahead,' said Jim, 'there's not much beach between the cliff and the sea. I bet you can't pass through when the tide is in.'

Tarin noticed only two could walk along together without getting their feet wet. She felt another sensation she couldn't pinpoint, but it felt like an invisible force was pushing her back. Tarin glanced at the sea and saw a boat with fishermen inside, but none were fishing just staring at them. 'Something's wrong, it's almost like the dagger doesn't want us to find it.'

'Probably because of the demons,' said Jim, 'we have company.'

Tarin glanced around but saw no one on the beach. 'Where? I can only see the men in the boat.'

'Look up.'

Tarin did and saw about thirty men and women looking over the cliff further up the beach. 'That's if they are demons, but what are they doing?'

'Look at their faces . . . they all have the same expression. It appears they were waiting for us I guess. I'd say you were right about them being able to sense the dagger's power.'

Tarin stared at the cliff face looking for somewhere it could be hidden. 'They can sense the dagger, but can't retrieve it. I wonder if the Gibson gang had any part in this. They knew Stokes and the hut he stayed in.'

'Yes, but from what the sergeant told us Stokes never breathed a word of it to anyone else. The Gibson gang might know some of the demons, but they would've stopped us coming here if they could.'

'True, but it's because of them we found the second hut. I don't believe we would've searched for a second if not for the gang chasing us. They may not have known we were searching for anything, just two cops who found their drug supply.'

'We need to get back up there before we're trapped down here.'

Tarin nodded. 'I'd rather search without them watching.'

They raced up the steps and onto the road. The demons, holding curved daggers, hurried towards them. Jim pulled out his gun and they stopped.

Tarin scratched her head. 'Demons don't fear bullets.'

'No,' said Jim, 'but gunfire might bring too much attention.'

'Maybe, but I think it's something else.' Tarin glanced around for any escape, and the only way was back over the ridge by the main road. She could see houses and what looked like beach front shops, but they were behind the demons. 'What we've been told about the dagger is it spreads a mist. If the mist touches a demon which has been shot, it'll send them back.'

'Could you use the dagger if we found it?'

'I doubt it. Elouise said only certain people can use it and little Jemima is one of them. It's still our best bet though as I don't believe we're going to run far.'

'We could get back to the ridge, but knowing our luck we'd bump into the Gibson gang.'

Tarin glanced at the demons and shuddered. They looked like normal men and women, standing still, staring at them. 'I don't think the demons like going down there because of the dagger.'

Jim raised an eyebrow. 'Are you saying we're safer down there?'

Tarin shrugged. 'I doubt very much we're safe anywhere at the moment. However, I don't believe they'll do anything until we find it.'

They climbed back down the steps and the demons moved forward. They stayed at the top blocking any attempt for them to go back.

Jim glanced back up at them. 'They must know we can run down the beach on the right.'

'Yes, they might be lesser demons, but they're not stupid. There must be a more powerful one leading them.'

The search along the beach was slow as neither knew what they were looking for. They inspected the cliff face, high and low, but found nothing.

'The demons are coming down,' said Jim, 'we might be getting close.'

Tarin carried on along the narrow beach. 'Yes, or we've walked straight past the dagger. The demons must've used people to look for them, and they never found it.'

Jim rubbed his eyes. 'I can't believe I'm saying this, but maybe the dagger didn't want them to retrieve it. You said it didn't want you to find it, but what about now?'

Tarin shook her head as the beach grew wider and the cliff ran inwards to a steep grass bank of about forty feet in length. 'I don't sense anything at the moment.' She glanced back at the demons edging closer. Behind them she saw others approach including some men on off-road motor bikes. 'The Gibson Gang have arrived.'

'Great,' said Jim, 'even if the dagger worked for us, it would have no effect on them.'

'What about the hill over there? Could you climb it in a hurry?'

'Of course, are you thinking of making a run for it?'

Tarin looked back towards the demons. They kept their distance and those on the bikes couldn't get past on the narrow beach. 'Not while there's a chance of finding the dagger, but at least I can't see any demons up there.' The strange sensation came back, and she saw a dark shadow on the cliff face. 'Something's happened . . . the dagger's waiting for us.'

Jim rubbed his head with the butt of his gun. 'Are you saying a knife has had a change of heart?'

'I can't explain it,' Tarin pointed at the cliff, 'but the dagger is hidden there.'

'Where? I can only see a shadow.'

Tarin ran over to the cliff. 'A shadow from what?' She saw the opening of a tunnel and entered. Tarin walked ten feet in the dark and saw something glow on the floor. She knelt and picked up a metal box.

'It's time to go,' Jim shouted.

Tarin ran out of the cave as the demons hurried onto the wider beach. She opened the box and pulled out the dagger. The demons stopped and a feeling of calm washed over her.

'I don't think it's working,' said Jim, with gun in hand. 'Get up the hill . . . I'll hold them off as long as I can.'

'Inspector Jim Murray, you'll do no such thing, we're in this together.'

Jim sighed. 'Fine, but run.'

They did as the demons gave chase. Tarin made her way up with ease as did Jim alongside her. She turned waving the dagger at the demons, and they stopped. The Gibson Gang rode onto the beach with two on each of the five bikes. Tarin knew the dagger wouldn't frighten them, and turned to run down the road when she heard the engines of more bikes. Nine bikers rode up and faced the beach.

One removed his helmet. 'Are you Tarin Barkley and Jim Murray?'

Tarin raised both eyebrows and glanced back at the demons which had stopped at the arrival of the bikers. 'We are.'

The biker opened his jacket and pulled out a broken spear. 'I'm Chains, and was asked to give you this . . . it's good at killing demons by all accounts.' He handed it over. 'You should turn your phone on as it took us ages to find you.'

'They're in my car,' said Jim, 'they blew it up.'

The biker nodded and grabbed a set of chains wrapped around the back of his bike. 'That would make it difficult to answer them. Would you like some help with those down there?'

Tarin gripped the spear and glanced down the slope. 'It would be most welcome, but they're not all demons.'

The bikers pulled out daggers of different shapes and sizes and rode down the hill. The biker who gave her the spear swung his chains turning any demon they hit into dust. Four of the bikers jumped off their bikes into the middle of a group of demons. Tarin watched as their speed sent half the demons back in seconds. She noticed the Gibson Gang pull out guns when a biker rode straight into them. Three off-rode bikes and their six riders lay on the beach. The other gang members rode forward when Jim fired his gun. He hit Snakehead in the shoulder, and they fled.

'Nice shot,' said Tarin.

'Thanks,' said Jim, 'but how did they know which were the demons? They never tried to kill any of the gang.'

'I've no idea, but at least they're on our side.'

Chains rode up the hill to them. 'Are you going back to the manor?'

Tarin stared at the clothes on the beach as the other bikers rode up. 'Yes, but we have no transport.'

'You can ride with us if you want,' said Chains, 'I've only known them a couple of days. It was Charles who asked me to give you the spear.'

Tarin smiled. 'I think that was just a way of getting you to come and help us, but I'm not going to complain at the moment.'

Chains nodded. 'You could be right, but it would be best if we get the dagger back safely.'

'The demons know we have it now, as there are some in a boat watching us.'

'I need to get in touch with my insurance company,' said Jim, and they both stared at him. 'They did blow up my car.'

CHAPTER TEN

The Hags of Harleston

Devon Fields glanced up from the table when Jack and Chloe entered the Prince of Wales pub. 'They're here.'

Benjamin turned his head. 'They were quick.'

Jack let Chloe sit before doing so himself, and drinks were already on the table. 'Thanks, I need this?'

Devon watched as Jack took a long swig. 'It went OK I take it.'

Jack put the glass down. 'Yeah, little Jemima is now on a plane heading to Australia for a long holiday with her parents. I needed a cold drink as I'm so hot.'

'What's the plan?' said Chloe, wearing a white t-shirt like Jack. 'Charles asked us to assist you but never said what you were doing.'

'We're seeking information on someone,' said Devon. 'We know he's from a wealthy family, and he owns a few businesses. We know nothing of his personal life, and he has no criminal record.'

Jack wiped his head with the back of a hand. 'What's he done to get our attention?'

'Last night, Chains and his friends sent ten of you know what back. Clive Montague,' she said quietly, as the pub was busy, 'owns the motorbikes they were using.'

'Are we not going to just ask him?'

Devon shook her head. 'Not yet, I'd like to find out what I can about him first.'

Chloe took a sip of her lager. 'A good place to get gossip, but it all depends on the type of person he is.'

Devon nodded. 'Let's hope people are not too frightened to mention his name.'

Jack leant on the table. 'So we sit in pubs waiting for people to talk, it could be worse.'

'No,' said Devon, 'we watch the premises of his main business and see who comes and goes. It might take days to find anything of interest, but I don't want to ask questions as it will reveal our presence.'

Jack rubbed his chin. 'Do you know any of the police here?'

Devon glanced around the bar. 'Not personally.'

'I know a couple of detectives,' said Benjamin, 'but they're all retired now. If we have no luck, I'll ask them what they know of the family.'

'We don't want to spend too much time on this,' said Devon, as she watched a man in his twenties drink back a pint at the bar. He picked up three more, and walked to a table near theirs with another man and a woman already sitting down.

'Fifteen years ago tonight it happened,' he said, and put the drinks down. 'My friend Stephen died that night in a sick and twisted ceremony.'

'Oh no, Darren,' said the woman, 'not this again. My friend Alice also died that night.'

'Yeah, and what did the police do? Nothing, that's what.'

'What could they do?' said the other man. 'They died in a fire.'

Darren sat down. 'Oh come on, Phil. Two children aged nine, and six old people unrelated to the children died in a barn fire. Everyone knew it was wrong but none said anything.'

Devon listened with interest and turned to the others who were also listening to the conversation.

'It's why you came back tonight,' said the woman, 'just so you can rant on about it.'

Darren shook his head. 'No, Sophie, I'm back because it's the anniversary of their deaths. I would like some answers as it has been fifteen years. Even now people are still too frightened to talk about it.'

'We know, but what's the point we can't do anything about it?'

'How about an investigation to find out what really happened? The families of the adults have never been questioned.'

Phil leant back in his chair. 'That's because they don't know anything.'

Darren waved a finger in front of them. 'You're wrong, all three of the women found had real teeth, yet two of them were known to have false teeth.'

'The Blanchards have gone . . . the last one died a year ago.'

'I know, and I'm going to the house later to take a look around.'

'That's against the law,' said Sophie, 'and just wrong.'

'Everything about it is wrong. The Blanchards may have gone, but the Culshaws and Montagues have questions to answer.'

Devon smiled at the last name as Benjamin, Jack and Chloe stared at her.

'It's not worth it,' said Phil, 'what are you hoping to find?'

'Evidence, maybe a room they perform ceremonies in.'

'Why would they have one of those?' said Sophie. 'You already said they performed it in a barn.'

Darren picked up his pint. 'Yeah, and while I think about it, why was there never a search for the murderer? They all died in a barn fire with the doors locked from the outside.'

An unshaven man put his phone away and approached the table. 'Did I hear you say you're going to the Blanchard house tonight?'

Darren looked up at him. 'Who's asking?'

'I'm Rick, and I'm desperate. My son went missing last night and I'm out of places to search for him.'

Darren turned to his friends. 'We have to help this man.'

'I'm in,' said Sophie.

'OK,' said Phil, 'it won't hurt if we're looking for a missing boy.'

Devon knew the man was lying. 'You will not go to the house.'

'Excuse me,' said Darren, 'who are you to tell us what we can or can't do?'

Devon showed them her warrant card. 'Police, trespass on that land and I'll have you arrested.'

'What about this man's son? We have to try.'

Devon turned to Rick. 'I take it you reported your son missing.'

Rick nodded. 'Yes, but not here. I'm from Metchly, five miles away.'

'It is unlikely for your son to be here, but if it eases your mind I will get the police to check out the house. None of you are to go trespassing.'

'That's wrong,' said Darren, as Rick walked back to the bar, 'his son has gone missing.'

Devon finished her drink. 'Then he shouldn't be in a pub drinking. We're going now so remember what I said.' Devon stood and the others followed suit as they walked out of the pub.

'What are you doing?' said Jack. 'That looked like a great opportunity to me.'

'Let's hope it still is,' said Devon. 'I saw something you didn't as it was behind your back. We just need to wait here a minute or two.'

Footsteps soon sounded as Darren approached with Phil and Sophie behind. 'Are you going to call your friends or was that a lie?'

Devon glanced around and saw a shop on the corner of a road to the left. 'Go over to the shop and keep out of sight from the pub.'

Darren scratched his head. 'What?'

'Just go, we will have to drive over there.' The three ran off as they climbed in the cars. She turned to Benjamin. 'Keep an eye on the pub to see if anyone comes out.'

Benjamin attached the seat belt and turned his head back towards the pub. 'What did you see?'

Devon drove off. 'I'll explain in a minute, but I'd like to know more of how those children died fifteen years ago.'

'So would I, and why wasn't it investigated.'

'Questions would've been asked, but it appears six of those who died were from the richest families around here.'

'If it happened fifty years ago I can imagine it being covered up, but not fifteen years ago.'

Devon turned left onto the road and right on the next as they passed the shop. She saw the three waiting in an alley and parked up. 'Yes, but if demons were involved it changes things.'

They climbed out as Jack and Chloe pulled up and all four made their way to the alley. The three from the pub hid by a skip, and looked somewhat nervous.

'We need to keep an eye on the pub,' said Devon, and the three walked over to them.

Darren rubbed his nose. 'What's going on?'

'I want some answers,' said Devon, 'and as I just saved your lives I'm sure you're going to give them to me.'

Darren stepped back. 'We don't know anything, and how do you mean . . . saved our lives?'

'You know a lot more than us, and I don't believe anyone else here would tell us anything.' Devon shook her head at him. 'You might want to be a little quieter when talking of certain things in a pub. I saw Rick make a phone call while he listened to your conversation.'

'I don't understand,' said Sophie, 'what difference would that make?'

'Why would he be sitting in a pub if he's meant to be looking for his son? Whoever he was talking to would've been waiting at the house for you. Only death waited for you there.'

'That's crap,' said Darren, 'are you really a cop?'

Devon nodded. 'I'm a Detective Inspector. This is my Uncle Benjamin, and my friends Jack and Chloe. None of us have ever heard of this fire which killed your friends. If what you say did happen, it would've made big headlines.'

'It's true, but it never made any front page. Are you gonna look in to it?'

'Rick just came out of the pub,' said Chloe, 'and four cars have just pulled up. He's with someone else.'

Phil walked out of the alley to take a look. 'That's Tony the barman.'

Devon watched as eight men climbed out of the cars and Rick spoke with them.

'Shit,' said Darren, 'are they after us?'

Devon checked the shard of glass which wasn't glowing. 'You touched a nerve in there, and they want to shut you up. I need to know what happened fifteen years ago.'

'Our friends died,' said Darren, 'Stephen and Alice burnt to death in a barn with six others, three old men and three old women. They were Cedric and Victoria Montague, Geoffrey and Cecilia Blanchard, and Roderick and Violet Culshaw. They had no connections with our friends and shouldn't have been there. Only nine years old, and they were miles from home. The fire was seen from a distance and when the first person arrived it was too late. The doors had been chained shut.'

Devon rubbed her chin. 'You mentioned false teeth.'

'Yeah, two of the women had them, but the bodies of the women found in the fire had real teeth.'

'Another six have arrived,' said Chloe. 'Rick and the barman have climbed into one of the cars and drove off. The other men have split up and some are coming this way.'

'OK,' said Devon, 'we best get these home.'

'Not until we take care of those coming this way,' said Jack, 'they'll only end up coming down the alley.'

Devon raised an eyebrow. 'How many are there?'

'Four,' said Chloe, 'it won't be a problem.'

'Is it wise?' said Benjamin.

'We don't have much choice as our weapons are in the car and can't get to them without being seen.'

Devon ushered the others behind the skip as Jack and Chloe stepped out of the alley. She heard a few thuds and the odd groan before Jack and Chloe returned. They both dragged a body each and hid them behind the skip before fetching the other two.

Sophie stared with open mouth. 'Is this normal police procedure?'

Jack sat an unconscious man up the wall. 'Probably not, but I'm not a cop.'

'Neither am I,' said Chloe, as she passed Jack a sheathed dagger which he attached to the back of his jeans.

'I used to be one,' said Benjamin, 'but I'm retired now. Devon is, of course.'

Darren scratched his chin. 'Wouldn't it be easier if you got the police here?'

Devon considered it. 'No, not if they're covering up those murders. We best get you home before you get deeper into something you would not like.'

'What about our friends?'

'They're dead,' said Devon. 'I will find out what happened, but don't expect to find the story printed in any newspaper.'

Jack hurried down to the end of the alley and glanced out making sure it was clear. 'Which way?'

'Left,' said Phil, 'then the first right, and our house is on the corner.'

Darren stepped out of the alley with the others. 'Why are you walking when you have cars?'

'We need answers,' said Devon, 'and when we get you to safety we will start asking these men questions.'

'We should come with you as we want answers too.'

Devon shook her head as she walked down the road. 'It's too dangerous and you live here.'

'I don't, I'm visiting.'

'You're stopping at ours tonight,' said Sophie, 'and we don't want trouble at our door.'

Devon noticed Jack stop further ahead and put up his hand. 'What is it?' she asked as they approached him.

'I just saw some of those guys go into a house over there. One of them kicked the door open.'

'Oh shit,' said Phil, 'that's our house. What are they doing?'

'What do you think?' said Devon. 'You might not know Rick, but someone knows you and where you live.'

'Yeah,' said Sophie, 'Tony the barman. What are we gonna do now?'

Phil took out his mobile phone. 'I'm calling the police.'

Devon put a hand on his arm. 'No, you do that and you will soon disappear. I know what we're dealing with here, and the only way to help you, is to stop them.'

Phil put his phone in a pocket. 'I know what we're dealing with, some rich crooks and their thugs.'

'They may be part of it, but it's much worse than that.' Devon rubbed her chin. 'What do you know of them?'

'Not a lot really, Clive Montague isn't the kind of person I socialise with. His grandmother was one of the women who died in the barn fire.'

'I presume he still lives in the family home, but what about his businesses? Does he have any around here?'

Phil nodded. 'He has a warehouse near town. You'll always find his thugs hanging around there.'

'Not tonight,' said Jack, 'they're out looking for you three. We have to go and check it out.' He turned to Phil. 'How far away is it?'

Phil scratched his head. 'About fifteen to twenty minutes if you're walking.'

'What about us?' said Darren. 'We're not waiting around here.'

'You come with us,' said Devon, 'but you do as we say.'

Jack patted Phil on the shoulder. 'You and I'll go ahead and clear the way.'

Phil's eyes grew big. 'Are you serious?'

'Sneaking past them will take too long and I don't like the idea of them being behind us. Darren can show the others the way.'

Phil shrugged and ran ahead. 'Come on then.'

'It's been a strange night,' said Benjamin, 'it's not going to plan.'

Devon watched the others run off. 'It wasn't going to plan when I went to the cemetery only to find you'd been hiding in the church all day. I prefer it all neat and tidy but you know we don't get that with whom we're dealing with. As for it going to plan we never really had one, but we got more information than I expected.'

Darren turned to them. 'I'm not sure I trust you. It's no coincidence you're here tonight.'

'No, we're investigating Clive Montague and came here to find out what we can about him. I did check with records but nothing and not a lot about the family.'

'You said there's something worse than him, what's that?'

Devon thought about it but decided not to tell him. 'I hope you don't find out, but I've a feeling you will.'

'That's not encouraging,' said Sophie, 'are you trying to frighten us?'

'A gang of men just broke into your home, you should already be frightened.' Devon put a hand on her shoulder. 'You're safe with us, you saw my friends in action.'

'They're frightening,' said Darren. 'Jack's gone to beat up any in front, and Chloe's behind hoping for others to sneak up on us. Are they robots?'

Devon laughed. 'No, but when you see them training they're something else. I can fight but not at their speed.'

They walked on for fifteen minutes and turned down another road. On the other side Devon saw trees halfway down. Jack and Phil waited at the end behind a hedge.

'Any problems?' she asked.

'It was amazing,' said Phil, 'he put four down before they knew we were there.'

'What happened to you?' said Sophie. 'You've always hated violence.'

'I still do, but they broke into our home.'

'The warehouse is around the corner,' said Jack, 'I saw a couple of men go in and there are cars parked outside.'

'We better forget going inside for now,' said Devon, 'we have no idea what else might be in there.'

'Back to my plan,' said Darren. 'If they're out here, they won't be at the house waiting for us.'

'What's the point?' said Devon. 'The last Blanchard died a year ago so whoever owns the house now would've changed everything.'

Phil shook his head. 'No, it was left to Clive Montague, and he hasn't changed anything.'

'Are you sure?'

'Yeah, everyone here knows it.'

Devon clasped her hands together. 'Where's the house?'

'Outside town, the three large country houses are close to each other. If we walk, it would take us nearly an hour.'

'Forget that,' said Jack, and turned to Devon. 'Give me your keys, Chloe and I'll get the cars.'

Devon took the keys out of a pocket and handed them over. 'We'll be in the trees over there.' She crossed over as Jack and Chloe ran down the road.

Darren rubbed his eyes. 'I think we got in over our heads. Coming back here after a few years and the last Blanchard gone, I really thought people would talk about what happened.'

Benjamin leant up a tree. 'It just shows how important it is to certain people to keep the deaths quiet. Eight people died, and we can assume at least five of them were innocent.'

'Only five?' said Devon.

'It could be all eight, but we don't know what roles the husbands had in the whole business.'

Devon turned to Darren. 'After the fire did any other members of the families arrive like distant cousins?'

'If they did I never heard about it.' Darren folded his arms. 'I said all along it was some sort of devil worshipping ceremony which went wrong.'

Sophie sighed. 'You know you're talking to the police, she'll have you sectioned.'

Darren shrugged. 'Something happened that night, and people are still keeping it secret. Even the police here believe they were all innocent in the barn, so it makes you think which side they're on.'

'I won't be keeping secrets,' said Devon, 'but I can guess what happened that night for the most part. I won't be disclosing it to you just yet as I need more information. You might be able to figure it out yourself if you concentrate on one piece of information.'

Darren screwed up his nose. 'What's that?'

'False teeth.'

'What about the Blanchards?' said Benjamin. 'How many children did the couple who died in the fire have?'

'Two, I think,' said Darren.

'No,' said Phil, 'they had three. The eldest, killed herself after her parents died, the middle one died when he crashed his car, and the youngest died last year from an illness. I say youngest but he was about fifty.'

'There's another car,' said Sophie, 'it's just pulled up outside the warehouse.'

Devon glanced through the trees and saw two men climb out the car. 'Are any of those Clive Montague?'

Phil shook his head. 'No, the one in the black t-shirt is Lloyd Culshaw, a right nasty piece of work.'

Devon watched the man saunter into the warehouse. 'Do you know that for a fact or just a rumour?'

'Everyone knows it. He once beat a guy and put him in a coma for parking in his spot. He was never charged for it and when the man made a recovery he moved away. Culshaw isn't the kind of person you want to get the wrong side of.'

Devon heard a twig snap. 'We're not alone.'

A figure stepped out from behind pointing a gun at them. 'You're quite correct.'

'Clive Montague,' said Phil.

'You have a big mouth,' said Montague, 'one which will cost you your life.'

'Wait,' said Devon, as she stared at the man who looked about thirty-five with neatly trimmed hair. 'You have to tell me who actually died in that barn all those years ago.'

'Big mouth there has already told you, six old people and two children.'

Devon needed to give Jack and Chloe time, that's if they hadn't been seen leaving. 'That's a lie, as the three women mentioned were not in the barn when it burnt down.'

Montague smiled. 'You're good, but then you are a detective. Start walking to the warehouse now and I might tell you all about the night of the fire.'

They walked through the trees into the street and crossed the road towards the warehouse. Men stood outside as the five were marched into the building and patted down. Devon wore a thin jacket and the man who checked her for weapons didn't notice the shard of glass in her pocket, although he took her gun. They were taken to a canteen where Rick and Lloyd Culshaw stood drinking beers.

Lloyd pulled a knife from the back of his jeans and grinned. 'This is new, Clive, you pay men to do the work and capture them yourself.'

Montague nodded as he indicated at the others to sit at the tables. 'I'm sure Rick will tell us he herded them here.'

Rick rubbed his neck. 'Yes, and the lads are out there looking for the other two.'

Clive raised an eyebrow. 'Another two?'

Devon breathed deep, as Montague hadn't seen Jack and Chloe.

'Yeah,' said Rick, 'a man and a woman are still out there.'

'This could be a fun night.' Clive turned to Devon and Benjamin. 'You were the ones with the guns, where are your friends?'

Devon shrugged. 'Like Rick said, they're running from your cronies, as there must've been eight of them.'

'They won't get far,' said Rick, 'the guys after them are good.'

Clive nodded. 'Soon as they get here we'll go to the house.'

'Whose house?' said Devon.

'Keep ya mouth shut,' Lloyd snapped, 'before I use my knife on you.'

'No,' said Clive, 'you won't do anything until we get to the house. I don't mind a little chat until we go and have fun.' He stared at Devon. 'The Blanchard House, of course.'

Devon rubbed her chin. 'I was told they all died.'

'Yet, you've already worked out that's not true.'

'For the most part, Cecilia Blanchard is still living, as were all three women after the fire. What I'm struggling with are the husbands.'

Clive clapped his hands together. 'Very good, but I'd hardly call it living.'

'The Hags of Harleston,' Lloyd laughed. 'They live together in their little coven.'

Devon felt repulsed by the man, she could sense his cruelty. 'So the ritual worked.'

'You could say that,' said Clive, 'but not exactly how they expected. Would you like to know what happened?'

Devon nodded.

Clive pulled out a chair and sat down. He put the gun on the table in front of him. 'It started years before the night of the fire. Three women, from the richest families around here, became friends. They had one thing in common, cheating husbands. My grandmother, Victoria Montague, blamed it on her age although she was only in her forties. Cecelia Blanchard and Violet Culshaw started to believe it of themselves. Life was passing them by and soon it would be all over. They were angry with their husbands, of course, but the thought of dying from old age consumed them. There was nothing they could do as death comes to us all. One day when the women were in their sixties a man came along with a spell which would make them young once more. Sacrifice a child and take their youth. They prepared in haste and paid certain people to get them what they needed. They made mistakes in their haste to get it done. The first was it should've been three children they sacrificed, but for some reason only two were kidnapped. They also sacrificed their husbands out of revenge, and three women to make it looked like they died.'

Clive rubbed his hands and smiled. 'As I said it didn't work out how they expected. I don't know if it was the missing child, the adults they sacrificed, or the spell was no good, but it backfired on them. They wanted eternal life and youth, they got eternal life but that was all. The women were the ones who chained the doors shut.'

'Why bother,' said Devon, 'if it didn't work?'

'The women had no idea at the time as the effects would not show until the following morning. No one could see the bodies until they were destroyed. I can still hear my grandmother screaming the following morning. She got eternal life but looked twice as old, and quite hideous.'

'This bores me,' said Lloyd, 'where are the others?'

'Patience,' said Clive, 'I've told them what happened and I want to know why an armed detective is here.'

'Rick,' Lloyd snapped, 'go and find them.'

'Well,' said Clive, as the unshaven man left the room, 'why are you here?'

Devon sat back in the chair. 'I was coming to see you but it was late, so we had dinner in the pub.'

Clive leant forward on the table. 'Were you going to arrest me?'

Devon shook her head. 'No, it's about missing persons, not that anyone knows who they are.'

Clive's eyes grew large. 'How can you know people are missing if you don't know who they are?' He rubbed his chin. 'What do I have to do with it?'

'A group of bikers have vanished and their bikes, purchased by your company, are on a pub car park.'

Clive shrugged. 'You're a cop and must know what bikers are like. They're probably drunk somewhere and will be back.'

Devon decided to test him. 'No, from what I was told they vanished, they're dust.'

Clive gripped the table as his manner turned sour. 'What do you know of them?'

Devon didn't answer as the door opened and Jack, with arms behind his back, walked in followed by Rick.

Lloyd grinned. 'About time.'

Jack's arms shot forward and pointed a gun at the man. 'Drop it.'

'Don't even think about it,' said Chloe from the doorway, as Clive reached for his gun. She stepped inside pointing one at him and Devon took his.

'Rick, you stinking coward,' Lloyd shouted.

'I had no choice . . . you should've seen how they beat your men.'

Lloyd ran at Jack with knife in hand. Jack sidestepped, tripped him with his foot and hit him across the back. Lloyd flew forward and landed on his front. He didn't move and Jack rolled him over to see the knife in his chest.

Clive stared down at the body. 'He's gonna be pissed about that.'

Devon stood. 'Come on, Clive has invited us to Blanchard House.'

Jack grabbed Clive's shoulder and stood him up. 'What about Rick?'

'He's coming with us, but we can drop these three off somewhere safe.'

'No way,' said Darren, 'I just found out my friends didn't die in a fire but were sacrificed, I have to go.'

'I don't want to go,' said Sophie, 'but I'm not going home when those men could wake up anytime.'

Devon sighed. 'OK, but when we get there you will stay behind us. I'll go with Clive, and he's driving.'

Clive raised an eyebrow. 'After what I said you still want to go there?'

Devon nodded. 'It's because of what you told me I want to go.'

Thirty minutes later Clive pressed a small remote and a set of gates opened. He drove through and up to a large house. Devon saw a faint light in one of the windows on the far right, but all the others were dark.

Clive parked the car. 'Welcome to Blanchard House.'

Darren, sat in the back, opened the door. 'You're way too cheerful.'

'I've spent many happy nights here, and you do know I own the place.'

They climbed out the cars and approached the old Gothic house. Clive opened the main doors to a large dark hall. The group followed him to a set of double doors at the end where he opened them to a large lit room. Devon stepped inside where five men, in hooded robes, stood near an altar. She knew without looking at the glass they were demons. Devon glanced left and saw three old women sat at a table.

'Welcome, Clive,' said the demon behind the altar, 'we were expecting you. However, it appears, they have the guns.'

Clive rubbed his hands together. 'I know, but they insisted on coming here anyway.'

'You might as well get over there,' said Devon, 'and you,' she said pointing the gun at Rick.

The three old women stood and moved around the table. Their faces had deep wrinkles of someone who had lived many lives. They moved unnaturally in jerky motions, with one bent over on hands with knees twisted out of shape.

'That's just too creepy,' said Sophie, as the women stopped by the demons.

The demon behind the altar clasped his hands together. 'Are you going to arrest them? They are murderers.'

Devon stared at the demon. 'I'm here for the one who coerced them into performing the ritual.'

'She knows about demons,' said Clive, 'she said as much. I bet she's one of those who have been hunting you down.'

The demons pulled their hoods back to reveal red eyes and pointed teeth. The one who spoke grew to eight feet tall.

'Stuff this,' said Phil, and turned to run.

'I don't think so,' said Lloyd, as he entered the room, 'no one's going anywhere.'

Jack pointed a gun at him. 'Get over there with the others.'

Lloyd scowled. 'Bullets cannot kill me.'

Jack shrugged. 'Maybe not, but I'm sure a bullet to the head will knock you out until all the fun is over.'

'What's the point in this?' said Clive, as Lloyd stomped over to him. 'All you're doing is prolonging your deaths, this is no game.'

Devon laughed. 'It is to your demon friends. As I said, we came here looking for you. I never expected you would make it easy and bring us straight here. Is that the Lord of Chaos?'

The large demon growled. 'How do you know who I am?'

'A demon dressed as a biker mentioned it before being sent back.'

Chloe opened a bundle she was carrying and removed two swords. She passed one to Jack who still held a gun.

The demon snarled. 'Do you believe you can defeat us with those?'

Jack shrugged. 'I do have a gun, and to be honest I'm a little tired.'

'Take them,' the demon shouted.

Devon pulled out the shard of glass and held it up as the demons ran forward. They stopped as beams of lights shot from the glass. All five demons were covered in white energy as were the three women, Clive, and Lloyd. The latter fell to the ground holding his chest where the knife had entered.

Clive stepped back. 'What just happened?'

Devon stared at the body. 'He just died from the knife wound he sustained not long ago. Whatever power the demon gave you to live forever has just been taken away.'

'Kill them,' the Lord of Chaos shouted, 'the light does not harm us.'

The four lesser demons ran forward as shots were fired and their robes soon dropped to the floor covered in dust. The Lord of Chaos was shot several times, but he still stood. It ripped off the robes as its hands grew into long claws. The demon strode forward and swung a long arm at Chloe. She ducked underneath as her sword sliced into its side. Jack charged forward and spun, beheading the demon as it reared back in pain.

Clive tried to run only for Rick to pick up Lloyd's knife and stab him in the chest. Rick dropped the knife and walked towards the doors.

Devon pointed her gun at him. 'Where do you think you're going?'

'To get my son, Montague kidnapped him so I'd do his bidding.'

Devon lowered the gun to let him pass. She glanced over at the three old women who stood motionless. 'Are they dead?'

Benjamin stepped over to the nearest and nudged her with his gun. Cracks appeared on the wrinkled face as she fell apart. Benjamin stepped back quickly. 'You could say that.' The other two dropped to the floor and turned to dust only a lot slower than a demon. 'I never expected that to happen, but at a guess I'd say time has taken back the years they stole.'

'How do you work that out?' said Devon. 'It's only been fifteen years.'

'I know, but they took eight lives and the ritual backfired and aged them.' Benjamin glanced around the room. 'I best call Charles to get this place cleaned up.'

Sophie walked over to them shaking her head. 'After all this you're going to cover it up?'

Devon nodded. 'Of course we are . . . you can't have this type of thing in the papers.'

'What about our friends?'

Darren nudged some of the dust with his foot. 'They've been avenged and those who killed them will never hurt anyone again.' He turned to Devon. 'Did you know this would happen?'

Devon shook her head. 'No, but I hoped it would. I'll have those men who are still out there picked up and you can all go home.'

Darren rubbed his chin. 'Is this something you do a lot?'

'It's becoming a habit.'

'Only I've been thinking.'

'No.'

'I was right about what happened all along.'

'No.'

Darren smiled. 'I was going to write a blog of what happened once I got home, but this is much better. You're driving me back and the conversation will be interesting.'

Devon sighed.

CHAPTER ELEVEN
Demon Slayer

Rachel Cooper stared at the computer screen. 'If anyone read my internet history they'd come to the conclusion I'm a right psycho.'

Sharon Keane nodded. 'I thought the same thing, but if anyone asks just say you're an author.'

Rachel smiled. 'I might even write a book when this is all over. What I need now is some inspiration on what to search for.'

'There are plenty here to ask, the Manor house is full of intelligent people. Charles, Elouise, Arthur, and Peter have been doing this for a long time.'

'I know, but I want to find something to show I'm contributing and Peter's not well at the moment.'

Sharon laughed. 'You got rid of a demon lord . . . I'd say that qualifies you.'

'Yeah, but others are out there risking their lives while I'm sat at a computer.'

'Have you tried the riddle from the poet?'

Rachel shuffled through some papers on the desk and found the riddle. She read through it and typed "Blood soaked earth from battles past" into the search engine. The page changed, and she saw many headlines but nothing she wanted and clicked on page two. She scrolled down and found something. 'What about this one?'

Sharon glanced over at the screen. 'Which one?'

Rachel put her finger on the screen. 'This one, it says five battles the church doesn't want you to know about.'

Sharon slid her chair over. 'I've not seen that one before, try it.'

Rachel clicked onto the site and five different stories appeared. She read each one while scrolling down the page. 'This is it, the first isn't too far away and you'll recognise the fourth.'

Sharon raised both eyebrows. 'Print it off, and we'll take it into the battle room.'

'It's not a battle room, just a room where they discuss everything.'

They walked into the meeting hall as many of them called it and saw Devon had returned. She was discussing the previous night's events with Charles, Elouise, Arthur, and Peter, the latter looking pale.

'When will they be back with the dagger?' Devon asked.

'Sometime today,' said Elouise, 'they could have arrived here yesterday, but decided to take a longer route to make sure no one was following them.'

Charles glanced up. 'Hello, my dears, any news from Sean and Rob?'

'They're investigating a sighting in the country side,' said Rachel, 'but we've found something.'

Charles sighed. 'Not off the devil's highway, you can't believe everything you read on there.'

Rachel smiled as she placed a printed copy of the page in front of each of those sitting at the table. 'I'm sure it was a much better system back in your day when information was passed by word of mouth, or even written in chalk. Of course, we don't believe everything we read on the internet, but we do find valuable information on there. Not every rumour is a lie, not every story is fake news. If you read the fourth article, you'll recognise it.'

Charles picked his glasses off the table and put them on before reading. 'Oh yes, it's where you defeated the demons at the hospital. How is it the one who owns the site knows of the place?'

Rachel shrugged. 'I've no idea, but the first article tells of a place which is less than an hour away, and we're going to check it out.'

Charles nodded. 'I'm coming with you.'

Devon stood. 'I will see who's available to go.'

Rachel couldn't help looking at Peter, whose face looked strained from pain. 'Are you OK?'

Peter stared up at her. 'I'm fine . . . my back's playing up is all.'

'Sharon and I are nurses . . . we might be able to get you something for it.'

Peter shook his head. 'There's nothing you can give me to ease the pain, there's nothing anyone can do for me. The hump was caused by demons, and the pain has got worse since the bang to my head.'

Rachel pulled up outside a set of gates to Colebrook Farm. They already knew it was empty, and she could see it had gone to ruin. She climbed out the car as did Sharon, Charles, and Dan. Another car pulled up behind as Devon, Jack, and Chloe got out.

Dan opened the boot and took out a bow and quiver of arrows. 'Wait here while we go and check it out.'

Devon sighed and took the glass shard from an inside pocket as Dan and Jack ran down the long path to the farm. 'There's a reason I carry this everywhere.'

Rachel followed down the path as the two men entered the farmhouse. 'I thought he was a builder not Robin Hood.'

Charles smiled. 'He is, but has an amazing talent with a bow. He had never used one until he fired the one he carries. I've never seen him miss.'

Dan stepped out the front door just as they arrived. 'It's clear . . . sort of.'

Devon raised an eyebrow. 'What's that supposed to mean?'

'We found a dead demon in there?'

Dan walked back inside and the others followed into what looked like a living room. Rachel stopped in her tracks at the site of the demon lying there. It looked about eight feet and had horns on the top of its head.

Dan scratched his chin as Devon stepped out the back door. 'Why didn't it turn to dust? I shot an arrow in its chest and still nothing.'

'Because it is dead,' said Charles. 'We usually just send them back, but they can be destroyed, so I have heard. I have never seen it, but I would say this is it. Although, I am sure the body should still turn to dust.'

'It's all too confusing for me,' said Jack, 'does it matter if it didn't turn to dust? I thought it was their spirits which were sent back.'

Charles nodded. 'You are quite correct, it is confusing. When demons are summoned a door opens, and they step through whole. When they get sent back, their bodies cannot travel with the spirit as there is no door so it disintegrates. You can see the other clothes around the room where other demons were sent back.'

'This one wasn't,' said Dan, 'it's still here.'

'I know and it disturbs me deeply.' Charles removed his glasses and rubbed his eyes. 'It appears the demon's spirit was destroyed and not sent back. It would take someone or something with great power to do such a thing.'

Devon stepped back inside. 'It was definitely a something, but why would another demon do this?'

'Demons have no loyalty to anyone, but they do have the same goal. The lesser demons will obey their masters for their own motives and protection. What makes you believe another demon did this?'

'Footprints, the ones outside are different to these on this thing. Each foot had three digits.'

Rachel glanced down at the demon's feet and saw it had two, pincer like toes, curved, and pointed at each other.

'So there's another on the loose out there,' said Dan, 'but what are we going to do with this one?'

'I will have it burned,' said Charles, 'this whole place needs destroying.'

~ ~ ~ ~

Dan sat at the table in the meeting hall, with Charles, Elouise, Arthur, Devon, and Benjamin. 'Is there any end to all of this? We keep sending them back only for more to appear.'

Charles glanced across the table at him. 'Don't lose faith . . . we have caused them a lot of damage. Some of those sent back were dangerous demon lords. Every little victory works in our favour if there is a final battle.'

'We have a lot more warriors,' said Elouise, 'and weapons to send them back.'

Dan shrugged. 'I wouldn't call myself a warrior.'

'Yet, like everyone else, you fought bravely.'

Devon held up a police report. 'I'm going to investigate a couple of murders.'

Charles rubbed his hands together. 'I read the report and couldn't find a connection to demons. I do believe one of the deaths was an accident.'

Devon opened her notepad. 'I was not convinced, so I called Inspector Doyle for extra information.'

Benjamin smiled. 'He got the promotion?'

Devon nodded. 'They needed someone to fill in while I'm here. I asked him to find out what he could, and although the murders happened in a different county, he got the information I needed. One man had his throat cut and the other was kicked to death by a horse. I thought it curious how a man who worked in computers and lived in the city ended up dead in a field where no horses had been on the day. Of course, horses with riders may have passed through without anyone else knowing, but I don't believe it to be so. The two men also knew each other and were part of a group interested in mythology which became demon mythology. I believe the other members are in danger.'

'The police there must believe the same as you do,' said Dan, 'or that one of the other members is the murderer.'

Devon shook her head. 'They believe the one was mugged after leaving a pub and had his throat cut, the other an accident. Of course, you are correct in saying one of the members could be the murderer.'

Charles put a finger to his lips. 'Do you believe they found anything in their interest of demon mythology?'

'I don't know . . . maybe something found them. One of the three remaining members of the group could be a demon as I only have information on one of them.'

'You have his address?'

Devon turned a page over in the notepad. 'Yes, and to his warehouse.'

'I'll go with you,' said Dan, 'we might get to send more back.'

Elouise smiled. 'These acts of bravery are the reason we will prevail.'

Devon stood. 'We leave in an hour . . . I don't want to get there too late.'

Dan watched her walk away. 'Where's Peter?'

'Having a lie down,' said Elouise, 'his back is causing him pain.'

'Can't we do anything for him?'

Elouise shook her head. 'He will not take anything and refuses to go to hospital.'

Dan glanced out the window as two black jeeps pulled up. 'We have company?'

Charles stood and walked over to the window as armed guards climbed out of the cars followed by a man in a suit. 'I wondered when they would show up.'

'Is it William?' Elouise asked.

'No, it's Bernard.'

Benjamin turned to the window. 'Who are these men?'

Charles returned to his seat. 'Sir William Conrad, a friend of ours, and Bernard is his right-hand man. He's the one who organises all the clean-up jobs.'

The door opened and a tall man, followed by an armed guard walked in. He nodded his head to them and placed a brief case on the table. 'Good afternoon, Sir William sent me to see if there was any news.'

Charles removed his glasses and wiped them. 'Good afternoon . . . and not a lot since I spoke to him over the phone earlier. We have news of two strange deaths which will be investigated later.'

'Sir William said you have the dagger here.'

'No, it has been found but hasn't arrived yet.'

'What? Why is it taking so long?'

'They took a detour to make sure no one followed them, but you must know this already.'

'Sir William believes it should be taken to the mansion where we can protect it.'

'I'm afraid we have no say in that.' said Elouise. 'The monastery has told us to keep the dagger until this business is resolved, and the person who retrieved it is the custodian.'

'Demons have been here a long time, it will never be resolved.'

Charles shook his head. 'No, and we will not always need the dagger. What we have now is different, the demon numbers are growing, and something out there is more powerful than we have seen before.'

Bernard frowned. 'Sir William will not be happy about this. He would like the other artefacts you have. As you say there are more demons appearing every day, and they need protecting.'

Arthur raised both eyebrows. 'The demons need protecting?'

Bernard turned a little red and looked flustered. 'No, the artefacts.'

'As Elouise told you,' said Charles, 'we cannot give what does not belong to us. Weapons and artefacts belong to those who find them.'

Dan rubbed his eyes and stared up at the man. He took an instant dislike to him. 'Whose side are you on?'

Bernard turned to him. 'Excuse me, what is that supposed to mean?'

'Locking up the few weapons which kill demons is only protecting demons. The only way to stop them is to send them back, so why take such weapons out of the fight?'

Bernard shook his head. 'I don't, but Sir William believes they're better off served at the mansion, and he is the one with the money.'

'I do not think so,' said Arthur, with almost a scowl. 'We three here, and Peter, have never asked him for a penny. Sir William pays for the clean-ups and some information, yet it is us who do all the work.'

Bernard turned scarlet. 'Are you forgetting his security force?'

'How can we?' said Charles. 'Every time you arrive it's with armed guards. William knows who finds an artefact decides on where it should go or uses it.'

'He will not be happy.' Bernard picked up the case and walked out of the room.

'I'm not over impressed with your friend,' said Dan. 'It's a shame Devon left when she did.'

'Reverend Simon's shard is in the cabinet,' said Charles. 'However, Bernard is not a demon. His behaviour was a little strange, almost as if they want to protect the mansion and forget the rest of the world.'

'I have never trusted him,' said Elouise, 'but I'm surprised at William.'

Dan picked up the quiver in the weapons room and inspected the arrows. Most were iron-tipped with two being the special arrows.

Jack walked in and took his sword off a shelf. 'Is everything OK, only I heard you sounded a little fed up earlier?'

Dan put the quiver over his shoulder. 'I'm fine, I've been thinking about my son. He's in America due to have an operation on his spine.'

'How come you're not over there with him?'

'I wouldn't be much help and besides I want to help make this a safe place for when he comes home.'

Jack nodded. 'I can understand that, I don't have any kids, just a younger brother.'

'Where's he?'

'With friends at the moment, I don't want him involved in this.'

Dan grabbed his bow. 'Does he know about the demons?'

'Yeah, he was there when I retrieved the sword, as were my friends.'

'I'd get them here as soon as possible.'

'I just said I don't want him involved.'

'He may already be involved. If the demons find out who you are they will attack your brother and friends. It's a lot safer here for them.'

Jack rubbed his chin. 'I never thought about that . . . let's hope there's enough room here with all the police and priests.'

'There's not that many, and there's plenty of room. I think the Elders had already sorted that before any of us came here.'

Jack smiled. 'The Elders?'

'It's what Joe calls them. Did they tell you about the visitor we had?'

'I heard he wanted to take all the weapons, well he's not having this sword.'

'Nor these arrows,' said Dan. 'I might not be the one who retrieved them, but they were given to me.'

'Yeah, because you're the best archer we have.'

'I'm the only one and I'd never used one before I came here, but I was good at darts.'

'Check your ancestry, as I hadn't used a sword before I picked this up.'

The door opened and Joe entered. 'Devon's waiting for you, but she said I can't go.'

Dan smiled. 'You're not ready yet, and we need you to look after Sarah.'

Joe frowned. 'I'm mad, not ten years old.'

'You're neither of those, but Sarah trusts you more than the rest of us.'

'She told me I'd be going to fight them soon, but she's not sure when.'

Dan raised an eyebrow. 'Sarah said that?'

Joe nodded. 'Yeah, and I have to be there or everyone dies.'

Jack patted him on the shoulder. 'We best keep you here, safe, until the right time.'

Joe scrunched up his nose. 'I walked into that.'

'It's for the best,' said Dan. 'You wouldn't want to go against Devon's wishes, would you?'

Joe threw his hands up in the air and turned around. 'She doesn't need a weapon, all she has to do is stare at them, and they'd run away.'

Dan laughed. 'Don't tell her that.'

~ ~ ~ ~

Two cars pulled up outside The Realm of Gadgets Warehouse. Devon climbed out the first with Jack and Chloe. Dan, Simon, Benjamin, and Arthur got out of the second.

Jack stared at the advertising posters in the windows. 'It looks like a nerd's paradise.'

'Oi,' said Chloe, 'I was a nerd . . . well I was always called one.'

Devon pushed on the door which opened. She glanced down and saw the lock hanging off. 'Be on guard.'

Jack stepped over to her with sword in hand. 'What is it?'

'Someone's forced their way inside.' Devon took out the glass shard which didn't glow. 'There are no demons here.'

They stepped inside to a warehouse shop and walked through a door behind the counter. Devon saw rack of shelves full with computers, laptops, and game consoles. On the floor lay clothes covered in dust.

'Over here,' said Arthur, running to the right where a man lay on his front. He checked for a pulse. 'He's alive . . . I need some water and a cloth.'

'There's a kitchen over there,' said Simon, 'I will get them.'

'Let me go first,' said Chloe, and they walked on past the unconscious man.

Dan helped Arthur turn the man over and put him in a sitting position up the racking. Jack walked off to check out the rest of the warehouse, while Devon waited to see if the man regained conscious and noticed a lump on his forehead. Simon and Chloe returned with a bowl of water and a towel. Arthur dipped an end of the towel in the water, rubbed it onto the man's head, and he stirred.

Devon noticed Jack on the far left. He waved his hand indicating he had found something. She hurried over and followed him down behind the racking. Lying there motionless was another large demon.

Jack tapped it with his sword. 'It's dead.'

Devon nodded. 'We best find out what the man knows.'

The man sat there with both hands on his face. 'I thought they were friends, but they were monsters. I never believed demons were real but that's what they were, and they wanted to sacrifice me.'

'You're safe now,' said Simon, 'they've gone.'

Devon crouched in front of the man. 'You're Glen Smith, and part of a group of three before the other two joined you not long ago?'

Glenn rubbed his eyes. 'Yes, it was all innocent fun before the others came along. I wanted no part in the demonology, as I like elves and dwarves. It was Brendon's idea to let them join as they promised to show him another world. All we had to do was summon up a demon with magic powers. Now my two friends are dead and now I know who did it. The other two came here earlier and said they were going to sacrifice me. The one changed right in front of me and grew. Another burst in here and knocked me to the ground. Where did they go?'

Devon stood. 'The ones who tried to kill you are dead, you're safe now.'

'What about the other thing? It could come back anytime.'

'No, it has no interest in you.'

'What are we going to do with the dead one?' said Jack.

Devon took out her phone. 'I'll call it in.' She tapped on a number in her contact list and heard a dialing tone.

'Hello, Inspector,' said Charles, 'is everything OK?'

'The place is secure, and we've found another dead one.'

'That makes three.'

'Three?' said Devon.

'Yes, Inspector Keane called not long ago and told us they found one too.'

'What should we do with this one?'

'Is there anywhere you can burn it? I don't think it would be a good idea to ask for a clean-up team at the moment.'

Devon knew Charles meant Bernard. She had not seen the man but knew what he was after. 'I'll sort it, but I don't like the fact three of these more powerful demons were already here. We had no idea they were until another demon killed them.'

'I know, and it worries me too,' said Charles. 'We will have a meeting in the morning as things are escalating faster than I expected.'

Devon ended the call and turned to Glen. 'The demon's body is still here, and we need somewhere to burn it.'

Glen struggled to his feet and shook his head. 'You can't do that, its body is proof they murdered my friends.'

'It's proof which could send you to jail for the rest of your life.'

Glen stepped back and bumped into the racking. 'What? I've never hurt anyone.'

'No, but when three men try summoning demons and only one of them is still alive, what do you think the police will do? The authorities would never allow this to go public and you would be a burden to them.'

Glen lowered his head. 'What about justice for my friends?'

'Their killers have been dealt with, but more will die if we don't stop the others.'

'There's a yard out the back, and by the back door is a can of petrol.'

Jack followed her as they walked back to the body with Dan. 'You were a little harsh on him.'

'You do know I'm with the police?'

'Yes, but I'm sure there's supposed to be a good cop too.'

Devon raised an eyebrow. 'I was being both. I want him to keep quiet about this as it might keep him alive.'

'How do you work that out?'

'As I told him the authorities would never let this go public. Even the demons wouldn't like a dead one on show. Let's just destroy the body, and he can get on with his life.'

Dan stared down at the demon. 'How are we meant to move this thing? I have no desire to touch it.'

'There are pallets on the racking,' said Jack, 'so there must be a fork lift truck somewhere.'

Devon shrugged. 'You two can sort it out . . . I'll go and find the petrol.'

CHAPTER TWELVE
Another Riddle

Joe stared out of Sarah's bedroom window. 'Peter's in pain again.'

Sarah sat in front of the dressing table as she brushed her hair. 'I know, but it'll be over soon.'

Joe saw what looked like a man by the trees near the stream. 'I can see someone out there.'

'Yes, he's waiting for you.'

Joe stared and saw the figure was wearing a hood. 'I'll give it a miss, it's a demon.'

Sarah shook her head. 'No, Joe, you have to go.'

Joe frowned. 'You want me to go out there to a demon?'

'You have to trust me . . . he has something important to tell you.'

~ ~ ~ ~

The nine bikers pulled up outside the manor house with two passengers and made their way inside. Chains saw Peter, ashen face and grimacing. Judy Miller held his arm and was followed by Elouise.

'Is he OK?' the big biker asked.

Elouise shook her head as she watched Peter go through the door of the meeting room. 'He's getting worse.'

They walked into the room and saw most of those from the manor were already seated. Tarin and Jim sat next to Benjamin, while Chains and Gyppo took seats by Devon. The remaining bikers stood with their backs to the wall.

'Welcome all,' said Charles. 'Refreshments will be supplied shortly. First let us get up to speed with what we know.' He turned to Tarin. 'You found it then?'

Tarin nodded and put the metal box on the table. She opened it so everyone could see the dagger. 'You can feel its power, but that's all I felt when I touched it. If it's going to help us someone else will have to use it.'

Charles tapped the tips of his fingers together. 'I am in no doubt one here will be able to do so.'

'We have a creature on the loose,' said Arthur. 'We believe it to be a demon, but as it has already killed three powerful demons we can't be sure. I would be grateful, but until I know its motive I cannot.'

Chains glanced over at the door, it opened as Joe and Sarah entered. Although the young man was smiling, Chains could sense he was nervous about something.

'I've been given a message for you,' said Joe, and passed over a letter to Devon. As the inspector took it, Joe grabbed the dagger and jumped across the table to Peter.

Chains leapt off his chair, but was too late as were the others who moved. Joe plunged the dagger into Peter's back, and the man fell forward onto the table. Chains couldn't reach as an invisible force blocked his way, and a bright light filled the room.

'Joe,' Jack shouted, 'what the hell have you done?'

'Wait,' said Sarah, 'just watch. Joe, you can take it out now.'

The young man stepped back, shaking his head and pulled the dagger out.

'Look,' said Judy, who was the closest, 'Peter's hump is getting smaller.'

Chains saw the back of Peter's jacket getting lower, and the hump vanished.

Peter stirred, sat up, and felt around for his hump. 'What happened?'

'I stabbed you,' said Joe.

'No,' said Sarah, 'you stabbed the hump. It's OK you did the right thing.'

Joe threw the dagger on the table as the glow around them faded. 'How can sticking a knife in someone ever be right?'

'No, the hump, it wasn't natural and would have killed Peter.'

Peter stood, no longer crooked, and put an arm around Joe. 'You saved my life, and made it better. I am now free from the pain the hump caused me. I did wonder if it would be you who could use the dagger.'

'I don't understand,' said Joe, 'Why would it work for me?'

'Your surname for a start, as I believe your grandfather . . . no, great-grandfather was Frank Wright who helped retrieve the dagger from Germany just after the war.'

'Come on, Joe,' said Sarah, 'they have a letter to read and discuss.'

Devon held the letter up. 'Who gave you this?'

'The demon poet,' said Joe, 'he was outside not long ago.'

Chains shook his head as they left the room and turned to Peter. 'You look a lot taller and will be able to ride your own bike now.'

Peter grinned. 'I will need a new jacket.'

Gyppo scratched his chin beneath his beard. 'Those young ones are not exactly normal are they?'

Peter shook his head. 'Far from it . . . I don't believe the demons knew it when they had them in their clutches. They need protecting at all costs.'

Tarin placed the dagger back in the tin. 'We should hear this message before going on with the meeting.'

'Indeed,' said Peter, 'I'm looking forward to solving a riddle right now.'

Devon opened the letter as those who had stood sat back down. She unfolded the paper from inside and read aloud.

'The game has changed with this new player, for it's no friend this demon slayer.

It takes the power from those it slays, and the final battle will be in days.

Demons will come through by the score, when the beast finds the door.

The power you have will not suffice, find the third and grow it thrice.

This clue might sound weak, but will help in what you seek.

For the children her life she gave, yet she's buried in an unmarked grave.

The die is set the die is cast, blood soaked earth from battles past.'

Devon put the paper on the table.

Charles sighed and rubbed the bridge of his nose. 'I'm sure it would be a lot easier if he just told us what he knows, and now I wonder if he knew anything in the first place.'

'He does,' said Elouise, 'but he is telling us the game has changed.'

Devon nodded. 'The new player taking powers from other demons, which means it will be more powerful than any we've faced so far. What we need to figure out is how to grow our power thrice. If we need to find a third we must already have two.'

'Arrows,' said Charles, 'we have two special ones.'

Devon shook her head. 'No, those are weapons not power. The shards of glass, we have two of them.' She took the one out of her pocket and glanced over at Simon. 'You have one of these.'

Simon nodded. 'It's in the cabinet.'

Charles stood and pressed a button on the wall behind him. A hidden drawer slid out. He took out the glass shard, and put it on the table with Devon's.

'Nice,' said Chains, 'do you have secret passages too?'

Charles sat down. 'I wouldn't call them secret as Joe found them on his first day here.'

Devon moved the pieces of glass around until they fitted together. 'It would make a small window if we had the third.'

Arthur nodded. 'A stained-glass one.'

'From a church,' said Tarin, 'one which has a cemetery with an unmarked grave.'

'Where?' said Jim, 'there must be thousands of them.'

'Backley,' said Rachel.

Devon turned to her. 'What makes you think that?'

'Blood soaked earth of battles past. He told us that line before. Backley is one of the places we found out about. There are two more, but one is a quarry and the other is just a road.'

'Backley,' said Raven, as she stepped away from the wall. 'I was there a few years ago and it does have a cemetery. It also has an unsavoury biker gang, and we had to fight our way out of there.'

Chains glanced up at her. 'Who were you with?'

'Tempest and Mistral. The guys were creeps, but we didn't want the police asking us too many questions, so we left.'

Blades grinned. 'That's one for us to check out.'

'I'll go to the nearest,' said Devon, 'and I want to take both shards in case we find the other.'

'Fair enough,' said Charles, 'but it's up to Reverend Simon.'

'Of course, and that's why he's coming with me.'

'As will I,' said Dan.

Devon shook her head. 'No, as much as I'd like your skill with the bow to be there you best stay here. Tarin and Jim can come with me.'

Dan scratched his head. 'Why would it be best if I stayed here?'

'Our new tasks have left us with a problem which we need to solve quickly. The letter states the final battle could be within a few days if not sooner, and we will be spread thin. Peter says Joe and Sarah need protecting. You, Jack, and Chloe have the skill and power to do that.'

'You'll have to give me an hour,' said Jack, 'I've got to go and fetch my brother.'

'The road is the closest,' said Rachel, 'I'll ask Sean and Rob to have a look at the quarry.'

Charles clasped his hands together. 'Where are they now?'

'Church, they've gone to see a priest who was found dead last night.'

'Tell them to only look and call us if they find anything . . . they don't have weapons to fight a demon lord.'

CHAPTER THIRTEEN
Millstone Quarry

The body of the priest lay outside the back of St Laurence church. Rob rubbed his chin as he stared down at the knife in the dead man's chest.

'No offence,' said Inspector Moore, 'but we have this under control. Why are you here? And why two inspectors?'

Carling smiled. 'I've only recently been promoted, and will most likely be removed from this case soon.'

Rob, who stood next to Carling, nodded. 'We're not here to take over the case, just to see if it matches any other strange murders.'

'Oh right, do we have a serial killer on the loose?'

'Probably, there's usually one or two about. This murder may be strange, but nothing to do with what we're looking for.'

Moore stared down at the body. 'Why is it strange?'

'How long as he been a priest and when did he find god?'

Moore shrugged. 'I've never seen him before, but then I don't go to church. Why do you ask?'

'Look at his hand . . . you can see part of a tattoo.'

Moore knelt and pulled the priest's sleeve back. 'This is a gang tattoo.'

'Yes, I thought so too. I doubt he was a priest, but here hiding, and this is a revenge killing.'

Moore turned to a constable. 'See if you can find anything with his identity on, and find out where the real priest is.'

'We'll leave you to it,' said Rob.

Moore nodded. 'Thanks for your help.'

'Should you rule it out so easily?' said Carling, as they made their way back to the car.

'I haven't ruled anything out, but I do believe it was another man who killed him. If it is part of it, the only information here is the tattoo.'

Carling looked over at the car. 'Where's Sean?'

Rob indicated with his thumb. 'Over the road, he's just coming out of the café.'

Carling turned as Sean crossed the road with a tray of drinks and a bag of food. 'Top man, I'm starving.'

'Don't get your hopes up . . . I've seen him eat more than that in one sitting.'

Sean walked over to them as they climbed into the car. He sat in the back and passed them a coffee each. 'I wasn't sure what you wanted, so I got you both a full house.'

Carling took both sandwiches and passed one to Rob. 'Perfect.'

Sean opened the wrapper to his own sandwich. 'Was the murder related to demons?'

'I don't know,' said Rob, 'but I don't believe we need to waste any more time here.'

'Good, we need to go and take a look at Millstone Quarry.'

'Why, what's there?'

'I've no idea, but it's one of the places Rachel and Sharon found. Rachel said things are moving fast and the final battle could happen within days.'

'The final battle,' said Carling, 'is that like the boss fight at the end of a level in a game?'

'Yes,' said Rob, 'only it's not a game. This time I believe we win and live happily, lose and this place becomes a demon world.'

Rob turned down a lane late afternoon and saw a sign pointing to Millstone Quarry. 'We're almost there.'

'They ought to take that down,' said Carling, 'it's been closed for years.'

Rob saw an eight-foot wire fence on the left of the road and pulled over. Attached to the fence were warning signs. Through the fence he could see three work huts. 'It's strange to leave those here.'

'Probably used by security guards,' said Carling. 'You know what kids are like for playing in places like this.'

They climbed out and walked towards the gates.

'They're open,' said Sean.

Rob nodded. 'There might be someone here, but I can't see any other vehicles.' He stepped through the gates. 'We best check out these huts first, I don't want anyone behind us.'

They crept over to the nearest and Carling looked through the window. He shook his head as Sean moved onto the next and did the same. Rob moved over to the third and glanced through the window. He could see a plate with a half-eaten sandwich, a radio, but no guard.

To the right of where they entered a dusty path vanished down a slope. He turned the other way beyond the huts and came to the edge of the large quarry. It sloped down to the left and stopped at what looked like a cliff face with a forty-foot drop. At the bottom he saw a pit entrance or a cave. To the right where the quarry went uphill he saw piles of rocks and a dirt path made for trucks.

'Get back,' Carling shouted, as the sound of a gunshot blasted through the air, and he fell to the ground.

Rob dived for cover by the hut. 'Shit, Carling, are you OK?'

'Yeah, the bastard just winged me. I saw two of them, both looked like bikers.'

Rob sat with his back to the hut and pulled out his gun. 'Where are they?'

'To your right but you won't get a chance, they have us pinned down.'

Sean leant on the other side of the cabin. 'Can you see them?

Carling rolled onto his front and crawled forward. 'About thirty feet away, I can just see the top of their heads.'

Rob watched as Sean picked up a rock the size of a football. He held it in both hands and threw it backwards over the hut.

'Not bad,' said Carling, 'a little more to the right.'

Sean bent over and picked up a larger rock. He adjusted his position and threw. As he did Rob reached over the edge with his gun and started firing.'

'That was close,' said Carling, and crawled forward to the edge. 'I can't see them. They've moved.'

Rob moved back while keeping low. 'As should we, they won't be able to see us if we keep away from the edge.

Carling crawled back as the three men moved around the quarry to see if they could get a better view of the bikers. They carried on for a few minutes when the sound of motorbikes roared.

Rob turned and saw two bikers ride out through the gates. 'Come on,' he shouted, and gave chase.

They ran to the car and climbed inside. Rob started the engine and drove off in the opposite direction to which they came. He could see the bikers in the distance and put his foot down.

Carling looked at the hole in his shirt sleeve the bullet made. 'You do know they might be leading us away from the quarry on purpose.'

Rob nodded. 'Yeah, and whatever they're hiding is in the mine.'

'What mine?' said Sean, 'I thought it was a quarry.'

'I saw a pit entrance on the left and I bet it wasn't here when the quarry was being worked. I'm not going in there without a proper weapon.'

'It's those two I want,' said Carling, as he took a plaster out of a first aid kit. 'One of them put a hole in my shirt.'

'I'll call it in,' said Sean, 'they'll want to know about the quarry.'

They drove on for an hour before losing the bikers in a town and Rob stopped the car. 'I've a feeling they're from here. Let's get something to eat and wait.'

CHAPTER FOURTEEN
The Bikers of Backley

The Lords of Night rode up to the Backley Arms on the night. It was a biker's pub as Raven told them, and they saw many bikes parked outside. They removed their helmets and stepped inside. It was a large room with many bikers sitting at the tables along the walls. Others were playing pool at the end of the room as heavy metal music blasted from the speakers.

Chains stepped over to the bar on the right. 'Nine lagers, please.'

The barman wiped his hands on a towel. 'Pints or bottles?'

Chains threw a couple of notes on the bar. 'Bottles.'

A younger biker approached but kept his distance. 'We don't like strangers coming in here.'

Blades turned to Raven. 'A friend of yours?'

Raven put a hand through her long red hair. 'No, he would've been too young to drink here at the time.'

The young man scowled as another biker with grey hair grabbed his arm.

'Don't be an idiot, lad, you'd be dead in seconds.'

The young biker pulled his arm free and walked off.

'I don't recognise any of them,' said Tempest, and turned to the barman who was putting opened bottles on the bar. 'The clientele has changed since I was last in here a couple of years ago.'

The barman shook his head. 'We've had a few new additions with the younger ones, but the regulars will be in later. Most of this lot are just wannabes, hanging around the Servants like a bad smell, hoping to become a member. Do you know them?'

'I met a few when I was last here,' said Tempest, as the barman nodded, put the change down, and walked down the bar to serve another customer.

Blades glanced around. 'Most of them are staring at us.'

'So I see,' said Gyppo, 'and the others are on their phones. Word will be getting around about our presence.'

Chains took a drink from a bottle. 'The barman called them the Servants.'

'The Servants of Satan,' said Raven. 'They appear to have groupies now so something has happened since Tempest, Mistral, and I were last here. Should we wait for them to arrive?'

Chains looked at the other bikers. 'No, we finish our drinks and go to the graveyard.'

'I'm not so sure,' said Gyppo. 'I agree we don't need the trouble while we search the cemetery, but something's wrong here. Bikers don't advertise for new members.'

'I know,' said Chains, 'and we'll find out afterwards. If we wait for this gang to arrive there will be a confrontation, and you know the younger ones here will join in.'

'The older biker wasn't here before,' said Raven, 'and the symbol on the back of his jacket is different.'

Jess indicated with her eyes. 'He's coming over.'

'I know you lot,' said the old biker, 'Gyppo, isn't it?'

Gyppo nodded. 'That's me.'

'I met you many years ago at a rock festival, not that you look any older.'

'Life's been good to us,' said Gyppo, 'although I'm a little greyer now. I'm sorry but I don't remember your name.'

'I'm Reg, and I look a lot older.'

Chains put his bottle on the bar. 'Are you part of the gang from round here?'

Reg shook his head. 'I was years ago, but I'm retired now.'

'I didn't know bikers retired.'

Reg smiled. 'I guess we don't really, but the gang packed it in. This new lot are called the Servants of Satan . . . we were the Scourge of Satan. '

'Have you come out of retirement?'

'No, I just worry about the young ones who want to join the gang. Frightening you off would score them some brownie points.'

Chains pushed his hair back. 'Wouldn't it be easier to start their own gang, there's enough of them?'

'Money and power, or so they believe, and the fact they have the police in their pocket. They'll be in soon to choose one of these as a member.'

'That's weird,' said Gyppo, 'someone should try dissuading them.'

'I've tried,' said Reg, 'but I'm just a silly old biker to them. The thing which worries me is that they only let others join if one of the gang goes missing.'

Chains frowned. 'I don't like the sound of that, there's no set limit to how many you have in a gang.'

Reg shrugged. 'I know, but it's how they work it.'

'It's no biker gang,' said Gyppo, 'not when one of their own goes missing, and they just replace them.'

'That's the thing,' said Reg, 'this isn't the first time. You can work out for yourself which ones do go missing.'

'The new members,' said Chains, 'the original gang are still together. These are not waiting to become members, but fodder in whatever this gang is up to.'

Raven rubbed her chin. 'Surely these must know this. Why would they want to join for that?'

'They're members for a couple of weeks,' said Reg, 'or so it looks, riding around with the gang as if they're royalty. The others see this and it makes them want to join even more.'

Gyppo glanced around the pub. 'We have to put a stop to this.'

'We will,' said Chains, 'after we sort out our other problem. I wouldn't be surprised if it's all linked together.' He turned to Reg. 'Thank you for the chat, but we have to go for now.'

Reg smiled. 'Ride safe.'

Chains stepped outside with the others and walked over to their bikes. 'Wait a moment,' he said, and grabbed the end of his iron links.

'We can't let you just leave,' said the young biker, as he and his friends hurried out of the pub. They lined up opposite, over twenty of them, young men and women. Five of them held knives. 'You have to pay for coming here.'

Ice laughed. 'Are they serious? I thought they didn't like strangers.'

'They're trying to keep us here until the Servants arrive,' said Chains. 'It means we don't have much time if we want to get there without being seen.' He whipped his hand forward and the iron links flew across the car park hitting the mouthy biker on the hand.

He screamed in pain and dropped the knife. 'You broke my fingers.'

Chains pulled the links back. 'Good, there's a chance you'll survive the night. The rest of you go home . . . fight for the gang and you'll die.'

'You don't frighten us,' said another young biker with a knife, 'we can take you.'

Chains turned to Raven and Tempest. 'Make it quick as we need to go, but don't hurt them too much.'

The two women leapt forward and somersaulted in front of the four lads holding knives. They spun, swinging their legs, knocking the knives out the hands of the closest two. They spun once more kicking each on the chest and the lads flew backwards. Raven dropped down kicking the legs from the next one. He fell back as she elbowed him in the face. Tempest grabbed the arm of the fourth as he lunged at her and threw him onto his back. The other young bikers ran back inside the pub.

Chains climbed on his bike. 'That looked painful.'

Raven walked back and straddled her own bike. 'They shouldn't be carrying knives.'

'Which way do we go?'

Raven turned and pointed up the road on the right. 'Up there is the high street where you go left. The cemetery is a couple of miles down the same road.'

Chains rubbed his chin. 'A busy high street I take it?'

Raven nodded. 'Yeah, there are a lot of pubs and restaurants which will be open this time of night.'

'We need another way, as I don't want anyone to know where we're going. This final piece, if it is there, may not be known by the demons.'

Gyppo held his helmet as if to put it on. 'What if they do know and are waiting for us?'

Chains smiled. 'We do what we're good at.'

'The road opposite,' said the dark-haired Mistral. 'It goes in the same direction of the high street between houses, and at the end there's a business park. Beyond that there's a field.'

'Won't the park be locked?'

Mistral shook her head. 'There are no gates . . . it's a public walk through. We would have to leave the bikes as the other side of the field is a fence with a wooded area.'

'OK,' said Chains, 'once we're out of sight from this pub turn off your lights.' He put on his helmet and rode off down the road.

They soon switched off their lights and carried on in the darkness. The business park came into sight and the gang rode to the end. Chains saw a path leading to the field and to his right were large industrial skips. He rode behind them and parked up. He took the iron links off his bike and walked over to the path, before carrying on to the field which he could see clearly. On the right, lights from cars leaving the high street shone in the distance.

'We could take the bikes over to the fence but there's a chance they might be heard.'

'We go straight across,' said Raven, and they ran without the darkness hindering them.

The Lords of Night reached the fence and climbed over. They made their way through the wooded area and came across the huge cemetery. Chains could see the graves going all the way to the road and just as far on the left to another set of gates near a church.

Doc scratched his chin. 'This might take a while, what exactly are we looking for?'

'You were at the meeting,' said Gyppo, 'a woman who gave her life to save the children.'

'I know that, but you'd think she'd have a large shrine. I also know she's in an unmarked grave, but I can see many without headstones.'

Chains stepped forward. 'We might as well ask. There are lights in the church so someone might be at home.' He walked on, dodging the graves, until he came to the double doors of the church. Chains pushed one open, and they entered where four people turned and stared at them. The priest put down pile of hymn books she was holding.

'We don't want your kind in here,' said another woman, with a feather duster under her arm.

'Beryl,' said the priest, 'everyone is welcome here, although there are more appropriate times.'

Chains stepped forward with the iron links still draped over his shoulders. 'I apologise for coming at this hour, and we have heard about the gang from around here. We are not like those, and we come in search of something.'

Beryl unfolded her arms and pointed the duster at him. 'And what do you know of the gang?'

'Only that they're a bad lot, an old biker called Reg told us.'

'The silly old fool, they laugh at him now but will soon tire of him.'

'His heart's in the right place,' said Chains,' and it doesn't look like anyone else is looking out for the younger ones.'

'What can you do if the police ignore what the gang get up to?'

'I am Reverend Caroline,' said the priest, 'you said you were looking for something.'

Chains nodded. 'A woman's grave, all we know about her is that she gave her life to save children.'

'Wrong cemetery,' said Beryl, 'I would know if such a woman was buried here.'

Chains glanced around the old church and noticed part of the wall behind the altar was more modern than the rest. 'Is there nothing in the records about such a woman? It may have happened a long time ago.'

'They only go back to the fifties,' said Caroline, 'the ones before then were destroyed in a fire.'

An older man approached. 'A woman died in the fire, it could be her.'

'That's ridiculous, Albert,' said Beryl, 'she was the one who caused the fire.'

'Reverend Michael never believed it to be so. It also saddened him he was not allowed to give her the last rites.'

'Isn't that a little harsh,' said Doc, 'refused a proper burial for starting a fire?'

Albert pursed his lips. 'There was more to it, but I was only a boy at the time.'

'I might have something,' said Caroline, 'give me a moment.'

Chains watched her go and turned to Beryl. 'You're worried about Reg?'

Beryl nodded. 'Of course, he's my brother. The bikers here years ago were nothing like this lot now. Some of them were charming, so I married one. These new ones are just scum.'

'We'll take care of them soon, but how is it they have the police on their side?'

'Not all the police, just some local ones who must be getting bribes.'

'We have many friends in the force who won't be happy about what's going on here.'

'I've found something,' said Caroline, as she approached with an old dusty book.

'I remember now,' said Albert. 'The woman, a spinster, was believed to have abducted six children. She died in the fire which many thought she started to kill the children. The children gave a different account and said it was men who wanted to kill them, but the woman wouldn't allow it. They said the woman set the men on fire, so they could run away. No one believed the children as only the body of the woman was found.'

'Father Michael believed the children,' said Caroline. 'This isn't a record, but the old priest's diary.' Caroline opened the book and turned the pages. 'I am having a personal crisis over the death of Elaine Turnbull, something which troubles me greatly. The children said horrible looking men were trying to kill them not Elaine. They also said the men had red eyes . . . it is not the first time I have heard about such creatures. It would also explain why only Elaine's body was found. I was ordered to have her buried in an unmarked grave without a Christian burial. My personal belief is she died saving the children from demons. I decided to bury her myself in the garden behind the church. I write this in hope that one day others will know about the demons and give her a proper Christian burial.'

'How horrible,' said Beryl. 'It might be a silly tale, but she should've been given a proper burial.'

'It's far from silly,' said Mistral, 'the woman was a hero. She saved those children and sent the monsters back.'

Caroline raised an eyebrow. 'You believe demons are real?'

'They're very real,' said Chains, 'we've been fighting them for a long time. Their bodies turn to dust when you send them back, so they would have never been found in the fire. We came here for another reason, but if she gets a proper burial it won't be a wasted visit.'

'Father Michael was the most honest person I know,' said Albert, 'and he was not one for flights of fancy. If he believed demons walked the earth I for one say it's the truth.'

'It sends shivers down my spine,' said Caroline. 'Demons or not, I'm going to give her the last rites. The testimonial of the children should've been enough. I will also make sure she has a proper burial.'

Chains nodded. 'So you have seen the grave?'

'Yes,' said Caroline, 'there's an old wooden cross, but that's all.'

'We should go out to it.'

'Why are you so interested in her?' said Beryl. 'What difference would it make now?'

'Because the demons are still here,' said Chains, 'and Elaine Turnbull may still have some part in getting rid of them.'

'It doesn't matter,' said Caroline, 'I would like to say a few words over the grave.'

The priest led them outside the church and around to the large garden. Chains could still see the cemetery over the small wall before turning back and saw three wooden crosses.

'Which one?' he asked.

'The one at the back,' said Caroline, 'the other two were pet dogs.'

'Not too bad then,' said Beryl, 'I'd like to be buried by my dogs.'

'I think you mean near your dogs,' said Doc, 'the other leaves a weird image.'

Caroline spoke as they gathered around the grave. 'Here lies Elaine Turnbull, a woman, whose life was taken in the act of incredible bravery. On the night of her death monsters came to kill children, but she alone stopped them. No one knew it at the time but this brave woman rid the town of evil and stopped many more murders. This is just a short mention of her deeds before a right and proper ceremony will be performed at a later time. We here are too few for such a ceremony, but we do thank you for your deed.'

A white glow emanated from the grave for a few seconds and disappeared. Chains knelt as he saw a shard of glass poke through the earth. He pulled it out and held it in his hand.

Caroline stared at him. 'What is that?'

'Part of a window,' said Chains. 'One from here which witnessed the deed of Elaine Turnbull, such a deed does not go unnoticed. Selfless acts of bravery create a force which does not die.' Chains heard the sound of engines.

'Bikers,' said Ice, 'lots of them.'

'You better vanish,' said Chains.

Ice, Raven, Tempest, and Mistral leapt over the wall and soon disappeared into the cemetery.

'What about us?' said Beryl.

'Go back to the church and let us handle them.'

'What if they have police with them?'

'We'll take care of them too.'

Caroline glanced across the cemetery. 'Shouldn't we take the glass into the church?'

Chains shook his head. 'No, it's what they're after, and will put you in danger.' The big biker walked them to the doors of the church before slipping into the shadows of the trees.

Rob stared out of the restaurant window as a group of bikers rode past. 'Come on, it's time to go,' he said, and threw money on the table before they hurried out to the car.

Carling climbed in and attached his seatbelt. 'There's a lot more of them, are you sure they're the same ones?'

Rob started the engine. 'Yeah, they got the same logo on the back of their jackets.'

They drove through the high street and saw a field on the left with houses in the distant on the right. They saw the bikers further ahead who slowed and disappeared to the left. As Rob drove closer, he saw they had entered a cemetery. He carried on past and pulled over. They climbed out and approached the open gates. Both Rob and Carling held guns while Sean carried an iron bar. They saw the bikes parked up but no bikers.

Carling leant on a gate post as he glanced around in the dark. 'Where are they?'

'Further ahead,' said Rob, 'they're going towards the church at the other end, and I don't believe their intentions are holy.'

Sean stepped through the gates. 'We have to stop them.'

Rob nodded. 'I know, but we can't just charge forward, there are too many of them. There's a hedge on the right, and if we keep low there's a chance we can get to the church unseen.'

~ ~ ~ ~

Chains watched the Servants of Satan run towards them in a line without trying to hide. The only thing which kept their pace slow was the gravestones they were avoiding. He counted twenty and some of them carried guns. The line of Servants became shorter as Ice, Raven, Tempest, and Mistral darted at them from the shadows. Chains couldn't see what they were doing from where he was, but watched as Servants of Satan fell without making a sound. The others grouped together around those with guns, and shots were fired. He heard a noise to the left as three men emerged from the shadows, with two holding guns.

One pointed it straight at him. 'Police, get over here.'

Chains whipped his arm forward and the iron links shot through the air. The end of the links flew at the hand holding a gun when the biggest of the men caught it.

'Attacking a police officer is a serious offence,' he said.

Chains pulled on the links but the big man did not yield.

'Sean,' said the one pointing a gun, 'you do know what you're holding?'

Sean glanced at the chains. 'Yes, of course.'

'Good, then you'll know who's holding the other end.'

Sean raised an eyebrow and stepped forward letting the tension on the chains loosen. 'I think we may have crossed wires.'

Chains nodded. 'I've heard of you, nice catch.'

'These are Rob and Carling, both police inspectors, and real ones.'

'I know that now, only we were told many of the police here are in cahoots with the gang. I guess you thought all bikers are the same.'

Rob shook his head. 'No, and I never saw the logo on the back of your jackets. To be quite honest I didn't know there were still a lot of bikers around.'

'We might want to discuss this later,' said Gyppo, as he stepped out of the shadows behind Carling and Rob. 'The other bikers are still coming this way.'

Carling stared at the grey haired biker. 'You were there all the time?'

Gyppo nodded as more shots were fired, and they ducked for cover.

'Hand it over if you want to live,' one of the Servants shouted.

Chains glanced over the top of a headstone. 'Hand what over?'

A bullet hit the edge of the stone. 'You know what I mean, and we have you surrounded.'

Chains ducked back down. 'I think it is us who have you surrounded. You are the ones cowering in the centre.'

'We are not cowering, but waiting,' said the Servant. 'You don't think we came alone do you?'

'Then why don't you wait up here with us?'

Rob sat with his back against a gravestone. 'Is that a good idea?'

Bullets flew past until there was silence. A few seconds later Doc and Blades appeared carrying three guns.

'They can wait where they are,' said Doc, 'I'm not carrying them up. He was correct in one thing they're not alone. Demons appeared from the way we entered and the four ghosts are taking care of them.'

'We have company,' said Gyppo.

Chains heard the bikes as they approached the gates closest to them. He stepped behind the stone as the others took cover. Another Twenty rode down the drive and pulled up followed by two cars.

The nearest biker removed his helmet. 'It's no good hiding, we have you surrounded.'

Chains laughed. 'You're wrong as your friends are no longer behind us. Would you be the leader of this rabble?'

The biker took a gun from the inside of his jacket. 'I am.'

'What happened to those young bikers who went missing?'

'Gone, I'm afraid, they couldn't handle the work.'

Chains grimaced. 'I don't like killing people, but you've earned it.'

'I don't think so . . . we have the police with us.'

'So do we . . . only these are the real police.'

'Not here they're not, this is our town.'

The car doors opened and four uniformed officers climbed out, followed by four more in suits.

'Demons,' Chains whispered.

Rob rubbed his chin with the barrel of a gun as hooded figures entered through the gates at the other end. 'I'm more worried about those with guns, there's gotta be at least twenty bikers ahead, and we don't know how many are behind us.'

Chains glanced back and saw hooded figures in the distance. 'Don't worry about any behind . . . we need to take care of those with the guns first. It's a lot harder to fight demons with bullets flying around.'

'Just hand it over,' said the lead Servant, 'and make it easy on yourself.'

Chains could see the bikers waiting, but not all had guns, many had knives. 'As I said to your friend, hand what over?'

'What you came looking for, the reason you are here, we know all about it.'

'Wrong church, you already know this or you would've found it yourself.'

'We never looked as it would not show itself to us. Now hand it over.'

Chains felt the shard inside his jacket. 'If I did have it, what do you think would happen if I handed it over?'

'We'd let you go free.'

Chains shook his head. 'Don't insult us, and I didn't mean that. The item you're talking about has a bad effect on demons, as it makes them vulnerable to normal weapons. We do have plenty of those.'

'I've waited long enough,' said the lead Servant, 'Kill them.'

Bikers fired at them and Chains ducked back as the bullets chipped away at the headstones, Rob rolled on the ground and fired his gun as did Carling. Doc and Blades threw knives although they had guns. Four of the gang fell to the ground and the others ran back for shelter. Chains noticed the demons had hidden behind the cars, and glanced back but could not see any of the hooded ones.

Rob reloaded his gun. 'Where the hell have they gone?'

'I wouldn't worry about them,' said Chains, as Mistral came into view.

Rob raised an eyebrow and heard the sound of more motorbikes. 'How many of them are there?'

'Oh look,' said the lead Servant, 'our young friends are here to impress us. You know I'm going to send them in first.'

Chains watched them approach the gates as the remaining Lords of Night joined him. 'Do so, and I'm coming for you. None of your friends will stop me.'

The new bikers rode down the drive at speed and straight into the Servants of Satan. It gave the others a chance to run in and help the younger ones. Chains ran at the demons and noticed Sean had the same idea. They both charged forward, Chains swinging the iron links, and Sean barging into the closest. He rammed an iron bar into the chests of the two he knocked down, and sent them back. Chains turned the first one he hit with the iron links to dust and wrapped them around the next one's neck. He turned to face the others and saw Ice and Mistral had beaten him to it.

Chains put the links over his shoulder and patted Sean on the back. He glanced over at the new bikers where the Servants of Satan were all sat on the ground defeated. The younger ones removed their helmets and Chains smiled when he noticed not all were young. Many had grey hair and beards.

'Hi, Reg,' he said, 'it looks like they finally listened to you.'

Reg shook his head. 'Not in the way you might think. They were so impressed with how you defeated them at the pub they asked me what I knew of you. I told them a few stories I had heard. They decided it would be better if they formed their own gang and called themselves the Scourge of Satan. I feel quite proud about that.'

The doors of the church opened and Reverend Caroline stepped outside. 'What just happened?'

'They came to take what we found,' said Chains, 'but we refused and stopped them.' He watched as three Servants were dragged over to the others, all three were dead.

'I know that,' said Caroline, as the others from the church joined them. 'What I want to know is why eight turned to dust.'

Chains pointed to the dusty remains of the demons. 'You'll find many clothes around the cemetery tonight where a lot more were turned to dust. They're what Elaine Turnbull was protecting the children and the town from all those years ago. You see what happens to them when they're stopped, and it's why everyone thought she was guilty.'

'They turned to dust and only her remains were found. The children said they looked like men but had red eyes.'

'Oh my,' said Beryl, 'she really was a hero.'

'Yes, she was,' said Caroline, 'and we will make sure people know about her. What I don't understand is why would they want the glass?'

'To stop us using it,' said Chains.

'It looks like the demons know more than we thought,' said Rob, 'or you were set up.'

Chains nodded. 'It sounds like the latter, and they were waiting for us to retrieve it.'

They turned to the gates as sirens sounded. Police cars and a van sped up the road and into the cemetery. Sixteen police officers jumped out followed by two men in suits.

The two in suits approached. 'What the hell's going on here?' said one.

Caroline stepped in front of him. 'I told you over the phone, Chris, the gang over there sitting on the ground came here with guns. If it wasn't for these men and women stopping them I have no idea what would've happened.'

'If I hadn't seen you standing there talking to them I would've waited for armed police, but it doesn't tell me what they were after.'

Rob pulled out his ID card. 'I'm Detective Inspector Rob Keane, and this is Detective Inspector Carling. We chased two of them here as they had already fired at us earlier today.'

'Sir,' said a constable, 'there are police uniforms on the ground here.'

'Check the IDs,' said Rob, 'you'll find they're fake. It's how they've been getting around the law.'

'I'm Inspector Chris Hughes, what happened to the ones who were wearing those uniforms?'

'They're demons,' said one of the Servants.

Another put a hand over his mouth. 'Shut up you moron, they're still around.'

'It looks like someone's been smoking something,' said Rob, 'I never saw anyone wearing them.'

'Sir,' said another constable, 'we have three dead bodies, it looks like they were shot.'

'The guns are over there,' said Chains, pointing to a grave. 'They belonged to the gang who were shooting at us from both sides, as you can see from the headstones.'

Chris looked him up and down. 'Are you sure this wasn't a gang fight?'

Chains shook his head. 'No we were talking to Reverend Caroline when they turned up. Many of them were wearing robes, which you'll find around the cemetery.'

'Robes?' said the other officer in a suit. 'Sounds like a cult to me.'

Chains shrugged. 'They do call themselves the Servants of Satan.'

Chris sighed. 'What have I walked into? Apart from devil worshipping maniacs, dusty clothes no one wants to claim, half the bikers here should be in an old people's home.'

'There's still some life in us yet,' said a grey haired biker with a ponytail.

'Norman,' said Beryl, 'I thought you had packed it in.'

'Yes, but something had to be done.'

Chains turned to Chris. 'You might want to check missing persons as some young bikers will be on there. Those Servants were the last ones to see them.'

Chris rubbed his eyes. 'This is going to be one heck of a report I will have to make.'

Rob passed him a card. 'Have a word with my super, or get yours to call him. It'll make things a lot easier.'

Chris took the card. 'Thanks, but I'm sure you'll give me an honest account of what happened.'

'Of course, but you might want to talk to those in charge before you put certain things in your report.'

Chris nodded and turned to a sergeant. 'I want more officers here to search the whole cemetery, and I want the gang taken to the station.' The inspector glanced at the card before walking over to his car.

Chains passed the shard of glass to Sean. 'Don't let anyone know you have this until the right moment. We'll ride elsewhere and if anyone did set us up they'll think we have it.'

Sean nodded. 'Where will you be going?

Chains shrugged. 'Not sure, but I hoped those at the manor might have somewhere for us to check out.'

'As Rob said we chased two of the gang who shot at us. We were taking a look at Millstone Quarry, and we're sure there's something they didn't want us to find.'

'We'll take a look,' said Chains, as an elder biker approached.

'So it's true, the Lords of Night are in town.' The biker, wearing a bandana, smiled. 'I am Eric, and was once known as Iron Arm until I met your gang all those years ago. I had never been beaten at arm wrestling until then.'

Chains rubbed his nose. 'Sorry about that.'

Eric shook his head. 'It wasn't you but the lady over there, Tempest, isn't it? I have to say she has fared a lot better than I, in fact you all have.'

Rob rubbed his chin. 'The one called Reg said he told the younger bikers of some of their fights.'

Eric nodded. 'I remember thirty years ago when they fought a gang a lot worse than these here. Outnumbered three to one, but all eleven of them came away from it unscathed.'

Rob glanced at Chains. 'There were eleven of you?'

'There still are,' said the big biker, 'The other two have another task.'

'It's time for us to go,' said Gyppo, 'it would be best if we slipped away before more police arrive.'

Rob nodded. 'Take care, we will most likely see you soon.'

CHAPTER FIFTEEN

Doom and Gloom

Dan stood outside the manor, and stared over the front of the land into the darkness. 'I've a bad feeling about tonight.'

'You're not the only one,' said Jack, 'I've been feeling uneasy for the last few hours. It might have something to do with the dagger.'

'It wouldn't surprise me after what it did for Peter earlier. The demons know we have it and it won't take them long to locate us.'

'With any luck they might believe we don't have anyone here who can use it.' Jack glanced back where Jamie leant on the frame of the front door. 'I wonder if the dagger is warning us.'

'Could be,' said Dan. 'We should be prepared and see how we can defend this place.'

'Cool,' said Jamie, 'can I have a gun.'

'They're no good against demons,' said Jack, 'and have you ever used one?'

Jamie shook his head. 'No, but it can't be that hard. Anyway, bullets can hurt them as we have the dagger here.'

Dan patted Jack on the shoulder. 'You might have been better off not listening to my advice.'

'It sounded good at the time, and there might not be any guns here anyway.'

'We best go check and get our own weapons.'

~ ~ ~ ~

Joe scrunched up his nose as he stared at Sarah. She sat on the edge of the bed with her eyes closed, and had done so for a while. He walked over to the window and glanced out.

'I might go out for a jog,' he said.

'What?' said Sarah.

Joe turned back to her. 'Oh, you're awake. I thought you were going to sleep all night.'

Sarah shook her head. 'I was not asleep, I was doing something.'

'You sat there for ages with your eyes shut. If that's doing something you should ask me as I'm good at it.'

'I was concentrating. I need you to stop joking as this is serious. The final battle won't be in days, but much sooner. We're in danger here and need help.'

Joe raised both eyebrows. 'I'll go and tell the others.'

Sarah shook her head. 'They already know, I told them.'

Joe scratched his head. 'You told them through your mind, like a message?'

'Not quite, it was more of a feeling, like the oncoming of doom.'

'You did that? I thought I was having a turn.'

'Sorry, but it was the only way I could do it, and they are getting prepared.'

'You sat there for ages when we could've just gone downstairs and told them.'

'I know, but I had to find help as well.'

~ ~ ~ ~

Doom rubbed his unshaven chin as he leant up the bar of the Forester's Arms pub. He listened to a conversation in the corner of the room. Four figures sat at a table, two he knew were demons. The two opposite were men, but he had no idea who they were.

'What's in it for us?' said a demon.

'You get all the other artefacts,' said the man with a moustache, 'but the dagger is mine. Once you have left I will go in with my men and claim it.'

'Our master would appreciate the dagger.'

The man frowned. 'All my men are armed with weapons which will send your kind back, and we also have other powerful artefacts.'

The demon clasped its hands together. 'If that is so, why not go in yourself and get them?'

'They have guns which my men are vulnerable to, where you are not. These people have been sending your kind back for a long time and I'm sure your master would be pleased if you got rid of them.'

'He would indeed be pleased, but you have already told us they have the dagger. It makes us vulnerable to their guns.'

The man shook his head. 'No, they haven't found anyone who can use it yet, and many of them are away searching.'

'How do I know this is not a trick?'

'Why would it be, I will be giving you an address your kind has been after for a long time. When you get there, you will know I speak the truth. If you're not interested I will get my men to do it.'

'No,' said the other demon, 'give us the address, we will do it.'

The man held up a piece of paper. 'I will need a couple of hours to organise my men, so do not go until midnight. I cannot risk anyone else finding out what you've done before I get there.'

Doom turned to Gloom next to him, tall, slim, with dark brown eyes, and wearing biker's leathers. He nodded and they left the pub. Outside he took her arm and walked to the side of the building.

'What are you playing at?' she asked.

'Let's wait here a moment, I want to see who comes out first.'

The two demons stepped outside and walked towards a car.

'You agreed too easily,' said one, 'they will try to kill us soon as we take care of those at the house.'

'Since when have we been frightened of humans? You know they cannot kill us, as we will come back.'

'Yes and how long will it take to come back?'

'That won't happen tonight as he needs time to organise his men. We will not be waiting but going in straight away.'

'Yes, but shouldn't we notify our master first?'

'If we do that, others with more power will go and claim the glory. Is that what you want?'

The other demon shook its head and climbed into a waiting car.

'Let's send them back now,' said Gloom, 'and the address dies with them.'

Doom shook his head. 'We don't know it will, and besides it's a little too busy here.'

'Then we follow them until it's quieter.'

Doom climbed onto his bike. 'Fighting them would only slow us down. We know they have ways of contacting each other without the use of mobile phones. Those two may just wait for their minions to do the dirty work.'

Gloom nodded as she straddled her bike. 'Those at the manor already know something will happen, but will be outnumbered.'

'How do you know that?'

'The young woman called Sarah told me.'

~ ~ ~ ~

Dan saw figures in the shadows as he glanced out the front door. They massed in a line facing the manor house. He turned to Jack, Jamie, Gary, and Elizabeth. 'We're not alone.'

'No,' said Sarah, as she walked down the stairs with Joe, 'they're out the back too.'

Judy hurried over to them. 'It's not safe for you down here . . . you should go back to your room.'

Sarah shook her head. 'People have been telling me that all my life, and I've never found it any safer.'

Jack stood with sword in hand. 'She's right . . . we can't protect her or Joe if they're upstairs. This place is too big with just a few of us. We're going to need those with guns at the windows.'

Dan turned as Charles, Arthur, and Peter stepped out of the meeting room. 'How many guns do we have?'

'Six,' said Charles, 'but not a lot of bullets.'

'What's going on?' said Elouise, when she stepped into the hall.

'Demons,' said Dan, 'there must be at least twenty of them out the front.'

Elouise's eyes grew big. 'How did they find us?'

'It's a big house,' said Dan, 'we've been coming and going for a while now.'

'No,' said Charles, 'they have never been able to find us before, someone has told them.'

'Oh shit,' said Jamie, looking out the door, 'they've lit torches, and some have guns.'

Jack turned to Joe sitting on the bottom step of the stairs. 'We might need to see the power of the dagger.'

Joe screwed up his nose and held the dagger up. 'I think it's broke.'

Dan took an arrow from the quiver. 'That makes the guns useless then.'

'No,' said Sarah, 'the dagger will come to our aid when we need it.'

'That might be now.'

'I doubt the others will be back in time to aid us,' said Arthur, 'they're too far away. Are you sure those out there are demons?'

'Quite positive,' said Dan, 'the red eyes are a big giveaway.'

'It's like a line of fireflies,' said Jamie. 'They're moving closer and it looks like they have a can of petrol.'

'They're going to set us on fire,' said Charles, 'and hope the dagger escapes unscathed.'

'Nice,' said Dan, 'and they'll just pick us off if we run.'

Charles nodded. 'It would appear so, and demons do not fear fire.'

'Shoot the petrol can,' said Sarah, 'and they will have a change of mind.'

Dan stared at her as Charles passed him a pistol. He crept over to the window next to the door and pointed the gun outside. He saw the can, fired, and the bullet hit the target. Petrol splashed up onto a torch and the can exploded. A demon screamed as flames engulfed him and clothes fell to the ground.

Dan turned to Charles. 'Are you sure about fire as it just sent one back?'

'I don't understand,' said the older man, 'it never worked for me.'

'Maybe it's the dagger,' said Jack.

'No,' said Sarah, 'it's the land. There's a power here and the demons became vulnerable to all weapons when they stepped onto it.'

Jack passed Jamie a pistol. 'Only use it if they get close.'

Jamie spun the gun in his hand. 'Where are you going?'

'They're not going to just come through the doors, they'll enter anyway they can. The guns will be best served here and at the back doors.'

Dan watched through the slightly open doorway. 'Who's watching the back?'

'Chloe, Rachel, and Sharon.'

'I will take some of the guns to them,' said Arthur, 'Chloe would be better off doing as you are.'

'I'll take a gun,' said Gary, 'if you have one spare.'

'We have,' said Charles, 'come with me they are in the meeting room.'

'What about me?' said Elizabeth. 'What should I do?'

'Go with Elouise,' said Jack, 'and get the staff somewhere safe.'

'The secret passages,' said Joe, 'you'll be safe in there.'

Gun fire shattered through the air. 'Quickly,' said Dan, as Gary returned with a pistol, 'they've started.'

The two women left as the windows either side of the door exploded and bullets flew into the hall. They ducked low as Jamie and Gary fired their guns out the windows. Dan released an arrow through the gap in the doorway as four demons turned to dust and the others backed away.

'Nice shooting, guys, you got four, and they've stopped.'

'Strange,' said Gary, 'they outnumber us.'

'They're nervous,' said Sarah. 'They were expecting the others to get back up and not turn to dust.'

Dan turned but couldn't see her. 'I don't suppose they'll go away now.'

Sarah poked her head around the stairs. 'No, it would be a much worse fate for them if they did. They will come again soon.'

'I'm going to watch the other windows,' said Jack, and left the room.

Dan watched through the gap and saw a demon giving others orders. Two of them ran forward. Jamie and Gary fired, but missed as the demons altered direction at the last moment.

'Shit,' said Jamie, 'they weren't supposed to do that.'

Dan pointed an arrow and released. It flew through the air hitting the demon giving orders, and it turned to dust. 'It's a ploy for you to waste what ammo you have.'

The demons charged again and once more changed direction at the last minute. It happened over and over for the next twenty minutes. Jamie and Gary both fired trying to guess which way the demons would turn. Dan had more luck with the bow, but he was low on arrows. He could hear gun fire outside and widows breaking. Dan knew the demons had got inside, and he grabbed one of the special arrows to fight hand-to-hand if needed.

'There were a lot more than twenty out there,' said Gary. 'I'm sure we sent back that many already.'

Dan nodded as he stepped over to the stairs and saw Judy, Joe, and Sarah sitting there. 'Is this the best you could do for a hiding place?'

'It's the safest,' said Judy, 'as all the rooms have windows, and these two wouldn't go in the passage.'

Sarah looked up and smiled. 'We didn't want to miss the action.'

Dan raised an eyebrow. 'You're not exactly seeing much as it's all outside.'

'For now.'

Dan realised it wouldn't be safe for much longer. He turned as Jamie fired the gun out of the window before ducking back down.

'I'm out of bullets,' he said.

Charles stepped out of the meeting room with Peter. 'There's too many, and I have no bullets left.'

The front doors opened as a demon rushed inside. Dan was too fast for it and rammed the arrow into its chest. Two more appeared as the dust fell to the ground. Dan saw the quiver leant up the wall by the door as Jack walked in through a side door, and the demons pointed guns at them.

~ ~ ~ ~

Doom rode through the gates and heard shooting. He pulled over and removed his helmet. 'They're already here.'

Gloom shook her hair loose. 'I'll take care of those around the back.'

Doom climbed off his bike and made his way through the trees behind the line of demons. He saw them running at the house in twos and others towards the windows to the right of the main doors. He pulled two curved knives from inside his jacket and ran forward like a dark cloud. The demons didn't see him until his shadow fell over them and one by one they turned to dust as he ran down the line. It took seconds for him to send those waiting back, but others ran to the house, and he saw two enter the front doors.

~ ~ ~ ~

Dan stared at the demon knowing none of them could cover the distance before it fired the gun.

The demons grinned. 'Our master will be pleased there will be prisoners to torture,' said one, and his smile vanished. His whole body vanished seconds later along with the other demon. Their clothes dropped to the ground and a tall slim biker stood in the doorway with a dagger in each hand.

'They've all gone,' said Sarah, 'all the demons who were here have been sent back.'

Dan sighed and glanced at the biker. 'Thanks, but I don't think we've had the pleasure as you wasn't with the others when they came here.'

'I'm Doom, and had other things to do.'

'Are all the gang out there?'

The biker shook his head. 'No, just Gloom and I, she's been taking care of those out the back.'

Jamie ran to the door and looked out. 'There were loads of them.'

Doom shrugged. 'I surprised them, and they're not the most intelligent of creatures.'

A door towards the back opened as Arthur, Chloe, Rachel, Sharon, and Gloom walked through.

Chloe smiled. 'It's clear out the back. I don't know how she did it but all I could see was them bursting into dust.'

'Indeed,' said Arthur, 'and she was not gloom for us as we had run out of bullets.'

'Doom and Gloom,' said Joe, 'we're Thunder and Lightning.'

Sarah frowned. 'They already know who we are, and we have to go now.'

Judy shook her head. 'You can't go anywhere, you just saw what happened.'

'Sarah speaks the truth,' said Gloom, 'You all have to leave as you are in danger.'

'What?' said Peter, 'I thought we just won.'

'This battle,' said Doom, 'but armed men are coming to take anything you have here. They set you up as we overheard two men talking to the demons. The men are coming after midnight to clean up once the demons have finished you off.'

Charles shook his head. 'We know who he is. They are correct, you must all leave now and go in different directions.'

'And go where?' said Jack, 'I'm not letting Jamie and my friends go off on their own.'

Charles rubbed his chin. 'I meant in groups. You might be noticed if so many cars were seen going in the same direction. You can meet up after a few detours. I would like you to take all the artefacts and weapons we have with you. As for where, I will call Devon and find out.'

'If you can get through,' said Elouise, 'I couldn't call out when the demons were attacking.'

Rachel checked her phone. 'I've got a signal.'

Charles nodded. 'It might have been something to do with the demons. I am going to stay here and wait for our guests.'

Doom shook his head. 'That would be too dangerous . . . the man told the demons to kill everyone here.'

'He will not kill us,' said Elouise. 'We know who he is and there will be no reason for him to harm us as we will have nothing left when you all go. I cannot leave until I see his face when he finds out the demons have failed.'

Doom nodded. 'Makes sense I guess. Gloom and I'll take Thunder and Lightning.'

Judy folded her arms. 'I don't think so, they need proper care.'

'No,' said Joe, 'we need to ride on motorbikes.'

'He's right you know,' said Peter.

'It's for the best,' said Sarah, 'they can take us off road as the dagger will bring those in the cars unwanted attention.'

'We won't be using roads until we need to,' said Gloom, 'and will meet up with you later. Our friends were going to take a look around Millstone Quarry, and we'll make our way there.'

'I think we should all go to the quarry,' said Dan, 'after what the others said. Has anyone seen Father Nick?'

'He's with the kitchen staff,' said Elouise, 'they were frightened.'

Jack glanced around the hall. 'Where's my brother?'

'He went outside with Gary,' said Joe.

Dan looked out through the doorway and smiled. 'Here they are.'

The two men stepped inside carrying a large bundle each.

Jamie put his on the floor. 'I thought we might need more guns, and they had quite a few.'

'It was Jamie's idea,' said Gary, as he put his bundle down, 'and I thought it was a good one.'

'So do I,' said Jack, 'good work.'

Jamie knelt and picked up a pile of arrows which he passed to Dan. 'I thought you might want these.'

Dan smiled. 'Thank you and I do. How did you find them so quickly?'

'They never went further than the clothes.'

Dan nodded and patted the younger man on the shoulder. 'You know it was my idea for you to come here?' He heard the sound of motorbikes as Doom and Gloom pulled up. 'When did they leave?'

CHAPTER SIXTEEN

The Demon Summoner

Devon sat in her car waiting for others from the manor house to arrive. The final location, New Hampton, Rachel had found came to nothing. All they found was an empty field and decided to drive back when Charles phoned her. Benjamin and Reverend Simon were also in the car and in the one behind sat Tarin and Jim. She glanced at the clock which showed twenty after midnight.

'I don't believe it's the right place,' said Benjamin, 'it doesn't look like anything had ever been built there.'

'Maybe,' said Devon, 'but the site never stated there would be a building here, just a road. However, I do agree the final shard is not here, nor does the place have anything to do with demons.'

'The Lords of Night may have had better luck,' said Simon, 'as they were going to search a cemetery.'

Devon noticed headlights in the rear view mirror. 'I know, and if they do find something it would mean four of the five sites are connected to the demons. I'm worried we're missing something here.' Devon saw the cars behind pull over, and she climbed out.

Dan walked over to her as Tarin and Jim joined them. 'You heard what happened?'

Devon nodded. 'Charles told me, where are the others?'

'Gone to meet up with Sean and the two detectives. We'll join up with them near the quarry. Did you find anything?'

'No, New Hampton is just a field near a housing estate.'

'Maybe we should try Old Hampton,' said Tarin, 'I doubt whoever put the addresses on the site are a hundred per cent sure of them.'

'True, but we can't go searching all night. We best make our way to the quarry.'

Devon slowed the car at a junction as a small coach approached from the right. She stopped and stared at the hooded figures inside. 'Did you see that?'

Benjamin nodded. 'Demons, it looks like they're going towards the quarry, and we need to stop them.'

Devon glanced over at a sign pointing to the right. 'Old Hampton, we need to find out where they're coming from.'

She drove right and the other cars followed down a dark country lane. Towards the end she saw an old house, the lights inside were off but could see lights flickering behind it. She stopped the car thirty feet away and climbed out.

Dan stepped out the third car and hurried over to her. 'What's wrong? The quarry is the other way.'

Devon watched as many of the others climbed out the cars. 'Did you see the coach?'

Dan nodded. 'Yeah, what about it?'

'It was full of demons.' Devon took the glowing shard from the inside of her jacket. 'They came from here.'

Tarin stood with the broken spear in one hand. 'Could this be the secret door the message mentioned?'

'I don't know,' said Devon, as a hooded figure walked from behind the house. It stared at them before turning to run back. An arrow flew through the air and turned it to dust.

'I wonder if it heard the engines and thought it was another coach.'

'Probably, but if it's the first since the last coach then I don't believe it's the doorway.'

'It does appear too slow,' said Tarin, 'but we best put a stop to whatever it is.'

Devon, Dan, Tarin, Jim, Benjamin, and Reverend Simon walked around the side of the house. Devon could see light from a fire at the rear and as they edged closer she saw four hooded demons standing in a line. In front of them were piles of clothes, and beyond the fire another demon by an altar. The demon chanted words they couldn't understand and a figure stepped out of the fire. A naked demon stood as the other demons noticed the new comers.

Devon raised the shard of glass as the four demons ran at them. Beams of light hit the demons as Dan released two arrows in quick succession. Jim fired his gun three times and five of the demons were sent back.

Devon stared at the one behind the altar. 'How many of these have you brought through?'

The demon grinned. 'Too many for you to stop. Not just those lesser demons, but bigger ones with a lot more power. The demon ripped off its robes and started to grow.

Tarin leapt over and rammed the spear into its chest. The demon screamed before turning to dust. 'Why do they grow? It doesn't make them any stronger.'

'They want you to see them in all their glory,' said Benjamin, 'before they kill you.'

'You don't believe it was the secret door,' said Reverend Simon, twenty minutes later.

Devon drove down a dark country lane without any street lights. 'No, it was the demon. It has to be in the quarry, something which has been hidden for a long time.'

'I'm surprised they need one if a demon can do it like that, and why not at the quarry?'

'I doubt he could do it for too many,' said Benjamin, 'and from what Peter told me, certain rituals are stronger in different places. He also told me they perform them around midnight.'

'Good,' said Devon, 'if that's true, only the one coach would have left the house.' She noticed a mist ahead.

CHAPTER SEVENTEEN
A walk in the Mist

Joe held on to Doom as they rode through fields and leapt fences on the bike. He had never felt so free, even when he was at the manor house. He had the freedom of the house, but he felt like a prisoner as he couldn't leave with demons looking for him. Doom rode the bike up a hill and stopped near a copse of trees. Joe climbed off and watched as Doom took a pack off the back of the bike. Sarah climbed off Gloom's bike as Doom erected a two birth tent.

'You two better get some sleep,' said the biker, 'it could be a long night.'

'I'll be fine out here,' said Joe. 'Let the ladies have it as I've never looked up at the stars before.'

Sarah raised both eyebrows. 'That's kind of you, best hope it doesn't rain.'

Joe watched as she entered the tent, and he smiled. He walked behind it and pressed both of his hands into the canvas.

'JOE, THAT'S NOT FUNNY,' Sarah shouted.

He strolled back to the front where Doom sat on the ground looking into the distance and sat next to him. 'I don't think she appreciated that.'

Doom glanced down at him. 'I won't ask.'

'What's it like living on the road?'

'We are not always doing this, as I do like a bed now and then. I won't deny this is my favourite way of living.'

'Have you rode bikes all your life?'

Doom shook his head. 'No, I was a child once. We also rode horses before bikes came along.'

Gloom stood over them. 'I'm going to get an hours sleep, don't keep Joe awake all night with your tales.'

Doom turned his head as she walked to the tent. 'I don't think she appreciated that.'

Joe screwed up his nose. 'It was lucky you came to the manor house when you did.'

'It wasn't luck, as Sarah was calling to Gloom. We already knew as a demon told us to be in a pub at a certain time to get information.'

Joe wrapped both arms around his knees. 'I bet he made it rhyme.'

'In the Forester's arms you will find, a secret plan of a treacherous kind.'

Joe scratched his head. 'Why does he do that?'

Doom shrugged. 'I've no idea.'

'Do you know what's going to happen?'

'There will be a final battle, the outcome none of us knows.' Doom glanced at him. 'You need to be there, does it bother you?

Joe lay back on the ground and looked up at the stars. 'No, I'm looking forward to it. Do you think the others are taking a rest before going to the quarry?'

'I hope so . . . it wouldn't be a good idea if they arrived at different times in small groups.'

~ ~ ~ ~

Charles swept broken glass into a pile when he heard cars pull up outside. He glanced out of the window and saw eight four by fours pull up. Armed guards climbed out of each and two opened the rear doors of the second car. A plump man climbed out and stared at the house before taking a handkerchief out of his pocket and wiping his neck. Bernard got out the other side and joined him.

'Sir William is with them,' said Charles.

'Good,' said Elouise, 'we best go and greet them.'

They walked to the front doors where William approached with Bernard and the guards.

'Good heavens, Charles,' said William, 'what on earth happened here?'

'Demons,' said Charles, 'we were attacked.'

William wiped his forehead. 'Are you and Elouise OK? Was anyone hurt?'

'Everyone is fine, just the damage to the house as you can see.'

'What about the artefacts,' said Bernard, 'are they safe?'

Charles nodded. 'Very safe, and far away from here.'

Bernard frowned. 'What do you mean?'

'We can worry about that later,' said William, 'right now I'm more concerned my friends were attacked. How did the demons know about this place?'

Charles shrugged, and lied. 'I honestly do not know, but then it was only a matter of time. They have a new leader who may well have the power to locate us or even the dagger.'

'How many demons were there?'

'At least thirty out here and the same out the back.'

William raised both eyebrows. 'Amazing, and you sent them all back?'

'Not personally, although I did send a few back. The warriors who were here fought magnificently, and our archer never misses.'

'Your message earlier said the final battle could be within days.'

Charles scratched his chin. 'Yes, but after tonight I believe it will be sooner.'

Bernard shook his head. 'We should've taken the artefacts to the mansion when we had a chance. I cannot believe you let them go.'

'As I said it was not up to me. The artefacts belong to those who find them.' Charles rubbed his chin. 'Although this is the safest place for them we would not have been able to withstand another attack. The last one was sent back with a knife as we had run out of bullets.'

'Bullets?' said Bernard. 'The dagger worked?'

'No, we never used it,' said Charles. 'Soon as a demon steps onto our land they become vulnerable to normal weapons.'

William wiped his neck again. 'You never told me that before.'

'I only found out tonight.'

'I only came tonight as I could not get through on the phone. I also wanted to see Peter stand straight.'

Charles turned to Elouise. 'Are the phones working now?'

'Yes, I don't know what the demons did, but they are working.'

'We're here now,' said William, 'maybe your friends will come back if we call them.'

'I doubt they will answer, as they've gone radio silent. Anyway, we cannot stand out here all night.'

'Indeed, I thought you were never going to invite us in,'

'You are always welcome here . . . it's just the broken glass.'

'That matters not, as we need to form a plan of action.'

'If they won't come back here,' said Bernard, 'we should go to them.'

Charles nodded. 'Yes, and it might be a good idea to find out where they are.'

~ ~ ~ ~

Devon noticed the mist getting thicker and slowed the car. 'This doesn't look natural.'

Benjamin closed his window. 'No, and I've read books about mist and fog, and the things in them wasn't pleasant.'

Devon glanced at him. 'I doubt we'll find anything nice in this either. I mean it feels like the demons have created it to hide what they're doing.' She stopped the car as the mist became too thick to drive in. she climbed out as the other cars parked up. They all climbed out and Tarin approached.

'I take it we're on foot from here,' she said.

'Yeah, but we're still a good distance away. It could take hours but at least the engines won't give us away. Have you heard from any of the others?'

'Rachel called me when she met up with Sean, Rob, and Carling. They're also on foot but headed there from a different direction.'

'Charles is on his way,' said Devon, 'with Sir William and his men.'

'I hope he knows what he's doing.'

'Me too, but we might need the extra guns.'

'Anyone heard from the bikers?' said Dan.

Tarin shook her head.

'Not a thing,' said Devon, 'and we don't have the third shard yet. We best walk in silence as we don't know what's out here.'

'True,' said Tarin, 'let's just hope their eyesight is no better than ours in this.'

~ ~ ~ ~

The iron links flew through the air and connected with the head of a demon. It turned to dust before its clothes fell to the ground. Chains pulled the links back to him as he moved forward in the mist. He saw Ice dart to the left as Jess came into view.

'This is fun,' she said, 'what do you think the demons are up to?'

'Patrolling, maybe, or waiting to ambush the others.'

'There's something here, I can sense it.'

Chains nodded. 'Yeah, Ice has just gone running to it.' He looked up and noticed a dark shadow outlined through the mist. When the creature came into view he saw it stood twelve feet tall and was broad. It had a large round head and wide mouth, but no nose.

The demon swung a huge fist down at Ice who side-stepped it. He sliced through its arm with his dagger and the demon roared in pain. Blades ran behind the beast and cut through the back of its legs and the demon fell onto its knees. Raven leapt onto its wide back and plunged two knives into its neck. She leapt off as the demon turned to dust.

Gyppo and Doc hurried over to them. 'It's clear down the left.'

Chains put the iron links over his shoulders. 'We'll wait for Mistral and Tempest before going back to the bikes.'

~ ~ ~ ~

'It's gotta be here somewhere,' said Rob, 'we were here not that long ago.'

'Yeah,' said Sean, 'it was also a nice sunny day.'

'There's something ahead,' said Jack, as he held is sword out.

They stopped as a line of figures approached in the mist. Eight demons, all with red eyes and curved daggers, stood in front of them.

'No guns,' said Rob, as he took out a knife, 'they would only give us away.'

Chloe stepped forward with her sword as Sean took out an iron spike. Jamie pulled out his knife and stood in front of Elisabeth.

'Stupid mistake, humans, but our master will be pleased when we kill y__'

The demon didn't get to finish as it turned to dust like another further down the line. Mistral and Tempest stood in their place. Both women swung their arms sideways catching the demons either side of them in the throat. Jamie tried to run forward but Jack pulled him back. The two women somersaulted in front of the remaining demons and stabbed them in the chest.

Mistral turned to the group as clothes and dust fell to the ground behind her. 'You've gone away from the road.'

Rob glanced down and saw dirt. 'Shit, we have too.'

'Turn right and walk straight ahead. Once you get to the road turn left and follow it. We'll go and search for more patrols.'

Rob nodded as the bikers disappeared into the mist, and he walked to the right. 'I'm a great detective, the only thing I can see is the ground and I didn't even look.'

'Yeah,' said Jamie, 'but did you see how hot those women are?'

'A little too old for you, mate.'

Jamie shook his head. 'No way, I'm eighteen, and they can only be in their twenties.'

'You can double that at least.'

'Hardly, that would make them fifty.'

Rob shrugged as he reached the road and turned left. 'I've no idea how old they are, but they were fighting with the Lords of Night thirty years ago.'

'I would say that was rubbish, normally,' said Jack, 'but I can believe anything at the moment.'

'I was going to help them,' said Jamie, 'but you stopped me.'

'Yes,' said Jack, 'and although your intentions were honourable, they had already worked out what they were going to do. I was not going to let you get in their way.'

CHAPTER EIGHTEEN

Thrice the Power

Devon saw shapes ahead as they walked along the road. She held the shard but didn't bother looking at the glass as it had been glowing since they entered the mist. One of the shapes moved towards them.

'Hello,' said Jamie, 'we're up here.'

Devon shook her head. 'You might want to be a little quieter as there are demons around.'

'I know, we saw some not long ago, and two hot biker chicks sent them back.'

Devon's eyes grew large. 'The bikers are here then?'

'I think so, but we only saw two. They've gone looking for more patrols and I really think they're hoping to find some.'

'If we see them again you might not want to call them chicks. Have you found the gates?'

Jamie shook his head. 'No, Jack decided not to go that way as it might be too risky, so he's cutting through the fence with his sword.'

Devon nodded thoughtfully. 'That's sound reasoning.'

They reached the others as Jack pulled part of the caged fence away. There was a lot of silent greeting with the nods of heads.

Jack stepped through the gap and poked his head back. 'There's no mist on this side.'

Devon followed as Rob held the fence open. 'The demons did create it then.'

'It would appear so.' Jack walked forward, stopped, and held up his hand. 'Watch where you go, there's a steep bank here.'

Tarin looked across. 'There's another hill opposite.'

'It's a path,' said Rob, 'for the trucks to take the stone away. The quarry is on the other side of the hill.'

'Wait a minute,' said Tarin, and ran off into the darkness.

Jim sighed. 'She will be the death of me.'

'This could be the death of us all,' said Jack. 'Did we need to bring so many?'

'Yes,' said Peter, 'all those here are important. They might not be warriors like you, or like I was many years ago, but they can fire guns. If we fail tonight, there will be no place on earth safe from these monsters.'

Tarin ran back. 'It leads to the opposite end of the quarry to the pit. You can see everything from there.'

Devon rubbed her chin. 'What did you see?'

'Demons, lots of them. Most of the activity is near the pit which you can see clearly as they have many flaming torches.'

'Good,' said Jack, 'it means their eyes are no better in the dark than ours.'

'Maybe,' said Peter, 'but it also means they found the secret door.'

'Could be,' said Tarin, 'but I don't think they've opened it as the demons weren't exactly pouring out of the pit.'

'No,' said Arthur, 'they would have to dig it out and drag it into the quarry.'

'There's still a chance we can stop them,' said Devon, and turned to Tarin. 'Is there any cover for us?'

Tarin nodded. 'There are piles of stone we can hide behind.'

'Why hide, humans,' said a voice from the other hill, 'when we already know you're here?'

Devon glanced over at the hill and saw a hooded figure disappear into the quarry. 'We go Tarin's way, and with any luck the dagger might show up soon.'

~ ~ ~ ~

Charles glanced out the window of the four by four as they entered the mist. They soon passed other cars parked up along the road. 'It's their cars, but where are they?'

'Gone on by foot,' said William, 'the mist must be too thick to drive in a normal car. We should be OK with the fog lights we have.'

'If they're still alive,' said Bernard, 'for all we know the demons have all the weapons and artefacts now.'

'You should not be so negative,' said William. 'It is also pointless as there is nowhere else to go.'

'I have the utmost confidence in them,' said Charles. 'The fact we haven't seen any demons is a good sign.'

The convoy of four by fours drove through the gates. The lead car slowed as the driver looked for the best way to go and drove down the makeshift road into the quarry. Charles saw mounds of stone and people standing behind them. The cars stopped, and he climbed out to greet the others and was joined by William, Bernard, and the guards.

'You made it,' said Devon.

'Yes, the mist out there is quite thick. Do you think they were expecting you?'

Devon shrugged. 'They may have been expecting someone as three of us were here yesterday. They had patrols trying to stop anyone who entered the mist.'

'Is everyone here?'

'Not quite, there are a few absentees.'

Bernard stared at her and glanced around at the others. 'Where's the dagger?'

'I've no idea,' said Devon, 'but it's not here.'

'Don't lie to me . . . you would not have come here without it.'

'Bernard,' William snapped, 'hold your tongue and have some respect. If the lady says the dagger is not here, then it is not here.'

'No, they have the dagger I know it.'

'Really?' said Devon. 'Take a look at the other end of the quarry. The demons are forming lines to attack us. They know we don't have it.'

Bernard shook his head. 'Give me the dagger and they will not attack.'

William wiped his neck with a handkerchief. 'What the hell are you talking about?'

'He made a deal with them,' said Charles, 'and hopes to make another. He was the one who set up the attack at my home.'

Bernard raised his gun at Charles. 'Maybe I did, and now hand over the dagger or my men will kill you all.'

'I don't think so,' said Dan, with an arrow pointed at him, 'you would die first.'

One of the security men pointed his gun at Bernard's head. 'I don't know what's going on, but we do not threaten our friends. If we're to stand any chance we have to fight together, now drop the gun.'

'You dare point a gun at me, O'Leary,' Bernard blustered, 'I'm the one in charge.'

'No, Sir William is, now drop the gun.'

William shook his head as Bernard threw his gun down. 'How did you know he made a deal with the demons?'

'He was seen giving them my address,' said Charles, 'and told them the time to attack.'

'You never said anything.'

Charles shook his head. 'No, as I didn't know how many of your men were involved. I knew you didn't have anything to do with it and now I believe it was only two of them. When you arrived tonight you were meant to find the scene of devastation and all of us dead. Bernard would have got his wish and took the dagger back to the mansion as you asked him to.'

'I did no such thing,' said William.

'I know, but he came for it all the same. I'm not sure what he was hoping to gain or if he thought the mansion would survive if the demons win.'

William turned to Bernard. 'You better start running as the demons will not be happy with you.'

~ ~ ~ ~

Devon watched Bernard walk up the path with another man, and she turned back to the demons. Over a hundred lesser demons lined up with larger ones behind.

'Form a line,' O'Leary ordered the other guards, 'either side of those from the manor house.' The guards, all with automatic rifles, ran into position.

Devon glanced down the line at Reverend Simon. 'Wait until they get halfway before holding up the shard.'

Jack and Chloe stood with guns pointing forward, and the swords stood in the ground ready to use. The demons moved forward at a slow pace before running. Devon raised her hand and held up the shard. Simon did the same and beams of light shot from them straight at the demons. Soon as they were close enough those with guns fired turning many of the demons to dust. The bigger ones were harder to stop, but the automatic rifles of the security force brought them down. Dan dropped his gun and fired arrows at the demons getting too close.

Devon glanced around and all the demons which attacked had been sent back. 'That was too easy.'

Arthur nodded. 'It was a test like they did earlier at the manor. They want to know what weapons and artefacts we have.'

'They used all those demons just to test us?'

'Yes, because of what they have found. The demons you have sent back will be able to return here through the gateway.'

'And now they know we only have two shards of glass and no dagger. There's still a lot more of them, so why didn't they try to kill us?'

'The demon lord wants us to see the gateway and the demons pouring out of it. They believe we do not have the power to destroy the doorway.'

Devon held the shard up. 'We don't, and this felt like it was fading towards the end.'

'As was mine,' said Simon, 'I don't know if it would last another onslaught like that.'

'Look,' said Tarin, 'they're bringing something out the pit. 'It's some sort of stone frame.'

Devon turned to the pit and saw demons dragging out what looked like half a wall. In the centre was a doorway, which was pitch-black. 'We need a plan, and fast.'

A large demon stood next to the gateway and held its hands upwards. Lights came from them towards the opening.

'Oh,' said Sean, and held out the third shard, 'you might need this.'

Devon ran over to him. 'You had it all along and never said?'

'Chains told me not to until the right moment, this might be it.'

Devon shook her head as she put the two shards together. 'I won't ask how you knew this is the right moment.'

'Good, because I can't tell you how I knew either.'

Simon handed over his shard. 'It appears the timing is perfect. Thy power will be thrice now.'

Devon placed the shard next to the other two and it knitted together as one. 'Seriously, you had to say, thy?'

'It seemed appropriate when saying thrice.'

'You might want to hurry,' said Dan, 'the gateway is opening.'

Devon stared back down the quarry and saw demons running out of the doorway. She held the small stained-glass window in the air and it glowed bright. A brilliant white beam of energy shot straight at the gateway and it exploded. Many demons close to it turned to dust.

The demon lord roared. 'Kill them, kill them all.'

Devon watched as hundreds of demons ran forward, some of them huge. The window in her hand glowed no more. 'Where the hell is the dagger?' She passed Simon the glass and pulled out her gun.

'Listen,' said Tarin, 'I can hear motorbikes.'

Demons, of all shapes and sizes charged forward. Simon held up the glass but only faint light came from it. Guns blasted and demons fell, but were soon on their feet again. Devon glanced up and saw nine motorbikes ride off the edge of the quarry at the demons.

A length of iron links wrapped around the neck of a demon three times bigger than a man as Chains landed. He pulled the links back and the demon toppled over before turning to dust. Devon saw Sean drop his gun as Demons were almost upon him. He pulled out an iron bar and batted them away. Dan stood with one of the special arrows and Tarin exchanged her pistol for the spear. They were out of bullets and would have to fight hand-to-hand. The Lords of Night had cleared the middle of the quarry, but would not reach those almost upon them. Many of the demons were faster than the others, but Tarin matched those closest to her. Devon could hardly see the spear as she swung it. Jack and Chloe stood in front of the older ones and dust flew everywhere with some of the guards dead on the ground.

Devon pulled out a knife as a demon lunged for her. It never reached as it turned to dust after being hit by a knife.

'It's no good,' said Dan, 'we're not sending enough back.'

'Look,' said Jack, 'a white mist.'

Doom rode through with Joe holding the dagger in the air. The quarry soon filled with a light mist and all the demons which had been shot turned to dust.

'Sorry we're late,' said Doom, as Gloom rode in with Sarah on the back. 'We were held up.'

'We have to help our friends,' said Gloom.

Devon nodded as Joe and Sarah climbed off the bikes. She glanced down the field where eight bikers stood around a fallen comrade. 'We're coming with you.'

They ran down the quarry to the bikers. Doc sat up rubbing his back.

'Is he OK?' Devon asked.

Chains nodded. 'He will be, and maybe he'll take more care of his bike in future. The front wheel fell off when he landed.'

Doc managed to stand. 'I've been busy running a pub.'

Chains turned back to the pit where the remaining demons stood, six of them, the demon lord, and five other large ones. 'Let's finish this.'

The bikers ran forward as two of the demons fell to two of the special arrows. Three more moved towards them.

'Watch out for the demon lord,' said Devon, 'its power is greater than these.' She watched the bikers bring down the three demons with ease. Chains swung his iron links, which Devon thought grew longer than they should, at the middle one. They wrapped around its lower leg, he pulled the links and the demon fell over. Blades and Tempest leapt on its chest and plunged their knives into it. Doom and gloom ran and appeared to change into dark clouds covering the one on the left before it turned to dust. Ice, Mistral, and Raven, sent the third back and Devon had never seen a person jump so high when they did.

The demon lord roared and raised its arms. Lightning crackled from all around as something appeared behind. It grew either side of the demon.

Devon realised what they were and turned to the other end of the quarry where the others remained. 'Oh shit, we better get back.'

'What is it?' said Dan.

'Wings, it has wings.'

The demon stood as huge wings flapped either side. It flew into the air as the others ran back but the demon flew fast and soon passed them. It headed straight at Joe and Sarah and landed in front of them. Judy, Rachel, and Sharon ran to them, but had no weapon to stop the demon. Joe pushed to the front with the dagger spreading the mist, but the demon shrugged it off. It lunged forward at him only to be blocked by an invisible shield.

'You have failed,' said a hooded figure coming into view behind Sarah. 'You will not harm these . . . you will not harm anyone again. You did not open the portal and because of your failure the gateway was destroyed forever.'

The demon hissed. 'I will have my revenge and take their souls.'

The hooded figure raised a hand. A bolt of energy shot from it and the demon screamed. It burst into flames before dropping to the ground and became dust.

Joe turned to the hooded figure. 'You never made it rhyme.'

He pulled back the hood to show the face of a plain-looking middle-aged man, and patted Joe on the shoulder. 'It wasn't necessary.'

Devon approached them. 'Who are you?'

'My name is Theodore Smith, my real name I forgot a long time ago.'

'Thanks for all your help, but why did everything have to be a riddle.'

Theodore clasped his hands together. 'I'm sorry, my dear, for not making it clear, but demons you know are very slow.'

Devon sighed. 'What's that supposed to mean?'

'I have had to mingle with them at times, so I could find out what they were up to. You know this, of course, as you saw me with them. Getting messages to you can be risky but demons do not like riddles, and they like things which rhyme even less. I know the rhymes were not great but I had to rush a few of them.'

'So it was just a code, are you a demon?'

'Yes, or I believe I was. I've been walking this land for a long time, and would pass as human with tests.'

Tarin scratched her head. 'How long have you been here?'

'I cannot say for sure as I wandered for many years with my mind just a blur. It was a different world back then, a dangerous one. I'm not sure how I got here but I wasn't like other demons, lusting to kill. I roamed the land keeping away from people until I realised humans were just like me. I travelled with gypsies for a while before I had to move, something I did many times over. Not ageing can cause you problems in the dark ages. It always came back to the demons and their cruelty. After certain people I cared about were sacrificed, I decided to send them back whenever I could.'

'Is it over now?' said Devon.

Theodore shook his head. 'No, it will never be over. You may have saved the world, but they will always be trying to get over here and people still suffer at their hands. Even now someone is most likely trying to summon one over. I should not worry about that at the moment and enjoy your victory.'

'I hear that,' said Chains, 'does the manor house have a bar as I could do with a cold drink right now?'

'There's one at the mansion,' said William, 'perfect for a celebration.'

Devon glanced up at the morning sky. 'It's a little early for that, and besides we should take care of the dead guards.'

William frowned and glanced over at the bodies. 'Indeed, and forgive me if I sounded callous. Defeating the demons is something I have wanted to do for a long time, but not at a cost of lives.'

Elouise stepped over to Devon as William walked away. 'Do not think harshly of him. His wife and son were sacrificed by demons many years ago.'

'What happens now?' said Dan. 'Do we all go back to what we were doing before?'

'Some will,' said Theodore, 'others will continue the fight. Joe and Sarah will still need caring for.'

Joe scrunched up his nose. 'You want to lock us up again?'

Theodore shook his head. 'No, you are not mad, but the demons know of you.'

'We can worry about that later,' said Devon, 'I need sleep, and after I will go to the mansion and drink to those who died, and to the victory.'

THE END